Praise for Abbi Waxman and her novels

"Abbi Waxman is both irreverent and thoughtful."
—#1 *New York Times* bestselling author Emily Giffin

"Move over on the settee, Jane Austen. You've met your modern-day match in Abbi Waxman. Bitingly funny, relatable, and intelligent, *The Bookish Life of Nina Hill* is a must for anyone who loves to read."
—Kristan Higgins, *New York Times* bestselling author of *Pack Up the Moon*

"Meet our bookish millennial heroine—a modern-day Elizabeth Bennet, if you will. . . . Waxman's wit and wry humor stand out."
—*The Washington Post*

"Abbi Waxman offers up a quirky, eccentric romance that will charm any bookworm. . . For anyone who's ever wondered if their greatest romance might come between the pages of books they read, Waxman offers a heartwarming tribute to that possibility."
—*Entertainment Weekly*

"It's a shame *The Bookish Life of Nina Hill* only lasts 350 pages, because I wanted to be friends with Nina for far longer."
—Refinery29

"I hope you're in the mood to be downright delighted, because that's the state you'll find yourself in after reading *The Bookish Life of Nina Hill*."
—PopSugar

"[Waxman is] known for her charming and comical novels, [and her] latest book stirs up all of the signature smiles and laughs."
—*Woman's World*

ADULT ASSEMBLY REQUIRED

BY ABBI WAXMAN

The Garden of Small Beginnings

Other People's Houses

The Bookish Life of Nina Hill

I Was Told It Would Get Easier

Adult Assembly Required

"An aptly and hilariously titled novel. . . . Waxman again delivers with her signature wit and laugh-out-loud writing, offering us authentic characters who feel like people we've met and loved in our own lives—all while offering sly commentary on the roller coaster that is the college application process for parents and their college-hopefuls." —Shondaland

"Abbi Waxman's warm, quippy novels explore familial dynamics with sarcastic wit and plenty of heart. . . . Being a teenager—or parenting one—is tricky territory, but Waxman steers her characters through it with compassion, snappy dialogue, and the right dose of zany humor. Things may (or may not) get easier for the Burnstein women, but the ride, literal and otherwise, is highly enjoyable." —Shelf Awareness

"Waxman shines at creating characters that feel like best friends, inspiring compassion, laughs, and cheers, and fans of Katherine Center and Linda Holmes's *Evvie Drake Starts Over* will adore this." —*Booklist*

"Waxman expertly navigates the fraught shoals of college admissions in this spot-on tale. . . . Waxman's alternating first-person narration from Jessica and Emily rings true, while a memorable supporting cast . . . provide excellent support. . . . This sweet treat doesn't require a college-bound child to enjoy, though anyone who has helped their offspring weather the admissions process will definitely appreciate this sharp send-up." —*Publishers Weekly*

"Funny and insightful." —Book Riot

Abbi Waxman, the *USA Today* bestselling author of *I Was Told It Would Get Easier, The Bookish Life of Nina Hill, Other People's Houses,* and *The Garden of Small Beginnings,* is a chocolate-loving, dog-loving woman who lives in Los Angeles and lies down as much as possible. She worked in advertising for many years, which is how she learned to write fiction. She has three daughters, three dogs, three cats, and one very patient husband.

You can keep in touch with Abbi through her website www.abbiwaxman.com, or via @amplecat on Twitter, @abbiwaxman on Instagram or abbi.waxman on Facebook.

ADULT ASSEMBLY REQUIRED

Abbi Waxman

REVIEW

Copyright © 2022 Abbi Waxman

The right of Abbi Waxman to be identified as the Author of
the Work has been asserted by her in accordance with the
Copyright, Designs and Patents Act 1988.

First published in the US in 2022 by Berkley
An imprint of Penguin Random House LLC

Apart from any use permitted under UK copyright law, this publication may
only be reproduced, stored, or transmitted, in any form, or by any means, with
prior permission in writing of the publishers or, in the case of
reprographic production, in accordance with the terms of licences issued
by the Copyright Licensing Agency.

All characters in this publication are fictitious
and any resemblance to real persons, living or dead,
is purely coincidental.

Cataloguing in Publication Data is available from the British Library

ISBN 978 1 4722 9361 9

Printed and bound in Great Britain by Clays Ltd, Elcograf S.p.A.

MIX
Paper from
responsible sources
FSC® C104740
www.fsc.org

Headline's policy is to use papers that are natural, renewable and recyclable
products and made from wood grown in well-managed forests and other
controlled sources. The logging and manufacturing processes are expected
to conform to the environmental regulations of the country of origin.

HEADLINE PUBLISHING GROUP
An Hachette UK Company
Carmelite House
50 Victoria Embankment
London EC4Y 0DZ

www.headline.co.uk
www.hachette.co.uk

When two people meet, each one is changed
by the other so you've got two new people.

—JOHN STEINBECK

Summer

ONE

Liz Quinn, the manager of Knight's, one of the few remaining independent bookstores in Los Angeles, was not someone you'd describe as softhearted. Yes, she had adopted a stray cat who'd had kittens in the store, and yes, she had a new relationship she sometimes blushed over, but generally speaking she viewed humanity with a jaundiced eye.

However, even Liz was having a hard time not feeling sorry for the customer standing in front of her.

To start with, the young woman was wet. It doesn't rain very often in Los Angeles, particularly in August, but it does rain, and ten minutes earlier the clouds had challenged themselves to dump as much rain as they possibly could. Liz had discovered a puddle in front of Douglas Adams and tracked it along the shelves to P. G. Wodehouse. There she found the *Homo nimbus* and spoke to her.

"Excuse me, would you care for a towel?"

The young woman turned to look at her, and Liz realized she'd been crying.

"Uh . . . yes, thank you. It started raining." She was still crying, albeit silently; the tears kept rolling down her cheeks, leaving cinematically visible tracks in whatever grimy residue they were washing away.

"I'd ask if you were OK, but clearly you're not," said Liz, whose mastery of the précis was unsurpassed. She raised her voice and called to the back of the store, "Polly, bring a towel, will you?"

A muffled voice called back.

"No, I'm not OK," said the woman. "I'm sorry about the floor." She took a breath, and reached out to shake Liz's hand. "My name is Laura Costello, and I'm having a bad day." She realized that made her sound like a member of a twelve-step group with an extremely low requirement for membership, but it's what came out.

"In what way bad?" asked Liz, always interested in other people's disasters. She wondered what was taking Polly so long with the towel, then remembered she herself had used it to dry Ferdinand the store cat, who'd also missed the memo about the rain. Her brow furrowed slightly as she tried to remember what she'd done with it . . . Had she left it under the cat? Oh well, Polly would work it out. Liz refocused on Laura.

"Well," said Laura, taking a deep breath and unloading at a rapid clip, "I moved here for grad school, but I came early so I could get settled and maybe line up some part-time work and today I had a job interview and it went well but I didn't get it so I guess not that well and then I went home and my apartment building was on fire." She paused. "Not *my* apartment building . . ."

Despite the narrative speed and slightly hysterical delivery, Liz was following. She nodded, her hands folded in front of her like a puzzled but hopeful maître d'. "I understood what you meant. I can see how that might put a kink in your knickers."

Laura Costello looked at her cautiously, not entirely certain what knickers were, and sniffed. "So I called my grandmother for suggestions but she snorted and called me a wuss, and to distract me told me a friend of mine had cheated on her boyfriend Dave with Other Dave. The one with the toes."

Liz was clinging to the thread, like the fantasy-genre jockey she was. "The original Dave was toeless?"

Laura shook her head. "No, he has toes, but Other Dave has *extra* toes."

Liz raised her voice again. "Polly! Towel!"

"And then she said I could always come home, which she knew would calm me down because obviously that's not what I want to do."

"Of course not," said Liz supportively, though she was beginning to regret even starting this conversation in the first place. Liz had what you might call resting approachable face, which meant this kind of detailed personal download got thrust on her all the time. It was a pity, because she really wasn't very interested.

Laura gathered her long wet hair into a makeshift knot and looked at Liz, wide-eyed. "So I was wandering around trying to think of what to do and it started raining so I got on the first bus that came along and here I am." She was trying to hold it together, and behind her head the twist of hair was slowly and silently unfurling like a cinnamon bun, expanding in the heat of the store. "I have no job, no friends, and now no apartment and no dry clothes or actually any clothes except the ones I'm wearing." Unexpectedly, she smiled. "But I'm still here and in another month I'll start grad school and then I'll have somewhere to live." She turned up her hands. "It's fine, I'm fine, everything's fine." There was a wobble hiding somewhere in her voice, but it was keeping its head down pretty successfully.

At that very minute, Polly Culligan, one of the employees of the bookstore, turned up with the towel. "Sorry," she said breathlessly, "the cat didn't want to let go." Then she noticed the drying tears and the soot and the expression on Liz's face and raised her voice. "Nina!" she yelled. "Put the kettle on."

Nina Hill was the co-owner of Knight's, and a bookish person of the first order. She had been spending the afternoon going through school reading lists for the year, making sure the store was completely stocked. True, most local parents would purchase their books online, the quislings, but you would be surprised how many copies of *The Outsiders* the store ended up selling at the last minute (*stay gold, Ponyboy*). Plus, if a local parent walked in and asked for *The House on Mango Street* or *The Great Gatsby* and some other parent had snatched up the last copy, there would be hell to pay (and Amazon would pocket the profit). Nina took this responsibility seriously and had been deep in concentration when the door suddenly burst open and a tall, damp woman accosted her where she sat. Nina leapt to her feet, yanked out the earbuds that had prevented her hearing the yelling, the knocking, or the requests for kettle assistance, and prepared to do battle.

"Hello," said the sudden arrival, who was, of course, Laura. She looked down. "How did you fracture your wrist?" She'd appeared so abruptly because the rain had made the door to the office swell, and she'd had to push rather harder than she'd expected and . . . you can imagine the rest.

"I'm sorry," said Nina. "Are you looking for a book?" She backed up a little, which caused her to step on the cat, who bit her on the ankle. Ferdinand had only just recovered from the loss of the towel, and being stepped on was a bridge too flipping far.

"Is it a Colles' fracture?" asked Laura, still standing there dripping on the carpet. The thing to know about both Nina and Laura—though they didn't realize it about each other at the time—is that they were both women of singular focus. Nina was obsessed with books, popular culture, movies, and anything meme-able. Laura was obsessed with sports, bones, muscles, and achieving a full range of motion. Unfortunately, Laura's specific area of interest was making her come across as a bit of a nutter. Especially when you added damp, smoke, and the wild hair that was reminding Nina of Scandinavian Hagrid, *which isn't even a thing*.

"I don't know what kind of fracture it is," Nina said crossly. "Are you from my health insurance company?" Her voice was surprisingly deep, and there was zero nonsense in her tone. Possibly even less than that.

Laura frowned. "No."

"Are you from the city?" LA's Occupational Safety and Health Division didn't normally get involved in nonwork-related incidents, but Nina was taking no chances.

"No." Laura took a step back and stomped on Polly, who was right behind her. She squeaked, but had more self-control than the store cat and didn't bite Laura at all.

"Hey, Cerberus," growled Liz dryly from beyond Laura's shoulder, "this person needs a cup of tea, not an interrogation."

"Liz?" said Nina.

"Yes," replied her friend and business partner, pushing past Laura, who seemed to be frozen in place. "Who else would it be? This is not a surprise attack, an insurance checkup, or even a random piece of Dada performance art, it's a damp customer who's having a bad day and needs a cup of tea." She bustled over to the kettle, flicking it on and turning around to raise her eyebrows at Nina. "Remember those people who sometimes come between you and your tidy shelves? The ones we depend upon for our liveli-hood?"

"Oh," said Nina, squinting dubiously at Laura. "Yes . . . I remember them."

Laura looked at the small, slender young woman in the fifties fit-and-flare dress and immediately worried they weren't going to get on. Nina was the kind of hip, geek-chic girl who'd looked over her vintage-framed glasses in high school and made Laura feel oversized and clumsy. "Sorry," said Laura, "I probably should have introduced myself before asking about your wrist, but I'm train-ing to be a physical therapist and a cast always catches my eye." She dropped her gaze to underline her nonthreatening status and im-mediately started being jealous of Nina's shoes, which were small and beaded. She had always wished she were "quirky" enough to wear vintage clothes, but she'd never been able to pull it off.

Nina looked mollified. "Well, I'm sorry for leaping to the conclusion that you were a health insurance spy."

"That's a thing?" asked Polly, whose expression suggested she was imagining something far more exciting than the reality.

Nina looked strangely pleased to answer. "Are you kidding? Insurance fraud—not counting health insurance—costs the indus-try over forty billion dollars a year. Health insurance fraud on its own is more like seventy billion." Nina raised her eyebrows. "And while life insurance dates back to the burial societies of ancient Greece and Rome, we also have evidence of insurance fraud dating back to the first century AD, which, if you think about it—"

"Enough trivia chatter," interrupted Liz, "I need tea."

Ten minutes later Nina still hadn't explained how she'd hurt herself. To be fair, that ten minutes had been taken up by Laura explaining about the fire, the apartment, the job . . . but Nina had made the tea left-handed without spilling, so Laura estimated she'd been in the cast at least a month.

"Thanks," Laura said, taking the tea. "But seriously, how did you fracture your wrist? I really want to know." She was sitting on a table at the back of the office, having politely asked the cat to move. The cat was beyond peevish by that point, and Liz had to intervene and give up her chair.

Nina rolled her eyes and said, "It's a super-boring story. I slipped getting out of the shower and my hand slid into the base of the toilet and bent the wrong way. *Very* elegant. The slapping sound of my wet butt cheeks hitting the tile will be the sound effect for every embarrassment I ever experience from here on out. It sounded like someone thwacking a porpoise with a fly-swatter."

Laura gazed at Nina and felt her jaw wanting to drop open. Laura had grown up in an opinionated and vocal family, probably more than most, but Nina didn't talk like anyone she'd ever met and it was freaking her out. Nina's pattern of speech was so quick and confident that Laura mentally withdrew a little. She herself was more of a doer than a sayer. At least, that's what her grandma used to tell her when she'd faltered into silence in the middle of a sentence again. Her tongue got tied and her brothers laughed, and she . . . couldn't.

"I don't think it's a boring injury story," said Liz. "It's like the librarian in *Library Lion*." All three booksellers then smiled in exactly the same way. Not in a creepy *Children of the Corn/Stepford Wives* way, but from habit.

Laura frowned. "Is that a book?" No flies on you, Costello, she chided herself. Here you are . . . in a bookshop.

"It's a wonderful children's book about a lion that comes to the library." There was a pause, then Liz added, "Nina would read it to you, but I warn you, she'll cry at the end."

They all looked at Nina, who Laura would not have thought was an easy crier, and she shrugged.

"Sorry, happy endings make me weepy. Sue me. There is a classic John Hancock commercial . . . *Grandma can have my room* . . ." She shook her head and looked at Laura, ready to change the subject. "You and I are not the same size, but—don't take this the wrong way—I have some of my boyfriend's clean clothes at my house, and his sweatpants are at least dry." She shuddered. "I do not enjoy wearing damp clothing. They made us swim in middle school and you had to dress fast before next class, and pulling knee socks onto wet legs is surprisingly overwhelming." She closed her eyes briefly, and added, "I'll run home right now and grab them. I live super close."

"You know," said Polly, "this is why I keep half my wardrobe in the back of my car. You never know when you're going to need a new ensemble."

"She didn't drive," said Liz. "She took the bus."

"She what?" asked Polly, frowning. "Where's your car? Did it burn, too?"

Laura shook her head. "No, I don't have a car. I've only been here a week or two, I keep meaning to get around to it."

Polly was aghast. "You need a car in LA," she said. "I mean, loads of people use public transport, but it's not like New York . . . it doesn't actually *work*."

Nina shook her head. "You're wrong, the MTA averages over a million trips a day and there are over two thousand buses on the streets, though probably not all at once." Then she shrugged. "Anyhoo, I'll go get you dry clothes and then we can have a very typical Los Angeles conversation about the relative merits of freeways and surface streets." She headed out the door.

"Thanks," said Laura dubiously, unsure how she could contribute to such a conversation. "You guys are being very nice to me."

"Slow afternoon," said Liz, adding fresh hot water to her tea. She peered out of the office to check the store, but there were only two regulars who would yell if they needed her. Liz was dressed in black, which was her preferred hue, and her T-shirt read *I would prefer not to*, which was confusing because she'd been exceptionally obliging so far. Laura could feel the beginnings of a headache.

Polly started bouncing up and down. "Oh my god, I can't believe I didn't think of this sooner. You can come and stay with me!" She corrected herself, "Well, not with me literally, but in the house where I live. Last week a tenant left to go on tour and his room is available." Polly was blond like Laura, but where Laura was all shades of fawn and gold and caramel, Polly was the palest straw, with blue eyes that saw excitement and drama everywhere. She was wearing rainbow-striped tights under a purple corduroy miniskirt, with yellow boots and a T-shirt with a Twinkie on it. It was a look.

Liz frowned. "On tour with what?"

Polly shrugged. "*Jesus Christ Superstar*? Does it matter?" Polly was not a detail-oriented person. She was a big-picture thinker. An idea person.

"Not especially," said Liz. "Simply adding color to my day." Liz liked ideas as well as the next guy, but also enjoyed getting lost in the weeds.

Laura was still feeling bedraggled, though the tea was helping. "Where do you live?" she asked Polly.

"Very close, in Hancock Park," said Polly. "It's a *great* place, you'll love it. It's a big old house and the owner lives there and rents out rooms." She grinned, kicking her sunny Doc Martens as she perched on the desk. "Her kids grew up and she got bored on her own. She's a trip."

Takes one to know one, thought Laura. "How big a place?" she asked curiously.

"Oh, big. There are five bedrooms," replied Polly. "Not including the landlord's own space, but she has a whole floor." She counted on her fingers. "Maggie has the top floor, she's the owner, then on the second floor there are three bedrooms, and on the ground floor there are two. I guess they weren't bedrooms to start with, they were a dining room and a sitting room, but now they're bedrooms." She smiled at Laura. "We share the kitchen and garden and there's a pool and pets and it's great."

"I don't know . . ." said Laura, feeling nervous about having roommates, especially ones who were so quick to take strangers home. "I don't think I even have enough money for a deposit. I mean, I have savings, but first, last, and security . . ." She pulled a card from her pocket. "The landlord of the apartment building was there, and he said he'd pay for a hotel for a few nights. Maybe I should call him." The card was wet, but the number was still legible. "I mean, you don't even know me, I could be a serial killer."

Polly laughed. "I doubt it, they're pretty rare."

Liz snorted darkly. "Or maybe they only rarely get caught, did you think about that?"

"Nope," said Polly. "Besides, there's something about her shoes that says *reliable*." They all looked down at Laura's admittedly sensible Hoka running shoes. Polly pulled out her phone and started dialing. "I'll call my landlady right now."

Laura opened her mouth to object but caught Liz's eye. The older woman shook her head.

"You can't stop her once she gets going," she said, getting to her feet and heading off to sell books to word-hungry customers. "Accept your fate, rest here, and dry off."

She and Polly left, pulling the door mostly closed behind them. Laura looked at the cat. The cat looked at her. Neither of them said anything, Laura because she didn't speak cat and the cat because she was mentally composing a letter to her senator.

TWO

An hour and a half later, dressed in a very soft pair of sweatpants and a hooded sweatshirt that said *Fight Evil, Read Books* on the front, Laura found herself sitting next to Polly on the way home. Polly had one of those adorable, bright orange Fiat 500s, and as her place was less than a mile away, the trip was mercifully brief. Laura was a nervous passenger but she did a good job of hiding it. Largely because Polly wasn't paying any attention to her but was instead providing a potted history of the neighborhood.

In the 1920s an oil baron called George Hancock developed the area of Los Angeles that still bears his name. Hancock Park remains one of the city's wealthiest neighborhoods, and Laura found her jaw scraping the neatly manicured sidewalks as Polly pulled up and parked on August Boulevard.

Laura had taken one of those bus tours of Beverly Hills when she'd first arrived in LA, and there the wealth faced the street and announced itself in expensive finishes and architectural details. In this neighborhood, five miles to the east, the wealth was hidden behind high walls and even higher hedges, all of it a deep dark green that made it clear the gardeners weren't concerned with saving water. In Los Angeles, a city built in the desert, the deep green of lawns and trees is a better indicator of true wealth than the pale green of dollars.

Polly lived in the largest house on the block, not that any of them were small. It looked like it had been moved directly from the South of France, the stone a soft butter yellow, the slate roof interrupted by three sets of dormers thrown open to catch the early evening breeze, the windows deeply set and mullioned. Roses clambered across the front and draped themselves lazily over windows and doorways. It was, without doubt, the most beautiful house Laura had ever seen. The front garden had no fence, and sloped generously down to the street, but a large gate at the side separated the driveway.

Polly had gotten out of her car and came over and smiled at her. "Nice, right?" She sighed. "I love it here. I lived in Studio City when I first got to LA, but Maggie was a customer at the bookstore, and we got to know each other. When a room opened up, she let me know. That's how she does it, all word of mouth."

As they approached the house, loud barking sounded from inside. More than one dog.

"By the way," said Polly, inexplicably lowering her voice and leaning closer, "I told Maggie we've known each other for years."

"Why?" said Laura. "I don't even know your last name."

"It's Culligan," said Polly, "but you call me the Polmeister."

"I do?"

"Yes," said Polly, her voice still low, "it came to me when I was telling Maggie about you." She frowned at Laura. "She goes by gut, but likes references. You're not actually a serial killer, are you?"

"No," said Laura. "I'm a grad student."

"So was Ted Bundy." Polly pondered, "I don't suppose you've ever done improv?"

"No," said Laura. She looked hopeful. "I was part of the theater club at school."

Polly perked up. "Acting?"

Laura shook her head. "No . . . lighting crew."

"Oh." Polly looked disappointed. "Well, go with it."

Laura wondered if she was overtired, because normally she would have balked, but she nodded and walked into the house. There was something very . . . convincing . . . about Polly.

The barking stopped instantly when they closed the front door, and a medium-sized dog waved a plumy tail and greeted Laura politely. He or she looked like a small Irish wolfhound, but speckly. Dogs always make things better, thought Laura, reaching down to pet him.

"This is Herbert," said Polly. "He's one of Maggie's dogs. There's another one somewhere, and a cat . . . You're not allergic, are you?"

Laura shook her head, looking around. The interior of the house was dark and cool and very simple. Laura had never been to England, but this house reminded her of every Masterpiece Theater show she'd ever binged. It smelled of fresh flowers, orange oil, and, distantly, baking bread. Heaven probably smelled like this. It was clearly a family home, and worn in places, but there were few photos or knickknacks around to suggest the presence of children. She was going to ask Polly for more information, but then they were in the kitchen and an older woman was coming forward and smiling.

"Hi there," she said, holding out her hand. "You must be Polly's friend Laura, how are you? I'm Maggie Morse, I'm Polly's landlord." She laughed, as if the very idea was funny, then said,

"Polly told me about the fire, how awful. That was literally today?" Her expression went from amusement to sympathy in the flicker of an eye; her face was as mobile as a child's. She was tall, though not as tall as Laura, with big brown eyes, short dark hair shot with gray, laugh lines and wrinkles and no makeup. If you had a problem and were scanning a crowd looking for help, hers was the face you'd stop at.

Laura shook her hand. "Yes, this morning. I'd left already, so I missed it breaking out, fortunately. By the time I got back this afternoon, it was extinguished and roped off."

Maggie clicked her tongue. "What did the landlord say?" She turned and flicked on a kettle, much as Liz had done earlier.

Laura shrugged. "He was there, he was handing out his business card and offered to pay for everyone to stay in a hotel while he sorted out the insurance." She thought of the landlord's sad and anxious face, like a basset hound who'd watched his investment go up in smoke (basset hounds are big speculators, surprisingly). "Not all the apartments were burned, but everything was damaged." The smell of bread was much stronger in here, with an undercurrent of good red wine, and she looked around for somewhere to sit. Then she realized they weren't alone.

The kitchen was generous and ran along the back of the house, opening onto a larger back garden than Laura had expected. The walls were yellow; the counters were pine. A long table, not fancy, but rough like a farmhouse kitchen table, was set for dinner. Two other people were already sitting at it, munching bread and watching Laura and Polly with interest.

Maggie reached up into a cabinet for a glass. "Do you want some wine?"

"I have brandy in my room," said one of the people at the table, a man with a long beard and twinkly eyes. "That might be better." He was wearing an extremely well-cut three-piece suit, which was confusing with the beard, and Laura found herself struggling to decide which external clue was more useful.

"Wine is fine, thanks," said Laura shyly, giving up on categorizing. She actually didn't like drinking very much, but it seemed impolite to say no.

"Since when do you have brandy?" the young woman at the table asked the bearded guy. "We played Scrabble last week, you didn't offer me any."

"I was already struggling to keep up," replied the man. "If I'd brought alcohol into the mix, it would have been all over."

The young woman laughed and smiled at Laura. "I'm Anna, I don't suppose you play Scrabble at all?" She was older than Laura, maybe thirty. Her skin was dark, her hair even darker. Although her expression was serious, her eyes had a definite twinkle, and Laura was sorry to disappoint her. About the Scrabble, that is.

"Not very well," she replied. "Sorry."

Maggie had been watching Laura's face, and now she raised her eyebrows. "Is wine what you actually want, or perhaps a cup of tea would be better? I'm already boiling the kettle for myself."

Another cup of tea was exactly what Laura wanted, and she nodded gratefully. Maggie bustled away, her shapeless charcoal linen dress wrinkled in the back, its pockets usually full of dog treats, judging by Herbert's close attendance. She reminded Laura of an anthropology professor friend of her parents', a frequent and welcome visitor. She'd always worn a highly pocketed fishing vest containing items ranging from pens to arrowheads to, one time, memorably, a light-up keychain of the Venus of Willendorf that played the eighties Bananarama classic "Venus."

The bearded guy waved at Laura from the other end of the table. "I'm Jay Libby, everyone calls me Libby."

"I'm not super good at names," said Laura, which wasn't actually true. She was extremely good at names, but the thought of adding anything more to her head right then was overwhelming. She felt herself starting to tremble slightly.

Maggie appeared with a cup of tea. "I went ahead and did regular British tea with milk and sugar, it's really the best thing for shock."

"And," said Polly, pouring herself a glass of chocolate milk, "it has so much tannin in it that when they dig up old British bodies, their stomachs are like little leather bags." The room fell silent. "Sorry," said Polly, "Nina told me that and it kind of stuck." She took a sip of milk and waved the glass. "I'm going upstairs to get changed. You good for a bit, Laura?"

Laura nodded, and Polly disappeared. Laura forced herself to take a sip, despite the steam rising from her cup. If hot tannins would help, she was all for them, leathery tummy or not.

Maggie went back to poking about on the stove, where something delicious was cooking, and Anna and Libby went back to their conversation. It was about a show Laura hadn't seen, so she let her attention wander. This was clearly the busiest room in the house, and the copper pans hanging above the island looked like they got a lot of use. Laura felt her heart rate slowing, her panic abating. Most of the details of this room were different from her own childhood kitchen, but there were enough similarities to offer touchstones: a recipe card box, a blue cylinder of salt—she'd dressed as that little girl for Halloween one year—a jelly jar with loose change in it.

Herbert the dog was standing to one side of the oven, watch-

ing Maggie stirring and tasting. Everything about him was relaxed apart from his eyebrows, which tracked his lady's every
move. There, thought Laura, is a dog who knows the value of patience. She heard a click and looked.

"Your rice cooker is finished," she said to Maggie, then blushed.
"Sorry, you probably noticed already."

Maggie reached over and unplugged the rice cooker. "Nope,
totally didn't, thanks." She looked over her shoulder at Laura and
smiled. "Do you want to help me?"

Laura jumped up. She took great comfort in being occupied,
being useful.

Maggie pointed to a wall cabinet. "The bowls are the big ones
in there, blue and white." She paused. "Or whatever there is, they
don't all match."

Actually none of them matched, though several were blue
and white. Laura counted heads and came up with five. She put
the bowls on the counter. "Forks and knives?"

"Forks and spoons," replied Maggie. "Top drawer near the table."

Polly reappeared, carrying a plush-coated gray cat. "Oliver
was in my room again," she said, sounding mildly annoyed.

"How is that possible?" asked Maggie, fluffing the rice with
a fork. "You shut your door, didn't you?" She waved her wooden
spoon. "Come and get it."

"Yes," said Polly, "but there he was, smack-dab in the middle
of the bed, like a fluffy gray brioche." She shook the cat gently; he
squeezed his eyes at her. "Shedding!" She dropped him gently on
the floor, where he re-smoothed himself and sauntered off, unconcerned.

"I guess he came through the window," said Libby, standing
up to get a bowl. "I saw him studying the ficus tree on that side the

other day. Was your window open?" He sidled past Laura, peering into the pot. "Yes, chili, precisely what the doctor ordered."

"Cilantro, sour cream, and cheese in the fridge," said Maggie, looking at Polly, who was closest.

Polly pulled the containers out and set them down on the counter, looking for a spoon. "Yes, my window was open, but that's because I live on the second floor and had mistaken Oliver for an elderly cat, rather than a fur-suited ninja who scales walls and climbs trees. My mistake." She looked at Laura. "Dude, you should grab a bowl and dig in before Libby steals it all."

"It's not stealing," said Maggie. "It's sharing." She smiled at Laura. "But she's right, please don't stand on ceremony."

Laura helped herself and discovered she was ravenous. She sat down at the table and started to eat, feeling better with every mouthful. It wasn't long before everyone else joined her.

Then the questioning began. It started innocently enough.

"So, Laura," said Maggie, around a mouthful of chili, "where did you grow up?"

"New York."

"State or city?" asked Anna.

Laura smiled. "Both."

Maggie frowned. "So how did you and Polly get to know each other?" She turned to Polly. "You said at college?"

Polly shook her head. "No, we met after." She turned to Laura, an expression of complete innocence on her face. "I'm not sure I even know where you went to college."

"Columbia."

"Polly said you're a physical therapist?" Libby asked curiously.

Laura shook her head. "Not yet, that's why I'm here, to go to graduate school. My undergraduate degree is in biology."

"Huh," said Libby. "Mine's in ancient history." He reached for more cheese. "Less useful, probably."

"So, how *did* you two become friends?" Maggie was not to be deflected.

"We met online first," said Polly, with her back to them, over by the oven. She radiated nonchalance, and Laura worried she'd come home with a sociopath. "On Amphibinet. We enjoy a shared love of amphibians."

Short pause. Everyone swiveled to look at Laura.

She smiled and nodded, silently. *Oh good lord, Polly's a lunatic.*

"And then she came to town for ReptileCon a few years ago and the rest is history."

The pause deepened, if that's possible. Laura was red-faced and had stopped eating. Libby and Anna were watching, their spoons held in midair.

"Really?" said Maggie thoughtfully. "I thought you said amphibians."

"Amphibians and reptiles, yes," said Polly, still looking as if she'd just come from rescuing orphans and baby birds. "We love them all."

"I had literally no idea." Maggie looked at her, then Laura, then back to Polly. "What's the difference between a salamander and a gecko?" she asked.

"It depends who you're asking," replied Polly defensively.

Maggie's lips twitched, but she turned back to Laura and said, "You'll tell me the truth. What's the deal?"

Polly gave up. "Don't blame Laura," she said. "It was all my idea."

"Shocking," said Maggie dryly.

"We met for the first time today," Polly explained. "But she was all wet and lost and sad and I felt bad, and what's-his-name left to go on tour last week, so I thought . . ."

"That's right," said Anna. "What did he go on tour with?"

"*Evita*?" said Polly, shrugging.

Maggie was still frowning. "You thought maybe she could stay here?"

Laura was mortified. "I'm sorry, Maggie."

Maggie smiled at her. "It's fine, Polly loves a story. She can't help herself. She lives in a rich fantasy world. It's part of her charm."

Polly turned up her palms and grinned. "Sorry! I thought you might be more open to it if she wasn't a complete stranger."

Anna laughed. "So, how long have you actually known each other?"

Laura swallowed. "I walked into the bookstore around four p.m."

Everyone looked at the huge kitchen clock hanging next to the sink. Half past seven.

"Nearly four hours," said Maggie, getting up for more food. "Sounds good to me."

THREE

When Laura followed Maggie into the available downstairs bedroom and saw the floor-to-ceiling windows, the deep rose walls, and the pink-and-cream flowery rug, she was filled with an incredible sense of peace. Her childhood home had been very cramped, and privacy had been fleeting. The studio apartment she'd had for the last week or so had been affordable but boxy, a seventies cube with little charm. This was a whole different ball of wax, an elegant, spacious room with high ceilings and long velvet curtains the color of a cold dog's nose. Assuming the nose was pink to start with.

She looked around and paused. "Wait, is that a real fireplace?"

Maggie laughed. "Yes. The animals will be forever underfoot when winter rolls around." She smiled. "Although I guess you'll be in student housing then."

Laura was surprised. "It gets cold enough to have a fire?"

Maggie nodded. "Sure, it can be chilly in the evenings, you'll see." She walked over to close the curtains in the room. "I know it's hard to imagine right now, but Los Angeles does have different seasons: There are three days of spring every May, an unpredictable and unpleasantly hot summer from then until three days of crisp and lovely fall sometime in November, then an unpredictable and unpleasantly chilly winter until the three-day spring rolls around again."

Laura laughed. "Well, New York isn't much better: Spring and fall last a month each and make you certain there's no better city on earth, then summer and winter are brutal and exhausting. Precisely when you decide it's time to leave once and for all, spring or fall shows up and you forget the pain all over again."

Maggie made a face. "I've known relationships like that." She turned to survey the room. "The furniture is nothing fancy, but hopefully you'll be comfortable here." She leaned against the door and folded her arms. "Here's the scoop. I rent out rooms because I like the company and extra income, but how much time you spend with the rest of us is totally up to you. I make dinner most nights, but not all, and if you want to join us you need to text me before noon."

"How does everyone . . ."

Maggie was clearly used to this conversation. "Pay for it? Dinner? Everyone throws a ten in the jar if they're there, doesn't worry about it if they're not. So far it's worked out. I'll let you know if you owe me money, but you'll have to take my word for it because I don't keep receipts or give it that much thought." She tipped her head to one side. "The rooms downstairs are bigger, but you share the bathroom, which only has a shower. If you want to take an actual bath in a real tub, the bathroom's upstairs." She mentioned a figure for rent that was much lower than Laura had been paying (though that rent had included an unshared bathroom, a kitchenette the size of a pack of cards, and all the cockroaches she cared to entertain). "I don't take a deposit because I don't like keeping track and want to be able to throw people out immediately and even capriciously, if I so choose. There's no contract, it's only me." She sighed. "It's definitely illegal, Los Angeles is pretty strict about these things, don't tell the mayor."

"I don't know what he looks like."

"Lucky for me. Washer and dryer are off the kitchen, you'll have to get your own detergent and stuff."

"So, Polly's upstairs, and Libby and Anna . . . ?"

"Also upstairs, and the other guy downstairs is Bob Polanco. He's a gardener who moved in three months ago." She raised an eyebrow. "You'll be sharing the downstairs bathroom with him, as I said, and I have zero tolerance for bathroom disorder. He knows Polly, too, not sure how, but lots of people know Polly. We don't see him very much, and when we do see him, he tends to be in the garden." She turned to leave, adding, "Not like a gnome or anything, he takes care of the garden as part of his rent. If you want to lock your door, I can give you a key, but most people don't." Maggie's brown eyes twinkled and crinkled at the edges. "Welcome to our house. I enjoy new tenants, I'm always around if you need me."

Laura turned to face the room again. "Thank you so much, Maggie," she said. "It's a beautiful room."

Maggie smiled. "Yes, it's one of my favorites. Wait till you see the garden, Bob's a genius, even if he doesn't say a lot." She turned to leave. "Do you need to borrow sheets?"

"No, I'm going on a Target run with Polly." Laura blushed. "I'm really sorry about earlier."

Maggie laughed. "Don't worry about it, I'm not. Most people are relatively decent, and many of them are wonderful, I've discovered. However, even if you're an asshole, you're only here for a month or so." She stepped into the hall but paused when Laura said her name. "Yes?"

"Did you know," asked Laura, "that Maggie Morse was an extremely important twentieth-century ornithologist?"

"No," said Maggie. "Really?"

"Yes," said Laura. "My parents are bird people, so . . ."

"Huh." Maggie started to smile, but Laura saw it coming.

"I meant ornithologists, not half-person, half-bird."

"Disappointing," said Maggie, closing the door.

A little while later, Polly and Laura stood inside the entrance to Target, each leaning on a cart.

"I don't need a cart, really," said Polly, casually scratching the back of one leg with the other foot, "but the thing with Target is there is always something . . . ideal." Polly quickly wheeled right and left like a cartoon race driver. "Which way? On the right we have women's clothing, accessories, shoes, and sportswear, straight ahead we have cosmetics, housewares, and—ultimately—the grocery section." Polly clearly spent a lot of time at Target, and who could blame her?

"I need a little bit of all of it," said Laura, heading right, "but if we start with clothes, then I'll have time to come to my senses at the end."

"It's the shopping that's fun, not the spending per se," agreed Polly. "I see we understand each other."

FINAL TALLY:

LAURA:
Dressing gown: fluffy.
Slippers: fluffy.
Underwear: not fluffy.

Usual bathroom stuff: shampoo, conditioner, shower
gel, mascara, lip balm, gray eye pencil, cover stick.
Towels: fluffy.
Other clothes: four pairs of leggings, four T-shirts,
four pairs of socks, two zip-up hoodies, two pairs
of running shorts, one extra pair of running shoes,
one pair of flip-flops, one pair of flat black slip-ons.
Sheets: flannel (this caused discord, as Polly failed to
persuade her LA was too warm for flannel sheets,
and Laura told her hell wouldn't be too warm for
flannel sheets, and they discovered a fundamental
disagreement about fabric in general that—
fortunately—they were able to move beyond).

POLLY:
Lamp in the shape of a dinosaur, tights with
pineapples, gold scissors with stork handles,
tampons, new coloring pencils, a packet of orange
Milanos, and an adorable little tin of safety pins
she would distinctly remember buying and never
be able to find when she needed them.

FOUR

The next morning Laura returned from her morning run to a quiet house. She looked at her phone—it was nearly 9:00 a.m.; everyone must have left for work. She hadn't slept that well in weeks, and the run had felt really, really good. She went into her room and levered off her shoes, telling herself she was supposed to undo them first, and not doing so. Padding into the kitchen, she found a note propped up on the counter:

> *Dear Laura,*
> *Coffee in the pot since 7, feel free to make more.*
> *Tea in the cupboard, cereal ditto. Animals have all*
> *been fed, don't listen to their lies.*
> *Maggie*

Laura looked down. The gray cat had arrived and curled his tail around his feet with the elegant precision of an Englishman furling an umbrella. Herbert the dog was behind him, his tail waving hopefully. Behind them, a sedate distance away, was a small ottoman in the shape of a pug. Her tail wasn't moving, and she fixed Laura with a boggling eye that said she'd resigned herself to the shortcomings of the human race and didn't expect this tall drink of water to buck the trend. Laura wondered where she'd been the evening before. At work? On a date?

All their liquid-eyed gazing was useless; Laura was not going to be the person who snuck food to the pets, no, ma'am. As a child she'd been terrorized by a tuxedo cat named Rollo who would wake her at 5:00 a.m. every day by placing a soft white paw on her eyelid and leaning on it. It's a surprisingly effective alarm. She remembered crying and pulling the sheet over her head, but he was merciless. He would put his tiny triangle nose next to her ear and purr like a Lamborghini until she got up to feed him. Laura wasn't going to let this happen again; when the gray cat—Oliver?—twirled around her legs and squeezed his green eyes up at her, she only petted him for a few minutes before ignoring him completely.

She found a mug and made herself some tea. She stepped out and took her first good look at the garden. She needed to stretch, and she might as well pick a pretty place to do it.

Maggie hadn't been overselling. The garden was lusciously verdant and beautifully kept, like the cover of *Better Homes and Gardens*. The roofs of other houses could be glimpsed through majestic trees and over weathered brick walls that presumably marked the boundary of the property. Where she was standing was a house-wide patio, with large flagstones nestling into dark green moss. A set of battered wicker chairs was grouped around a table where sections of the newspaper were still spread out. Abandoned coffee cups suggested a sudden noticing of the time, and Laura resolved to take them in and wash them. Might as well make herself useful.

She was still hot from her run, so she started stretching her ankles and wrists, moving her mug from hand to hand. When she'd left the house it was cloudy overhead, but already she could feel the heat of the day beginning to warm the stones. Good luck beating summer in New York, she thought, because unless you can recapture the smell of rotten milk and diapers that wafts through every apartment building on the Upper West Side, you're not even trying.

There were low, wide steps down into the garden, and flagstones like the ones she stood on picked their way across the lawn to a large, fenced-in vegetable garden that abutted the brick wall that separated them from their nearest neighbor. It appeared to be a riot of growth, with tomatoes visible even at this distance tangled over bamboo tecpee trellises. A tall ornamental arch stood at one end, overrun with pink and cream roses. It was beautiful, and Laura started to walk in that direction.

Something moved low behind the tomatoes and a man stood, wearing pajama pants and nothing else. No . . . he must have had earbuds in, because when Laura squeaked for absolutely no good reason whatsoever and whirled around to go into the house so fast she spilled hot tea on her feet, he didn't look up. Laura made it to her room in record time and gingerly peeped through the curtains at the garden and the guy.

What on earth is wrong with you? You're allowed to be here. You're not twelve.

The man walked along the row of tomatoes and then turned away to crouch and look at whatever was growing in the next raised bed.

Laura was forced to admit the guy did nice crouching work, with a very pleasing set of muscles and adorable pajama pants that were wearing a little thin over the butt. Christmas pajamas, Laura noted, Snoopy and Woodstock with holiday lights, a timeless classic. When he stood again and turned to walk back into the house, she found herself reluctant to look at his face.

But she did.

Huh. Laura turned away and listened to the sounds of the man coming in, talking to the dogs, and heading into the room down the hall from hers.

The door closed.

Laura stood and considered. You didn't need to be Sherlock to work out he must be Bob the gardener guy. Identification wasn't the issue. The issue was that he was absolutely, in every single way, her type.

It was really the face that was the problem. No one that good looking could possibly be available / interested / not a douchebag. Wide cheekbones, dark hair and eyes, a ridiculous dimple on his chin. No. Not happening. Been there, done that. The fact that he spoke to the dogs was anomalous. He couldn't look like that and be a nice guy.

She looked in the mirror and reminded herself she wasn't interested in romance. You've had quite enough of that, she told herself, you're here to focus on your studies, your life, and your independence. The last thing you need is some guy swanning around and telling you what to do. Plus, she thought, regarding herself critically in the mirror, he's out of your league. Laura wasn't pretty, as she was reminded every time she went online. She tried not to care about this and was sometimes successful. She knew she wasn't hideous—it wasn't like children screamed at the sight of her—but she was well informed about the ways in which she could be improved upon.

She read numerous articles on how to dress better and apply makeup more skillfully (or at all), and had a vast Pinterest board of girls who had the same coloring as she did but somehow managed to make it pop. It was easy to see where she and they diverged: They were waifish, she was muscular. They braided their hair in interesting ways, she had a ponytail. They had symmetrical faces, she had one eye 2 percent larger than the other and a nose that was eleven degrees from perpendicular. (She knew these last two facts thanks to a helpful app that allowed you to map your face in excruciating detail—sponsored by a plastic surgery company.) She'd also discovered her waist was too low and her measurements a little bottom heavy to be ideal. She was glad to know these things, though she couldn't do anything about them except be painfully aware and self-conscious. She'd purchased a variety of clothes designed to make the most of her "good bits," but always ended up back in leggings and T-shirts, feeling colorless, uninspiring, and comfortable.

Every so often she'd try one of those apps that sent her daily affirmations and genial encouragement, but she found their friendly typefaces and hand-drawn platitudes easy to ignore. She knew she wasn't the only young woman to feel disappointing, because social media was filled with badasses insisting all bodies were good bodies and urging her to reject the patriarchy, but then she felt ashamed of not being stronger and shallow for caring what other people thought. It's hard to love yourself while simultaneously striving to become the best you you can be, which implies your current version could use some work. Laura couldn't decide what was worse—the mental contortions needed to balance these competing self-images or the emotional pretzeling required to feel happy about it.

She heard Must-Be-Bob go into their shared bathroom down the hall and then, later, the front door open and close. She scuttled down the hall herself, clutching her new towels with their tags still attached. The bathroom was still slightly steamy, with some droplets of water on the shower door and a faint scent of cedar and lemon. The room itself was very simple. White subway tile, a gray stripe, a built-in shower tiled in the same gray. A large mirror hung above the sink, with glass shelves on either side. One side was empty; Laura assumed it was for her.

She wasn't going to look at his stuff.

She looked.

There wasn't much to look at. Ibuprofen, still with a seal on it. A razor that looked old and battered. One of those actual shave brushes with a bowl. Laura concluded either he was old-fashioned or his grandpa had given it to him and he was sentimental.

She looked at the things she'd bought for herself at Target. Toothpaste, toothbrush, shower gel, shampoo, conditioner . . . etc. None of it purchased with the thought it might be on display. Fortunately, she'd also grabbed a big pouch to keep it all in, so she'd leave the shelves bare and remain a mystery to him. Her mouth twisted wryly at her assumption he'd give her more than a passing thought.

She showered and dressed, pausing to look at herself naked in the mirror. She looked better; a little roundness was coming back, softening the lines of muscle. She ran her fingers over her scars, which covered the side of her torso, with others on her hips and knees. There were more on her back she couldn't see, and several under her hair, but she didn't need to see them to know they were there. For a while now she'd been able to look at her scars and be grateful, but some days her grasp on gratitude was slippier than others. She leaned forward and examined herself closely in the mirror.

"You could be dead, and you're not," she whispered to her reflection, "so quit your bitching and get on with it." She stood back up. "Whatever *it* is." Then she grinned at her reflection and stood like Superman—she'd seen it on a TED talk—and threw her toiletries in the big sack.

Once she was dressed, Laura sat down at the patio table to sort out her life, at least that part she'd thought to cover with renter's insurance. She called her insurance company and spent an hour on the phone with a very nice lady (or possibly gecko) named Amanda who helped her list her losses and start the claim. Laura prayed the check would come before her credit card bill. She called the utility companies that hadn't even sent her a first bill yet and closed those accounts. She called her credit cards and changed her address. She called her student loan people. Finally, having fetched herself a fresh cup of coffee and taken three deep and cleansing breaths, she called her mother.

Laura's mother, Dr. Eleanor Costello, taught at Columbia and lectured at home. She had been wrong on maybe three occasions in Laura's childhood, and each time she'd blamed it on erroneous source material. She was a woman of deep intellect and cast-iron certainty, who never went farther south than Forty-Second Street if she could help it, and believed that pigeons held the secrets of the universe. Those last two parts were unique to her; the other attributes are found in most mothers.

One of Laura's brothers answered the phone.

"Hey, doofus," he said on hearing her voice. It was Jake, the brother just above her in age. He was married, lived as far downtown as he could, and taught at NYU. Laura was literally the only noneducator in her family, a mysterious exception frequently discussed in her presence.

"Hey, loser," she replied, because he was her favorite brother. "What are you doing there?"

"Nice," he said. "Can't a man check on his aging parents from time to time?"

"Not if he normally never wants to come within twenty blocks of the apartment. What's up?"

"Actually, it's your fault I'm here, sort of."

Laura rolled her eyes. "Explain yourself."

"Well," replied Jake, "Mom has taken to texting all of us to ask if we've heard from you, although I bet she hasn't reached out to you at all."

"Not a word," said Laura. "That's why I'm calling. Is she OK?"

"Well, you know . . ." said Jake, and then his voice changed. "Here she is. Bye, goober." And then he was gone.

"Laura! Baby! Are you OK?" As always, her mother sounded concerned.

"Hey, Mom," said Laura, taking a deep breath and reminding herself she was thousands of miles away. "I'm totally fine." She paused, closing her eyes. "But I have a new address to give you . . ."

"Why?" her mother's voice went up into a higher register. "What happened to the other place? Did you get thrown out?"

Laura frowned. "There was a little fire, so I moved into a friend's house, the landlord lives on-site, there are plenty of people . . ." She waited for her mother's reaction. She didn't have to wait long.

"*A fire?*" Her mother's voice would soon only be audible to dogs.

"I wasn't there, no one was hurt"—Laura hoped this was true—"and I found another place immediately." It was always best, people had discovered, to present Dr. Costello (female, senior; there were four other Dr. Costellos in their family, all male, three of them younger) with a problem that had already been solved, as otherwise she was inclined to freak out and demand to be involved.

"Who started the fire?" Her mother's tone was a familiar one to Laura, a combination of concern and imminent judgment.

"No idea," said Laura. "Maybe it was electrical, you know."

"Hmm," said her mother, clearly preferring a team of highly trained arsonists. "Is the new place in a safe neighborhood?"

"Yes, very," replied Laura. "Hancock Park."

"Never heard of it," her mother sniffed. "Is it near Beverly Hills?"

When Laura had decided to move to Los Angeles for grad school, her parents were mystified, then concerned, and then irritated. Born and raised in New York, neither had ventured far outside of the state, though both traveled abroad every year for fieldwork. Her mom was a professor in the psych department, specializing in pigeons. Not that pigeons need a lot of therapy— they're actually very self-actualized—but they are excellent subjects for behaviorists to study and tend to be easily obtained and generally willing to give it a go. Laura frequently wondered if her mother liked pigeons better than people, but never plucked up the nerve to ask.

"Yes," lied Laura, "pretty close. Anyway, I'm not alone, so that's good."

"Yes," said her mom in her teacher voice, "solitude isn't good for social organisms."

"We're flock animals," said Laura, patiently anticipating her mother's next point.

"We're flock animals," said her mother, rolling over her. "We need the company of our own kind, particularly members of our immediate family grouping." She hesitated. "Who is this friend, anyway? You don't have any friends in Los Angeles."

Ouch. "Her name is Polly. I met her in a bookstore." Laura changed the subject. "How's Dad?"

"Fine, I think." Her mother's voice went in and out slightly, and Laura could imagine her looking around vaguely in case her husband was lurking nearby. "I haven't seen him in a while."

This was also par for the course. Laura's parents had met on literally the first day of college, when they got roped together as lab partners in their mandatory dissection class. Laura's dad taught in the biology department, not the psychology department, and his area of specialization was smaller: hummingbirds. But her parents' fascination with feathered creatures drew them together, and after falling in love, they quickly got married in order to get back to their labs and keep working. They were a strange combination of total commitment to each other mixed with utter disinterest in the other's daily whereabouts or activities. If you asked one about the other, they would look around and shrug if they weren't immediately in sight, and almost as quickly forget the question. When they ran into each other around the apartment, or even on campus, they would start talking as if they had literally been in the middle of a sentence not two seconds earlier, rather than hours or even days apart. It wasn't a very traditional marriage, but it worked for them, even as it confused everyone else.

"And Grandma?"

"Great," replied her mom shortly. There was a pause. "I'm fine, too, thanks for asking."

Laura rolled her neck from side to side and then all around, trying to prevent herself from tightening up. "That's good to hear, Mom. How's work?" This was a safe question to ask, and Laura and her brothers had learned early on that the best way to deflect their mother was to ask her about her work. For her brothers this had led naturally to their own teaching careers, but though Laura had been a strong student, she'd never loved sitting in a classroom.

"Excellent," replied her mom. "One of my grad students is up for an award, and we got funding for another remote camera. Plus Morris and Ethel have a new clutch of eggs, it's very exciting."

Morris and Ethel were a four-year-old bonded pair who lived on the roof of their apartment building, in an aviary her mother had had since before Laura and her brothers were born. Pigeons mate for life, and Morris and Ethel had raised several sets of chicks together. Her mother had once witnessed Morris literally bringing Ethel a flower while she sat on their eggs. Admittedly, Ethel had eaten it, but still, couple goals.

"That's awesome," said Laura. "Look, I have to go now, but I'll email you the new address. Say hi to Dad for me, alright?"

"You're still not going to change your mind about grad school?" asked her mother incredulously, ignoring Laura's clear desire to end the call. "How do you know the fire wasn't the universe's way of telling you to come home?"

Laura sighed. "Mom, there were fifteen apartments in that building, the message could have been for anyone. And yes, Mom. I'm already enrolled, I'm going to grad school here." She paused. "Nothing's going to change."

Her mother became fractious. "Everything already changed! You had your whole career mapped out, you showed such promise, there were so many fields open to you."

Laura didn't say anything because she was tired of repeating herself. Besides, she knew her mom wasn't finished. The first line of attack was always the originally planned future, the road not taken. If that didn't work, her mom would zig and bring up the recent past, still hoping this change of direction was a blip and Laura would return to her previously scheduled programming.

As predicted, her mom changed her tone, doing her best to sound gentle and caring. "Maybe you need to take more time? After all, it hasn't been very long since the accident. You're still, you know . . . unstable." Laura's mom was not a bad person, but she wasn't naturally gentle or caring, and her tone wasn't convincing. A couple of years earlier Laura had been involved in a very serious car accident, and although her mother accepted the accident itself wasn't Laura's fault, responsibility for subsequent changes of life plan and a variety of embarrassing mental health problems landed squarely in Laura's court. Her mother had found the whole thing deeply irritating.

"It's been nearly two years, Mom. Please can we stop rehashing this?"

Her mom made a noise Laura was all too familiar with, a click-tongued hissing sigh that conveyed several different emotions in one sound, none of them positive. Third and final plan of attack: Laura's stubborn irrationality. "You can go to grad school *here*, Laura. Why must you leave the nest in such a dramatic fashion? What's wrong with Columbia? I'm sure it has an excellent program for whatever it is you're doing. Plus here you can take public transportation, which is so much easier for you. God knows how you're planning to get around out there."

Laura closed her eyes. Her mother knew exactly what program she was doing, she just didn't approve of it, and anything her mother disapproved of became magically inexplicable. The public transportation dig was simply her mom being bitchy. Laura stood up and walked over to the kitchen door. Knocking on it, she said, "Mom, someone's at the door, I have to go."

"Make sure you see ID before you open the door . . ." said her Mom immediately.

"Yes, Mom, I'll call you later." Laura hung up, then leaned her forehead against the wall and stayed there, banging it gently.

FIVE

Having gotten that out of the way, Laura stole two of Bob's ibuprofen and headed to Larchmont. Stepping off the bus, Laura felt . . . happy, despite her mother's best efforts. Larchmont Boulevard reminded her of the Upper West Side, the bustle of cafés and stores and people. Laura realized she was hungry and headed to the bookstore to see if Polly was there.

"Roomie!" said Polly, looking up when Laura came into the store. "Have you come to whisk me away to lunch?" She paused. "I think we're too old to call each other roomie."

"I agree, but yes, lunch."

Nina was standing there, gift wrapping a book for a waiting customer. Polly looked at her and raised her eyebrows. Nina grinned and nodded.

"We're not busy right now, off you go."

Laura spoke up. "Thank you again for last night, I'll bring your clothes back tomorrow."

Nina waved a hand and grinned again. "You left one of your socks in the office, it's still wet, amazingly. Did you know raindrops aren't actually raindrop shaped, but more like tiny, watery hamburger buns?" She made a lifting gesture with her hands.

"They start out as spheres, but their bottoms flatten out as they fall."

"Probably true for all of us," said Polly cheerfully. "Come on, I'm hungry."

Outside she turned to Laura. "What do you feel like eating? Burgers, sushi, pizza, salad, Italian, Greek, bagels, vegan, poke, Thai?" She shrugged. "There's even American-style home cooking, if you want to go a little farther north." She was wearing bells somewhere on her person, because every time she hopped from foot to foot, she jingled. "Hurry up and choose, I'm hungry."

Laura laughed. "All of that's here on this street?"

Polly nodded. "I forgot Mexican."

"Ooh, Mexican it is."

They headed north and ordered tacos. Then they sat on a low brick wall nearby and waited.

"So," said Polly, "did you see Maggie this morning?"

"No," Laura said, and shook her head. The taco place called their number, and Polly went to grab the tray. As always, the food made everything better. Dogs and good food: universal improvers.

For a while they munched in silence, and then Laura said, "So, tell me about Maggie. What's her deal?"

Polly looked at her and finished chewing before answering, "How do you mean?"

"Is she married?"

"Divorced."

"Happily?"

"No clue." Polly took a sip of her drink. "She's chatty but not informative, if you know what I mean. And besides, we're not friends or anything. She's got to be, like, sixty. And she's a therapist, so, you know. I always end up saying more than I mean to."

Laura said, "I don't know. I've never seen a shrink." This wasn't *entirely* true, but there was no need to go into it then and there.

Polly looked surprised. "You haven't? What's wrong with you?"

Laura made a face. "Nothing. That's the point."

Polly considered this. Then she said, "I go to the movies with Libby and Anna sometimes."

"Are they dating?"

"No," Polly replied. "It's a romance of the mind only. I think, anyway."

"Lots of Scrabble?"

"Yeah. And other games. Do you play bridge?"

Laura nodded. "Yes, actually. My grandmother taught me when I was a teenager, so I could make up a four when one of her friends failed to show up for their weekly game. I'm no good, but I do love playing cards."

"Well, don't admit it unless you want to play. They're hustlers."

"Bridge hustlers?"

"Making tricks and taking money." Polly grinned. "They play competitive bridge as a team, which strikes me as bizarre. Not to mention how weird it is that the universe put each of them in a house with the only other young person in Los Angeles who was looking for a bridge crony."

Laura shrugged, not finding it all that weird. "Maybe the universe likes card games?"

Polly said, "Doubtful," and stuffed another taco in her face. That done, she said, "And did you meet Impossibly Handsome Bob?"

Laura coughed, having inhaled a piece of lettuce.

"I'll take that as a yes," said Polly, thumping her on the back.

"Yup, he's disarmingly attractive." Her smile was benign but her eyes were sharp as she watched Laura coughing.

Laura got her breath back. "Sorry, yes. Or at least, I think I saw him in the garden."

Polly raised one eyebrow enviably high. "Laura, if you've seen Bob, you'd know it. The fact that you nearly choked to death tells me everything."

"And what's his deal?" asked Laura, purely interested in information gathering.

"Fancy him, do you?" said Polly, looking unsurprised. "I don't blame you, though he's not my type."

Laura was blushing. "What is your type?"

"Eclectic," replied Polly airily. "Bob's only been there a few months, and he's a cool customer, I know that." She drank some more of her horchata. "What's your deal, while we're discussing deals? Boyfriend? Girlfriend? Neither or both?"

Laura stayed red. "Neither. I was . . . engaged, kind of, but we broke it off before I moved here."

Polly widened her eyes. "Ooh, a tragic past, tell me all about it."

Laura laughed. "It's not tragic at all. We'd known each other a long time, we'd grown apart, I wanted to take a break, he didn't, so I came here." She hoped she sounded more confident than she felt. "I'm pretty sure he doesn't think I'll make it and will show up back home in a few months."

"Why?" Polly was amazed. "You're going to grad school, right? Not joining a death cult."

Laura tried to decide how to frame it. "I know, but he wasn't the only one. My family is pretty certain I'm making a huge mistake."

"Los Angeles," said Polly owlishly, "is often the wrong choice, but it's never a mistake." She tapped the end of her nose and then pointed at Laura.

"What does that mean?" Laura asked.

"Wait and see," said Polly. "Everyone comes here for one thing and usually ends up finding another." She grinned, then looked at her phone. "Crap, I have to go back. Where are you parked?"

Laura laughed. "I take the bus, remember?"

Polly stared at her. "And it brought you right here?"

Laura nodded. "Honestly, Polly, you should expand your horizons a bit. Public transportation is better for the planet, cheaper, easier . . . you should try it."

They started walking back to the bookstore, and Polly shook her head. "I already drive an electric car, and I love it like a brother. It's my traveling capsule hotel of happiness." She looked at Laura. "You don't really like driving, do you?" Before Laura had a chance to say anything, Polly added, "Speaking of Bob . . ."

"We weren't," said Laura, surprised Polly had been able to tell how uncomfortable she'd been in the car the night before.

Polly ignored her. "He and I are having a small interpersonal beef right now and you need to pick a side."

Laura shrugged at her and said, "Your side, of course. What's the beef about?"

"Daisy."

"Daisy who?"

"The pug."

"OK, yes. I met her this morning. She's very . . ."

"Plump? Rubenesque? Well covered?" said Polly. "She appreciates fine dining, it's true. She's always slept in my room, or at least she did until Impossibly Handsome Bob showed up."

"Why do you call him that?" asked Laura. "I mean, apart from the fact that it's accurate."

Polly wrinkled her brow. "It's what Nina calls him. I guess I caught it from her. Anyway, a few weeks ago I came downstairs around eleven to get a snack and a glass of water. Normally"—she stressed the word—"*normally*, that was when Daisy would follow me upstairs and settle in for the night. She's like a professional hot-water bottle, that dog. She goes under the covers and I rest my toes on her and love her deeply. But that night I came down in time to see madam swishing into Bob's room, with him holding the door open like a velvet rope." They had reached the store and Polly paused outside the window. "I said, *Hey, Daisy sleeps with me*, and he said—"

"Wait," said Laura. "You said that to him?"

Polly was indignant. "Yes! Daisy is my dog."

"Literally?"

"No, of course not literally." Polly was unabashed. "But emotionally. And he had the balls to say, *I noticed it's hard for her to get up the stairs. I got her a heating pad.*"

They stared at each other.

"Yeah," said Laura, "I see your problem."

"Right?" Polly sighed. "Like I said, cool customer."

Inside the store Laura could see a short line had formed at the register and pointed it out to Polly.

"Gotta go," Polly said. "See you later. Dinner?"

Laura nodded. "Will you tell Maggie? I forgot to get her number."

"I'll text it to you. She wants only first-person dinner reservations, it's one of her rules." Polly went in, then turned around and said, "Try and think of a good plan to thwart the dognapper."

Laura nodded. "I'm not sure 'dognapper' is the right term, he only gave her a warmer welcome."

Polly narrowed her eyes. "Remember who brought you in, Laura. Love the one you're with."

Laura grinned and nodded, waving as she turned to head home.

Polly hurried back into the store and smiled at Nina. "Sorry, I got chatting."

"Nooo," said Nina quietly. "How unusual, you're normally such a Trappist." She helped another customer, handing them their book and adding, "Although, you know, Trappists don't *literally* take a vow of silence, they simply maintain a pretty radical silence, generally speaking."

"Radical Silence is an excellent band name," said Polly. "I think the new girl fancies Bob."

Nina frowned. "Everyone fancies Bob, he's empirically fanciable. Doesn't mean she actually wants to, you know, date him."

Polly shrugged. "I'm going to stick my nose in."

"Don't do it," warned Nina. "It never works the way you want it to."

"I won't do anything drastic," said Polly, ringing up a customer who was buying a romance novel and drinking in this conversation.

"Pol, don't stickybeak. Remember what happened in Ventura."

The customer leaned forward, her eyes wide. "What happened in Ventura?"

Polly shook her head. "My lips are sealed."

"Yeah," muttered Nina. "By court order."

They fell silent until the customer left, and then Nina turned to Polly and fastened her with a firm stare. "Polly, you don't know Bob very well, and you don't know Laura at all. Stay out of it."

Polly sighed, and perched on the counter. "Nina, I am not a super-educated person, as you know." She held up her hand to interrupt Nina's immediate contradiction. "Dude, I didn't go to college, it's OK, I didn't want to, I'm happy I didn't, and I've never regretted it for a second." She pointed a finger. "Don't get brainwashed by the hegemony, Nina. Not going to college doesn't make you an idiot, and going to college makes you a debt-burdened lemming. Think for yourself!"

Nina didn't have an immediate comeback to this, as she hadn't been expecting that turn to the conversation.

Polly pressed her advantage. "But that doesn't mean I don't know people, because I do. There is nothing I know better than attraction—getting it, causing it, losing it, ruining it. I have done them all. Laura Costello—and props to me for remembering her last name—has a broken heart."

Nina frowned. "She does?"

Polly nodded. "She does. A broken engagement she pretended to be all cool about, but I could tell. As you know, the best way to get over someone—"

Nina interrupted her, waving one hand and putting the other over her ear. "Don't say it, you know I hate—"

Polly ignored her. "Is to get under someone else."

Nina made a furball sound. "There is so much wrong with that, I don't know where to begin."

Polly shook her head. "No, it's provably true. I've proved it. The best cure for a sad heart is a—"

"No," said Nina.

"Happy vagina."

"Stop."

"I've got more."

"Please don't."

All of a sudden they realized there was another customer standing on the other side of the graphic novel shelf, staring at them in wonderment. He was maybe thirteen and had understood only a fraction of what he'd heard until he'd very clearly heard the word "vagina" and looked up just as Polly and Nina looked at him, causing him to suffer such an extreme anguish of embarrassment that he literally turned and left the store, never to return. This was a pity, because he had plenty of allowance to spend on books and had been a pretty regular customer.

Nina hissed like a swan. "Now look what you've done. I just got him started on Percy Jackson, I had him on a book-hook for *months*."

She turned and headed to the back office, and Polly realized she was genuinely a little ticked off.

Nina turned back at the door. "Listen, Polly. I love you dearly, you're a local celebrity and a moderately good employee, but you are not a matchmaker. Stay out of it."

Polly nodded. "OK, Nina."

Nina closed the door fully aware she'd been snowed. Oh well. Laura was a grown-up. She could handle Polly.

Hopefully.

SIX

When Laura got home the house was quiet, apart from the animals who trickled in from three different directions and congregated in the kitchen, interested to see what thrilling diversions she was going to provide. She did her best to ignore them and opened the refrigerator door and stared into it as everyone does, hoping something would metaphorically leap out at her. She wasn't even hungry, she was simply thinking something sweet might be nice. She shut the fridge and opened the freezer.

Popsicles! Marked very clearly: *For sharing, help yourself, love, Libby*. She looked on another shelf and spotted a box of frozen mini-pizzas, with a label: *For anyone, love, Polly*. A container of ice cream was a gift from Anna, and a nearly empty bottle of vodka was from Maggie, with *Happy Holidays* on a label around its neck. Ah, thought Laura, I see how it is. Conspicuous and competitive generosity. I can play that game.

She reached for a Popsicle and shut the freezer door. She turned and realized that Daisy the pug was the only animal left, waiting patiently to see what she'd found in the Cold Cupboard of Food. Laura looked down, Daisy looked up. One tooth underbit her top lip on the right. Her ears were folded like rose petals, but one was flipped inside out. Both of her bulging eyes were a bit gummy and slightly misty, but her focus on Laura was laser-esque. Laura narrowed her eyes and took a bite of the rocket-shaped Popsicle, which promptly separated as if directed by mission control. The jettisoned tail section was caught before it hit the ground, yet Daisy appeared not to have moved at all. After holding Laura's gaze for a few seconds, she swallowed.

Laura finished the Popsicle and wandered out into the garden again, wanting to explore further. Tiny high feels followed her, and she turned to see Daisy in determined pursuit, curved toenails clacking on the flagstones. She really was shaped like a footstool, or a loaf of very dense bread. She walked like a woman wearing a too-tight dress and too-small shoes, but she had gravitas.

The two of them crossed the terrace and descended the shallow stairs to the lower lawn. It was late afternoon and the sun was gilding all the flowers as they made their way across the grass. Daisy wheezed a little and Laura slowed her pace. No need to make enemies at floor level.

The lawn was dotted with dandelions and daisies despite being cleanly mown. Presumably they were spared on purpose, and it reminded Laura of the rug in a preschool. She wandered past the vegetable garden, checking to make sure no one was hiding in the tomatoes, and through a narrow gap between two tall hedges. At first she'd expected to find a garage or maybe a guesthouse, but it was actually a small rose garden, arranged around a pair of benches and a low table. In the distance she heard the front door closing and paused to listen, but there was no further sound.

It was summer and the roses were in full bloom. Her grandmother loved roses, and her apartment was always full of flowers, her balconies dangerously heavy with containers. Laura bent over to sniff, and the first rose was so deeply rich with scent she found herself literally pushing her nose into it, like a large, flightless bee.

"Oh, hello," said a voice from behind her, and Laura turned to see—of course—Bob the whatever it was Polly called him. Impossibly handsome. Which he was, especially in the soft low sunshine of early evening.

"Hi," said Laura, backing out of the flower quickly, embarrassed. "Sorry, I was, you know, smelling them."

Bob frowned at her in puzzlement. "Uh, you're allowed to smell the roses. I think there's even a phrase about it." He was taller than he'd seemed at a distance, and broader.

Laura wasn't understanding him and could feel a blush creeping up her neck. *Fantastic self-possession, Laura.*

"*Take time to stop and smell the roses?*" Bob said, possibly wondering if he'd come upon a concussion victim. He could feel himself going pink, his usual shyness around other people— particularly women—starting to take over.

"Oh, right," said Laura, giving up and going for a big smile. It usually worked.

After a slight pause, Bob smiled back and stepped past her, going closer to the roses. He touched a flower, pulled off a brown petal here and there. "They do smell great, but you can also smell night-blooming jasmine." He turned and pointed at a nearby shrub. "I'm Bob, by the way." He stuck out his hand, and Laura shook it.

"I'm Laura," she replied. "I think we share a bathroom."

He grinned, which was honestly a little painful because it made his nose crinkle. "I know, but so far you're tidier than the last guy."

"I stole two of your Advil," said Laura. *Tidier, but more larcenous.*

"That's OK," he said, unable to come up with anything cleverer than that to say.

"I had a headache," she added.

"That's OK," he said again, then shook his head. "I don't mean OK that you had a headache, OK that you borrowed Advil."

"Right," said Laura. "Although I won't be giving them back." *Stop talking, stop talking.* "Because I swallowed them."

Bob's mouth dropped open a little as his brain struggled to come up with a response to that. After five seconds it came up with something: Change the subject.

"I have to pick roses for Maggie," said Bob, pulling a pair of pruning shears from his pocket and waving them. He looked at Laura. "Which ones do you like?"

Laura looked around. "Which ones smell best?"

He pointed at a creamy yellow one. "That one's nice, very lemony." He walked over and snipped a long stem, then a couple more. He sniffed them, and Laura came over to smell them for herself.

She looked up from the flower and smiled a question. "Will lemons go with dinner?"

Bob shrugged, noticing her cheekbones, her eyelashes, a splattering of pale freckles across her nose. He went over to a dark yellow rose with red petal edges and added a couple of those. Then another bush gave up two dark red flowers, more tightly furled than the others. He looked around, finally adding three white roses. He considered the bunch in his hand. "That should do, I think." He held the bouquet out to Laura. "What do you think?"

I think you standing there holding out a bunch of roses looks like the search results for "romantic images of handsome men," thought Laura, but what she said was, "Beautiful, she'll love them," then she turned and headed back to the house. Bob watched her hair swing as she turned, and felt his stomach drop. Maggie had said there was a new tenant. She'd said Laura was nice, from New York, and recently arrived in Los Angeles. She had completely neglected to mention Laura was gorgeous. He willed himself not to stare at her back view, but as she walked across the lawn ahead of him, it was unavoidable. She was tall, strong, and absolutely, in every single way, his type. When she'd smiled at him not three minutes earlier, he'd been momentarily stunned, tiny bluebirds circling his head like in an old cartoon.

Daisy looked up at Bob, then followed Laura. Bob said, "I see you've made friends with Daisy." He fell into step alongside Laura, the scent of the roses trailing them like a veil. "I warn you, she's demanding."

"She seems pretty low-key to me," said Laura. "What's she going to do, run over my foot?" She laughed. "Even if she jumped up and down it wouldn't hurt."

Bob paused and bent down to scratch Daisy's head. "Don't listen to her," he said. He straightened up and grinned at Laura. "You'll see." He loped up the steps to the house ahead of her, and Laura realized she was standing there staring after him. He was even more attractive close up than he had been at a distance, and she was grateful she wasn't looking for a relationship of any kind.

Otherwise she'd be in real trouble.

Despite the fact that Laura had forgotten to text Maggie about dinner, there was plenty to go around. Anna and Libby were out at a movie, so it was only the four of them. Not counting the dogs, who sat supportively nearby in case anyone needed help with their chicken, or advice on gravy ratios.

"So, you have to go to grad school to become a physical therapist?" asked Polly. "Isn't it just massage?" She made a face in response to Laura's expression. "I'm going to guess not, don't shoot me."

Laura relaxed her face and pondered, because the answer could be simple or complicated. She finished her mouthful of mashed potatoes and gravy and went for simple. "Physical therapists are experts in the way people move and operate their bodies. Humans are biological machines, right? We have levers and joints and tendons and muscles, and everything works together. Break one part and the whole machine falls out of whack, break more than one and it can crumble completely. PTs help people regain strength and function after they've had an illness or accident." She shrugged. "That's simplifying it, but even a small injury can have a huge impact if it stops you from living your life the way you want to."

"I broke my big toe when I was pregnant," said Maggie, helping herself to more vegetables, "and firstly, it was almost as painful as childbirth, I'm not even joking, and it took forever to heal. Walking was impossible for weeks."

Laura nodded. "The big toe is completely pivotal to walking upright, and gets no respect until it's injured." She stood and kicked off her sandal. "Watch." She took a slow step and demonstrated. "You hit the ground with your heel first, then roll forward through your foot, and then you actually push off using your big toe. Break that puppy and walking is really hard." She sat back down. "And of course injuries can be much more serious and complicated, and sometimes you need a team of PTs and other therapists working together." She blushed. "I don't really know that much yet. I start the program next month."

"How long is the program?" asked Maggie.

"Three years. It's a doctor of physical therapy, it's pretty intense."

"What made you want to do it?" asked Maggie. "And why here?"

Laura sighed. She didn't want to go into it in detail, but there was something about Maggie that made it easy to talk. "Well, my undergraduate degree is in biology, like I said, and originally I was going to keep doing that, getting my PhD and going into research or something." She felt her chest start to tighten up the way it did when she had to explain herself, and wondered if it would get easier soon. "But then, before graduation, I got into an accident and was badly hurt. I was in the hospital for weeks, and it took a really long time to walk again and things like that. It made me, you know, reevaluate."

"Is that why you have a limp?" Polly asked, mildly ashamed of being nosy, but not enough to not want to know. It's not the kind of thing you can ask about immediately, at least not once you leave preschool, but she'd wondered.

Laura nodded.

"What kind of accident was it?" continued Polly, hoping for something interesting like being crushed by a falling piano, or attacked by a tiger.

"Car crash," said Laura, laughing when she saw Polly's disappointed expression. "Sorry. I was driving back from snowboarding upstate. I hit a truck." She swallowed, feeling her heart speeding up. "I don't remember much, because several other cars got involved and I was unconscious for a while, and then I was awake but not totally . . . you know . . . together." She shrugged again, as if nothing could be less important. "It wasn't ideal."

Polly, Maggie, and Bob stared at her, and she felt herself getting redder. "I'm fine now." She added inconsequentially, "It was on the news."

Maggie had such an expression of sympathy on her face that

Laura couldn't look at her. Instead she looked down at her legs and waited through the silence. She'd learned there really wasn't anything good to say about the accident, and that no one was really sure how to react.

Bob, however, coughed and said, "That's terrible, could you pass me the potatoes?"

Laura passed the bowl. She could tell, as her eyes met his, that he knew she didn't want to talk about this and was happy to change the subject. *I don't need the details,* said his face. *I can tell it hurts.*

Polly wasn't as ready to move on. "Wow, how long did it take you to walk again?"

"Months," replied Laura, "and that's how I found out about PTs and what they do." She thought of her therapist's face, his kind eyes, his certainty. "My PT never quit on me, and after a while I was fine." *Well, physically fine, anyway.* "I decided to pay it forward very literally by becoming a PT myself. I guess I lack imagination."

"That sounds extremely stressful," said Maggie.

"I guess," replied Laura breezily. She looked around. "What about you guys? Did you all grow up here?"

Maggie looked at her thoughtfully, but let it go. "Not me, I'm from the Midwest. Detroit, I came here for college and never left. My husband and I met here, raised the kids here, and here I still am." She shrugged. "I love my house, I love the weather, my business is thriving, why would I leave?"

Laura wanted to ask about her husband but didn't. She turned to Bob. "And you?"

Bob grinned. "Genuine Angeleno. Born and raised in Echo Park, east of here." He pointed at Polly. "She will claim to be one, too, but she's from Long Beach."

Polly pulled a face. "You're jealous because I had the beach."

Bob shook his head. "Not a beach guy." He stood and started clearing the plates and serving dishes. "We'll clean up, Maggie. Go enjoy the garden."

"I will, thanks." The older woman refilled her wineglass and headed outside. This was how it worked; she cooked, they cleaned. She considered it more than a fair trade, because who wouldn't rather cook than clean?

Loading the dishwasher, Laura decided to ask some questions of her own. "And you're a gardener? Or a landscaper? What's the difference?"

Bob smiled. "Not a lot. I guess a landscaper works with more than plants, and a gardener focuses on what grows. Maybe?"

"Did you go to school for it?" That sounded vaguely insulting, but a quick glance at his face showed he hadn't taken it that way. *I am such a klutz.*

"Yeah, I have a degree in horticulture." Bob looked unconcerned about Laura's opinion of his education, and something inside her relaxed a little. He reminded her of her brother's friends. She was the youngest of four, and the only girl. Her brother's friends had been everywhere throughout her teens, some of them quite consistently. But even if she'd liked any of them, and once or twice she did, she'd gotten the impression they considered her off-limits. Bob had that same reserved energy, the same quiet vibe.

"That's how I met him, kind of," said Polly, who'd helped clear the table but was now sitting at it eating a bowl of ice cream.

"Kind of?" Laura was interested.

They both laughed and Polly rubbed her eyebrow and said, "You explain it, I've got brain freeze."

"No," said Bob, looking under the sink for the dishwasher tablets, "it's too confusing."

Polly swallowed her ice cream and looked at Laura. "Follow this if you can: His teacher from college is dating Nina's boyfriend's brother's sister-in-law. That *same* woman, Lili, has a kid in one of Nina's book clubs at work, so they met that way, and then Nina met her boyfriend at Lili's wedding."

Laura was struggling and frowned. "Wait, the mother's boyfriend?"

Polly shook her head. "No, her own boyfriend, Tom. Lili's sister was marrying Tom's brother. That's how it all fits together."

Laura was still confused. "And where do you come into it?" She looked at Bob. "Were you at the wedding, too?"

"Nope." He'd started the dishwasher and was wiping down the counters. "But I'm close with my old teacher and Lili and her sister, met Nina a few times and then Polly, and Polly told me about the room . . ." He shrugged. "Friends of friends of friends. It's confusing to me, and I'm part of it."

"It's just backstory," said Polly. "All you need to remember is I am a good person to know when you need somewhere to live."

"As you proved within twenty minutes of meeting me." Laura sat down at the table again.

Bob hung the dish towel on the oven door handle and turned to leave the kitchen. "Uh . . good night, ladies."

Polly and Laura watched him leave. Daisy got up and followed him. Then Polly turned to Laura and made a combination facial expression and hand gesture that somehow conveyed everything Laura was thinking. She realized it was one of Polly's trademarks, using her body to express things her words couldn't. Maybe it was an actor thing, or maybe it was a Polly thing.

"Don't worry," Polly said. "After you've known him awhile, the handsome wears off." She licked her ice cream spoon. "You don't stop seeing it, you simply accept it's part of the totally normal and mostly friendly dog thief who lives in the house."

"The one who looks like a movie star?"

"Yes. The totally normal and mostly friendly dog thief who lives in the house and looks like a movie star." Polly carried her dish over and rinsed it. "And starts the dishwasher before I'm ready and is possibly trying to steal my emotional support dog." She washed and dried the dish and looked at her watch. "I've got an hour to kill before meeting some friends. Do you want to watch some peak TV?"

SEVEN

As Bob walked away from the kitchen, he heard the gentle clicking of claws and turned to see Daisy trickling along behind him. He slowed down to let her catch up. He heard Laura saying "movie star," back in the kitchen, and let his imagination fill with the sound of her voice. He'd watched her across the table, looking up from under her ridiculous lashes, like a giraffe, or the soft unicorn toy of one of his nieces. He'd observed that she was quick to smile and slower to laugh. She had a heavy hand with the salt. She didn't drink a lot; she still had half a glass of wine left when the dinner was over. She was wearing hummingbird earrings. She didn't mention a boyfriend. She liked animals and he'd noticed her slipping food to the dogs more than once. She'd been hurt badly and didn't want to talk about it, and he could relate to that.

The women had lowered their voices and Bob couldn't hear anything else from the kitchen. Daisy came to a gentle halt in front of his door and turned back to look questioningly at him.

As he held the door for her, Polly came out of the kitchen and saw the tableau. She made a tongue-clicking noise, presumably by clicking her tongue.

"I see how it is," she said, coming to her own gentle halt at the bottom of the stairs.

Bob grinned at her shamelessly. "You're welcome to change rooms with me, I don't have a problem climbing stairs." Daisy looked at Polly for a second, then trundled in.

Polly narrowed her eyes. "Your room is bigger."

"Yes, but your room is in the back. It's quieter."

Polly turned and headed up the stairs. "True, but then you'd be farther away from our lovely new tenant, and wouldn't that be a shame?"

Bob wasn't sure how to respond to this, and as she reached the first landing, Polly turned a little and said, quietly, "She's single, you know." She carried on up the stairs, not looking directly at him. "She was engaged, but now she's not, FYI."

As she went into her room, Polly decided that sharing factual information couldn't possibly be considered sticking her nose in. Nina, of all people, would support that . . . right?

Bob closed his bedroom door and looked at Daisy, who was turning circles on her heated bed and occasionally poking it with a firm paw.

"She's single," Bob said to her. "She was engaged, but now she's not."

Daisy looked at him and said nothing.

"I completely agree," said Bob, wondering if there was a baseball game on. "But the chances that a girl who looks like that would be interested in me are pretty small."

Daisy disagreed, but wasn't sure how to phrase it.

Bob sat down on his sofa, opened his laptop and found the baseball game, then texted his big sister.

"Hey," he said.

A pause, three dots, then, "Yo."

"'Sup," he responded. There was a longer pause, then three dots, then his sister texted him again.

"What's wrong?"

He smiled wryly at the screen. He'd typed all of six letters.

"Nothing's wrong," he replied.

"Money, work, or girls?" she texted.

Bob gave up pretending. "Girl."

"Spill."

"New housemate. Gorgeous."

There was a very brief pause, then the phone rang. He grinned, and answered it.

"Hey," he said.

"Robert," his sister said, "I hope I don't have to remind you of the danger of shitting where you eat."

Bob made a face. "Firstly, that's a horrible saying, and secondly, I've always taken that to mean don't have a relationship in the workplace."

Roxana made a familiar snorting noise. "Don't argue semantics, you know what I mean."

"She's literally across the hall. We share a bathroom."

"No, really, you cannot take this any further. You can't live with someone and *then* start dating them, it's backward." Roxy was only semi-joking. She didn't want her baby brother getting his heart broken again.

Bob's smile faded. "She probably wouldn't even be interested." He leaned down and undid his laces. One of the knots had gotten wet, and he had to wedge the phone under his ear and use both hands.

His sister made another familiar noise, this time more sarcastic. "Right, because women are never interested in you."

Bob shrugged. "At first, maybe. Then they get to know me and it's all over. I'm not flashy enough for LA girls." He worked his foot out of the first boot and tossed it in the corner, startling Daisy.

"Oh, quit it." Roxy knew this was genuinely an issue for her brother, who was as cute as a bug but suffered from PPST: piss-poor small talk. No matter how relaxed he was, how confidently he started the evening, the minute an attractive girl spoke to him, his tongue turned into a wooden spoon. He could no more make lighthearted and humorous conversation of a seductive nature than he could have sprouted a jet pack and blown out of there. His looks were a big initial draw, but then—as his best friend in college had bluntly pointed out—he choked in the clutch. This was great for the friend because he was less attractive but quick and funny, so going to a bar with Bob was like bringing a golden retriever puppy; girls simply materialized. While Bob blushed and answered in monosyllables, his friend turned on the charm and got lucky a lot more frequently than Bob did.

"Are you watching the game?" Bob wished he'd never reached out to his sister. She meant well, but her encouragement reminded him that he *needed* encouragement, and it was giving him a stomachache.

"Don't change the subject, but yes." Roxana sighed. "What's the girl's name?"

"Laura."

"Grandma's name?" Roxy sounded uncertain. "Great, another layer of weird."

"Really . . . let's change the subject." Bob's voice was quiet.

Roxy relented. "Could you believe that double play?"

Bob leaned back into the sofa, relieved. "When? I only turned on the game thirty seconds ago. What did I miss?"

"Oh," said his sister, settling into her own couch, miles away. "Get comfortable, I'll bring you up to speed."

EIGHT

The next morning after she'd run, showered, and dressed, Laura made herself a cup of tea and called her grandmother.

Laura's grandmother (her father's mother) lived three blocks away from Laura's childhood home. Every summer her parents went away to do fieldwork—Laura's mother ran a longitudinal study on family groupings in London's Trafalgar Square (pigeons, not tourists), and her father returned to the Andes each year to anxiously count endangered puff-leg hummingbirds—and Laura's grandmother would move in to take care of the kids. Barbara Costello was not a scientist like her husband and son, but only because her slender generation of female scientists stopped working when they got married and became mothers; people assumed their brains fell out along with their placentas.

"Hey, baby," said her grandmother, clearly glad to have a distraction. "Did you find a job yet?"

"Nope, I'll get right on it after I finish breakfast."

Her grandmother laughed. "Don't tell prospective employers you burned down your apartment building."

Laura made a face. "Mom told you, huh?"

Her grandmother laughed again. "Are you kidding? When

she called, it took me a while to work out you weren't in the hospital."

"I wasn't even there when the fire started, Grandma."

"How convenient," joked her grandma. Laura heard the sound of a kitchen chair being pulled back, and the satisfying sigh her grandmother gave as she sat down. A fork rattled on a plate, and Laura wondered if Grandma had cake or pie. There was always one or the other, under a big glass dome on her kitchen counter. Laura was suddenly overwhelmed with homesickness and took a deep breath, letting it out slowly and, she hoped, silently.

"Don't freak out," said her grandmother, apparently having developed bat-like hearing. "She didn't literally imply you'd become a fire starter." The fork noise came again. "You know, I made a peach pie and you're not here to help me with it." She chewed and added, "Your mother is sending you a box of clothes, by the way."

Laura frowned. "Why?" She shook her head. "Because of the fire, you mean?"

"Exactly. I pointed out these were clothes you'd chosen to leave behind, but presumably she thought something was better than nothing."

"Does she think I'm walking around Los Angeles naked?"

Her grandmother coughed on a crumb, then said dryly, "Your mother has been married to my son for nearly forty years and I'm still not completely sure what she thinks about anything. She's not exactly forthcoming."

Laura changed the subject. "I spoke to Jake yesterday, he seemed good. How's Marc?" she asked, referring to her other brother.

"Marc and your mother are feuding," replied her grandmother breezily, "although as of this morning no one else has been dragged into it."

Laura rolled her eyes. "I'm scared to ask . . ."

"Marc suggested crows were more skilled than pigeons at facial recognition."

Laura's jaw dropped open. "You're kidding."

"No," her grandmother sighed. "Corvidae versus Columbidae, will the madness ever end?"

Laura shrugged. "Well, other families probably draw swords over sports teams." Then she made a face at herself; this was a sore topic, as Laura and her grandmother were the only sports fans in the family.

"Well, you ran away to the circus and left me on my own," said her grandmother. "If the Knicks don't make the playoffs, I know who I'm going to blame."

"They haven't made it since 2013, so that's really not fair. Maybe I'll start supporting the Lakers, they're far more successful."

"Huh," grunted her grandmother. "Do so, and it will be good you're on the other side of the country." She'd been born in 1946, the year the New York Knicks came into existence. Laura's great-grandparents had taken that coincidence seriously and run a strict local-teams-only household. Knicks. Yankees. Jets. Rangers. End of story.

Laura laughed. "Honestly, I'd be totally down for a visit, even if it meant getting a slap across the back of the head." She looked at the time, and added, "I should get on with my day, but I'll call you again soon. I love you."

There was a fractional hesitation. "You haven't asked me about Nick."

"No," said Laura, "I haven't."

"Have you spoken to him?"

"No."

"Are you going to?"

"No."

"I thought it was all friendly?"

Laura took a deep breath. "Grandma, Nick and I grew up together, went to college together . . . the romantic part is over, but we're always going to be friends." She waited, but her grandmother didn't say anything. "Honestly, though, I'm trying to start a fresh chapter over here, and Nick is not part of it."

"Does he know that?"

Laura shook her head, unseen. "Grandma, I gotta go. I love you."

"I love you, too, baby."

Laura was about to hang up when her grandmother added, "Wait, did you get a car yet?"

"No, not yet. The buses are fine, and there's a subway. Kind of."

Her grandmother's voice softened. "Baby, you'll have to drive sometime. You knew that when you moved there."

"I know," Laura said, a little crossly. "I went in a car only the other day. It was fine." *Mostly fine.*

Her grandmother sighed, then said, "Go, Knicks!"

"Go, Knicks," replied her granddaughter, and hung up.

NINE

After the call Laura took a bus to Larchmont to return Nina's clothes. When she arrived at the bookstore, Nina was engaged with a customer, and Laura ducked behind a shelf to wait. She looked along the rows of spines, tipping her head like you do in a bookstore, and saw she'd accidentally selected the science section. Familiar favorites caught her eye, books she hadn't read in years but knew by heart. *The Panda's Thumb*, a classic (and hugely entertaining) collection of essays about natural history, leapt out at her, the same edition she'd had on her bedroom shelf at home. The sight of its cover comforted her, and while she leafed through it, she peered over the top of the shelf at Polly and Nina.

Nina was wearing a soft red sweater over yellow cigarette pants, an outfit she'd been pretty happy with until Liz said it reminded her of Winnie the Pooh (Disney, not Shepard) and then Nina couldn't unsee it. Chagrin had taken the bloom off her morning and she had yet to regain it. She should have dressed in gray, because now she felt like Eeyore.

However, the customer in question was asking for recommendations for Golden Age mystery writers and had apparently hit a nerve. He'd read one left in an Airbnb and it had awoken a passion he'd never dreamed existed.

"Which book was it?" Nina's eyes were beginning to sparkle. Golden Age mysteries were one of her many literary jams. Possibly the jammiest.

The guy beamed. "It was *Gaudy Night*, by Dorothy L. Sayers."

Laura watched Nina's face fall. "Damn," she said loudly, then apologized when the guy looked worried. "Sorry, sorry, but that is the *worst* place to start Dorothy Sayers, the worst." She sighed. "Let me be clear, it's an amazing, incredible book, great plot, satisfying denouement, and I can totally see why it got you here, but it's the final book in the all-important Whimsey-Vane romantic subplot. You'll have to cleanse your reading palate with something equally good but different and go back and start over with Sayers later on, maybe in a few years." She turned and led the customer away. "Let's stay in the genre, but leap the ocean and a decade or two . . . Rex Stout to the rescue, I think. Not *strictly* speaking Golden Age, but . . ." Her voice faded away as they disappeared into a separate part of the store, through a doorless doorway.

Laura crept out from behind the bookshelf and approached the checkout desk, where Polly was going over an inventory list.

"I could totally see you," said her new friend, not even looking up. Today Polly was wearing a black turtleneck (the AC in the store was very efficient) over vintage patchwork jeans, with her hair in the jaunty pigtails Sandra Bullock wears when she kicks Benjamin Bratt's butt in *Miss Congeniality*. Laura noticed the pigtails, but wouldn't have gotten the reference. Not a huge movie fan. Looking at Polly, though, made Laura painfully aware she was wearing leggings, running shoes, and a black Columbia University T-shirt that was faded almost to gray (it had escaped the fire by being on her at the time), and that she basically wore the same thing every day. Maybe she should get some fashion advice from Polly? Or Nina? Although there was something slightly familiar about Nina's outfit today, and Laura couldn't place it.

Nina reappeared with the customer, who was carrying a small armful of books and looking encouraged. "This is Polly," Nina was saying. "She'll take your information and I'll be in touch." Then she turned to Laura and said, "Hey, I knew you'd be in. I'm going to get my cast taken off this afternoon."

"Great," said Laura, because that seemed like an appropriate response. "It will feel weird for a while." She hesitated. "Your skin might be dry. You can soak it in warm water, then gently brush your arm." That sounded wrong. Who brushes their arm?

Nina looked interested. "Did you know the average person sheds several pounds of skin every year?"

Laura shook her head. "No, sorry, I didn't."

Nina raised an eyebrow and said, "It's not a test," and then both of them felt awkward.

"They'll give you exercises to do," said Laura. "It's important to do them. Did you know your thumb is controlled by nine distinct muscles, which are themselves controlled by all three of the major hand nerves?"

"No, I didn't know that," said Nina, "but I do know a quarter of all the bones in my body are in my two hands."

Laura stared at her. "Why do you know that?"

Nina shrugged. "I remember things, I can't turn it off. You probably know a lot, too." She froze, a faraway look coming into her eyes. Sadly, Laura didn't know Nina well enough to spot a red flag when she saw one. "What was your undergraduate degree, out of interest?"

"Biology." Laura wasn't quite following the direction the

conversation was taking, but she was determined to make her point. "The human hand is capable of an incredible number of motions and movements, and if you don't look out, you'll lose some of it."

Nina looked unconvinced. "You mean I might not be able to flip someone off?"

Laura nodded. "Or turn the page in a book."

"Good lord," said Nina. "Wash out your mouth."

Polly came back and looked at Laura. "What have you done now? You've got Bob all worked up and now you're upsetting Nina." She sighed. "You seemed so gentle and friendly."

Laura pointed at Nina. "She's not taking care of herself."

Nina turned enthusiastically to her colleague. "Polly, I think we've found our new Carter."

Laura looked at Polly, who snorted with laughter and headed back behind the counter. "Oh my god, did you reveal a deep inner well of knowledge?"

Laura frowned. "Uh, we were talking about how important it is to do physical therapy on her hand." She turned back to Nina. "Your hand uses thirty-four muscles simply to move your fingers and thumb, and all of them have been stuck in those casts. You need to do simple stretches and specific exercises every day." She made a stern face. "I'm not asking you to run a marathon. Spend half an hour."

"Science, plants and animals, probably organic chemistry, sports . . ." Nina broke off and spoke to Laura again. "Are you athletic?" She shook her head and muttered at herself, "Of course she's athletic, Nina, look at her, so, yes, sports, and the Olympics . . ."

Laura held up her hand. "I'm sorry, what on earth are you talking about?"

"Trivia," said Nina, grabbing that hand and shaking it. "Welcome to Book 'Em, Danno, a currently-trailing-but-destined-for-greatness trivia team in the East Los Angeles Pub League."

Laura stared at her. She'd understood all the individual words in the sentence, but had completely failed to grasp the larger meaning. "I'm sorry?"

Polly leaned across the checkout desk. "Nod. You'll enjoy it." She shrugged. "Plus you don't have much choice, she's relentless about this one, *extremely nerdy*, pursuit." This was clearly an old topic.

"What is it, exactly?" Laura wasn't ready to nod.

"It's a highly exciting, intellectually oriented social bonding exercise for people who'd rather look at a piece of paper than each other." Nina seemed pretty darn eager about whatever this was, and Laura recalled how easily she'd run off to loan a total stranger warm clothing. She owed this girl a debt of gratitude, and here was a chance to pay it off.

"I'm sorry," said Laura, blushing at her own slowness, "I still don't have any idea what we're talking about. Is it a club?"

"It's a bar trivia league, you drink, eat pistachios, and answer trivia questions on a variety of subjects."

"For money?"

Nina looked horrified. "No! For honor!"

"And an occasional ugly T-shirt," said Polly, "which is why I don't do it. That and my inability to remember anything for longer than thirty seconds."

Nina smiled at her. "However, you are an excellent cheering section, despite your gnat-like hippocampus." She turned back to Laura. "How about this? Come over to my place Friday night, and I'll explain the whole thing. You'll really do it?"

"I'll try," said Laura, "if you promise to rehab your wrist."

"Deal," said Nina. "Wait till I tell the rest of the team!" She hugged herself and then added, "And you can also explain what Polly meant when she said you had Bob all worked up." She looked at Laura and grinned wickedly. "Or did you think I'd missed that?"

TEN

An hour and a half later Laura was trudging along Third Street, carrying a bag full of books. She'd waited fifteen minutes for a bus, but none had shown up and she'd grown impatient. The weight was hardly a challenge but the sun was pitiless and Laura was starting to realize why LA had developed such a robust and air-conditioned car culture. A truck pulled over ahead of her, and when she drew level and peeped in, Bob was leaning on the steering wheel and smiling at her. Of course, because she was sweating through her T-shirt and was 87 percent certain her period had just started. Which would also explain the giant spot on her nose and the bursting into tears in the bookstore two days earlier.

All these thoughts raced through her head in the few seconds it took Bob to say, "Uh, I'm heading home, do you need a ride?"

Laura hesitated, because she really, really didn't like being in cars since her accident, but then a trickle of sweat rolled down her back and she decided she could handle the incredibly brief drive home.

"That would be great, thanks so much." Laura opened the door as Bob leaned over and swept everything from the front seat onto the floor. Then he made a strangled noise as he realized he'd massacred a small tray of seedlings that had been peacefully sitting on the seat, enjoying the breeze in their leaves. He looked up at Laura, who had paused in the act of getting in, and said, "Crap. Hang on two seconds, would you?"

She nodded and leaned over to help him salvage whatever they could. Bob righted the little tray and she replaced the spilled dirt with her cupped hands and he gently found and picked up the seedlings and she made little holes for them and he tucked them in and he could smell her hair and his fingers touched hers over and over in the earth and thirty seconds later it was all done. Laura picked up the tray, jumped in the truck, put her bag of books on the floorboard, did up her seat belt, and put the baby plants on her lap. She turned to Bob and smiled, and in that moment he realized he was deeply, deeply attracted to her.

Laura, of course, had no idea this was going on and merely kept smiling and hoping she wasn't bleeding on his seat because, well, that would be a challenging early conversation, despite the fact this was the twenty-first century. She looked at the plants in her lap and not out of the window; that way it was easier to pretend she was somewhere else.

It's entirely possible that Bob's mind was on Laura's face, so to speak, but it's also possible what happened next wasn't his fault at all. He looked briefly in his mirror and pulled out onto Third, and with a sound like a thousand giant lightbulbs exploding at once, another car sideswiped his truck and ripped off his side mirror.

When the body experiences a sudden shock, it actually freezes for one twenty-fifth of a second and then deploys intense psychological curiosity, mobilizing every neuron and nerve, every sense, every possible input to work out exactly what just happened. In a microsecond or two the brain gathers the intel, sorts it, analyzes it, cross-references it, and is ready to issue directions for what to do next. It's a miracle, really, and while it might not definitively prove the existence of God, it certainly deserves an enthusiastic round of applause.

Bob's brain, which was in pretty good shape generally speaking, came almost instantly to the conclusion that everything was fine and the world hadn't come to a sudden and inexplicable end. The other driver had hit his brakes and pulled over with his hazard lights on, so Bob turned to Laura and leaned over to grab his insurance card from the glove box.

"Shit, that scared the crap out of me, you OK? Welcome to Los Angeles, home of the worst drivers in America." His voice tailed off as he got a good look at Laura and realized she wasn't OK. At all.

Her eyes were completely dark, her pupils dilated almost to iris width, and he could see she had twice as many freckles as he'd previously noticed, her skin was so pale.

"Laura," he said, "are you hurt?"

She shook her head, then shook it again. "No. Am I?"

Bob looked her over quickly. No blood.

"No, you're not hurt," he said, his voice firm. "We're both fine, the guy knocked off my side mirror is all."

She nodded and stared at him. Her breathing was shallow, and he remembered her accident and wondered if she was still maybe a little freaked out. He looked through the windshield; the other driver was now out of his car, pointedly looking at his watch.

"Listen, I have to go and exchange insurance info with this asshole, but I'll be right back." He racked his brain for ideas, and thought about his nieces and nephews and what worked to calm them down. He scrabbled on the floor and handed her a flower catalog, and then pulled a pen from his jacket pocket.

"Could you do me a favor and go through and mark all the yellow ones?" he said, giving her the pen. "Circle the names, put an X by them, whatever." He smiled at her, noticing her eyes looked a little less out of focus. Not much, though, and she was still as pale as ever. He squeezed her hand quickly. "Laura, I promise, everything is fine."

She nodded.

"Only the yellow ones," he said mock seriously. "No other colors."

She nodded and opened the catalog.

"Yellow," she said. "Got it."

Bob got out of the car, and Laura started looking, her hand shaking as she held the pen.

Fortunately, there are a lot of yellow flowers.

By the time Bob returned to the car, Laura had pulled herself together and was deeply embarrassed. He handed her his registration and insurance.

"Could you put those back in the glove box?" He smiled at her, shaking his head. "I'm really sorry about that. I suspect it was his fault for not paying attention, but maybe I should have checked my blind spot better."

"These things happen," she replied. "I'm sorry I freaked out, what a wuss."

He was surprised. "Not at all, it was completely shocking."

She wouldn't look at him. "You didn't freak out."

He wasn't sure what to say. "Uh . . . it's, like, the third dumb, small fender bender I've had in the last year. Maybe the drivers in Los Angeles aren't the worst in the country, but they have to be up there." He looked carefully over his shoulder before slowly pulling out again.

Laura, unseen, shook her head a final time and looked out of the window. Her head was starting to pound, overwhelming chagrin snuffing out the hope she'd had that maybe things would be different here.

She was an idiot. Her parents had been right. She never should have come.

ELEVEN

When they pulled up in front of the house, Laura turned to Bob and smiled broadly.

"Thanks for the ride," she said. "I was getting pretty hot walking home, I won't lie." Yes, she thought, let's pretend nothing else happened, I'm totally good with that. It's always worked before.

Bob smiled back at her. "My pleasure. Are you sure you're OK?" Her color was completely back to normal, and he noticed how her honey-colored hair literally glittered where the sun hit it.

Laura nodded and opened the truck door, climbing out and heading to the house. "Sure, totally. Thanks again." One more smile, and she was gone.

Bob sat and watched her walk into the house, pretty sure he'd just been lied to.

As Laura came out of her bathroom a few minutes later—she hadn't gotten her period, which was *so freaking annoying*—she almost collided with Maggie, who was heading out for a walk with Herbert.

"Come with me," said the older woman, not posing a question so much as issuing a request. Laura nodded and turned; she hadn't really cooled down yet, so she might as well keep going. Bob was still in the driveway, pottering around in the bed of the truck, organizing tools and supplies. Laura had to squint to look up at him.

Maggie paused. "Home for dinner, Bob?"

He nodded. "If it's not too late."

"It's not," she replied, clipping the leash to Herbert's collar.

Bob looked at Laura. "Feeling better?" he asked.

"Sure," she replied quickly, "completely fine." She still wouldn't look at him, and hurried after Maggie, who was letting Herbert decide which way to go.

It was by now late afternoon, and it was dappled and pretty under the spreading trees of August Boulevard.

Maggie was excited. "My son will be here for dinner tonight."

"That's nice. Does he live in LA?"

"For the last four years he's been living and working in Japan, and I've seen him precisely once in person. We chatted online and Skyped once or twice a month, but the time difference between here and there was very challenging."

"Where was he?" Laura blushed. "I mean, Japan, I get it, but which city?"

"Tokyo. They're sixteen hours ahead of us, so I can only really call him in the evenings, which is the next morning for him. If I call him in the morning here, it's the middle of the night there, and that took me a minute to get on top of. But now that I'm completely used to it and can finally calculate the time zones without a piece of paper, he's coming home."

"To visit?"

"To stay, I hope."

"What does he do?"

"He's in finance, sadly."

Laura looked curiously at her. "Why sadly?"

"Oh, I don't know," said Maggie, waving at someone across the street. She raised her voice. "Did it all work out with the cabbages?"

"Yes," called back the woman, also raising her voice for this strange exchange of vegetable news. "We needed twelve in the end, so we were both wrong."

"Wow," called Maggie, then turned back to Laura. "That's a lot of cabbages. Anyway, there's nothing wrong with money, I guess. I thought Asher was going to be something more . . . interesting." She looked quickly at Laura. "That sounds wrong, it's fine that he's a businessman . . ." She tailed off.

Laura wasn't quite sure what to say here. Was Maggie genuinely sad her son was successful? "What did you think he was going to be?"

"A musician."

Herbert needed to do his more serious business and was trying to go behind a tree, so they stopped. Laura said, "But presumably he can be a businessman and a musician, it's not like those two are mutually exclusive."

"Sure," said Maggie, keeping half an eye on the dog, "but when Asher was young, he was full of creativity and fun, and then he went to college and came back all grown up and much less amusing. Then he got his heart broken and ran away to Japan to recover." She looked cross suddenly.

They resumed their walk, and every so often Maggie waved at other people, presumably neighbors and old friends. It reminded Laura of crossing the Columbia campus with either of her parents;

students and other professors would continuously stop and chat, or simply launch into complicated questions that made no sense to anyone but her mom or dad. Maggie was more casual than that, waving or saying hi, but it was clear she was plugged into Hancock Park as firmly as Laura's family was into the Upper West Side of Manhattan. Little tiny countries, with little tiny populations and even tinier politics.

They turned back toward home, and Maggie changed the subject again. "So, are you settling in? Do you need anything?"

Laura shook her head. "No, thanks, I'm good. I need to find a job, but something that'll work around school." She paused. "I should get my class schedule soon, which will make it easier."

Maggie shot her a sidelong glance. "And why was Bob asking if you were feeling better? Were you not feeling well?"

Laura shook her head again without realizing it. "No, I was fine. He was giving me a ride home and someone hit his truck and took off the mirror. It was very loud." She shrugged. "I'm fine."

Maggie said, "Accidents are by their nature shocking."

Laura nodded.

"And it wouldn't be surprising if you found any kind of car accident a little harder to take, because of your own experience."

"No, it's fine," said Laura.

"So you keep saying," said Maggie gently.

Laura switched on a smile she kept for occasions such as these, when her words failed her and she wanted to declare a subject closed. From Maggie's point of view, she might as well have written an essay.

They reached the house and Maggie unclipped Herbert and let him race up the slope to the front door.

The two women looked at each other, and Maggie smiled.

"Try and be gentle with yourself," she said, following the dog at a much more reasonable pace. "You've been through a lot. Rest. Pet the cat. Walk the dogs. Run and get strong."

Laura smiled at her. "You're all being very nice to me."

"You're likable," said Maggie simply. "Besides, being able to competently make your way in the world is an incredible achievement in and of itself, especially after trauma. If your story had happened to an elven princess, it would be a legend." She turned and walked away. "I'm going to lie down before dinner. I suggest you do the same. Even the legendary need to nap."

TWELVE

Laura took Maggie's advice and lay down, intending to give it five minutes. Two hours later she woke up sweaty and anxious, with a vaguely nauseated, spacey feeling. She'd been dreaming of the accident, she could tell, though she couldn't remember the details. She got up and stretched, her back clicking in a satisfying manner and the stiffness in her neck easing. She opened and closed her mouth a few times, trying to loosen her jaw. She opened her drawer, and her entire wardrobe slid to the front. She needed to either do some laundry or go back to Target. For a moment the smell of metal and gasoline and fear pushed into her mind, but she frowned and shooed it away. No, she told herself firmly, we're not doing that anymore.

Twenty minutes later, showered and dressed in essentially the same outfit, but cleaner, Laura made her way to the kitchen. It was immediately obvious something special was underway. A beautiful arrangement of roses and peonies took center stage on the butcher block counter, and the room was filled with the smell of roasting tomatoes. Maggie was pottering around putting things in little dishes and talking to Anna and Libby about the year 1000, for some reason. As Laura walked in, she was saying, "Really? King Steve?"

"Yup," said Libby. "I mean, it's not strictly speaking my period, but I'm pretty sure he was the first king of Hungary *and* crowned on Christmas Day."

Maggie raised her eyebrows. "You deliver that level of granularity on things you don't specialize in?" She turned and saw Laura coming in. Maggie smiled and reached out to give her a welcoming hug. "Hey there, Asher's going to be here for dinner." She was clearly very jazzed. "We're making pizzas." She paused. "I told you that already, sorry."

"Not the pizza part, that was new," replied Laura, smiling at Libby. He offered her a glass of wine, and poured it for her when she said a rare yes.

He looked at her as he handed it over, and asked, "Who's your favorite character of ancient history?"

"Uh . . ."

"Betty Rubble," said Polly, bouncing in through the French doors, wearing pajamas and carrying an empty glass. "That chick was underappreciated in her own time." She opened the fridge and grabbed some cranberry juice, which she mixed with soda. Then she added an umbrella, two straws, and a maraschino cherry. She makes everything a party, thought Laura. I wish I was like that.

Polly's arrival had made it five in the kitchen, and Maggie shooed them all out.

"I don't like people underfoot when I'm cooking," she said, slightly huffily. She looked at the wall clock, wondering if she needed to change the batteries.

One by one, Laura, Polly, Libby, and Anna stepped over Daisy, who'd planted herself in the middle of the doorway to the garden.

"The question is," said Anna, last in line, "whether Daisy is attempting to stop people from getting *into* the kitchen or *out* of it."

"I don't think," replied Polly, "she's thinking about anyone else at all. I think Daisy pleases Daisy." They'd all settled around the table outside, and she looked around at them. "Did I mention Ollie left part of a dead mouse in my room? It was waiting for me when I got home."

Anna made a face. "I think that means you two are dating."

Polly looked concerned. "Damn, I didn't get him anything."

"Which part of the mouse was it," asked Libby, "and how did you know it was a mouse rather than, say, a vole?"

Polly turned and looked at him scornfully. "One, a vole? Really? Two, it was the face part, that's how I knew it was a mouse." Then she added, "Plus I found a tiny pair of red shorts with white buttons."

Libby laughed and raised his glass. "OK, Pol, you win."

Laura gazed at Polly and wondered if she would get funnier if she worked with Nina all day, too, or if Polly was the one who'd been funny first and had influenced Nina. Laura always wanted to be quippy, but usually by the time she thought of a good thing to say, it was too late. Like, three days too late. Then Bob appeared, looking like a million bucks and carrying a bottle of beer. His hair was still damp from the shower, and he stood by the doors, making a fuss over Daisy. He looked up at Laura and smiled. She felt a little less overwhelmed. A friendly guy with a nice face, that's all. Then she remembered what a fool she'd made of herself earlier, and looked away.

The dogs burst into a frenzy of barking, and Maggie ran out into the hallway. Seconds later they heard excited voices, and the front door closed.

Polly stopped talking and Laura asked, "Do you know her kids?"

"No," said Polly, "I met her daughter once, she lives in Beverly Hills, but I've never even seen Asher."

They all watched quietly as a tall man walked into the kitchen, carrying a large duffel bag, which he dropped on the floor with relief. This was his childhood home, realized Laura; this house was as familiar to him as her own family apartment was to her. She and the other tenants were interlopers, and Asher might not be completely on board. Maggie was right behind him, talking a mile a minute, and before long she dragged her son outside.

"Everyone," she said, "this is Asher."

Asher looked a great deal like his mother, the big brown eyes, the wavy dark hair, though in his case it was neatly cut. He also had the same wide mouth as Maggie, and it was clear he was as quick to smile as she was, despite his jet lag.

"Hey there," he said. "I've heard a lot about all of you." He looked around. "I bet I can put names to faces . . ." His gaze came to rest on Polly, who was suddenly regretting putting on her pajamas. "You must be Polly."

She nodded. "Yeah, that's me. How could you tell?"

He laughed. "My mom's good at descriptions." He turned to the others. "You must be Libby"—Libby raised his glass—"which makes you two Bob and Anna." He looked at Laura. "And you're the new kid." He had another important thing in common with his mother—her ability to make people feel welcome.

Laura smiled. "That's right."

His mom came up and hugged him, and he turned easily and gathered her into his arms, lifting her off the ground.

"Don't squeeze me, I'll fart," she warned, and he laughed and put her down. She beamed up at him. "Dinner's nearly ready. Are you hungry?"

He nodded. "Yup, or at least I think so. It's tomorrow in Japan, and my body isn't sure what's going on yet." He grinned and shrugged, clearly happy to be home. The only one happier than him and Maggie was Daisy. She was hopping around on her claws, making tiny noises of frustration. Asher looked down and sat right on the patio, welcoming the little dog into his lap. She went nuts, rubbing her wrinkly face on him, spinning around and making whiffling sounds.

Polly looked at Bob. "See? Hurts, doesn't it?"

A couple of hours later, with Cheshire cat smiles of pizza crust all over the table and wineglasses and beer bottles fighting for space, Polly was riveting the group with tales of the Larchmont excitement of the previous year. She was on her third cranberry and soda, but was pacing herself and had dropped the maraschino cherries.

"So, Nina found out she had an extended family she didn't know about?" Laura was finding this hard to imagine.

"Yes," crowed Polly, clearly still delighted by it. "She knew she must have a dad somewhere, she's not a changeling, but her mom never talked about him. Then last year he died and she found out she had, you know, a million relatives in the city. It was a total trip."

"She wasn't as pleased as you might think," added Anna sympathetically. She had a younger brother she would have swapped for a kitten at almost any point in their childhood. Possibly still.

"She was horrified," clarified Polly. "Totally horrified."

"Why?" asked Asher, who knew Nina only vaguely but was obviously no stranger to Knight's and Larchmont.

Polly shrugged. "Nina's shy."

Laura was about to express disbelief when Maggie leaned out

of the kitchen door. "Anyone want an ice cream sundae? Show of hands."

Asher moaned and looked at his mom. "Did you make . . . the sauce?"

She nodded, counted hands, and went back inside.

"A small one," called out Polly, then hoped Maggie hadn't heard her.

Asher looked at her. "I take it you haven't had the sauce yet?"

"I'm not sure . . ." Polly looked thoughtful. "She makes one that tastes like eating toffee on the beach, all salty and sweet at the same time—I've had that one."

A small smile started to play across Asher's face, and he nodded. "Yes, that's a good one, but hopefully not that."

"Then there's the one that smells like it's going to be all strawberries but actually has a hint of rhubarb in it, which for one second makes you panic that it's going to be sour but then the ice cream chimes in and everything's lovely again."

Asher shook his head. "That was my sister's favorite, but not mine, so I don't think that's what she made."

Polly grinned. "Then no, I guess not."

Asher closed his eyes. "The chocolate sauce I *hope* she made reminds you of that birthday where you got everything you wanted, even the things you hadn't dared ask for, and where the chocolate cake remains the cake you measure all other birthday cakes against."

Polly laughed, while everyone else stared at them.

Laura leaned over to Bob and whispered, "Does everyone here talk like that?"

Bob grinned. "No, I would have said caramel, strawberry, and chocolate, but, you know, maybe they're made for each other." He sat back and gave a very subtle shrug at Polly and Asher, who were now recounting tales of best birthdays ever. It turned out that eight had been a high point for both of them.

Once dinner was over, Maggie started gathering plates, and they all leapt up to help her. She raised her hands. "Could you pick me some more roses, Bob?" she asked. "I want some for upstairs and I forgot to do it earlier."

"Where did you get the ones on the counter?" he asked. "They're not from the garden, and peonies aren't even in season."

Maggie clapped her hands to her mouth. "Oh my god, I am so sorry, I completely forgot in all the excitement." She smiled at Laura. "Those are for you! They arrived today and I put the card somewhere . . ." She got up. "Hang on." She went into the kitchen and came back out, holding a tiny square envelope. She handed it to Laura, who was blushing deeply. She was pretty sure who they were from.

She was right. Opening the card, she read the message and closed it. "Thanks, Maggie."

There was an expectant silence.

Impatiently, Polly broke it: "Well, who are they from?"

"Nick," said Laura. "A friend from home."

"The brokenhearted ex-fiancé?" crowed Polly.

"No," Laura replied firmly. "He's not brokenhearted, he's stubborn." She turned to Maggie. "You're welcome to break up the bouquet."

Bob was already on his feet. "I'll cut some more roses, we have plenty." As he turned he added, "Those roses have no scent anyway."

"Go off," said Polly, raising an eyebrow. "Don't hold back. Diss the roses."

He pulled out his clippers, sauntering down the stairs to the rose garden. "I'm a rose snob." He turned and looked at Laura. "Want to help me choose again?"

"Sure," she replied, happy to get away from the table, where Polly and Anna looked like they were revving up to ask her searching questions about her nonrelationship. Indeed, as she followed Bob into the garden, she could feel Maggie, Polly, and the others watching them closely. She put her hand behind her back and raised her middle finger. Polly snickered.

It was later than the previous evening, and the scent in the rose garden was heady.

Laura said, "I can't decide what smells better, the roses or this thing." She poked at a plant with white flowers.

"The jasmine?"

"Yeah, sorry, not good with plant names."

He was quiet and stepped closer to her, selecting the blooms he wanted. She moved back to give him room and abruptly felt uneasy. The flowers had thrown her; Nick had always loved a splashy gesture and he'd sent her flowers more times than she could count, but the fact that he'd sent them here was irritating. She hadn't given him her address, which meant her mom had given it to him, which meant her mom was still talking to him, which meant her mom was still on his side.

"I'm going back inside, it's colder than I thought," she said.

"I'm nearly done," he said, pausing to look at her. But she had already started moving away, and he watched her go, wondering if he'd said the wrong thing, despite having literally said three words. Regardless of what Polly might say, Laura had blushed over the flowers, so even though she said "ex-fiancé," maybe she still cared a bit. Bob kept clipping roses and tried not to feel crestfallen. He was used to being alone, it was fine, plenty more fish in the sea. They could still be friends.

As Laura approached the patio again, the conversation stopped and Polly's voice was slightly concerned as she said, "Everything OK?"

"Totally," said Laura as she breezed past them. "I got cold. I'm going to get a sweater."

Maggie and the others turned to watch Bob crossing the garden, holding his roses.

"What did you do?" asked Polly accusingly.

THIRTEEN

Once in her room, Laura threw off her clothes, grabbed her fluffy dressing gown, and sat on her bed cross-legged. First she texted Polly to tell her she was tired and had headed to bed. Then she took a deep breath and texted Nick. It was pretty late there, but if she was lucky she'd wake his ass up.

Her fingers flew. "I got your flowers."

There was a pause, then the three dots appeared. Dammit, he'd been awake.

(heart emoji) "That's great. I hope they were beautiful."

(three dots)

(flower emoji) "Like you."

Laura rolled her eyes so hard she almost dislocated an eyelash.

"Nick. We broke up. Please do not send me flowers."

"We're still friends."

(three dots)

(over-the-top crying sad face emoji) "Aren't we?"

Laura took an even deeper breath and hit FaceTime. She hated texting with Nick; he liked to send multiple short texts instead of one longer one, which meant she would start to answer the first whatever he'd said, then a second one would come in so she'd have to erase the first one and write an answer that addressed both whatevers, and *then he'd do it again*. And it wasn't like he couldn't see she'd started to answer; he could see her dots! Laura once told her grandmother this single personality trait would have been the final straw had his habit of calling her irritating nicknames and telling her what to do not already done the trick.

However, when his sleepy but familiar face loomed up on her screen, she smiled despite herself. This was the difficulty with Nick; he was charming and largely harmless, but also spoiled rotten and convinced of his own arguments. Everything was easy with him except, it turned out, achieving escape velocity.

"Hey, dollface," he said. "You look as gorgeous as ever. Burning the midnight oil?"

Laura frowned at him. "No, that would be you."

"Really?" He checked the time. "Oh, yeah. What time is it there?"

"Three hours earlier than you."

He grinned at her. "Sweetie, please tell me. Don't torture me." He snuggled down, and Laura realized he was in bed, which shouldn't have been a surprise. "You know how bad I am at math, honey bunches of oats." This was an old joke. His father had won the Fields Medal when he wasn't much older than Nick was now, and the fact that Nick was getting his PhD in biophysics had been viewed by his family as a compromise because he couldn't handle "real math." They still referred to him sometimes as "poor Nick."

She shook her head. "I mean it, Nick. Yes, we're friends, we've known each other forever, but we're not going to stay friends unless you back the hell up. If I can quote Taylor Swift, 'we are never, ever, ever getting back together.'"

Nick rubbed his face with his hand and pouted. "Yeah, yeah,

so you keep saying. Look, I can't help it if I want to try." He smiled, one of his melting smiles that made grandmas hand over their babies and babies hand over their ice creams. "You can take all the time you want, sweet cheeks, I'll wait patiently till you're certain."

"I'm certain," said Laura firmly. "This is what certain looks like."

"Who knew certainty was so sexy?"

Laura frowned at him. "Quit it. Seriously." She paused and sighed. "OK, seeing as we're on FaceTime . . . can I see him?"

Nick grinned and gently lifted the duvet.

"Androcles!" Laura said to the obese one-eared cat who'd been fast asleep against Nick's body until the comforting warmth of night had been ripped away. "Hey, baby, how you doing?" Her tone was soft and loving, and the cat blinked. He could hear a familiar voice, and if he wanted to, he could probably work out where it was coming from, but he didn't really want to, so he closed his eyes, lowered his head, and went immediately back to sleep.

"Aw, baby," said Laura. "You're not going to forgive me?"

Nick covered him up again. "I guess he needs time, just like you."

Androcles was named after the ancient dude who pulled the thorn out of the lion's foot because Nick was a physicist, not a historian. He'd found the cat in Riverside Park, wet, cold, and apparently dead under a tree. One ear was hanging off, one paw was hugely swollen and clearly infected, and fleas were holding a swap meet on his spine.

"And then," Laura remembered Nick saying several years before, "the vet pulled this huge freaking piece of wood out of his foot and all this disgusting crap came out and that's when I thought of his name."

Laura had looked at him. "But Androcles was the one who *pulled* the thorn, not the one who *had* the thorn."

Nick had shrugged and called the cat Andy for short. He was pretty much the only thing Laura missed about New York.

"Are we clear?" asked Laura one last time. "No more flowers, no more nothing. We are old friends, that's it."

Nick looked at her and seemed irritated. "I get it, Laura. But you can't change the way I feel, and I still want to be with you." He thought of something. "Besides, you need taking care of, whether you like it or not."

Laura shook her head. "I really don't, Nick. I'm totally fine."

"Really?" He looked skeptical. "Done a lot of driving yet?"

Laura frowned at him. "No more flowers."

"No promises. It's a free country, baby bear, I can send flowers to any beautiful woman I want to."

"Go right ahead," replied Laura, "but take me off your list or I really will cut you off completely."

He shrugged, clearly not believing a word of it. "Night, sugar cube."

"Night, Nick."

She disconnected, then picked up her pillow and screamed into it silently.

Earlier, back on the patio, Polly had put down her phone and addressed the others.

"She's going to sleep, she's tired." She looked at Bob. "I guess it wasn't your fault after all."

Bob turned up his palms and shrugged.

"She's been through a lot," said Maggie. "I'm not surprised she's tired. The accident, moving across the country, losing everything in a fire . . ."

Anna looked at Polly. "Have you ever been engaged?"

"Nope," said Polly. "I was briefly married, but we never got engaged."

"How long were you married?" asked Asher curiously.

"Thirty-six hours," said Polly. "I was married and separated in the space of a weekend." She gazed out into the garden. "It seemed like a completely brilliant idea at the beginning, but it wore off." She squirmed around in her seat and tugged down the top of her pajama pants. There, on her hip, was a tattoo of two rings and a date, with the date crossed out and *JK!* tattooed next to it in ironic Comic Sans.

"It's a very important commitment," said Polly. "You have to be sure you're ready, 'cause you're living with it forever."

"Yeah," said Bob. "I guess that's why most people get engaged first."

Polly looked surprised. "I suppose . . . I was talking about crappy tattoos, but you're not wrong."

A little later Bob walked quietly down the hall as he headed to bed. Passing Laura's door, he overheard her talking sweetly on the phone, asking someone to forgive her. As he'd been tidying the kitchen he'd seen the card from the flowers in the trash. Unable to stop himself, he'd read it:

> *I love you, please come home.*
> *—Nick*

His mouth tightened and he hurried to his own room, ready to close the door on the day and on any hopes he'd ever had about Laura. No big deal. It didn't matter at all.

FOURTEEN

Back in the garden, Asher looked across the table at his mother and wondered when she'd gotten old. She was as lovely as ever, full of beans and vivid curiosity, but she looked . . . tired in a way he'd not noticed before.

"So," he said, pouring himself the last of the red wine, "what else is new? I've heard all the neighborhood stories, what about you?"

Maggie shrugged. "You know all there is to know, which is to say, nothing. I play cards with my friends, I work, I read, I cook, nothing's changed."

"Just new tenants."

She nodded. "Just that. New tenants, new clients, same old me. It's like a soap opera; every so often there's a cast change, but the show keeps on running." She smiled. "I'm not sure that made sense." She rubbed her forehead and tried to summon more energy. She'd been incredibly excited to see her son and she was still filled with joy that he was home, but she was also really tired and it was way past her bedtime.

Asher laughed. "I got it. How's Ollie? I haven't even seen him."

Maggie said, "He's probably in Polly's room. She's slightly allergic, I think, so of course he tries to spend as much time on her as possible."

"Who wouldn't?" said Asher, and immediately kicked himself. He didn't dare look at his mother.

"Huh," she said, and waited for him to elaborate. He didn't, so eventually she said, "So, what's the plan, now that you're back? When does the new job start?"

"Next week." Asher examined one of the more generous pizza crusts, and decided it was worth nibbling. "Do you want to help me find a place to live?"

"You're not going to live here?" Maggie was disappointed. "I can throw out a tenant, say the word." She paused. "Not Bob, though, because look at the garden."

Asher grinned. "My attic room is twice the size of my Tokyo apartment, it's fine. I'll probably be here for a month or two, but I'm a grown-up, Mom, I'm too old to live at home. I'm thinking of buying a place, maybe."

"You are?" Maggie failed to keep the surprise out of her voice.

He nodded. "Yes. Japan was expensive, but as I pretty much worked, slept, and ate ramen, I saved money." He looked at her, steadily. "I'm ready to take my place in the adult world, buy a home, get married, have kids, get into debt—you know, the American dream."

Maggie laughed. "Fair enough, but you'll need to go out and find a girlfriend to start with."

Her son smiled at her. "Any suggestions?"

"None you haven't thought of already."

Asher looked into his wineglass and shook his head. "I'm jet-lagged, my mind isn't working very clearly."

"Polly's very attractive," said Maggie.

Asher shot her a quick glance, but she didn't say anything further.

"I hear a *but* coming," he said, tipping his head to one side. "What is it?"

"No but," said Maggie, drawing circles on the tablecloth with the edge of a spoon. "I'm not sure Polly's looking for the complete American dream, picket fence, babies thing." She stopped spoon circling. "But of course I could be totally wrong."

"What kind of guys does she like?" He caught himself. "Or girls, of course."

Maggie frowned. "Absolutely no idea. Guys, I think, but don't quote me. She's never brought anyone back, so I couldn't tell you. She goes out a lot, and she certainly parties, but maybe she's super fussy." She looked worried. "You're not thinking of reaching out to Madeleine, are you?"

Asher broke off a piece of pizza crust and offered it to Daisy, who was snuffling around the table legs like an ankle shark. "No," he said firmly, "not at all. I'm sure she's married by now anyway."

"Good," said Maggie. "I hope she trips and breaks her nose. More than once."

"Wow," said Asher, "so you're over all that then?"

Maggie leaned across the table and patted his hand. "You hurt my kid, you hurt me."

"I've forgiven her," said Asher.

"Good for you," replied his mother. "I am less emotionally mature than you. I never forget." She uncrossed her ankles under the table, subconsciously getting ready to stand up in case she needed to punch someone.

There was a long, long pause. Then Asher said, "Have you forgiven Sarah?"

Maggie looked at her son, her eldest child, and nodded. "Yes," she sighed. "But that's not really the point, is it? She doesn't appear to have forgiven me."

Asher stood and started gathering the few remaining dishes, thinking of his sister. "I called her from the airport, she hasn't called me back yet."

Maggie watched her son and gave an almost imperceptible shrug. He carried some dishes into the kitchen, and when he returned, he was ready to change the subject.

"Have you been dating at all?"

Maggie hooted with laughter. "Me? Are you mad? Why would I risk my hard-won peace and quiet?" She ran her fingers through her hair, leaving one side sticking up in pieces like the Sydney Opera House.

"I don't know," he replied. "A desire for physical intimacy? Someone to keep you company? Someone to travel with?"

Maggie looked off into the garden and shook her head. "I'm too old for physical anything, and the thought of traveling is exhausting. As for company, that's what dogs are for." She tipped her head toward the house. "And all these tenants. It's rare there's no one else in the house, there's usually someone to talk to."

"You dated when I was younger."

Maggie stood up. "No, Asher, this old lady is not interested."

"You're not old."

"I'm sixty."

"Sixty is the new fifty."

"Really? It feels like the old sixty to me, and I wasn't all that interested at fifty, either." She headed into the house, saying over her shoulder, "If sixty becomes the new thirty, let me know."

He watched her go into the house, and looked at his phone.

His sister still hadn't responded to his earlier text. He frowned, and texted her again.

"I'm home, when can you get together?"

He finished clearing the table, loaded the dishwasher, and set it going. He stood and looked around the kitchen he'd grown up in, very tired and glad to be home. As he headed up to the guest room, he checked his phone one last time. Nothing.

FIFTEEN

The next morning Laura was up at seven and did a fast three-mile run. Walking back to the house, she pulled out her phone and called her mother.

"Dr. Costello," said her mother, in the tone of voice she used when she was working. Clearly Laura had caught her on campus. Laura took a deep breath.

"Hi, Mom, it's me."

"I hear that," said her mom, then waited. Laura swallowed. There was something about her mother that made Laura feel like she'd messed up before she'd even begun. Possibly by just being born.

"Mom, why did you give Nick my address?"

"Because he asked me for it," said her mother readily. "Why shouldn't he have it, you guys are still friends, right?" She paused. "Or have you left that behind as well?"

Laura rolled her eyes. "Mom, I haven't left anything behind, I just moved out to the West Coast for grad school, I didn't embark on a continuing five-year mission to explore strange new worlds." Her mother was a sucker for a *Star Trek: The Original Series* reference.

It didn't help. Her mother sniffed, "Well, I'm still hoping you'll come to your senses."

"I'm fully sensible, honestly," replied Laura. "Please don't share my personal information with anyone else, OK?"

"Who else would want it?" said her mother carelessly.

Wow, thought Laura, thanks for the vote of confidence, Mom.

"I'm grading papers," her mother continued. "Did you need anything else?"

"No, Mom." Laura had reached the house, and headed to her room.

"OK, goodbye." Her mom hung up.

Laura threw the phone on her bed and looked at herself in the mirror just to remind herself she was a grown-ass woman.

"She's not the boss of you," she said aloud, and then headed to the shower.

All clean and dressed, Laura took a cup of tea to the patio, found it deserted, and sat on one of the faded yellow chairs. Despite her mother being a major downer, she felt a lot better than she had the night before; a good night's sleep had clearly been called for. She closed her eyes and leaned her face back to catch more early sun.

"Good morning," said Bob, appearing through the French doors to the kitchen. Laura opened her eyes and snapped her head up.

"Hey there," she replied, never at her wittiest first thing.

Bob was wearing an extremely faded T-shirt with a logo for a seed catalog and sweatpants that looked suspiciously like they got slept in. He was moving slowly as he came over to join her, but Daisy fairly flew over the doorstep and trotted down the stairs.

Apparently, she'd already finished her double espresso, fresh juice, and croissant, and was ready to seize the day.

Laura looked at Bob, slightly rumpled and puffy from sleep, and realized Polly was right—she was getting used to his face. It was a relief, she realized; she really wasn't ready for any . . . thing.

Bob smiled gently at her. "Feeling better this morning?"

OK, the smile is still a bit of a stunner, I won't lie. "Yes, thanks. I guess I was tired."

"Uh-huh," replied Bob. They fell into companionable silence, though the morning soundscape of Los Angeles was loud enough. The birds were singing with a great deal of verve, a pool pump was growling away in the distance, and three competing leaf blowers were coming to blows somewhere close.

Apparently inured to the noise, Bob sipped his coffee in silence, watching Daisy and not looking at Laura until he felt totally conscious. As he'd walked onto the patio, her eyes had been closed, her head tipped back, and she'd looked very much as she had in his dreams the previous night. It had been a little startling. Bob tended to wake up feeling good in the mornings, ready to work, ready to get outside and get going, but not in any way ready to chat. One of his favorite things about his work, for him, was that he rarely needed to speak to anyone first thing in the morning. Sitting across from Laura was a challenge, though, because he very badly wanted to talk to her and couldn't think of a single thing to say. *I dreamed about taking you to bed last night* probably wasn't the best opener.

"Right." He stood and stretched. "I need more coffee." He held out his hand for her cup. "Want some?"

"It's tea."

"I can make tea," he said, taking her cup.

Standing at the kitchen counter, Bob found himself in a bit of a quandary. It had been at least six months since anyone had seriously stirred him, and well over a year since he'd slept with a woman. That experience had been brief but pleasant, and he and she were still friendly. He hadn't gone to her wedding or anything, but it was cool. Possibly as a result of being the youngest child and only male in a family run by his mother and grandmother, both of them unrestrained masters of life, he was thoughtful about women, and liked them, even though they often rendered him mute. It was conceivable that never getting a word in edgewise his entire childhood had led to his social shyness, but more likely it was simply the way he was. He frowned, moving to pour the now-boiling water into Laura's cup.

"Sugar?" he called out, turning his head to hear her answer.

"One, please," she replied, and her voice hit his heart like a bell. Oh crap, he thought to himself. That is not a good sign. He stirred the sugar, pressed out the tea bag, and poured the milk, all while trying to think of something pleasant to talk about. When he returned to the patio and handed her the cup of tea, his fingers touched hers briefly. Not that he noticed.

Polly burst through the kitchen door, carrying Ollie under one arm. As usual, she started talking as soon as she saw another human face. "I had the most terrible nightmare that I was Raquel Welch in that old movie about getting all small and going into that guy's body. Remember that movie?"

Bob and Laura shook their heads.

"You're missing out," continued Polly. "Anyway, I was her in the movie and there's this bit where the bad guy gets all smothered by a white blood cell, and Raquel Welch gets all these antibodies all over her, but it's fine because they dry out and snap off like twigs once she gets back in the sub, and anyhow, in the dream I was her but being smothered by the white blood cell and

I woke up and Oliver was sitting on my chest staring at me!" She took a breath, the first in quite some time, and dropped the cat onto the patio. "He was the blood cell!"

The blood cell sat down and radiated insouciance. Polly sighed dramatically, then moved on to the next thing. "What are you guys up to today?"

Bob got to his feet and picked up his cup. "Nothing as exciting as that, I'm afraid." He headed into the kitchen, looking back to smile at Laura, and said, "Have a good day." Then he was gone.

Polly turned to Laura. "He definitely wants to date you."

"You are definitely delusional," replied Laura, "and I am definitely not interested. He seems like a nice guy and he's cute and everything, but I'm not open for business, so to speak. I'm closed for the season."

Polly shrugged. "Trying to bring a little joy into your life."

"I'm plenty joyful, thanks. Are you off to work?"

Polly nodded and grinned. "Bored?"

Laura laughed. Polly seemed self-absorbed and generally on a planet of her own creation, but she saw through Laura every single time.

"Is it that obvious?"

Polly stood up and shook her pant legs down over her boots. "Come to work with me, Nina will press more books on you. It'll make her so happy."

The bookstore cat, Ferdinand, was sitting in a box on the floor of the back office. Ferdinand had arrived the previous Christmas, theoretically to deal with a rodent issue the store was having. While the rodents had indeed moved out, Ferdinand had moved in and revealed herself not to be an enormous tomcat, but a very,

very pregnant ladycat, and several families in the neighborhood now had bookstore kittens. Liz had already named her Ferdinand, inspired by the cat's commitment to stationary contemplation, and decided not to change it. Ferdinand was no longer pregnant, but she was still built along capacious lines, and the box she had selected—which was the tray-like lid of a box of printer paper—was not. She overflowed enough to obscure the box but didn't reach the carpet, which was making Nina think of the speeders in *Star Wars*.

Nina looked up and saw Polly and Laura coming in. "Good afternoon, Polly," she said, pointedly looking at the time.

"Pfft," said Polly, dumping her purse and phone under the register. "It's barely ten a.m., the tourist slowed me down."

Nina looked at Laura, who shrugged, having already learned that clarifying anything Polly said was a waste of time and effort. The brief drive to Larchmont had been uneventful, and Polly had talked the entire time about other great movies featuring Raquel Welch, of which there were many more than Laura had realized. Perhaps she could take Polly everywhere so scary thoughts wouldn't have a chance to get a toehold. Laura turned to Nina.

"I was thinking of getting a jump start on school. Is there anywhere good around here to study?"

"How close?"

Laura shrugged. "Walkable."

Nina nodded. "Sure, but you'll need to narrow it down. Larchmont has a walkability score of eighty-five."

"You don't say," said Laura weakly, not completely sure what that meant.

"I do say. Are we talking coffee shops or libraries?"

"There's a library?"

Nina fixed Laura with a basilisk eye and raised her eyebrow.

"Are you expressing surprise there are libraries in Los Angeles? Did you think we were all illiterate cultural dilettantes?"

Laura shook her head. "Uh . . . no?" She was pretty sure she knew what a dilettante was, but she wasn't taking any chances.

"Fair enough." Nina looked mollified, and continued, "There are actually two—yes, two—public libraries within walking distance of Larchmont, though one is much closer. I'll find you the addresses." She made a face. "And the hours. There have been a lot of cuts, and one of them was only open two days a week for a while."

"Doesn't the library kind of steal your business?"

Nina looked surprised. "No, because there are lots of people who want to *read* books but don't want to *acquire* books." She shook her head. "Those people go to the library, and if they want to own something they've fallen in love with, they come here. The books want to be read, I don't think they care much beyond that."

"I guess so," said Laura, having never considered the inner motivations of books.

"Well, of course," said Nina, who thought of little else. She paused. "Of course, you could take the bus down to the central library, which is an amazing place." She looked curiously at Laura. "Are you going to get a car? It's going to be very challenging to live here without one, although, of course, lots of people do it. In fact," she said, her face brightening in the way it did every time a fact popped into her head, "Los Angeles has a lower rate of car ownership than Seattle."

Laura hesitated. "I was planning on it, but honestly, the buses aren't that bad, and owning a car is so expensive." *And ever so slightly terrifying.*

Nina nodded but Polly was horrified. "Dude, you can't not have a car here. How will you make a getaway?"

The other two swiveled to look at her. "What do you mean?" said Laura.

Polly seemed genuinely concerned. "What if you need to blow the joint, flee the scene, get out of Dodge?"

"Make like a tree and leave?" asked Nina, always up for a bad pun.

"Make like an atom and split?" added Laura, also ready to play this game.

Polly made a tutting noise. "It's all very well to joke around, ladies, but a woman needs the independence and freedom of her own mode of transport."

"I could get a bike," suggested Laura.

"Oh great," said Polly. "Sure. You escape a dicey situation and then immediately get mown down by a distracted driver. Have you seen how people drive in this city?"

The noise. The mirror. "Yes, actually, only just recently."

Nina cleared her throat, but Polly held up her hand. "I can tell you're about to tell me which other cities have worse drivers, or what the actual number of accidents per square yard is . . ."

"Well, you wouldn't measure in yards . . ."

"But it doesn't matter. My point is that riding a bike is dangerous, taking public transport is slow, and walking from here to UCLA isn't practical."

"Well, I won't be here once school starts," said Laura reasonably.

"Exactly!" said Polly. "There's the problem. You have to get a car, so you *can* be here."

Laura shrugged. "I'll get around to it."

"I have a mechanic friend who can help," Nina said surprisingly. "He'll help you find a good used car, he's nice like that."

"Uh, OK," said Laura. "I'm going to head to the library, so . . ."

"Oh, that's right," said Nina. "I'll draw you a map."

Polly had been pulled away by a customer, and Laura hoped she'd let the car conversation go. The thought of driving in Los Angeles, with the traffic and unfamiliar roads, was genuinely making her break out in a sweat. She hadn't been able to get behind the wheel in New York, but she'd been hoping it would be a different story here. And hopefully it would be, she just needed to work up to it. This, she told herself, is a problem for future Laura. For now she was going to go hide in the library.

Laura left the store with directions to the closest library, along with far too much information about it. (It was built in 1927, was of architectural significance, and had a fireplace, which Nina considered daring for a place filled with paper. Nina had then started telling Laura about a terrible fire at the Los Angeles Central Library, but fortunately a rush of customers—three at once—had come in, and Laura headed off to get an early lunch, not having had any breakfast.)

Now she was waiting in a strangely long line for a sandwich, farther up the boulevard. Surely the sandwiches couldn't be that good? Suddenly three people ahead of her wimped out and went to Chipotle instead, and she vaulted forward in an instant, realizing once she was inside the store and could smell the bread that it was 100 percent going to be worth it.

Nina had told her about a little park a few blocks farther east, close to one of the libraries. She'd seemed incredulous that someone would willingly walk that far in August, but Laura was used to walking hot streets to reach cool parks. Maybe the heat would keep people indoors, and she'd have the park to herself.

She could not have been more wrong. Dozens of kids ran around joyfully on the sandy surface of a fenced-in playground, with giant shades like kites above and nannies and parents alongside. The sounds of glee mingled with horns and engines from Beverly to create a level of ambient noise that made Laura glad she was headed to the library later. For now, though, she pulled out her notebook to give herself a flat surface for her sandwich, and unwrapped it. Prosciutto, Brie, tomatoes, aioli . . . luckily the sounds of the playground hid her gluttonous moan of pleasure.

A shadow fell across her book, and Laura looked up to see Bob, who also carried a sandwich in the now-familiar white paper. She held her hand over her eyes and he stepped to the side, putting her face in shade.

"Larchmont Wine and Cheese *and* Robert Burns Park in the first week?" he asked. "That's hard-core local knowledge." He paused. "Can I join you?"

Laura nodded, not being able to come up with a good reason why he shouldn't. She didn't dig very deeply, to be honest; if two consenting adults like park benches, there's no reason they shouldn't share one. He sat down and unwrapped his own lunch.

"Nina at the bookstore told me about the park." Laura kept eating her sandwich as Bob started his. She couldn't tell what he'd ordered, and was that too personal a question to ask?

"I got the vegetarian," he said, having swallowed the first bite and apparently developed telepathy. "I'm not a vegetarian, but I love roasted peppers and goat cheese."

"I'll get that next time," said Laura, who was enjoying her prosciutto. "Ooh, they gave me some of those tiny little pickles, I've never had one." She blushed, realizing she sounded like a country bumpkin rather than a suave Manhattanite. They'd had plenty of pickles at home, but not these bumpy little babies.

"Cornichons," said Bob. "I'm scared of them, they're very . . ."

Laura made a face at him and bit into one. Immediately her face screwed up, and Bob laughed. "Sour."

"I thought you were going to say 'hot' for some reason, and I like spicy." Laura had swallowed the tiny, puckersome gherkin, and regarded the one that was left with some respect.

Bob looked at her. "What did you end up deciding to do?"

"Study," said Laura, feeling a breeze stir her hair for the first time that day. "It's pretty much my default setting. Studying, working out, watching sports, that's pretty much me in a nutshell."

Bob smiled at her, and Laura couldn't help smiling back; there was something so appealing about his face. It was as handsome as ever, but it was now *him*, and every interaction made him less overwhelming and more . . . Bob. They ate their sandwiches in silence, watching the kids and dogs making enough noise for both of them.

Once they were done eating, Bob rolled his sandwich wrapper into a tight ball and overhanded it a pretty good distance into a trash can. He crowed as it sailed in, and made the noise of a roaring crowd. Laura laughed and crumpled hers, taking time to get it evenly dense. Then she stood, said, "Off the tree, three pointer," and lobbed it easily, banking off a nearby tree and into the trash. She whirled around. "Knicks take Lakers, no contest."

Bob laughed. "In an imaginary contest, sure." He looked at her. "I don't suppose you shoot hoops, do you?"

Laura laughed. "Thanks for phrasing that as a question. Most people look at me and assume I play basketball, or volleyball. I can shoot hoops, but I'm more of a swimmer."

Bob grinned. "Well, I can barely swim, but I would definitely love having someone to shoot hoops with. No one else is interested." He shrugged. "If you'd like to."

"That would be great," said Laura.

Bob stood up, checking his pockets for wallet and phone. "I'm going back to work," he said. "Can I give you a ride anywhere?" He paused, remembering the previous day. He looked at her, but her face gave nothing away.

"No, thanks," she said. "I'm going to the library and it's only a few blocks away."

"See, you learn something every day," said Bob. "I didn't even know there was a library near here." He looked at her. "Let me guess, Nina told you that, too."

Laura laughed. "Yes, along with a lot of other facts I've already forgotten."

He was hunting for his keys and finally found them. "She's a walking information booth, that girl."

"I wish I was like that," said Laura.

Bob made a face. "Really? She makes me feel dumb." He corrected himself. "Not on purpose, she doesn't mean to, she reminds me of being in school."

Laura looked at him. "Not a big fan of school?"

He shook his head. "Not really. I mean, it was alright, but, you know . . . I'd rather be outside."

"Me too," said Laura.

"But you're going to grad school?"

She nodded. "Yeah, but I'm looking forward to it. Once I realized what I wanted to do for work, going to grad school became part of getting there." An expression crossed his face she couldn't quite place, and she worried she was boring him. "So," she said, "you grew up here, right?" Bob nodded, and she continued, "Did you go away to college and come back to LA?"

He nodded. "Kind of, but I didn't go very far." He perched on the arm of the bench. "I went to Pierce, I loved it. They have a huge farm on campus, it's an amazing place. In fact," he continued, "I'm seeing my old professor this weekend. He teaches a public class in vegetable gardening, for the city."

Laura nodded. "Sure." He seemed to need encouragement, and she was always ready to focus on someone else (so much easier than talking about herself).

"Well, he started doing this thing where the whole class goes over and redoes one of their gardens." He frowned. "That sounded wrong." He took a breath and tried again. "He goes to one of the people's gardens and . . ." He could feel himself blushing.

Laura grinned. "I get it. They take turns to work on each other's gardens?"

Bob nodded and felt the color in his cheeks receding. "Right. Anyway, sometimes I go help him if I'm not busy, and this Saturday I'm not busy." He corrected himself. "I mean I am busy, but doing that. Because I wasn't too busy to do that." So much for not blushing.

"That sounds like fun," said Laura hopefully.

"Yes," said Bob, getting to his feet. "Well, I'll see you at home. There's a hoop over the garage door, if you feel energetic."

"Always," Laura said, and smiled. "Besides, an East Coast versus West Coast thing might be fun." She coughed and added, "For me, anyway."

He narrowed his eyes. "I see how it is. Fine. See you later."

She nodded and watched him walk out of the park. She told herself she was studying his gait, and that might even have been part of it.

SIXTEEN

When Laura walked through the front door later that day, Polly was coming down the stairs in a bikini.

Laura raised her eyebrows and made a wild guess. "You're going swimming?" She failed to keep the surprise out of her voice, and Polly frowned at her.

"Listen here, Sporty Sporterson, running every morning doesn't make you the only athlete in the house."

Laura felt bad. "I'm sorry, you're completely right. Can I join you?"

Her pique immediately forgotten, Polly nodded. "Yes, of course, but I'm really going to float about like a jellyfish. No laps or anything, I just got home from work." She frowned. "Wait, do you even have a swimsuit?"

Laura had already turned to go back into her room, but she stopped and looked stricken. "No! You told me there was a pool and everything, I should have gotten one at Target." She frowned at herself. "Dammit! I love swimming."

Polly laughed. "Don't cry, you can borrow one of mine," she said, going back upstairs. "I've got loads. Come on."

Laura looked dubiously at her figure as she headed up the

stairs. "I'm not sure we're the same size . . ." But she followed any-way, curious to visit Polly's room. She was also interested in seeing the rest of Polly's swimsuit collection, because the one she was wearing was an adorable gingham 1950s two-piece with a kicky little belt made of plastic hoops. Laura had always wanted to be the kind of girl who could carry off vintage style, who could wear hats and interesting shoes, but she wasn't. She'd gotten used to it, but seeing Polly—and Nina, who also rolled her own style—was re-minding her how much fun clothing could be.

Polly's room was a surprise. It was directly above Laura's, and while it also overlooked the garden, it lacked the floor-to-ceiling windows and fireplace. It was painted a pale shade of sage, with white furniture, and was immaculately tidy and uncluttered. Every surface gleamed, and the floor was polished to a high shine, a cloud of flokati floating in the center. A collection of snow globes stood on a bookcase, and a long, clearly handmade flag with a big P in the middle was covered with dozens of enamel pins, ranging from Zelda to axolotls. It was a gorgeous room, and absolutely the last thing Laura had expected. Polly saw Laura's expression and laughed.

"Dude, the inside of my head is such a circus I need my envi-ronment to be Zen." Then she threw open the doors of an enor-mous walk-in closet that was entirely stuffed with clothes, boots, coats way too warm to ever be worn in Southern California, and what appeared to be a fairly sizable collection of plush Pokémon. She grinned at Laura. "But this is where all the magic happens."

Polly didn't have *loads* of swimsuits, but she did have half a dozen. Most of them were barely there bikinis, but there was a single poppy-red one-piece. There were enormous cutouts on both sides and the suit dipped dangerously low in the back, so it was really a one-piece in name only. Laura pulled it on in the privacy of Polly's closet and tied the halter neck under her hair. She braided and twisted her hair into an efficient chignon, and stepped out of the closet.

"Well," said Polly in a resigned tone, "that's yours now. There's no way I'm ever wearing it again."

Laura stepped in front of the mirror and was taken aback. She'd swum competitively since high school and usually wore simple suits in black or blue. She was dismayed to see that despite her no-nonsense hairstyle, her appearance suggested *Playboy* rather than *Sports Illustrated*. Of course, her scars would have been an unusual feature on a model, but she'd never minded them. Everything else about her appearance bothered her, sure, but the scars that proved she'd been close to death and survived, she actually kind of liked. No one ever lost money betting against the consistency of human beings.

"Huh," said Polly, standing behind Laura as they both looked in the mirror, Laura frowning and Polly grinning. "I guess your boobs are a bit different than mine." She looked down at her boyish figure. "Insofar as you have them."

Laura was dubious. "I could put a T-shirt over it, maybe?"

Polly shook her head. "No, you look amazing. But don't do any backflips into the pool, I'm not sure those straps will hold." She giggled. "Wait till Bob sees you."

Laura looked at her. "Polly, there is nothing going on with me and Bob, quit it."

Polly shrugged. "I'm merely entertaining the possibilities." She paused. "And I have to say, your possibilities look pretty entertaining."

"Right, I'm definitely wearing a T-shirt," said Laura, looking around for something.

"No," said Polly, poking her. "You look great, own it." She paused, then added curiously, "Do your scars hurt?"

Laura shook her head. "They itch sometimes."

"Huh," said Polly, still gazing at her with frank curiosity. "Those muscles must take effort. Do you work out every day?"

Laura blushed and nodded. "After the accident I spent a year doing rehab, right?"

Polly nodded.

"Well, it became a necessity. Not because I wanted more mobility, but because I feel less . . . freaked out when I exercise a lot." She sighed. "Honestly, the accident kind of messed me up."

Polly moved her head to indicate Laura's scars. "I see that."

Laura shook her head. "No, my body is the easy part. It's the shit you can't see that worries me." She hesitated, not sure if Polly was going to understand. She seemed so confident and certain of herself. "I'm sure it will be fine, never mind."

"How long has it been?"

"Nearly two years. I really should be over it by now."

"Says who?" asked Polly.

Laura looked at her and shrugged. "Says me, I guess."

"Maybe you should stop listening to yourself," said Polly. "It sounds like you're maybe not giving yourself the best advice." Her tone was light, but her expression was serious. "I've learned recently that my mind isn't the safest neighborhood to go into alone." She grinned. "Still want to swim?"

Laura nodded. "Yes, but really, Polly, should I wear something else?"

"No," replied her friend and new personal stylist, turning to leave the room. "Stop worrying. It's ninety degrees out and you're wearing a swimsuit at a swimming pool, not lingerie at a board meeting." Laura wasn't sure this was a valid point, but Polly said it so firmly she decided to go along with it. Grabbing a towel from the bathroom, she followed the other woman out of the cool house into the hot sun.

As Laura padded across the grass after Polly, she could smell rosemary and the beginnings of the jasmine. Laura couldn't believe she'd been here for several days and hadn't seen the pool yet. When Polly pushed open a gate at the far side of the rose garden—a gate Laura hadn't even noticed—she caught her breath.

It was old, this pool, as old as the house, and its elegant lines were edged with broad flagstones interspersed with moss in a way that would probably be banned under current safety regulations. Lilacs and hydrangeas enclosed the space in tall, fragrant walls, and the pool itself was lined with green vintage tiles that gleamed like the eyes of the gray cat, Oliver. With a small "yay," Laura threw her towel to one side, skipped past Polly, and dove neatly into the deep end. With long, powerful strokes, she swam the length of the pool underwater and popped up at the shallow end, where Polly was settling down with her lower legs in the water.

Polly grinned at her. "You have a lot of beans, don't you?"

Laura nodded. "Aren't you going to swim?" She started spinning in circles in the water happily.

"Yoo, of course," said Polly, sliding gracefully into the pool and hunching her shoulders as the warm top layer gave way to the cooler water underneath. "Huh . . . not as warm as I expected." She began a slow and gentle breaststroke across the shallow end. "I view swimming as a water-based meditation practice," she said as she turned over and floated on her back. "I am reminded of our small place among the elements, our speckishness in the grand scheme of things."

"Which is a good thing?" Laura said.

"Yes," replied Polly, reaching the far side and holding on to the edge. "It's good to be rightsized every so often, to remember that I'm a swimmer among swimmers." She turned and launched herself in the other direction. "It can be a challenge to deal with the kind of physical beauty and incredible charm I possess." She passed Laura and grinned. "I've come to terms with it."

Laura flicked water at her. "I'm not really sure how to respond to that," she said. "I'm going to put in some lengths, is that OK? I'll keep to one side."

Polly waved a hand. "Knock yourself out, I'm making myself one with the universe."

Laura swiftly put distance between herself and the floating unicorn. She relaxed into her stroke, plowing up and down until her lungs burned. Ten lengths, twenty, more. She was able to turn off her mind and focus on the rhythm and effort of swimming, on the balance of her movement, on her turns and direction. She didn't think at all, and that was a blessing she never tired of.

When she finally felt she'd done enough, she swam to the side of the pool and rested her arms on the edge, breathing hard and smiling at Polly, who had apparently finished communing with the universe and was sitting on an old wicker chair at the side of the pool. Maggie and Anna had shown up with wine, and Maggie had spread out that morning's paper and was reading it section by section. Polly was wearing a cotton kimono she had apparently found growing on a tree, and looked as comfortable as she always did.

"You're an amazon," she said to Laura amiably. "I was never friends with girls like you in school. Jocks scare me."

"I'm not really a jock," replied Laura, wiping the water from her face and shaking the drops onto the side of the pool. They immediately disappeared. "Or maybe I am, I don't know."

Polly looked skeptical. "That's easily settled. Were you on any teams?"

"Uh, in high school?" replied Laura. "Yes."

"Captain of any?"

Laura nodded. "Sure."

Polly shook her head, her blue eyes bright in the reflected light of the pool. "Jock."

"One of them was the chess team."

Polly snorted. "Overachieving jock."

"And the Science Olympiad."

"Nerd-jock hybrid. Rarely seen, but definitely possible."

Laura grinned. "What were you into in high school?"

"Theater kid," said Polly.

"Of course," said Laura. "Why doesn't that surprise me?" She turned to Anna. "What were you, Anna?"

"Art nerd," she said. "President of the Anime Society *and* the Photoshop Club." She made a face and giggled. "Strangely enough, my social life never got in the way."

Laura smiled. "And you, Maggie?" she asked. "What was your crowd in high school?"

"Stoners," said Maggie, without looking up from her paper.

The gate to the pool area swung open, and Asher, Bob, and Libby appeared. Asher was carrying a platter.

"Hey there"—he smiled around—"Mom put me in charge of dinner tonight, so I made sushi for everyone." He looked at his mom. "Wasn't sure if you wanted it poolside . . . ?"

"Why not?" replied Maggie. "It seems appropriate." She paused. "You know, fish, water . . . never mind." She put the paper aside and looked over the platter. "It's very pretty."

Asher put it down and smiled at Polly. "Did you swim already?"

She nodded, hesitated, and then reached for a roll. "Did you learn to make sushi in Japan?"

Asher laughed. "No, Venice Beach."

Laura was cooling off and wished she'd brought a wrap, too. "I think I need to run in and get changed," she said. "It's getting cooler."

"I'll grab you something," said Bob, getting to his feet. "I have to go back in."

"That's OK," replied Laura shyly. "I'll come with you." Then she realized she'd have to get out of the pool, and hesitated. Pull yourself together, she thought. You're not wearing lingerie at a board meeting, remember? She pulled herself up and out of the water, quickly tugging and pulling on all planes, making sure everything stayed where it was supposed to.

"Wow," said Maggie, looking over her glasses at the younger woman, "that's quite the swimsuit."

"Uh, it's Polly's," replied Laura, heading toward the house quickly, trying not to catch anyone's eye.

"It doesn't look like that on me," said Polly nonchalantly. "I'd need to work out much more than I do." She laughed. "Or at all." She looked over at Bob, who was staring after Laura with a fairly obvious expression of astonishment on his face. "Weren't you going in, too, Bob?"

"Yes," he said, "yes, I was." He started after Laura, who'd reached the gate and was nearly out of sight. "Wait for me."

Once they were both gone, Polly turned to the others and grinned.

"I'll open the betting at two to one in favor of them hooking up by the end of the summer."

Everyone started reaching for their wallets.

. . .

Laura went directly to her room and quickly changed into sweats. The suit had made her feel self-conscious and exposed, so now she reached for big, soft, and baggy. Returning to the kitchen, she found Bob standing at the sink, measuring sugar.

"Are you cooking?" she asked, and he turned and smiled at her. She looked warmer and more comfortable than she had at the pool, and while he wasn't likely to forget what she looked like with fewer clothes on, he could see she felt better like this.

He turned back to the sink. "No, I'm making nectar for the hummingbird feeders. Maggie keeps several by the pool, and I noticed they were empty." He finished with the sugar, and added warm water, stirring to dissolve the crystals. "I should probably have brought them, too, to clean them, but . . ." He shrugged. "Not the sharpest knife in the drawer."

Laura frowned. "Because you forgot the feeders? That's a little harsh."

He said nothing, just lifted the glass jug he was filling in order to check it was clear. Then he smiled at her and said, "Are you going back out?"

"Yes." She nodded. "Can I help with the feeders?"

"Sure," he said. "I already made another jug. Can you carry that one?"

They made their way back to the pool, where the others were sitting and arguing about sushi.

"It's not real wasabi," Asher was saying. "It's horseradish dyed green. Real wasabi is a horse of a different color."

"Not green?" asked Polly, who was watching him closely while also trying not to watch him closely.

Bob and Laura passed the group, and Laura missed Asher's

answer. They went over to the first feeder, which was on the far side of the pool, and Laura watched Bob reach up easily to take the feeder out of the tree where it hung. Normally she was the one who reached for the high shelves, was called to fetch the rarely used glassware or unusual ingredient. The rest of her family was bemused by her height, a throwback to some earlier, more robust ancestor. Her mother was five four in heels—not that she wore heels—and her dad would only have hit six feet if he stood on a step stool.

Bob said, "Could you open this up and check it isn't completely disgusting inside?" He went over to gather the others, each a blown-glass globe with flecks and streaks of color. Laura looked around for a hose, spotted one, and went to wash out the feeder. Soon he joined her, and together they cleaned the feeders, refilled them, and hung them back up.

They stood together, waiting to see if a bird would appear.

"I swear I see the same one every time," said Bob, "but that's probably not true."

"It could be," replied Laura. "They're very territorial." She turned her head at a whir, and spotted one. "Hey, that's an Anna's, they're pretty much only found on this coast." She pulled out her phone. "I have to show my dad . . ." She raised it to take a shot, but the bird immediately zoomed away. "Huh, I guess that one was shy."

Bob was looking at her curiously. "You're a bird nerd?"

She laughed and nodded. "Kind of. I mean, yes, of course, who doesn't like birds? But actually my dad is a bona fide hummingbird expert. He's written books on them." The tiny bird reappeared, and she managed to take a quick photo. She paused, sending the text, then looked up at Bob. "Thanks for letting me help."

He was surprised. "Of course, thanks for helping."

She turned and went to join the others, asking if there was any sushi left or had they eaten every roll. Bob watched her go, coiling the hose and hanging it back up. Then he pondered the hummingbirds for a while, until he felt ready to look at Laura again.

SEVENTEEN

Much later that evening Laura was in her room, scrolling through her phone mindlessly, when she thought she heard whimpering from the garden. She paused, and listened carefully.

Yes. Definitely a dog complaining persistently about something.

She got up and went out to the kitchen. The French doors to the garden were closed, and framed in the lower right pane was Daisy's face. If she'd had a wristwatch, she would have been tapping it.

"Oh, Daisy!" said Laura apologetically. She opened the door and Daisy trundled over the stoop, not pausing to say thanks or anything, beetling through the kitchen toward the hall, where she ran into the feet of Bob, who had rounded the corner.

"I thought I heard you," he said to her, then looked up and smiled at Laura. "Thanks for letting her in."

"I think I could hear her more clearly from my room," replied Laura. "I don't know how long she was out there."

"Too long, apparently," said Bob as Daisy pushed past him and headed down the hall. After a moment they both heard the thumps and claw rattles that meant she was hopping up the stairs. Bob smiled. "And now she's punishing me by spending the night with Polly."

Laura smiled and stretched, looking at the wall clock. It was earlier than she'd thought, a little after nine.

Bob looked at her. "Wanna shoot some hoops?"

Laura thought about it, then nodded. "I'm getting tired, but sure, why not?"

"Great," said Bob, gesturing for her to precede him through the door. "Maybe I have a chance then."

"I said I was tired," said Laura, "not too tired to win."

Bob laughed and led the way around the side of the house. There, behind the gate that could be seen from the street, was the carport area. The covered driveway made a perfect court for the hoop on the side of the house.

"What's good about this hoop," said Bob, scouting around for a ball under the various pots and hedges, "is that it's my room behind it, so hitting the wall doesn't bother anyone but me."

Laura looked up at a window above. "And whose room is that?"

"Upstairs bathroom," replied Bob. "Maggie put the hoop up when her kids were teenagers, and gave the location a lot of thought." He found a ball and bounced it a few times to test it. "She's no dummy, that one."

Laura shook her head. "She's really nice, I like her a lot."

"Me too," said Bob, stretching his shoulders and lofting the ball into the hoop. "One to me."

Laura was already moving, catching the ball as it fell and scoring easily, all in one movement. "And one to me," she said, catching and bouncing the ball, spinning around and evading Bob's attempted interception. Another throw. "That's two."

Bob shouldered her out of the way and got the ball this time, then stopped. "Shit, sorry, didn't mean to knock you."

"Oh, please," said Laura, snatching the ball and dodging away from him, pushing him aside and making another basket. "Three to me. You're being polite to make up for your poor defensive skills."

"I see," said Bob, giving her a more serious shove and stealing the ball as it came down. "Fine, gloves off."

For another twenty minutes they played pretty hard, pushing each other out of the way and getting happily sweaty. The trash talk continued, but slowly died away as they got breathless. Eventually Bob caught the ball and stopped, bending at the waist and holding up one hand.

"You win," he said. "I'm confident enough to admit you're a far better player than I am. I may have a slight height advantage, but you are twice as fast." He wandered over to the wall and slid down it, sitting at the bottom with his legs folded in front of him. "Did you play on a team?"

Laura nodded. "Wait, I'm going to get water. Want some?"

"Yeah, thanks." Then, as she walked away, he tipped his head back and closed his eyes. He'd just gotten his ass kicked.

Laura came back with two tall glasses of water. She lowered herself onto the ground next to him and they sat there in silence, cooling down.

"That was fun," she said eventually.

"If you find getting your ass kicked fun," he agreed, still with his eyes closed.

She grinned and finished her water. "You're pretty good," she said. "More athletic than you look."

He turned his head and frowned at her. "Are you saying I'm out of shape?"

She turned to face him, and grinned. "Gotcha." She laughed. "I need more water, you coming in?" She got to her feet and turned, holding out her hand. "Need a lift?"

He reached up and took her hand, pushing up as she pulled, which resulted in a pretty substantial overshoot on her part. He crashed into her and they both stumbled.

"We're strong, but klutzy," said Laura, giggling.

"Fast, but uncoordinated," agreed Bob, letting go of her hand, which he abruptly realized he was still holding. For a few seconds they smiled at each other, acknowledging for the first time they found each other attractive. It was all there in the smile, but had also been there from the beginning, and they knew it.

Laura turned and headed into the house, Bob close behind.

After gulping more water, Laura washed her glass and reached for Bob's. He grabbed a dish towel and picked up her glass to dry it, arguing with himself internally before speaking.

"Hey, you remember I said I go help my old teacher on the weekends sometimes?"

She nodded, handing him the second glass. "Yeah, doing people's gardens."

"Uh-huh. Well, the one this weekend is a bird and butterfly garden. I thought maybe you might like to come, you know, being a bird fan. And butterflies, probably."

She nodded easily. "I've got nothing against butterflies, it's true."

He felt himself starting to go red again, and turned away, adding, "You probably already have plans."

"No," said Laura. "I think that would be fun. This Saturday?"

He nodded.

"Great," she said. "I'd love to. We didn't have a real garden at home, you know, being in an apartment."

He looked shyly at her. "It might be hard work, it'll be hot."

She frowned. "Are you suggesting I'm not strong enough for hard work?"

He grinned back. "Gotcha."

She laughed, and flicked water at him. Then she turned and walked away, saying good night as she did so. It was only after Bob realized that (a) he was standing there grinning like an idiot and (b) he'd almost dried a hole in the second glass that he put it away and went to bed himself.

EIGHTEEN

The next day Laura spent the morning studying at the library and then met with a temping agency. The woman there alternated between encouragement and pessimism—*I expect we can find something, although, you know, the market's pretty tight right now, plus you can only do part time, but I'm sure it will be fine, probably*—and by the time the meeting was over, Laura wasn't entirely sure how she felt. She also didn't know how much time she was going to have once grad school started up, so all in all she headed home feeling perplexed. At least she had plans for the evening, going to Nina Hill's place for the trivia discussion. Maybe a nap first? She liked Nina a lot but she was . . . a lot.

She walked into the kitchen, and there, as if by magic, but really only by the United States Postal Service, she found a large cardboard box on the kitchen table. Maggie was sitting next to it, sipping a cup of tea.

"This came for you," said Maggie, tapping the box. "I've exercised extreme self-control and only shaken it once or twice. I was hoping it was full of puppies."

"Why would someone send me a box of puppies?" Laura tipped her head to one side. "Is it even legal to mail puppies? I hope not."

Maggie shrugged. "No reason. I'm always hoping for puppies."

"Sorry to disappoint you," said Laura. "My grandmother told me my mom sent me a box of clothes, and this is probably it."

"Does she think you've been walking around in a feed sack since the fire?" Maggie shook back her bangles and charm bracelets. There were a lot of them, and while they were as heavy as shackles, Maggie used them more as percussion instruments. Attitude is everything.

"My mother despairs of me," said Laura lightly.

"Oh," said Maggie, "that's unfortunate." She looked with interest at the box, instead of asking the questions she wanted to. Timing is also important.

Laura examined the box. Her mother had printed her name and address very carefully, and the sight of her handwriting made Laura's tummy clench with longing for home. Shopping lists, notes to teachers, reminders in her lunch box . . . she'd seen that handwriting a million times, its careful cursive perfectly formed and unassailably legible. Her mother viewed life in black and white; information was right or wrong, feelings were justified or not, decisions were good or bad. Laura longed for that certainty because her brain felt like a kid's kaleidoscope, one colorful emotion shifting and bleeding into another, the only constant being flux. But at the same time her mother's way was often a very narrow path, and exploration was not encouraged.

Fetching scissors, Laura opened the box and started by pulling out a note. She opened it, saw her mother had started with, *Laura, don't forget to . . .* , and put it to one side.

"I'll read that later," she said to Maggie. *Or maybe never.*

The first thing she pulled out of the box was a skirt, an item of clothing she only rarely wore. Laura sighed and held it up.

"She lives in a dreamworld where I dress like Strawberry Shortcake." She reached into the box again. This time it was a pair of jeans, and Laura looked surprised.

"Wait, no, I take it all back. I thought I'd brought these and they'd burned. I love these jeans." She hugged them briefly and turned back to the box with more enthusiasm.

Maggie spoke. "Mother-daughter stuff is very complex."

Laura's eyes met hers and she nodded without comment. Maggie watched the young woman pulling out a pair of pajamas she was clearly happy to see, a pair of shoes she'd apparently been hoping never to see again, half a dozen pairs of socks, a flannel nightgown with rabbits on it, and finally, at the bottom of the box, a giant oversized hoodie. Laura paused.

"Huh," she said, eventually reaching in and pulling it out. Stuyvesant High School, the transferred decal wearing very thin. Laura laughed softly. "I think I wore this every single day junior and senior years, my mom was sick of the sight of it. I can't believe she sent it."

Maggie looked curious. "Why didn't you bring it with you?"

Laura carefully folded the sweatshirt, giving it a surreptitious squeeze with her fingers. "Well, high school was a long time ago, it's not like I wore it that much in college." She shrugged. "Not even sure that girl exists anymore, she didn't stand up for herself very much."

There was a pause, then Maggie said, "Well, I doubt you can blame the sweatshirt for that."

"Good point," Laura said. "It was probably only doing its best."

Maggie nodded. "Do you think you stand up for yourself more now, then?"

Laura started to answer, then remembered Maggie was a

therapist. She heard her mother's voice loud and clear: *People with mental and emotional problems need to get busy and stop indulging themselves. Everyone has problems, Laura, people can't just roll over and give up.* Even as a teenager Laura was sure her mother was wrong about this, but arguing with her was pointless. When Laura had fallen apart after the accident, her mother had struggled for weeks to find a physical cause for her constant crying and panic attacks, and in the end had to accept that some things simply couldn't be reasoned away or ignored to death. But she hadn't liked it, and she'd argued Laura out of seeing a therapist.

"They're not even PhDs," she'd scoffed. "Psychotherapy isn't real science."

Now, sitting in a kitchen thousands of miles away from home and fully free of her mother's influence, Laura wanted to talk to Maggie about how she felt but could feel old habits dying hard. *Nobody wants to hear you whining. Pull it together.* Luckily, there was one thing Laura's mother had been right about: Psychotherapy isn't simply a science. It's also an art, and Maggie could read Laura's closed face like an open book.

"So," she said, getting up to make tea and not eye contact, "what do you think of Los Angeles so far?" She filled the kettle and kept talking. "Apart from your apartment building catching fire, which could have happened anywhere." She smiled at Laura, and lobbed an easy opening. "You've had a challenging couple of years, right?"

Laura shrugged. "I guess."

Maggie shook her head. "For most people, a major car accident, a cross-country move, graduating college, a broken engagement, a house fire—these are once-in-a-decade or even lifetime events." Her tone was remarkably cheery, as if she were discussing the weather. "You've had all of those in the last couple of years."

Laura unconsciously shook her head. "It's fine."

"Great," said Maggie, watching the kettle. "So, what happened with Bob the other day?"

"I'm not sure what you mean," said Laura carefully. "Someone knocked his side mirror off."

"Yeah, I saw," said Maggie, putting tea bags and sugar in the mugs. "I wish I could say that rarely happens, but actually little fender benders like that happen all the time here, largely because we're all in our cars so much."

"Not me," said Laura, without thinking.

"No," said Maggie neutrally, "not you." She looked over at Laura and pushed a little. "It must have been shocking."

Laura nodded and said nothing. Maggie waited patiently.

As if sensing his presence was required, Oliver the cat sauntered in and jumped onto the table, taking a circuitous route across the top in order to demonstrate his mastery of foot placement and tail arching. Laura visibly relaxed, reaching out to pet the plush and friendly head.

"I think I was surprised at how loud it was," she said, "and I guess I freaked out a little bit. More than I should have, I mean." Oliver pushed against her hand, and she tipped her head a little to let him sniff her chin.

"More than you *think* you should have," corrected Maggie gently. "There isn't an actual international standard for freaking out."

Laura looked at the clock. Still time before she needed to go to Nina's. Then she said, "I guess you're right. I feel like I should be recovered from the accident, and I thought I was." She shrugged. "It's fine."

Maggie poured the hot water into the mugs. "So you keep saying." She carried the tea over to the table and nudged Ollie out of the way to put down the mugs. She settled herself at the table, then got up again to go fetch cookies from the cupboard, shaking the sleeve out onto the table and helping herself to a couple. She sat in a chair and curled her feet around the legs comfortably.

Then she looked at Laura and said, "Tell me about it."

One of Laura's plans when she came to Los Angeles was to investigate seeing a therapist, but so far she had avoided it as carefully as she had avoided getting a car. She knew those two things were related; she wasn't totally in denial. But Maggie wasn't precisely a therapist, she was a doctor, her mother would probably approve . . . not that it mattered . . . Suddenly Laura found herself talking.

"After the accident," she said, "I didn't have to drive or be in a car for months, so it never occurred to me it would be a problem. Once I was out of the hospital we took the subway all the time."

"Reasonable," said Maggie. "New York has a largely functional transportation system."

Laura smiled briefly. "You know, the LA buses work fine." She frowned. "Maybe if you all got behind the system, it would work better."

"Are you saying we have the public transportation we deserve?" asked Maggie.

Laura shrugged. "You said it, I didn't."

Maggie laughed, and took another cookie. "Fair enough. Well, carry on with the story. Presumably you eventually needed to get in a car."

Laura nodded. "Yes, my parents and I were driving to visit a family friend who lived upstate." She cleared her throat. "It wasn't far."

Maggie's face remained neutral, and everything about the

position of her body expressed still and focused listening. It made Laura want to continue.

"Anyway, as soon as we crossed the George Washington Bridge and got on the parkway, I started to flip out."

Maggie leaned forward and said, "I'm sorry if this is hard to talk about, but can you define flipping out?"

Laura took a deep breath, trying to control her body. "It started with a smell, the smell of the brakes. I was back in the accident, in my head, and I couldn't pull myself out. I started feeling really sick and we had to pull over." She flushed. "I threw up all over myself, it was terrible."

Maggie shrugged. "They're your parents, it probably wasn't the first time you'd puked in their car."

"Sure, but I was twenty-three. They probably thought those days were over."

Another shrug.

"Besides," said Laura, still blushing, "it was embarrassing. I couldn't make myself get back in the car for an hour, and then I had to keep my eyes closed the whole way home."

"And then?"

"Then I started having nightmares and random panic attacks on the street."

"Were they really random?"

Laura looked at Maggie sharply. "No, not at all. I looked on-line about, you know, problems after things, you know, when you can't deal with . . . when you're not strong about . . ."

"Post-traumatic stress disorder?" said Maggie helpfully.

"Yes," said Laura, stammering a little, always feeling intense embarrassment about that term, which she'd thought only applied to soldiers who'd risked their lives, or victims of terrible crimes. "That kind of thing, and I realized the attacks were always triggered by something. A siren, a screech of brakes, a horn . . ." She shrugged. "But there's an awful lot of that in New York, so it happened all the time."

Maggie nodded and waited patiently.

Laura took a deep breath. "But anyway, I pushed myself and pushed myself, and it got better. I reached the point where I could take a cab, and thought it was done. Then I got here and planned to get a car but I keep putting it off and then the thing in Bob's truck . . ." She looked at the table, and pushed a crumb around with her fingernail. "I don't know what to do."

Maggie was reflective. Then: "Can I ask you something?"

Laura nodded.

"Why Los Angeles? It's famous for its traffic, not famous for its public transportation, and it really is quite difficult to exist without a car."

Laura sighed. "It's hard to explain."

Maggie smiled very sweetly. "Give it a whirl," she said.

Laura nodded, and tried. "My family is . . . a little bit hardcore. Expectations are high, and standards are even higher. I was a good student, but I also enjoyed things my parents didn't understand, like sports. They thought sports were a waste of time, time I could have spent studying. But if I always won, if I was the best, they could understand why I did it. So that's what I did. I pushed myself really hard." She made a gesture of frustration. "Ironically, the time in the hospital after the accident was the first time I could remember where my days weren't scheduled to the last minute. I realized I didn't want to spend my life studying, and ever since, my parents and I have been fighting about it. When I started to have these . . . issues . . . my parents used it as ammunition to try and stop me from doing what I want. I decided to get away from home and convinced myself I could manage." She looked at her hands, which were trembling slightly. "So here I am. And now I'm worried that they were right and I was wrong and I'm going to fail and have to go home and they're going to tell me they told me so."

Maggie sat back and stretched out her arms. "Good lord," she said, "that's a lot of pressure to put yourself under."

Laura laughed nervously. "My mom used to say pressure makes diamonds and irritation makes pearls."

Maggie made a face. "Well, sure, but pressure also makes nervous breakdowns and irritation makes ulcers." She looked at Laura and patted her hand gently. "Let's find you a therapist and put getting a car on the back burner for now. Take things one step at a time."

"Maybe," said Laura. *Or maybe I can push harder and make it work.* She looked at her phone. "Oh crap, I have to go to Nina's house."

"Nina from the bookstore?" asked Maggie.

Laura got up, nodding. "Yes. She wants me to join her trivia team."

Maggie smiled up at her. "Try not to focus on winning."

Laura frowned. "I think that's the point of asking me."

Maggie pushed herself to her feet and gathered the mugs. "Well, sometimes it's enough to simply do your best."

Laura nodded, but doubted Nina would agree.

"I'll pull together a list of possible therapists," said Maggie, heading back to the sink. "You've picked a challenging city for yourself, but at least it's stuffed to the brim with anxious people and highly qualified therapists."

You're moving to crazy town, her mother had said. *You'll be balancing your chakras and putting crystals in your colon before you know it.*

"Thanks," Laura said to Maggie, and headed to her room to get ready for Nina's. She felt shy and exposed now, and wished she'd kept her mouth shut. *Someone offering to help you doesn't mean you're helpless, does it?*

Maggie watched Laura leave the room and sighed. It was a sad truism of her work that not everyone who needs help wants help, and not everyone who gets help uses it. She leaned over and stroked Ollie, who squeezed his eyes encouragingly at her. *You did your best*, he seemed to say, *keep that shit up.* Then he added, *And I'm hungry, if you happen to be passing the cupboard.*

NINETEEN

Nina Hill lived in the neighborhood immediately surrounding Larchmont Boulevard, commonly referred to as Larchmont Village or, more occasionally, Windsor Square. It was less formal than Hancock Park and the houses were smaller. However, it had actually been built earlier and its more casual appearance—a wide variety of styles, differently sized lots—was equally as studied as its sibling. Many of the houses had guesthouses, largely small, separate buildings in the back gardens, giving rise to the phrase *back house*. Nina lived in one such back house, and it took Laura quite some time to find it. And when she did find it, there was a large tabby cat sitting on top of the gate, judging her.

She paused, but when he didn't move, she pushed the gate gently, expecting him to jump off. He kept his eyes locked on hers the whole time as he slowly moved with the gate, maintaining a cast-iron loaf position without a single wobble. Apparently he had fur-welded himself to the gate some time earlier and had been hoping someone would trickle along so he could show off his skills. Once this strange experience had played itself out, Laura nodded her appreciation and headed up a flight of stairs to a red front door.

Nina swung it open and Laura was about to step forward, when the tabby shot underfoot and caused her to stumble. He'd disengaged his docking clamps, clearly.

"I see you guys have met," said Nina. "That's Phil, he's showing off because there are people here."

"Hmm," said Laura, hesitating when she realized there were two other people in the room. But she went in, because her mother didn't raise a quitter.

Nina Hill's apartment was basically a bookcase with a bed and a chair in it. Laura gazed around, impressed.

"So," she said, "books then?"

"Mostly," said Nina, "but also movies and TV."

Laura came all the way in and found a place to sit on a rug with a tiger on it. She smiled at the other two women. "Hi there, I'm Laura."

"Oh, for crying out loud," said one, looking at Nina. "Another L name?"

Nina shrugged. "I didn't even notice."

"Firstly," said the woman, "you notice everything, it's one your defining characteristics, and secondly, hi, my name's Lauren."

"And I'm Leah," said the final woman, who was sitting up against the end of Nina's bed. The room was beautiful, but with four people it was a little cramped.

Lauren had dark hair with a natural wave, and a sardonic sense of humor. She wrote for TV and mined everyone's life for material. She was single and generally horrified by the human race, particularly that segment of it that lived and dated in Los Angeles. Leah, on the other hand, was recently engaged and currently freaking out.

"Also," continued Lauren, "Leah, Lauren, and Laura sounds like a singing trio from the 1960s."

"I think it would be Laura, Lauren, and Leah," said Nina, interrupting. "Alphabetical."

"Or Lauren, Laura, and Leah, that's the best one," said Leah.

"Now none of them sound like names at all," said Nina. "Can we get back to the point?"

Laura realized she'd walked in on the middle of something. Nina turned to explain.

"Leah got engaged a month ago."

"Congratulations," said Laura, because that's what you say.

"Thanks," said Leah, because that's what they say.

"But," continued Nina, "now she's flipping out because she isn't sure she wants to get married." She sat down in the armchair and pulled her legs up under her.

"To her fiancé, or at all?" asked Laura.

"She doesn't know," said Nina.

"I don't know," said Leah.

"Both," said Lauren.

"Huh," said Laura. They all looked at her, as if waiting for her opinion, which they couldn't possibly want. She plucked at the fabric of her yoga pants and looked down.

"Well? What do you think?" asked Nina.

They *did* want her opinion. Laura swallowed. "Uh, well, being engaged and being married are two different things. Do one at a time."

Leah gazed at her, then looked at Nina. "You didn't say she was Yoda."

"Or Forrest Gump," said Lauren, raising her eyebrows. "No offense meant," she added.

"Never saw it," said Laura, "so no offense taken."

Leah sighed. "I think that's probably good advice, though." She smiled at Laura. "Thanks."

"You're welcome," said Laura, not sure how she'd managed to say the right thing.

"Right, then," said Nina, "here's the deal. Trivia teams play in leagues, and theoretically the winner of each round in the league goes forward, but in practice it's largely disorganized and ad hoc." She leapt up and pulled a T-shirt from a basket under her bed. It read *First Loser* in a classic baseball-type script. "This is the T-shirt my boyfriend, Tom, got when they came in second last year."

"They call second place First Loser? Wow, that's harsh." Laura was surprised. Who knew trivia could be so competitive?

Nina shrugged. "I guess someone thought it was funny."

"And you guys won?"

Leah hooted derisively. "We did *not* win, we did not even get through the semifinals because someone caused a minor riot and got us banned from one of the few venues that had a working *Galaga* machine."

"I'm sure they'd let us in now." Nina sounded confident.

"No, I tried last week."

Nina changed the subject. "So, anyway, the point of this meeting is to introduce ourselves to Laura, learn a bit about her, her strengths, trivia-wise . . ." Her voice trailed off. "What?"

The other women all looked at her, wide-eyed.

"This is a meeting?" asked Lauren. "I brought beer."

"I brought cupcakes," said Leah.

"Is there going to be a test?" asked Laura. "I have not prepared for a test."

Nina started laughing. "Alright, it's not a meeting. It's a new team member party, with beer and cake." She explained, "Leah's ex-boyfriend, Carter, got a new girlfriend who was jealous of him spending one evening a week with his ex-girlfriend . . . but Carter wasn't any better than any of us at sports or science, two areas I'm hoping you can crush in." She paused to take a breath, having not taken one for quite some time.

Laura was impressed by her aerobic capacity. She grinned at Nina. "No pressure." Lauren handed over a cold beer and Laura took it. "When's the first competition?"

"Next week," said Nina. "Next Friday." She reached for a cupcake and started peeling the paper liner using the pinch and pull method. "We have seven days to practice."

Laura nearly spilled her beer. "Practice? How do you practice?"

"By asking a lot of questions in rapid succession, of course." Nina raised her eyebrows. "It's not like *American Ninja Warrior* or anything, but you do need to warm up your brain." She paused. "And potentially your buzzer finger. You never know how tech savvy the organizers will be."

"What if it turns out I know nothing?" Laura was starting to feel anxious.

Nina shrugged. "Then I guess we'll see who's more embarrassed about it, you or me."

Laura was surprised. "It's going to be me, you don't seem to get embarrassed."

Nina made a face. "Oh, don't be fooled. I'm completely mortified seventy-two percent of the time." She tugged down a sock and scratched a bug bite. "Honestly."

Leah nodded. "It's true, she's deeply awkward on the inside."

"I'm doing better," said Nina, "but, you know, we've all got something, right?"

The three women gazed at her expectantly.

Laura smiled back at them and held her tongue. Suddenly, Nina pounced.

"So, what's the deal with Impossibly Handsome Bob?"

Laura felt herself getting red. "Nothing, there's no deal. I just got out of a relationship, I'm not interested in dating."

"You don't have to date him," said Leah. "You could . . . you know . . ."

"Hook up?" asked Laura. "Nah, no interest in casual sex, either." There was silence in the room. "Sorry, never been that kind of person." More silence. "So far, anyway."

Leah turned to Nina. "We're talking about the same Bob that came to trivia that one time?"

Nina nodded.

"The supercute one?"

Nina nodded again. Leah turned to Laura. "You have enviable self-control."

Laura shook her head. "No, I'm . . . taking a breath. I was with my ex since high school. I really want to be single for a while."

"But you admit Bob's a good-looking guy?" Leah seemed keen to reassure herself she wasn't wrong about this.

Laura nodded. "Sure, if you like tall men with dark eyes and incredible bone structure."

Lauren laughed. "Personally, I've always favored potato-headed men with cranky ex-wives and bitey children, but that's me." She looked around pleadingly. "Can we order food? All this chat about handsome men and casual sex is making me snackish."

Later, after Leah and Lauren went home, Laura helped Nina tidy up. She'd been able to answer most of the human biology and science questions Nina had prepared, and ended up feeling pretty pleased with herself. She wasn't good at the button pressing—particularly as Nina had a duck-quack buzzer that made her giggle every time—but Nina didn't seem worried about that.

"So, you're a neighborhood kid?" she asked Nina. "You grew up here?" She gazed around the room at all the pictures and artwork, the endless rows of books. There was a lot of color and pattern in the room, a lot of content. It wasn't exactly restful, but it was comforting.

"Well, not literally *here*, but this side of town, anyway." Nina shrugged. "My mom's a photographer and traveled all the time, so I was raised by my nanny, Louise. She's awesome. My mom would appear every so often, evaluate where we were living, and move us if she thought we needed more room. Then she'd leave again for months at a time." Her tone was light, but Laura wondered how that had actually felt. Her own mother had been a constantly hovering cloud, which had felt largely oppressive . . . but also provided cover.

Nina got to her feet and pointed to a photograph on her wall of a young man showing a crowd of small children how to load film into a camera. "That's one of hers," she said proudly. She walked over to her tiny kitchenette and opened the fridge. "Do you want more beer? Or something else?" They'd ordered Chinese food, and as always, it had made her thirsty. She'd probably wake up with puffy eyes and a vague sense of regret . . . but the pork buns had been worth it.

"No, thanks," said Laura, getting up to look at the picture. "Where's your nanny now?"

"In Georgia, with her own kids and grandkids."

Laura turned away from the photograph. "And your dad? Polly said something about your dad . . . ?" Laura couldn't remember what it was.

Nina laughed. "That he's dead?" She looked at Laura's stricken expression. "Don't worry, I never met him. I didn't know he existed until he didn't." She sat down in her enormous armchair and examined Laura with curiosity. "What's your family like?"

Laura shrugged and looked around for another chair. "Not very exciting. My parents are professors, my brothers are professors, I was supposed to be a professor." No other chair; she sat on the floor and tucked her legs under her, crisscross applesauce, folding over to stretch her back. "I spent most of my life on the Upper West Side of Manhattan, with daily voyages downtown for school. New York is a big city, obviously, but the Upper West Side is a small world, especially the way my family does it."

Nina look interested. "Ooh, academics. What do they teach?"

"Birds, largely. My dad is a professor in the biology department, studying the mechanics of flight, and my mom is a professor in the psychology department, studying the social lives of birds." Laura smiled. "We had birds all over the place, literally and figuratively. The one part of my childhood that was like yours was that both of them went away every summer to do fieldwork, so we stayed with our grandmother, or rather, she stayed with us."

Nina stared at her and said, "So . . . you know a lot about birds as well then?"

Laura grinned at her. "You're extremely single-minded about the trivia, aren't you?"

Nina nodded. "Yes, sorry. My boyfriend says it's irritating, and refuses to join my team. He was on an opposing team when we met, but he says I take the trivial out of trivia, which ruins it." She narrowed her eyes. "I really do like him a lot, but he's not very competitive."

Laura laughed. "Where is he tonight?"

Nina smiled. "Tom? He went bowling with his brother." She paused. "He'll come by later." She looked down and picked at the rug, slightly sheepishly. "We don't live together, but we see each other a lot."

"You met him through trivia?"

Nina started to nod, but then shook her head. "Yes . . . no . . . kind of. We met because of trivia, certainly, but we . . . I don't know. I wasn't interested in him at first because I didn't think he was a reader, which is kind of a deal breaker, but . . ." She paused, and blushed slightly. "I got over myself." She brightened. "Did you know that if you bowl four strikes in a row, it's called a hambone?"

"No," said Laura levelly, "I did not know that." She smiled. "Are you trying to change the subject? I didn't mean to be nosy."

"It's OK. It's a new relationship, we're still working things out."

"Does he live close?"

"Pretty close, we're both homebodies. He's traveled more than I have, I haven't even been to San Diego." She pulled a cat toy out of a drawer and starting playing with Phil. "One time he and I were supposed to drive to Mexico, like this fun, spontaneous thing, right?"

"Yes," said Laura, beginning to like Nina more and more. She might be small and cute, but there was no reason to get mad about it.

"Well, we made it as far south as Carlsbad, which is coincidentally the home of Legoland, and ended up spending the weekend there instead. It was pretty awesome." She giggled.

Laura grinned. "You spent a romantic weekend building things out of Lego?"

"I don't think anything was actually completed, but it was fun." Nina looked at her phone. "It's after nine, I guess we better call it a day."

"Wait, you promised to work on your hand."

"I did," said Nina calmly. "I scooped ice cream earlier and read for an hour at a good clip, and I turned each page twice."

Laura clicked her tongue. "Will you let me stretch your hand, at least? I learned how to do it for myself when I was recovering, and I promise it'll feel good."

Nina rolled her eyes but held out her hand. Laura shimmied over on the rug and took hold of it in both of hers, gently stretching and massaging. Inside her head she was listing the bones and muscles of this most elegant of small machines, visualizing the diagrams and charts she'd already spent hours looking at. The human body never failed to astound her; the intricate interdependence of structures hard and soft, the tension and torque of fascia and sinew.

Laura's hair slid forward as she bent over Nina's hand. "You don't need to spend hours on it, you simply need to be consistent." She interlaced her fingers with Nina's and spread them apart. "You'll be glad you did, I promise."

Nina looked dubious. "My wrist feels fine, honestly."

Laura looked up at her and went back to stretching. "Well, great, don't you want it to stay that way?"

Nina regarded the other woman thoughtfully as she bent over her hand. Living in Los Angeles meant Nina—and everyone else—saw a lot of good-looking people. Beauty queens of every gender arrived to make their fame and fortune, and Angelenos developed an extremely warped sense of average. By Los Angeles standards Laura was pretty but not outstanding. Her features were even, her nose neither small enough for cute nor big enough for interesting, her mouth pleasant and often smiling. Her coloring was unusual: Her hair and skin were shades of caramel while her eyes were gray, her irises ringed with black. What was truly remarkable about her was a considerable physical presence, both in terms of height (Nina thought she had to be nearly six feet tall) and strength (her arms and shoulders were defined and muscular, her legs even more so). Admittedly, when Laura had burst into the bookstore office all tall, damp, and smoky, she'd startled the applesauce out of Nina, but now she could see Laura used her powers only for good. She wasn't exactly . . . forthcoming about herself, but Nina could relate to that. She wasn't a podcast of personal feelings herself.

"Alright," said Laura, straightening up, "that wasn't so bad, was it?"

Nina flexed her hand. "I'll be honest, that was amazing. I'm going to have to rethink massage completely."

Laura frowned. "You don't like massage?"

"No," replied Nina, "too ticklish."

Laura opened her mouth, but then closed it. If she herself won the lottery, she would 100 percent spend it all on massage, but to each his own. She got to her feet and brushed herself off. Clouds of cat hair tumbled and caught the light.

"Sorry about that," said Nina, smiling ruefully, but Laura shook her head.

"I don't mind. Fur is much easier to live with than feathers, which have an unfortunate tendency to stick into you when you least expect it."

Nina opened her apartment door. "Thanks for joining our merry band," she said, rubbing her hands together. "We're going to pulverize the competition."

Laura wished she shared Nina's optimism. "Well, thanks for inviting me, and try to at least stretch your wrist and hand every day." She walked carefully down the steps. "Your cat is on the gate again. Is he going to bite me?"

"Doubtful," said Nina. "But he may give you venomous side-eye, it's his specialty."

Laura turned the corner toward the gate, disappearing from Nina's view. Nina listened to Laura's footsteps on the gravel, then a creak as the gate opened and closed. She could imagine Phil's expression of concentration.

Laura's voice floated back. "He hates me."

Nina grinned. "He doesn't. He takes his time to get to know people," she called out. "Like me," she muttered under her breath.

"I'm the same way," replied Laura, more distantly. "Maybe he and I will become friends eventually."

Nina smiled and went inside.

TWENTY

On Saturday it was hot before eight in the morning and Laura skipped her run for once, saving her energy for whatever heavy lifting was involved in gardening. She and Bob met up in the kitchen, and she hoped she'd dressed appropriately. She'd borrowed loose cotton pants from Polly and hoped they would keep her cool enough. Bob was wearing his usual jeans and a T-shirt from some gardening-related company. Laura wondered randomly if she would have to wear physical therapy–related T-shirts once she was working. Did such things even exist? She hadn't forgotten the connection she and Bob had shared the other night, but she was trying to. No time for distractions this year. Or probably next year, either.

"So, where exactly are we going?" Laura looked at Bob, who was pouring coffee and tea into two to-go cups.

"Culver City," he said. "It's maybe half an hour away." He hesitated. "Are you comfortable going in the truck? I got the side mirror fixed."

Laura made a scornful noise and nodded. "Of course. I was only surprised the other day." This wasn't entirely true; she was feeling a little nauseated with anxiety about being on the road, actually, but she was in no way ready to show it. She'd spent ten minutes in the shower telling herself not to freak out, and was hoping she was going to take her own advice. You're a tough cookie, she told herself over and over and over. This cookie is not for crumbling.

Bob looked at her, but she was bending down to pet Herbert the dog, who was waving his tail gently, stirring the air to get a better sniff at it. When she lifted her head, Bob smiled at her, relieved she was OK, his own nervousness about the day starting to fade away. Laura wasn't like most of the women he met in Los Angeles. She was easier to be with, less . . . demanding. Everything about her was self-contained, and everything she said and did made it clear she valued her independence. He wondered what it took to get under her skin, and then he found himself wondering about her skin, and told himself to snap out of it.

They headed out of the house, and Laura took a deep breath before opening the truck and climbing in. *I'm fine, it's fine, everything is fine.*

Bob turned on the engine, and looked at her. "OK?"

She nodded and gave him one of her big smiles. If he knew how scared she was, he would lose all respect for her, she was certain.

"I'm great, let's go."

Bob reversed out of the driveway and swung into the street. Laura's tummy lurched, but she breathed deeply and threatened herself to calm it down.

Let's talk about something else. "So, tell me about this teacher of yours. He sounds interesting."

Bob paused, waiting for an opportunity to make a turn across traffic. Because he wasn't looking at her, she let herself gaze at him. He had a little break in his nose, clearly very old, and a hole in his ear where he used to wear an earring. She felt tension pulling her ribs together, and decided to focus on the corners of his mouth instead. They lifted up, creating successfully distracting dimples.

He said, "You'll like Edward, he's great. He's literally a world expert on soil, and his family is one of the largest horticultural dynasties in Europe."

Laura laughed and hoped he didn't notice the shake in her voice when she said, "Are there a lot of horticultural dynasties?"

Bob looked serious. "Yes. But the Bloem company has been dealing in flowers since before the Dutch tulip mania."

"The what now?"

Bob shot her a glance, then explained. "In the seventeenth century, people in Holland became obsessed with tulips."

"The flowers?"

"Yes. Different varieties, different colors. It was a national obsession, then a problem, as people bought and traded bulbs and flowers at vastly inflated prices. Eventually the market collapsed, and people lost fortunes. The Bloem company managed to keep going, and still does."

"Huh," said Laura, not sure what else to say. "How weird."

Bob shrugged. "I find it easier to understand getting obsessed with plants than cars, or the latest phone. People *are* weird." He looked across at Laura.

"I guess." She fell silent, and then, as she became aware of the sound of the road under their wheels, said, "And you don't mind helping him out with this kind of thing?"

"Not at all," he replied, noticing her voice seemed a little tight. He tapped the brakes gently. "First of all, I like doing it. I'm much happier outside, I've never been good at being indoors."

"Me neither," said Laura, "but I haven't done much gardening."

"No problem," said Bob easily. "I'll tell you what to do." He paused. "I mean, you know, I'll let you know . . ." Nooo, his brain said, stop talking before it's too late. "Not, like, you know, a boss, but . . ."

She looked over at him and laughed, feeling her tension abating a little. "It's cool, I know what you meant. I'm here to help, right?" She spotted another potential topic. "Hey, what's that crazy tree?"

He looked. "That is a weeping bottlebrush tree, for obvious reasons."

Laura said, "You mean because of those bright red things that look exactly like bottlebrushes?" The tree had long, bright red blooms with hundreds of tiny hairlike stamens. They reminded her of something Dr. Seuss might draw. "Los Angeles is far more colorful than I expected."

"You came at a good time." Bob pointed at a huge purple tree. "There are still a few late-blooming jacarandas around, and orchid trees everywhere. We had a good wet winter, so this summer has been amazing." He shot her a look. "Sorry. Talking about the weather."

She shrugged. "I'm into weather. My whole family spent a lot of time outside, peering at various flora and fauna." She made a face. "Although I was the one running around while everyone else oohed and aahed over leaves and birds."

"Really?"

"Yeah, I was good at taking notes and holding things for

them. Other than that I was a massive disappointment to them, I'm afraid."

He looked at her very briefly. "You're kidding."

She reddened, and shook her head. "They don't understand why I don't want to be a scientist." She looked out of the window. "Professionally, I mean."

"Aren't you going to be kind of a doctor? Isn't that science-y?"

"I guess, sort of." She fell silent.

He paused, and redirected the conversation a little. "So was your house full of animals, growing up?"

"Not really," she replied, her voice still soft, "unless cockroaches count. Our apartment was pretty small, it was already a source of controversy that I had my own room while my brothers had to share; there really wasn't space for pets. But we had pigeons on the roof, and often had injured animals in boxes around the place." She thought back. "We had a juvenile squirrel one winter, but we weren't allowed to keep it." She remembered that scene very clearly, her begging her parents to let her keep Nutty, and her mother's disdain for the idea. *It's a wild animal, Laura, it has a place, a contribution to make, we have no right to stop it from being who it is.* Strangely, when she'd made a similar argument about her own career choice, her mother had mocked her: *People don't make a contribution, they're an infestation that threatens the whole system.* But to be fair, her mother wasn't a complete misanthrope. Laura could think of three other scientists her mom liked, one of whom was still alive. Her lips twitched; worrying about her family's opinion was fruitless.

Bob looked over at her, catching the corner of her smile as she looked away. Her skin reminded him of the underside of petals, luminously soft. She was wearing tiny butterfly earrings that for some reason touched him. Laura was a strong woman, but the earrings showed the sweetness she wouldn't show everyone. He wanted to see that side of her. He wanted to look through the bathroom door when he was getting undressed for the night, and glimpse her taking her earrings out before coming to bed. *Oh my god, I have lost my mind. I have skipped straight from dirty dreams to sharing a bathroom . . . although we do share a bathroom.*

Bob slowed down for a light. "My parents aren't thrilled with my life choices, either, but that's cool." He made a turn, and added, "I stopped caring about that a long time ago."

Laura said, "Me too, but my parents don't seem to care about my opinion of their opinion. They'll probably be giving it to me twenty years from now." She took a deep breath and realized her tension was nearly gone. "Honestly, my mother is mystified . . ." She shook her head, then changed the subject again. "Do you know what we're doing today?"

Bob nodded. "Today we're taking out a little patch of crappy lawn—Edward's description, not mine—and replacing it with a couple of raised beds filled with native plants and flowers for the butterflies and birds to enjoy."

"Does he do that for all his students?"

Bob shook his head. "Just any that let him."

They drove quietly for a while, and Laura gazed at the people they passed. Los Angeles was much less dense, people-wise, than Manhattan, but there was a similar energy. And apparently a similar level of passion for sports: Everywhere she saw Dodgers shirts. Or Rams. Or Lakers. She was about to ask Bob about it when he spoke again.

"You're also going to meet Lili, Edward's fiancée, because I think he said she was coming." He smiled broadly. "And you'll meet her kids, who are a total trip." He reconsidered. "Well, the younger one is a trip. The older one is pretty normal." He turned and started looking for house numbers. "Ah, there it is." He pulled over and parked.

The house in question was a small, one-story building on a side street, clearly much loved. The paint was fresh, the curtains bright, the front path decorated with chalk flowers. A little girl was sitting outside, chalking away.

I made it, thought Laura. I made it all the way and he didn't know how scared I was.

Bob and Laura got out of the truck, and the child looked up and hailed them.

"Bob! Noble friend! Trusty sidekick!" She stood up, an elementary-age kid wearing leggings with rainbows and a T-shirt with a sloth on it. Her shiny hair was cut in a bob, and her face was filled with delight. She ran over and threw herself on Bob.

"Queen Clare," said Bob, lifting her up and swinging her around. "How are things in the kingdom?"

"Fine," she replied, looking at Laura. "Who's this?"

"This is Laura," said Bob. "She's a new friend."

Clare reached out and shook hands with Laura, her little grip firm. "Are you a gardener, too?"

"No," said Laura, "I'm studying to be a physical therapist."

Clare was interested. "What's that?"

"She'll help people who've been injured or sick or whatever," said Bob, going back to grab tools from the back of the truck, "teaching them to walk, things like that."

Clare's eyes brightened hopefully. "Could you teach them to fly?"

Laura shook her head. "No," she said, but then thought about it for a second and added, "unless they could fly before, I guess."

"And if they could?" Clare was completely ready to pursue

this line of conversation, viewing reality as, frankly, a creative impediment.

Laura shrugged. "Then, yeah, if they could explain how they did it before, I could probably help them do it again." Laura wondered how she'd found herself saying this, but Clare seemed to take it in stride.

"That's cool," she said, filing away the information, "but today you're going to help Bob?"

Laura nodded. "Gardening, not flying."

"Right," said Clare, sitting back down to continue her chalking. "Because he can't fly anyway." She seemed to think his feelings might be hurt by this extremely factual statement, and quickly added, "But he's good at other things." She waited a hair too long to add, "Probably."

"Thanks for the vote of confidence," said Bob, pausing on his way into the house. "Is everyone here already?"

Clare shook her head and lowered her voice. "The people are nice, but the garden is too small for me to do anything except get in the way, my mom said. So she gave me chalk." She looked up at them. "What shall I draw now?"

"A cat," said Laura.

"You're like my mom," said Clare complainingly. "She always says draw a cat."

Laura shrugged. "They're cute, they're easy to draw."

"Do you know a cat's whiskers help them not get stuck in things?" Clare started drawing a cat. "That's what my friend Nina told me. She knows lots of things."

"Nina from the bookstore?" Laura asked.

"Yes," nodded Clare. "She's going out with my uncle's brother, you know."

"I don't think Laura's interested in Nina's love life, Clare," said Bob.

Clare frowned at him. "Everyone's interested in other people, Bob."

Bob rolled his eyes at Laura. "Coming in?"

Laura hesitated. "Why don't you go see what the plan is, I'll wait here."

After he'd gone, Clare looked up at her. "Is Bob your boyfriend?"

Laura shook her head. "We live at the same house. With Polly, from the bookstore."

"I know Polly," said Clare, faintly scornfully. "My sister goes to a book club at the store, you know." She added ears to her cat, then drew a flower behind one of them.

"I heard," said Laura. "Everybody seems to know everybody."

Clare sat back on the path and looked at her. "Bob used to be my aunty's boyfriend, you know."

"No, I didn't know."

"Yes," said Clare. "She called him Impossibly Handsome Bob."

"Oh, is that where that comes from?"

Clare nodded. "Yes. Then she got married and now he doesn't have a girlfriend." She smiled at Laura. "Maybe you can be his girlfriend. He's very strong, you know, he can lift me up over his head." She wrinkled her nose. "I don't get why he's impossibly handsome, he looks regular to me."

Regular Bob appeared from the house. "We're around the back," he said to Laura. "Feel free to join us if you like."

Clare looked at him. "Maybe she'd rather draw with me. I'm very good company, my mom said so."

Bob laughed. "Your mom is very wise. Laura can do what she wants, she's a free woman."

"For the time being," said Clare very archly, narrowing her eyes.

Bob raised his eyebrows at her. "You're a strange child, Clare."

Clare sighed, and relaxed her face. "Yeah, my mom says that, too."

TWENTY-ONE

As Clare said, the backyard was pretty small. A tall, broad man with an accent, whom Bob introduced as Edward, was directing activities. There were a couple of people working on removing sod from the small lawn, while another pair was assembling a raised garden bed. Laura looked at Bob and smiled.

"How can I help?"

Bob had been put in charge of the lawn and was using a sharp edging tool to divide the lawn into narrower strips so they could be lifted up with wide, flat shovels. Laura couldn't help noticing he was doing an excellent and efficient job of transferring weight while maintaining his core and protecting his lower back, and then she admitted to herself that she was simply ogling, and in pretending it was academic, she wasn't even fooling herself. A very pregnant woman standing nearby overheard the question and answered for Bob.

"You can help me, if you like." She came closer and stuck out her hand. "I'm Lili, you probably met my daughter Clare outside."

Laura nodded and smiled. "I'm Laura, it's nice to meet you. Your daughter is adorable."

Lili smiled and turned up her palms. "She's her own little bird, that's for sure."

"Bob said you had another daughter, an older one. Is she here?"

Lili shook her head. "No, Annabel's at a play rehearsal. I'm no use for digging right now, and the planting won't happen until the raised bed is done. However, I noticed some little corner beds . . ." She pointed and Laura saw what she meant: two little flower beds, or rather potential flower beds. They were currently growing old leaves and candy wrappers. "I was going to suggest I work on those, but I need to check that it's OK."

"I'm in," said Laura, following her over to where Edward was standing with a middle-aged couple who were clearly the owners of the garden.

"Hey there," said Lili, smiling at everyone. Laura saw the tall man turn and see Lili, and watched in half envy, half admiration as his face transformed at the sight of her. He reached out his hand and cupped Lili's shoulder, gently drawing her closer.

"Hello there," he said, his voice soft. "Jon, Sandy, this is Lili, my fiancée."

The couple smiled and nodded, and Lili said, "I was wondering if Laura and I could do a little rehab on those flower beds?" She pointed, but Sandy and Jon looked confused.

"Those corners?" Jon looked surprised. "They're not really flower beds, are they?"

"They easily could be," said Lili. "I promise." She looked at Edward. "Did we bring anything that would work there?"

Edward rubbed his head. "No, but you can ask Bob if he has anything, it's possible."

"He has some little flowers in trays, I saw them in the truck," volunteered Laura. "I don't know what they are or anything."

"Bob"—Lili raised her voice—"do you have any flowers?"

Bob stopped digging and stood there with his T-shirt clinging to him. He wiped his forehead with his arm and thought about it.

"I think I have one flat of color, but if you're talking about those corner beds, they won't do. Rose campion"—he looked at Edward—"needs full sun. You want something like *Brunnera*, or maybe *Dicentra. Trillium*, maybe?"

Edward frowned, and turned to Jon and Sandy. "How do you feel about ferns? Or leaves in general?"

Both Jon and Sandy looked confused. "Uh," said Sandy, "I'm pro-ferns, I guess."

"Honestly," said Jon, "never given ferns a single thought."

Edward nodded, taking the insult to ferns on the chin. "These main beds will be filled with flowering plants to encourage pollinators like hummingbirds, bees, and butterflies, but ferns also provide a place to hide for ground-feeding birds or other foraging creatures. Those two corners are in full shade, so ferns or hostas will be more suitable." He turned to Bob, who looked more interested in debating planting choices than digging in the hot sun. "Hostas, Bob?"

"Great, if these ladies can create some kind of soil for them." He smiled at Laura. "It's all about the soil, as Edward will tell you."

"Don't get him started on soil," said Lili to Laura. "He'll never stop." She took a breath, having reached that point in pregnancy where the baby was taking over internal real estate to the detriment of lung capacity, and said, "Laura and I will go to the garden center and get a few plants." She looked at Laura. "If that's alright with you?"

Laura looked at Bob, who smiled at her. She really didn't

want to get in another car, but there was no way she was going to let this thing get out of control. She would push herself and get over it. "Sounds good to me, let's go."

Edward fished in his pockets and threw some keys to Lili. "Be careful, *schatje*."

Lili smiled at him and turned to go. Laura looked once more at Bob, who was still standing there looking at her.

"Yeah, *schatje*," he said, "be careful." There was something affectionate and touching in his face as he looked at her, and Lili and Edward shot each other a quick look. They were both very fond of Bob.

"Don't worry, Bob," said Lili. "I'll look after her."

Edward's car was a long station wagon, and once they were inside, Laura realized the back seats were already folded down to make room for a wide variety of tools, bags of seed, textbooks, and papers.

"Your fiancé is a teacher?" Laura asked as they settled in. Lili had invited Clare to join them, but she'd been engrossed in her drawing and demurred.

"Yes, at Pierce." Lili lowered the window and addressed Clare. "Are you sure you don't want to come?"

Clare looked up at her. "Mom, we go to the garden center all the time . . . wait . . . is it the one with the good candy?"

"No, that one's closer to our house."

"Then no, thanks." She went back to drawing, muttering, "If it doesn't have sugar dots on paper, I'm not interested."

Lili looked dubious. "Well, if you need anything, Edward's in the back."

Clare waved her hand dismissively. "Have fun, Mom." Looking up, she added, "And Laura." She looked at her mom. "Laura's interested in Bob, you can tell her all about him."

Laura went bright red. "That's not true." Her embarrassment pushed her anxiety away briefly.

"And she teaches people to fly."

"Also not true," said Laura quickly.

Lili laughed, and closed the window. "Laura, if I took Clare literally, I'd have been lost years ago." They pulled away from the curb, and Lili turned to Laura. "Honestly, though, are you and Bob . . . ?"

"Only friends, and recently that," said Laura. "We live in the same house, that's all." Lili nipped into traffic, and Laura's hand tightened on the door handle.

Lili's face brightened. "Oh, are you in the house with Polly?" She looked over at Laura and grinned.

"Yes!" Laura tried to smile, waiting for Lili to look back at the road. "You know Polly, of course, Clare said so."

"The bookstore is pretty essential to the neighborhood, and Polly's pretty essential to the bookstore. Everyone knows Polly." Lili navigated the streets deftly, but drove fast and changed lanes in a darting, non-indicating fashion. Laura tried to ignore it and focus on Lili's face. She was quite a bit older than Laura and slightly round-faced with pregnancy, but there was something warm and youthful about her that Laura found appealing. Lili's long, dark hair was piled on top of her head and secured with one of those grabby clip things, but several large chunks were coming undone at the back, and there was a general messiness about her that was disarming.

"How long have you been at the house?" Lili asked, trying to get comfortable behind the wheel, wriggling a bit and sighing frequently. Pregnancy never looked supercomfortable to Laura; it looked adorable on the covers of magazines and in movies, but up close it seemed like several servings of pain in the ass.

"Not long." Laura explained about the accident, about moving to Los Angeles, about the fire, about grad school. She thought she breezed through all of it with equal emphasis, but Lili shot her a look and said, with startling bluntness, "My husband died in a car accident. I was a wreck for months afterward, couldn't even sit in a car without freaking out a bit. Have you found it hard?"

Laura's mouth dropped open. How was this woman saying all this to a total stranger? She felt the blood rushing to her face.

"It's been . . ." She couldn't continue, her voice cracking. *Jesus, what is wrong with me?*

Lili clearly wasn't thrown by this conversation and had more pressing concerns. She said, "I'm sorry, but I really need to pee. Can we stop at this Starbucks?"

Laura nodded. "Sure." She had her voice back, even if she still wasn't certain how to answer Lili's question. How do you say, *Yeah, it's been really hard, and—funny you should ask—I'm starting to think I'm losing my mind, thanks for asking?*

"Thanks." Lili pulled into a parking spot outside the coffee place and unbuckled her seat belt with relief. "I'd forgotten how much you pee when you're pregnant. It's not a plus."

"When's the baby due?"

"September." Lili was already out of the car and hopping a little from foot to foot. "Which is about six years from tomorrow."

"Are your kids excited?" Laura got out of the car and followed Lili through the swinging doors.

"Sure," said Lili, putting on a sudden burst of speed. "Can you get me an iced coffee with lots of room for cream?" She rushed up to the counter for the bathroom key and swiftly made her way across the room, navigating the crowd of overcaffeinated people in a mad, slalom-esque dash. The sales assistant looked at Laura. "I guess she really needs to go, huh?"

Laura grinned, and ordered their drinks.

Having successfully acquired ferns at the nursery, Laura and Lili returned to the house and found Clare and Bob playing hopscotch on the pathway.

Lili grinned and turned to Laura. "Clare has had a soft spot for Bob ever since he let her drive a tractor in our gardening class. That's where I met Edward." She watched her daughter openly cheating and Bob pretending not to see it. "Bob's a really good guy, you know." She turned to Laura. "It's not his fault he looks like that."

Laura laughed "I know, it's a bit distracting."

"It is. But try not to judge a book by its cover."

"OK."

Lili hesitated. "Or by its tendency to blush and stammer."

Laura smiled. "OK."

"Or by its fondness for talking about plants."

Laura's smile widened. "Are we still talking about a book?"

Lili opened her door. "Yes, of course. Crap, I need to pee again—can I leave you to unload the car?"

Bob was already coming over to help, and Laura smiled at him. "Of course," she said. "I'll see you in the back."

Edward had been right, the ferns and hostas looked beautiful in the corners. Lili regaled Laura with bizarre stories about her kids, her dog, her work, while Laura did most of the digging. Bending over wasn't easy for Lili, so she mostly sat on the ground against the wall and chatted while Laura dug, loosened the ferns from their pots, and placed them in the spots Lili pointed to. Time passed easily, and Laura relaxed. She'd been worried Lili was going to pursue a line of questioning about the accident, but Lili seemed to have moved on. Or maybe she was just an astute judge of people and could tell Laura didn't want to talk about it. Not being that astute a judge of people herself, Laura wasn't sure.

After several hours, and once the two delighted garden owners had expressed their thanks for way longer than necessary, Laura found herself happily helping Bob load the extra plants and tools back into the truck. She always felt better when she was active, even though she'd developed a secret habit of imagining her own muscles while she used them, which was probably weird. When she was going through rehab, her PT would talk her through everything her body was doing, and it stuck. She would bend to lift a fifty-pound bag of soil up into the truck, for example, and visualize her own quadriceps, glutes, and abdominals working, then her shoulder girdle and arms as she lowered it onto the truck bed . . . weirder still—and this she was never going to tell anybody—she always imagined her muscles as a highly trained team of miniature hers, little Lauras in leotards looking focused and dedicated and crushing it like an amazing internal flash mob.

"What are you thinking about?" asked Bob, who had finished loading the last of the tools and was hunting in his pockets for his keys. "You're smiling."

Laura dusted her hands off on her jeans. "Nothing. Daydreaming."

She walked around to get in the truck, and Bob watched the sun warm the honey tones of her hair. Get a grip, Robert, he told himself. You barely know this woman.

They climbed into the truck, and Bob turned to Laura. He

was full of the energy he always got from finishing hard work, and for once he was able to talk without thinking about it.

"Are you hungry? We kind of worked through lunch . . ."

Laura looked at her watch. "It's four thirty."

"Early bird special?" Bob grinned. "Denny's? Or Larchmont?"

Suddenly Laura was hungry, too. Ravenous, actually. "Denny's," she said. "I'm feeling a little homesick for diner food."

"You grew up in a diner?" Bob was still grinning as he checked over his shoulder and pulled out into traffic.

"Yes," said Laura, surreptitiously holding the armrest, "but behind the counter, so, you know, it was private."

"Plus all the ketchup packets you could ever want."

"Exactly."

TWENTY-TWO

They pulled into the Denny's parking lot and made their way to the entrance. The Denny's smelled the same as every other Denny's—pancakes, coffee, relaxed good humor. You know the smell.

Bob and Laura sat in a booth, and a friendly waitress came to take their order. That accomplished, and coffee received, they sat across from each other and smiled. Away from the work of the garden, Laura felt awkward. She started studying the surface of the table, which was remarkably consistent with every other diner table she'd ever sat at. She looked at the condiments: ketchup, check; sugar, check; little creamer things, check. Yup, everything appeared to be in order.

Come on, she told herself, say something. "That was fun," she said, possibly a little too brightly. "Everyone seemed very happy with the garden." She folded the menu and put it away, wondering if she would ever reach the point where conversation came easily to her.

Bob nodded, adding five little creams to his coffee. "I think they were. It was a perfect spot with plenty of sun, and we'll monitor the pH levels and soil composition over time, obviously."

Scintillating conversation as ever, Bob, he thought to himself. What beautiful young woman doesn't want to ponder soil composition?

Laura raised her eyebrows. "Do you taste the coffee anymore, or is it just flavored creamer at this point?" She sipped her coffee. It was unbelievably hot, but she managed not to scream and thought she carried it off pretty well.

He frowned, then realized what she was referring to. He tucked the little cream pots one inside the other. "They only hold enough to bathe an ant."

Laura was puzzled. "Why would you bathe an ant? I think of them as pretty clean already."

"No idea." He wished he could think of something funny, but he kept noticing her eyelashes, or her freckles, and forgetting what he was going to say. Besides, he wasn't really all that knowledgeable about ants. He tried to change the subject.

"What do your parents do?" Bob tried his coffee, too, and flinched. "How are you drinking this? It's like lava."

"They're teachers, what about yours?"

He laughed. "They're teachers, too!" He held up his hand to high-five, and they swatted at each other with moderate success. "Or at least, my grandmother, mother, and three sisters are all teachers. I don't know about my dad, he left when we were young." He didn't seem bothered by this, as indeed he wasn't. All those women had provided more than enough guidance, plus the half-dozen uncles and male cousins in his extended family were always around if he'd had a question that only someone with testicles could answer.

Laura asked, "What do they teach?"

"My mom teaches middle school everything, mostly social studies. I can name all fifty states in less than a minute."

"Prove it."

"Another time. Your turn."

She looked at him and smiled. "Mom and Dad teach psychology and biology, my three brothers teach entomology, zoology, and botany." She paused. "I not sure I could name all fifty states, but I can rattle off the Linnaean system of taxonomy." She shrugged. "Animal kingdom only, probably, but I could take a swing at plants."

"Wow," said Bob, his hand still warm from the high five; he could feel it tingling. "I . . . uh . . . couldn't." He shook his head. "Not even sure what you said, all I heard was a lot of 'ology.'"

"Yes," laughed Laura, "we have lots of ology in our house." She was feeling better. Bob really was easy to talk to, once she got over her fear of saying the first thing. "You have three sisters?"

He nodded. "All older."

Laura laughed. "Wow. Were you incredibly spoiled or totally pushed around?"

He pulled a face. "I had a choice? I got both, depending on the day."

"What's the gap?"

"Small, between all of us." He smiled and sipped his coffee. "My mom is very efficient."

"I hear that, my mom is, too. I'm the baby, my three brothers are all older." She grinned at him. "We're a matching pair: teachers' kids, baby of four, only one of our gender . . . Did you have a dog growing up?"

Bob nodded. "Yes, a mutt called Rusty."

Laura crowed, "We had a mutt called Lemon." She held up her finger. "Wait, let me clarify, we didn't have him, my grandmother had him, which was nearly the same thing." She could still remember long summer afternoons lying on her bed with

Lemon, the smell of his fur when she buried her face in his side, which she did quite frequently. She realized there was a little of Lemon in Herbert; they both had that kind of erratic fur that looked like they'd accidentally gotten thrown in a hot dryer.

It was at that moment that a kerfuffle broke out over by the entrance to the Denny's. They both looked around. A small crowd had formed around the claw machine, and judging by the crowing and yelling, someone had just won something.

Bob grinned. "One of my sisters once won five hundred dollars on a claw machine."

"I thought they were all rigged," said Laura. "I read an article that said the power is only sufficient to win a fraction of the time."

"You shouldn't believe everything you read," said Bob. "It's absolutely a game of skill."

"No way," said Laura.

"Yes way," said Bob.

They looked at each other and then, as one, got to their feet.

The simple fact of the matter is that claw machines *can* be rigged. The owner is able to alter the power of both the grip and the lift, but that's a blade that cuts both ways. It's possible the owner of this particular Denny's was feeling generous, or that the claw machine had just been filled, or that a magical alien race had come down and souped up the machine for their own intergalactic reasons, but regardless of why, it was paying out big-time. The three teenage girls who were playing the machine when Bob and Laura walked over were giddy with success, despite the fact that they'd each won a toy none of them would have taken for free, had someone offered it to them. The first girl had a sort-of unicorn (the horn pointed backward; possibly the manufacturer had only heard unicorns described), the second had a stuffed rabbit that could have spawned a horror franchise, and the last one was clutching a stuffed mushroom that might have been video game inspired, but ended up looking like an inappropriate drug reference.

As Bob and Laura walked up, the girls stepped back.

"We won," said the first one, looking up at the very cute guy who had just shown up. He was too old to be genuinely appealing, obviously, but still worth talking to. She was wearing a T-shirt for a band that had broken up seven years before she was born, a fact she was completely unaware of.

"I see that," said Bob. "Do you think you used up all the luck?"

The second girl shook her head. A small cloud of glitter settled on her shoulders. "It's not luck, it's skill." She was the one with the mushroom.

"My point exactly," said Bob, pulling a pair of quarters from his pocket.

"It's completely rigged," argued another of the girls, the one with the unicorn. Now that she'd had a chance to look at it properly, she was uneasy . . . the backward horn made it look bad-tempered, and she wondered how her other stuffed toys were going to respond to it. Then she remembered she was sixteen and shouldn't even have stuffed toys, then she felt guilty about the ones she did have, and then her brain short-circuited in a soup of hormones and neurochemicals and she went silent. Fortunately for her, nobody noticed any of this at all.

Bob stepped up to the machine and put in his money. The timer started to count down, and he moved the claw back and forth a few times.

Laura laughed at him. "What, feeling it out?"

Bob was unconcerned. "Yes. I am getting a sense of the mechanism, the timing, the power."

Laura snorted. "Please."

Bob took his hands off the controls and circled the game cabinet. He crouched and evaluated; he rubbed his chin and raised his eyebrows at Laura.

"Stuffed cat in the corner pocket," he said.

Laura looked. "The pink one with a bad attitude?"

"I think that's just the way its face is glued on," said Bob, "but yes, that one." He rubbed his hands on his legs, checked the timer, and moved the claw. In one movement he dropped, grabbed, and raised the claw, dragged the cat out of the pile of toys, and dropped it into the chute.

Laura goggled. Literally. Stood there with her mouth open and her eyes wide.

"No freaking way," she breathed.

Bob laughed and handed her the cat. "Your turn."

When they sat back down at the table to eat, Laura was down four dollars and was pretty vexed about it.

Bob reached for the ketchup. "Look, you did your best."

"It's rigged," she insisted, the cat still clutched under one arm. "It works some of the time and you got lucky."

"Me and the teenage ninja turtles?"

"Yes," she said firmly, pouring syrup onto her pancakes. "Every so often it's set to win like that so everyone gets excited and plays."

"For, like, eight turns in a row?"

She laughed, and again there was that . . . something . . . between them. Less than an open declaration of attraction, more than a one-sided fancy. A silent acknowledgment they could leave unsaid, at least for now.

As Laura watched Bob eat, she realized she liked him more and more; he didn't ask her challenging questions, he didn't dominate the conversation, and he didn't make her feel nervous. He was simply very present. Plus he was ready to drop everything and play the claw machine at a moment's notice, and who didn't love that?

Bob cleared his throat, and Laura looked up at him. "So," he said, having spent a few minutes formulating this conversational nugget, "are you looking forward to grad school?"

Laura nodded. "Yeah, I am. Did you go?"

He shook his head. "Nah. I wanted to, kind of, but you know . . ."

"Why not?"

He shrugged. "Money? Time? The whole complicated process." He colored slightly. "I'm not a big fan of paperwork."

Laura smiled at him. "It's not that hard once you get started. What would you do at grad school?"

"Flunk, probably," he said, looking away, out of the window. Laura frowned; had she said something wrong? She surreptitiously checked her phone. No messages. For a second she felt sorry for herself; when she'd been with Nick, she always had something to do. He loved to organize their time together, and she'd let him. Now that she was trying to build her own life, she realized she'd need more tools and materials than she'd thought.

She looked up and found Bob smiling at her. His smile was slightly goofy, making his face crease and his eyes crinkle. It canceled out the smooth planes and sharp angles of his resting face, replacing them with a warm and approachable humanity. All at once Laura felt grateful she was making friends in Los Angeles. Throughout her life her friendships had come through other people, through more popular and charming girls at school, through older students of her parents, and then, largely, through Nick. Bob and Polly and Nina . . . these were friends she'd made for herself. She was on a trivia team, for goodness' sake; that had to count for something.

"Everything good?" asked Laura.

"Yup," said Bob easily. "Do you want anything else to eat? More coffee?"

Laura shook her head. "I'm fine, thanks. Can we go home?" She noticed how easily she'd said that, but how strange it sounded.

Bob didn't smile. "Sure, of course." He gathered his stuff and turned around. "I'll go pay the bill."

"Thank you for dinner," said Laura, following him. She twisted her hair around her finger, then realized what she was doing and stopped. She stuck her hands in her pockets instead, and then worried she was looking too casual. Then she desperately tried to stop thinking at all.

"Of course," he replied. "Thank you for coming today and helping."

He faltered into silence and gazed around, having temporarily lost the ability to look at Laura. His attraction to her had grown so much during the day, and he was wondering how to navigate literally going home together. For a split second, when she'd asked to go home, he'd let himself imagine she was his girlfriend, that they were going to go into his room and she was going to let him undress her and take her to bed. He was taken aback by how much that appealed to him, but it wasn't really that surprising. He'd enjoyed her company so much, despite the fact he found her so physically attractive. Pretty girls normally made him feel clumsy and inarticulate, and he'd always blamed himself for that. For the first time he wondered if maybe it hadn't been his fault at all. Laura was beautiful, but when she smiled at him, he felt . . . seen, not evaluated.

A few minutes later they turned out of the Denny's parking lot and joined the stream of evening traffic heading along Sunset Boulevard. Traffic was heavy but moving steadily, and the sidewalks on either side of the street were thronged with people. Laura watched the people move and clump, marveling at the way they flowed and accommodated one another. A horn suddenly blared very loudly behind them, and seconds later a siren came screamingly close. Bob looked in the mirror and pulled to the side. An ambulance shot by, making the truck rock slightly, followed seconds later by a fire truck easily doing seventy.

Laura felt her heart starting to pound. *Breathe.*

As the sirens receded, Bob pulled back out into traffic, hitting the brakes to avoid a speeding car slipstreaming the ambulance. *There's always one.*

Sirens. The pressure of the seat belt. The smell of gasoline, the shocking gut-panic fear of fire.

Bob realized something had changed, and shot a glance at Laura. Pale again, a visible dew of sweat on her forehead. He pulled over and turned the engine off, angling himself to face her.

"Laura, you with me?"

She looked at him without really seeing him, trying to claw herself back to the current moment.

He reached over and took one of her hands, rubbing it between his own. "Laura, everything's fine, you're totally safe."

With a cold shiver settling over her skin, Laura nodded. "Sorry . . ."

"Don't be sorry," he said, letting go of her hand as he felt her tugging away.

"I'm fine now," she said, sitting back. "Sorry, the siren made me jump is all."

He looked at her and a line appeared between his brows. "We can stay here as long as you need."

Her voice was sharp. "I don't need to, we can go. Ignore it, I'm fine."

Now his eyebrows went up, and he tipped his head slightly. "Laura, it's really . . ."

"No, let's go." She turned away and wound down the window, letting the warm evening air into the car, closing her eyes where he couldn't see her, waves of nausea receding as she breathed. *This is not happening.*

Bob hesitated, then decided to take her word for it and turned on the engine. He noticed her hands were gripping the edges of the seat, and wondered if it would be better to go faster and get home sooner, or slower, which might be easier on her nerves.

"Laura . . . ?" he began. "What . . ."

"Please," she said desperately. "I'm a nervous passenger, please ignore me."

"But it would . . ."

"No. Please drive."

I'll drive then, thought Bob, wondering what she was thinking about that made her so anxious. The accident, presumably. He tried to drive sensibly and calmly, which was pretty much all he could do to help her. All she would let him do.

Laura was thinking about the things she thought about to stop herself from thinking. She started mentally listing the bones of the foot, of which there are twenty-six. She started reciting organs of the body in alphabetical order, followed by major nerves, and was halfway through the glands of the endocrine system when they arrived home.

It worked, as it often did. Laura was able to turn to Bob as they pulled up and say, without a shadow of tremor in her voice, "Thanks so much for today, I really had fun." Her face was composed; nothing had happened at all, nothing worth discussing.

"Are you feeling better now?"

She gave him a broad smile. "Of course! Sorry, I guess I'm more easily startled than I thought." Then she opened the door of the truck and walked toward the house.

Bob rubbed the back of his neck and opened his own door. He was pretty sure he'd just been lied to again.

TWENTY-THREE

As they approached the house, loud music spilled out to the street, and Laura hesitated. "Wait . . . what's that?"

Bob literally clapped his hand to his forehead. "I forgot. It's Poker Night."

Laura stopped walking. "Sorry?"

Bob gazed at her, and a slow smile spread across his face. "Your first Poker Night at Maggie's, and I'm here to witness it. There is a God."

Laura snorted and headed into the house. Someone was playing the Pointer Sisters and leaning on the volume. *Top ten song of all time.*

Bob watched her go and frowned. On the one hand, now he didn't have to worry about a clumsy good-night, but on the other hand, his time alone with Laura was over. He stopped on the lawn and looked up at the night sky. Despite the humidity and heat of the day, the darkness was unclouded and the stars bright diamonds on velvet. He needed to breathe and settle himself down. He'd been attracted to Laura, and then worried about her, and then confused by her. He'd had a relationship in college with a woman who'd become emotionally unstable, and it had put him through the wringer. He saw how strong Laura was, but twice now she'd freaked out and then pretended nothing was happening. It wasn't the freaking out that worried him so much. It was the pretending.

Bob shook his head at himself and followed Laura inside.

The Larchmont Booster Club was a small but determined organization. Founded in the sixties by a very bored woman with time on her hands, its goal was the "beautification and improvement of the Larchmont Shopping District." Largely and not all that secretly inspired by Anne of Green Gables and her Avonlea Village Improvement Society, it raised money for things like median flower plantings, repainting the lampposts, repainting the benches, repainting the curb, and generally repainting anything that stood still too long. On the one hand it wasn't important, but on the other hand it really was, because there was no getting away from the fact that Larchmont Boulevard was easy on the eye.

In the six decades since its founding, the LBC had transformed several times. In its first decade alone it had gone from a Phyllis Schlafly–esque twinset-and-pearls affair to a hippie counterculture collective and then into second-wave feminism and turtlenecks. It had languished a little in recent times, but when Liz at the bookstore was voted in as its new president—in absentia, or they never would have dared—she decided to hold meetings at her friend Maggie's house every month, and to hold them in the form of Poker Nights. All proceeds to the boosters, of course, and potluck offerings strongly encouraged and discussed over text for days beforehand. Within six months the booster club had enough operating capital to take the rest of the year off, but Maggie kept the Poker Nights going with her own core team.

As Laura walked into the kitchen, she was greeted by the dogs, who got to their feet and kept looking at her face and then at the kitchen island, their tails a blur of hopeful motion. No wonder: The whole surface was covered with small food. A quick scan showed bacon-wrapped dates, those little goat cheese puff things from Trader Joe's, individual s'mores . . . It was a thing of beauty, and Laura cursed the pancakes she'd eaten. Bob came in behind her and immediately reached past her for a s'more.

She turned to him. "Do you play poker?"

"No," he said with his mouth full. "One, I don't know how, and two, Poker Night is women only."

"Ah," said Laura, and hesitated. "Do you mind if I . . . ?" She blushed, unsure of the right thing to do. They'd been on a date, sort of but not really, and he'd taken her home, but had also brought himself home, and she'd embarrassed herself . . . Laura could feel her internal rainbow wheel spinning, her social software stalling out.

"Go ahead," said Bob. "I've got an early start tomorrow."

"OK, well, thanks again for dinner," she said, bending to pet Herbert, who thought maybe this was a precursor to dropped food and leaned into her legs.

"You're welcome, thanks again for helping," Bob said quietly.

"Of course," said Laura, shooting for jaunty yet nonchalant, but missing and hitting slightly manic instead. So she turned and headed out to the patio.

Bob sighed and looked down at the dogs. Then he took a piece of bacon from around a date and broke it in half.

Holding the pieces above Herbert and Daisy, he said, "She's

very pretty, and she makes me nervous. Don't tell anyone." He dropped the bacon fragments.

They never reached the ground, and his secret was safe.

The round table had been given a green cloth, and five women were sitting around its edge. Laura saw Liz from the bookstore, and Maggie she knew, of course. The other three women were Nina, Polly, and Anna.

As Laura stepped out onto the patio, the game paused and all the women swiveled in their seats.

"Hey, Laura," said Maggie, looking back down at her hand. "Don't mind us, we're wasting our youth gambling and drinking."

"Go right ahead," Laura said, stepping closer. "What are you playing, ladies?"

"Hold'em, of course," said Liz. "Do you happen to play?"

"A little," said Laura.

The heads swiveled again, but this time it was for Bob.

"Good evening, lovely ladies of Larchmont," he said, surprised by how suavely the phrase came out.

Anna and Polly giggled, and Liz made a low hooting noise.

"Ignore her, Bob," said Maggie. "Menopause does terrible things to a woman's libido."

Bob laughed. "Does anybody need anything from the kitchen?"

"I'll take another beer," said Nina, who hadn't raised her eyes from her cards.

Laura pulled a chair closer and sat down to observe. She'd learned poker (and bridge and canasta and gin rummy and crazy eights) from her grandmother, who'd learned cards from her late husband, a mathematician and card counter banned from Atlantic City. Laura still loved the feel of playing cards in her hand, the easy privacy of strategy and observation. She felt a wave of gratitude. Her parents might have taught her to rattle off kingdom and phylum, but her grandmother had given her practical, quotidian abilities. Card games. Knitting. Cooking. Sports. Nine times out of ten those were the skills she turned to when things got hard. The secret to happiness isn't always in your head. Sometimes it's entirely in your hands.

The ladies were finishing a game, which Maggie won, and Laura asked if they could deal her in.

She said, "What are we playing for?" and hoped the stakes weren't prohibitive.

"Bragging rights," said Polly. "And candy. Each mini York Peppermint Pattie is worth ten bucks, and the Starbursts are a dollar each."

Laura scanned the table. There were piles of candy at every place, with a suspicious pile of wrappers under most chairs. The players were literally eating into their profits.

Based on the relative height of the pattie stacks, Liz was winning and Nina was close behind. Polly clearly wasn't all that committed, as she was absentmindedly eating her stack, but Anna and Maggie were still in with a chance.

Maggie turned to Liz. "Blinds are five ten, you're small."

Liz threw in five Starbursts, then unwrapped one and ate it. Maggie dealt the cards.

"You seem to be doing well," Laura said, taking her hand as it was dealt. She peeked: ace, king, spades. Good start.

"No trash-talking," said Liz.

"That wasn't trash-talking," said Laura. "That was an observation." She picked up a peppermint pattie to see if she could flip it around her fingers as easily as she did a regular chip.

Liz narrowed her eyes at Laura. "I am growing suspicious of

your girl-next-door persona, miss. You handle that pattie like a pro."

Laura shrugged. "Play and see."

Liz looked at her cards and opened with two patties.

"I'm out," said Polly, and tossed her cards. She unwrapped a pattie and ate it cheerfully.

The other two also folded, leaving Nina, Liz, and Laura in the hand.

Laura looked at her cards again, looked at Liz, and then said, "Raise you a pattie."

Nina said, "I'm out, this is too rich for me." She put her cards down and then said, "Did you know . . ."

Liz said, "Stop," quite loudly, and stared at her cards. "No poker trivia, we made a rule."

"Oh yeah," said Nina, subsiding.

Liz called the pattie, and threw in five Starbursts.

Laura made a mocking noise. "I smell a bluff." She tossed in five Starbursts to call.

Maggie rolled her eyes and dealt the flop. The three cards lay in the center of the table: seven, eight of spades, nine of hearts.

"Check," said Liz, rapping her knuckle on the table.

"Me too," said Laura. "Check."

Maggie sighed and dealt another card. Ace of clubs.

Liz, who was displaying the worst poker face in the history of the game, grinned and threw in two more Starbursts and another York pattie.

Laura, whose face was as calm as a pond, called.

The final card was dealt: jack of spades.

Liz literally made a crowing noise and pushed her candy across the table. "All in, baby."

Calmly, Laura called again.

"Read 'em and weep, Knickerbocker, jack high straight." Liz started clawing back her candy, but Laura raised her hand.

"Not so speedy there, Hollywood." She laid her cards down. "That would be ace high flush, winning hand."

"I knew it," said Liz, throwing her cards on the table hard enough for them to bounce. "She's a total shark, I can't believe I fell for the angelic face and sweet disposition. I'm ashamed of myself." She addressed someone behind Laura. "Bob, be a dear and go put the kettle on. If I don't switch to peppermint tea right now, I'm going to be crabby in the morning."

"Sure," Bob replied, and Laura turned, surprised to hear his voice. He was sitting on the floor in the open kitchen doorway, leaning back on his hands and watching the game. Daisy was next to him, and Herbert was lying by his feet. Laura hadn't even realized he was there, and she watched him get to his feet and go into the kitchen. Every single woman around the table noticed her body language change. Except her, of course.

"I'm getting tired, too," said Nina, tossing her cards toward Liz, who was gathering the pack. "I have to open the store tomorrow." She looked around. "Where's the bowl?"

Maggie reached under her chair and pulled out a big blue-and-white-china bowl that Laura had previously seen holding fruit. It was full of candy, and Nina swept her winnings off the edge of the table and into the bowl.

"Wait, you don't even keep the candy?" Laura asked, surprised.

The women all shook their heads.

"It's for fun," said Liz as she passed Laura, and patted her on the arm. "This is California, baby, there's always more candy."

Maggie raised her eyebrows. "That's the worst state motto I've ever heard."

Liz snorted. "Better than *California: We hunted the grizzly to extinction*, or *California, home of a hundred thousand earthquakes a year*."

Maggie gazed at her friend. "You're really wasted in retail. You should be working for the governor."

Bob had meant to go to bed, he really had. After sharing another bacon-wrapped date with Daisy and Herbert, he'd even turned in that direction. But then he'd heard Laura's voice and turned back again.

He'd picked a spot in the doorway where he could see her but could also slide backward into invisibility if he wanted to. He watched her remove her shoes under the chair and toe-pull her socks off. Her toenails were painted the pale pink of a lemonade berry flower, one of his favorite native plants. He looked at Laura's profile, her forehead slightly wrinkled as she focused on her cards. She pulled at her lip when she was about to make a bet, and although her face and torso were absolutely still, her feet were kicking and flexing like mad under the table. He watched her hands as she held and played her cards. Long fingers, deft and accurate. He found them beautiful. She wasn't the prettiest girl he'd ever seen, he told himself, trying to be objective, trying to rein in his runaway horse a little, but there was something about her face that made him want to stop looking at anyone else.

He went to turn on the kettle for Liz, pulling down a mug and hunting in the cupboard for a peppermint tea bag. When he returned to the patio, the ladies were breaking up for the evening.

He frowned slightly. "No tea, Liz?"

She shook her head. "No, I'm fine," she said. "You stay here and make sure Maggie doesn't clean up." She and the other ladies chatted and laughed their way through the kitchen, followed by Maggie and trailed by the dogs. Bob turned to help Laura, who was already clearing the table.

She grinned at him. "I don't know if I'll be invited back," she said, handing him a stack of plates. "I may have blown my cover too soon."

Bob carried the dishes inside, and Laura went back and forth quickly, clearing the patio before the hostess had even finished saying goodbye to her guests. Maggie, Anna, and Polly came into the kitchen and started protesting, but Bob waved them away.

"Let the downstairs people take care of downstairs," he said. "Go to bed, we're nearly done anyway."

Anna and Polly needed no encouraging and headed upstairs right away, but Maggie looked around, and sighed. "Fair enough, I see there's no point in arguing with you." She peeped out at the garden, where Daisy was Roomba-ing around under the table for dropped candy, sighed again, and then snapped her fingers. "Oh, Laura, I forgot. I put some names for you on a piece of paper and slid it under your door."

Laura frowned. "Names?"

"Of therapists," said Maggie blithely. "You can call any of them, they're all good."

Laura flushed red, and turned away. "Uh . . . thanks," she said, and headed out the back door to the garden. "I'll go check for more dishes."

Maggie frowned slightly, then turned to take the back stairs up to her floor. "Thank you, Bob, sleep well."

"You too." Bob started the dishwasher and joined Laura on the patio. She was standing looking up at the moon, which was full and bright enough for her eyelashes to cast shadows on her cheeks. The moonlight filtered the red from her skin, and she looked completely composed.

"It's so clear tonight," she said. "I thought LA was always covered in a haze of pollution, but I see many more stars than I ever saw back home."

He looked up at the moon, then nodded. "Yup." *Come on, Bob, say something pretty about the moon, something romantic.* "Los Angeles is a desert and the day-to-night temperature variation can be pretty big, although there are several areas in the city where there is so much asphalt that the heat is retained far longer than is natural." *Or, alternatively, say something both unromantic and boring, totally your call.* "The nights are often completely cloudless."

"Huh," she said, wishing she'd brought a cardigan, or that she was near one of those asphalt patches. She liked the way Bob spoke to her. It reminded her of her family, informative like they were, but without the implicit criticism that she didn't know this information already. She was about to turn and say something, when she suddenly remembered she had a list of therapists lying on her bedroom floor and felt ashamed.

"Do you want anything to drink?" Bob asked. "I think there's beer left." He noticed her shiver. "Or I could make some more tea?"

She turned. "No, thanks, I should really go to bed." She kept her eyes down. "I had a really good time today, you were right about Edward and Lili, they're lovely. And Clare might be my new favorite person." She hesitated, wanting to apologize again for panicking, but decided to pretend it never happened.

Bob nodded and stepped back to give her room, resisting the impulse to reach out and touch her as she walked by, close enough for her hair to brush his upper arm. By the time the thought had even formed in his head, she was through the kitchen and in the hallway.

"Good night, Bob," she said, her voice drifting back.

"Good night, Laura," he replied, not even sure she'd heard him.

TWENTY-FOUR

The next morning Laura woke to the sound of birds and for a minute forgot where she was. Her childhood bedroom had been in the middle of her family's apartment, with a small window that opened onto the building's central air shaft. She'd woken every morning to the feathery elbowings of pigeons roosting on the air conditioners that lined the interior of the building. If it was summer, those air conditioners would be humming, and if it was winter, the pigeon conversations would be drowned out by the clanking and hissing of radiators. In the distance the cadences of sirens would rise and fall against the frequent singing, yelling, or uncontrollable laughter of neighbors.

The light had always been dim in her room, the lamps on throughout the day. Here the sun poured through the windows with almost indecent enthusiasm, pushing the curtains open. The birds were beside themselves with excitement about something, and she felt herself wanting to leap up to go see what it was. She could hear someone whistling in the garden, and wondered if it was Bob. She stretched luxuriously all the way down to her toes and debated whether to get up and go to the pool or turn over and go back to sleep. Then her phone rang. Laura looked at it. *Huh, nearly ten.* She didn't recognize the number, but it was an LA area code, so she answered.

"Good morning!" The voice sounded much more awake than she did, and it clearly had goals. "It's Nina, did you have breakfast yet?"

Laura propped herself up on her pillow and warily hit the speaker button.

"No, I'm still in bed."

She could hear Nina suck in her breath. "Alone? Or with Bob?"

"Nina, one, you're on speaker, and two," said Laura firmly, "Bob is not a thing. Don't get pulled into Polly's reality-distortion field."

Nina rolled on. "Whatever. I woke up surprisingly early this morning and thought I could possibly tempt you to do trivia practice in return for another wrist massage. Or do you already have exciting plans for the day?"

Laura frowned. "No, I have no plans, exciting or otherwise. I was thinking maybe I would swim . . . but that was as far as I got." She paused. "Bring a swimsuit and you can do some rehab in the pool."

"Nope," said Nina cheerfully. "Think of me as a cat carrying original engraved plates from *Birds of America* by John James Audubon. Water and I are natural enemies, sworn to keep each other at bay."

Laura looked at the ceiling. "Do you always wake up talking like this?"

"No," said Nina honestly. "I am not a morning person, but the possibility of winning the trivia tournament is strangely motivating." She paused. "I've been up since six. I've had three cups of coffee. I'll bring bagels."

Good lord. Laura said, "I do enjoy a bagel, but I am definitely going to swim."

Nina laughed. "Great, I will shout questions from a safe, splashless distance. I'll see you in a little bit. Go wake up Polly, she loves an everything bagel." She hung up, clearly on the move and getting shit done.

"Will do," muttered Laura as she levered herself out of bed and reached for her dressing gown. She found herself smiling— she'd forgotten how much she enjoyed the friendship of other women. Nick had taken up most of her time, and she was saddened to think how few girlfriends she actually had back in the city. Her mother had been right when she'd said no one else would want her contact info.

Laura was stiff and achy from gardening the day before, but it wasn't too bad. She'd loosen up by the time she was dressed, and in fact started feeling better as she clumped upstairs to knock on Polly's door.

"Urmph?" said a voice from beyond the door. At least, Laura assumed it was a voice; it could have been some polite but ungainly monster who was in the middle of eating Polly and wasn't going to talk with its mouth full.

"Polly?" said Laura gently.

"Wahrphs?" said the voice, now sounding like it was coming from under a pile of leaves.

"Nina's coming over," said Laura.

"Humph," said the voice. There was a definite subtext of *So?*

Laura raised her voice slightly. "And she's bringing you an everything bagel."

Two seconds later the door flew open and Polly stood there in immaculate silk pajamas—which were NOT what Laura would have guessed Polly wore to bed. They were daffodil yellow and had her name embroidered on the pocket.

"Well, in that case," said Polly, in a completely awake and totally compos mentis tone of voice, "I'll be right there."

There was a rose in a bud vase in the bathroom. Laura paused. Had it been there the night before? She wasn't sure. She bent to sniff it, not even needing to get too close to be overwhelmed by the buttery lemon scent. It wasn't one of the ones from Nick, so Bob must have put it there. She smiled, touched.

Once she was clean and dressed, Laura felt more ready to face the day. Or at least to face trivia. When she walked into the kitchen, Nina had arrived and she, Polly, and Maggie were milling around, preparing bagels and filling the room with the pleasing scent of toasted sesame seeds and onions.

"Aha!" said Nina, holding yet another cup of coffee. "There she is, our sports and science expert. Trained since birth in batting averages and world records, she will lift our team to greatness!"

Laura gazed at her. "Nina, I have to tell you something. I don't do well until I've had a cup of tea. You are welcome to talk to me, at me, over me, whatever it is you have in mind for this, but until I've achieved optimal blood caffeine levels, there is no point in expecting an answer."

Normally, Laura wouldn't have said something like that, but Los Angeles was doing something to her. Her mother would say it was giving her an attitude, which wasn't a good thing, but Laura thought maybe all the sleep and good food had something to do with it.

Nina immediately understood. "Sorry," she said. "I do sympathize, I'm totally aware that I'm a bit over the top this morning." She looked at Polly, who was leaning against the sink eating a bagel and occasionally shaking it over her shoulder to loosen the crumbs. "You know how I get."

Polly chewed her bagel, then said, "We usually cut her off after two cups at the store, but this being a Sunday, she had no structure in place." She shrugged. "I'm going to keep my head down and pray for your kidneys."

"Caffeine is processed by the liver," replied Nina.

"I'll expand my prayer coverage."

Laura looked at the bagels. They did look delicious, but she went to the fridge instead. She pulled out unsweetened Greek yogurt and berries, then added granola and finished it with a drizzle of raw honey.

Everyone else had fallen silent as she did this, and eventually she lifted her eyes from her breakfast and said, "What?"

Polly swallowed. "We're all eating bagels and you're making us feel bad by choosing something healthier."

Laura shrugged. "Look, I grew up in a kitchen with a metal sign that said 'If it isn't bacon, it isn't breakfast!'" She took a mouthful of yogurt and honey and spoke around it. "California is supporting my healthier habits, and I'm fine with that." She shrugged. "Sorry not sorry."

Maggie, who had balanced smoked salmon, capers, onions, and tomatoes on a bagel half and then successfully eaten the whole thing without losing a single element, nodded. "Los Angeles changes people, what can you do?"

Nina stared at them and then blurted out, "Did you know that capers are actually little flower buds and are stuffed with antioxidants?"

"Is this on the test?" asked Polly.

. . .

An hour later Nina was looking at Laura with such anticipation it hurt. They were still in the kitchen, still sitting around the table, but with only half an onion bagel left. Herbert had his eye on it and Daisy would have, too, if she'd been able to see the top of the counter.

"Can we stop yet?" asked Laura. "I really want to swim." She'd run out and purchased a regular swimsuit on Friday and was keen to try it out.

"Not yet," said Nina. "You're doing so well."

"I didn't get any of the movie ones," said Laura, sighing. "How is that doing well?"

Nina took a breath. "Firstly, we don't need help with movie trivia, I was simply checking the range of your knowledge." She paused, and was clearly torn between good manners and curiosity. "Can I ask . . . did you grow up without cable?"

Laura reached for a banana and peeled it. "We had cable, but we only watched documentaries and approved movies."

"Shocking," breathed Polly, who was still recovering from the discovery that Laura had never seen *Saved by the Bell*.

Nina flipped through her stack of cards. "Fine, I'll focus on your strengths: What are the three smallest bones in the body?"

"The ossicles," said Laura. "They're three tiny bones in the middle ear." She turned to Polly. "The smallest one, the stapes, is only three millimeters long." Polly was smiling encouragingly, so she added, "That's about the same size as a sesame seed."

"Amazing," said Polly, who really couldn't have cared less, but enjoyed being supportive. "Did you ever watch *The Big Comfy Couch*?"

202 · ABBI WAXMAN

"No," said Laura. "Was that a TV show?"

"Yes, and pure nightmare fuel. Speaking of which, *Scary Stories to Tell in the Dark*?"

"Yes. Books were totally encouraged."

"Focus, people," said Nina. "What is a pyrogen?"

"Something that gives you a fever," said Laura.

"In what year was the first female referee featured in an NFL game?"

"Twenty twelve. That was a sports question, I thought we were doing human anatomy?"

"Laura," said Nina, "the whole point of trivia is that they can ask anything."

"What is a male swan called?" said Polly. "For example."

"Or what was Alexander Graham Bell actually working on when he discovered the telephone?" added Maggie, who was an occasional stand-in member of the team. She was reading the Sunday *New York Times* and working on her second cup of coffee. Daisy was curled up by her feet, having been given the end of Maggie's bagel.

"Or which US state name ends with three vowels?" finished Nina. "You have to be light on your feet, ready for anything."

"Well, I'm not, as we already proved," said Laura. "I have no idea what a male swan is called. Mr. Swan?"

"A cob," said Polly. "Female ones are called hens."

"Good to know," said Laura. She turned to Maggie, who said "the hearing aid," and then to Nina, who said "Hawaii."

"Can I swim now?" said Laura calmly.

"Where was the world's first parking meter installed?" asked Nina, with a slightly cheeky expression on her face.

Laura got to her feet. "One, I don't care, and two, if you want to keep questioning me, you'll have to follow me to the pool."

Nina looked at her laptop. "Fine, I have plenty of charge, let's do it."

The pool was very different under the midday sun than it was in the evening, but the water was as cool and invigorating as ever. Laura dove straight into the deep end, and while the others arranged their towels and computers and newspapers and dogs to their liking on the loungers, Laura swam lengths and woke herself up completely.

Eventually she climbed out and went to sit by Nina, who was as much in the shade as she could be.

Nina frowned at her as she approached. "You're a little bit too energetic, I'm not going to lie. You're not going to try and talk me into getting fit, are you?"

"No," replied Laura, "although you might like it." She reached out. "Can I see your wrist, please?"

Nina let her examine her forearm. "It feels fine, I doubt we need to do anything."

Laura ignored her and started gently stretching and massaging Nina's hand.

"That definitely feels sore," said Nina, then added, "How's it going with Bob?"

"They went gardening yesterday," said Polly. She raised her eyebrows. "Which is my personal nomination for worst date idea ever, but to each his own."

"It was fun, I met people, I did things." Laura shrugged. "But it was in no way a date."

"Did you eat food together?" asked Polly.

Laura nodded.

"Date," said Polly.

"I hate dating," said Nina firmly. "If Tom and I break up, that might be it for me. I don't think I can go through the first part of a relationship again." She shuddered.

"I like dating," said Polly, "because I'm only really interested in, like, a quarter of a person."

Nina looked at her. "Do you mean a quarter of people? Like, one in four people?" Laura was stretching her fingers apart, having interlaced her own fingers with them, and it felt amazingly good. *Just think how fast I'll be able to turn pages after all this loosening up!*

"No," Polly patiently explained, "I mean like a quarter of a person. When you're dating, you only share a small part of yourself, right? You don't use all your material, you bring out your best stuff, the top twenty-five percent. You dress well, you think about what you're saying, you're a considerate lover . . . Once we start digging into more established, everyday personality traits, I start wanting to bounce." She sighed. "I remember one time I was about six weeks into a dating thing, and we decided to go away for the weekend. Up until then the guy had been hilarious, charming, and devoted to oral sex. So, I'm lying next to him in bed and he starts booking the trip. Twenty minutes later I'm hopping up and down pulling on my jeans because he turned out to be a cheap, fussy traveler who needs to use air miles whenever possible and reads every single review, starting with the ones that give one star." She lay down on the lounger and closed her eyes. "Most guys I've dated are only about twenty-one percent interesting, which is usually good for about three months."

There was a small silence, and then Nina said to Laura, "The thing to remember about Polly is that she's a scientist at heart. The rest of us are merely subjects for study."

TWENTY-FIVE

A little while later, after Nina headed off to meet her boyfriend and Polly left to do whatever it was she did on a Sunday afternoon, Laura found herself standing outside her bedroom door. She was still in her swimsuit and needed to get changed, but she was conflicted. Without a doubt the noises coming from Bob's room meant he was watching the baseball game, a game she was about to go into her own room to watch. On the one hand she'd spent most of yesterday with him, and he was probably sick of the sight of her, and on the other it's much more fun to watch a game with someone else. As she dithered, Daisy trundled past her and paused briefly, looking up at Laura and apparently reaching some internal conclusion, because she then beetled on and scratched loudly at Bob's door. Bob opened it, and saw Laura.

Holding the door for Daisy, he said, "Hi there, is the game too loud?"

Laura shook her head. "No . . . what's the score?"

Bob's face lit up. "It's three-two Phillies, top of the third, you want to come and watch with me?" He blushed slightly. "I'm actually rooting for the Yankees in this game, but only because the

Dodgers need them to beat the Phillies . . ." He faltered, looking at her face. "Not a Yankees fan?"

Laura looked horrified. "Of course I'm a Yankees fan. I was making a face because I realized you're probably a Dodgers fan and it's going to make for tension around the breakfast table." She assumed a tragic expression. "Not everyone deals with failure very well."

Bob narrowed his eyes. "You'd think Yankees fans would be used to it."

The rivalry between the New York Yankees and the Los Angeles Dodgers was one of the oldest and fiercest in the country, and Laura was delighted at the prospect of keeping it alive on a super-local level, i.e., across a hallway. She smiled. "I'd love to watch, let me get changed and I'll be right there."

Bob looked genuinely pleased. "I'll get some chips and dip." Wow, Bob, he told himself, you really know how to show a girl a good time. Chips AND dip? Yet strangely, Laura looked equally as happy as he did at the prospect, and as she went into her room to get changed, he hurried off to the kitchen to gather snacks. If anyone had been listening, they would have heard him humming.

Laura tugged off her swimsuit and wondered if it was weird to be so excited about watching a baseball game while eating chips and dip. Throughout her teenage years she'd watched her friends go nuts about proms, dances, house parties, and other social events. She'd join them to get ready and be mildly amused by all the clothes and makeup and tissues in bras. Laura wasn't antisocial; she went to everything and had a reasonably good time. But she didn't like drinking or smoking pot, and she really, really hated drama of all kinds. While her friends seemed energized by scandals and intrigues and romances, she got a stomachache and the urge to run for miles. Her happiest times were spent at Yankee Stadium with her grandmother, or curled up in front of the TV, yelling at the game. Her parents ignored her sportiness as long as she was the best at whatever she was doing and kept her grades up, much as other parents ignored occasional drunkenness or a deep and abiding commitment to Korean boy bands. She'll grow out of it, they assured themselves, she'll narrow in on an area of academic study and all this running around and sweating will fade away. It hadn't.

When she came out of her room, she nearly ran into Bob, who was on his way back from the kitchen carrying a tray and hurrying to return to the game. She opened his bedroom door for him, and the two of them sat on the sofa and gazed at the score.

"I was out of the room for four minutes," said Bob. "How did I miss two home runs?"

"They'll replay it," said Laura confidently. She reached for a chip and dipped it, looking at the score. "I'm amazed the score is this close, the Phillies have been having a terrible season." She laughed, and popped the chip into her mouth. "The second game against the Rays was mortifying, but that's what happens when you play small ball against a big team, right?"

Bob gazed at her silently, trying to dampen the glow of joy he felt, the relief of knowing he'd reached solid ground and found something they could really talk about. Sometimes, on dates, he'd hear himself rattling on about this game or that team and notice the light fading from the eyes of the woman across the table. He'd panic and try to change the subject, but before long they'd both falter into silence and he'd panic all over again and find himself talking about plants, which was even worse. There had been many late nights when he'd come home alone and rehashed all the things he could have said, the interesting topics he could have reached for, if only he'd been able to stop his skittish brain from reaching for familiar subjects. But Laura liked plants, and she liked sports, and something about her smile told him maybe she liked him, too.

The game continued, and Laura and Bob argued about plays, second-guessed the referees, and generally enjoyed every minute of the remaining innings. Every time one of them jumped up to curse at the screen or yell at a play, they'd sit down a little closer to the other, and before long both of them were very aware they were essentially pressed up together on one end of the couch. During pauses in play, Laura surreptitiously checked out Bob's room and was surprised; it was tidy and organized, with a large drafting table against one wall. She wanted to ask about it, but waited until the game was over. Then they both sat back and grinned at each other.

"Why do you have a drafting table?" asked Laura, getting up and wandering over to it. Her thigh still felt warm where it had pressed against his, but she focused instead on the thin pieces of paper attached to the table. Looking closely, she realized they were plans of some kind.

Bob stood and came over. "I use it for planning gardens," he said. "I found it on the street ages ago and dragged it home." He gestured. "That's actually this garden. I was thinking of adding a water feature." He looked at her. "I'm really lucky, Maggie doesn't mind if I try new things here, so I get to test out ideas."

Laura leaned over the plans, noting the mix of symmetry and wilderness, the little symbols becoming clear: circles of all kinds for trees, tiny bushes and pathways, indications of light and shade. "You don't do this on your computer?"

"Yes," said Bob, "I do that sometimes, but I like to start by drawing. It gives me time to think about it, if you know what I mean."

Laura nodded, then noticed something else sticking out from under the plan. It was a printout from a website, and as she pulled it out, she read the header, *Cornell Graduate Program in Public Garden Leadership*, and turned to look at Bob. "Oh, is this the grad school thing you were talking about yesterday?"

He nodded, and reached for the paper. "Yeah . . ." He tailed off.

Laura frowned at him. "When do you need to apply?"

Bob turned away. "I don't think I'm going to. It's a lot of work."

"The program?"

He shook his head. "No, the application. The program is amazing."

"What is it about?" asked Laura. "I mean, what is public garden leadership?"

Bob dropped the papers onto the table, next to his computer. "It's what it sounds like. It's for people who want to run parks or botanical gardens, things like that."

Laura picked up the papers again and sat back down on the sofa. Bob seemed vaguely uncomfortable talking about this and she wanted to know why. "And that's what you want to do?"

Bob was silent, then took his spot at the far end of the sofa. "It's not very interesting."

Laura shook her head. "I think it is, tell me about it." When he paused, she added, "Bob, anything's interesting when it's explained by someone who cares about it. I know absolutely nothing about public garden leadership, but I honestly want to hear, so spill it." He still looked uncertain, so she leaned back and folded her feet up under her. "There isn't another game on, and I have no plans, so there's no point trying to avoid it."

Bob sighed. "Don't say I didn't warn you." He looked down at his hands. "I have this dumb idea to open public vegetable gardens all over the city. Like, a small public park you can dig and weed and plant in, if you want to." His voice got more confident. "I got the idea from the vegetable course, with Edward. People want to interact with nature, but it seems overwhelming, especially if you live in a city, and there aren't a lot of opportunities to show how simple it can be." He looked up at Laura, and his eyes were bright with enthusiasm. "It used to be that most towns had some kind of public allotments, open spaces people could rent and grow vegetables on . . . and there were victory gardens during the war . . . and people could take classes and do projects . . . kids, of course, but also adults . . . regular gardens and maybe greenhouses . . . or you could come in and sit and enjoy the plants and get fresh produce or flowers. Anything extra would be donated to a food bank. There are community gardens in some places already, but it would be different, you wouldn't be responsible for any of it, it would be open for everyone." Laura nodded, understanding what he meant and smiling at how excited he was getting. "You wouldn't need to make some big commitment, you could wander in and pull weeds for an hour if you felt like it." He faltered, and said, "Like I said, it's kind of a dumb idea."

"Why?" said Laura forcefully. "I think it's a great idea! In New York the public parks are filled with people all the time, Central Park, Riverside Park . . . they're one of the best things about the city."

"Yeah," said Bob, "and LA has several fantastic public parks for hiking and exploring, and obviously the botanical gardens and other wonderful arboretums, but these would be much smaller, and dotted all over the place." He smiled crookedly at her. "You don't think it's stupid?"

"Not at all. I think it's fantastic." She read over the information. "So, why don't you go do this program?" She looked at him. "It's only a year, and you have all the requirements." She read further. "Presumably Edward would write you a letter of recommendation." She frowned. "What's stopping you?"

Bob shrugged. "I . . . I'd have to write a proposal, and pull together a résumé."

Laura nodded. "Sure, but that's no big deal."

"I'd have to apply for financial aid."

"So?" said Laura.

"And I would lose all my customers."

Laura shrugged. "Which would matter if you wanted to keep doing what you're doing, but it sounds like you want to do something different."

"And I'd have to move to Ithaca for a year." He shivered thinking about it.

Laura laughed. "I get that. It's unbelievably cold in the winter there, but it would make a change from all this lovely sunshine."

Bob smiled. "I guess I can stand anything for a year."

"Of course," she replied. "Hey, you want help with the application? I had a part-time student job in the admissions office at school, forms and applications hold no fear for me." She leaned forward and waved the papers at Bob. "Honestly, Bob, it's easy. You're super qualified, and I'll help you with the financial aid forms, I just went through the whole process myself."

"Maybe," he said, feeling shy again. Why did Laura have to be so considerate, on top of being so attractive? There was something about the planes of her face, the way the light hit her jaw, her eyelashes, her voice . . . He could even overlook the fact that she was a Yankees fan, because they were her home team, after all. You couldn't help where you were born.

As he was about to speak again, there was a sudden jolt in the room, and pencils started rolling off the drafting table. In the distance they heard china falling and breaking, and as the shaking in the room increased, Daisy started barking, echoed by Jasper somewhere else in the house. Outside, in chorus, a variety of car alarms went off, going in and out of time with each other.

Laura realized what was happening and reached out for Bob, who was reaching out for her. They gripped each other silently as the earthquake rocked the room, causing books to tumble from the bedside table and the lamp in the ceiling to swing. With a final, hard judder it stopped, and Bob let go of Laura's arm.

"Are you OK?" He looked at her eyes, which were still very wide. "That was a pretty good one, but not too close . . . maybe 4.0?" He stood up. "I'm going to check on the others."

"That was my first earthquake . . ." she said, laughing shakily. "It wasn't like I expected . . . the room actually moved." She stood, but wobbled a little. He took her arm again, and smiled at her.

"Don't worry, you'll get used to them." They could hear voices in the hall: Maggie, Asher, and Libby. Bob went to open the door, and found Maggie right outside.

"Bob," she said, breathlessly. "We've got a problem in the garden. You'd better come and see."

TWENTY-SIX

When they all walked out into the garden and saw that a section of wall had collapsed on the vegetable garden, taking the rose-covered arch with it, Laura heard Bob swear under his breath. Not angrily. Sadly.

"It's kind of incredible," said Libby, who had been consulting his phone, "that the wall fell at all, because that was not a big earthquake."

"It felt big to me," said Laura, who was still a little bit thrown. Weirdly, she wasn't anywhere near as discombobulated as she had been in the truck. Mind you, earthquakes had a certain novelty value, whereas the danger of cars felt painfully familiar.

Libby looked up. "It was a 4.2, which is minor."

Bob opened the gate of the vegetable garden and headed toward his tomato bed, which resembled the aftermath of a pretty serious food fight. "I think the tomatoes might be done for." He stared at the wall, the trellis, and the massacred roses.

"Poor Cécile," Bob said softly. He stepped forward and tried to move the trellis, sighing and picking bricks from between the branches.

"You named the roses?" asked Laura, coming over to help.

"That's their variety," he replied, "Cécile Brünner. She's been around for a long time, and she's pretty indestructible." He bent down to look at the roots, then looked up at Laura and grinned. "If we can get the trellis back up, I think the old lady might make it."

Laura stepped next to him and reached for the trellis.

"Careful," he said. "She's not completely thornless."

"Who is?" muttered Laura, carefully placing her hands to avoid the worst of the spiky branches, and closing one eye against a trail of roses that threatened to blind her. "This thing is heavier than I thought."

Bob nodded. "I'm glad you're here to help with it, I'm not sure I could manage on my own." He looked at her, noticing her hair was filling with petals, the loosened pink curves settling in her curls.

They got the trellis upright, and Laura held it while Bob ran to get wire. The fence around the garden was still totally solid, and in a few minute the trellis was firmly attached again. Bob pulled clippers from his pocket and lopped the damaged branches, ending up with an enormous armful of pink blooms.

"I think you deserve these," he said, "for surviving your first earthquake and saving my favorite roses."

Laura smiled easily. "Thanks. Not sure I have a big enough vase, but I like the thought."

They smiled at each other until they heard a cough, and remembered they weren't alone.

They turned to see Maggie, Asher, and Libby staring at them.

Maggie was smiling. "Bob, once you guys have finished posing for the top of a wedding cake, will you check the wall to make sure it's not going to collapse any further? We'll call someone to-morrow."

Laura and Bob turned to each other and realized they were still standing under the arch, dotted with a confetti of petals and leaves, Laura's arms filled with the blooms Bob had handed her. They both blushed and nodded, and Maggie headed into the house, followed by Libby mumbling something about checking on Anna. There was a pause, then Asher changed the subject.

"Where's Polly?" he said to Laura. "She was here earlier, right?"

"She said she was going to meet some friends," replied Laura. "Not sure where, though."

"Do you guys need any help out here?" asked Asher.

Bob looked around the garden. "Nah, I think we can manage." He looked at Laura, who had already put down the roses and started picking bricks out of the tomatoes. Asher nodded and went back inside the house, and Bob stood for a minute or two surveying the damage.

Laura straightened and looked at him. "So, bricks out, what then?"

"Triage the plants and go from there."

Laura nodded, and turned back to the bricks. This she could do. Bob watched her for a little while, then went to get some stakes and ties. As he sorted through the shed, he was surprised to find himself whistling.

When Asher went back to the kitchen, he found Maggie angrily sweeping the floor. He was perplexed by his mom's reaction; she'd been through many earthquakes, some quite serious. He remembered half a dozen quakes and power outages in his child-hood, including one that had turned into an overnight pillow fort and flashlight fest, a definite five-star memory. He'd always found earthquakes slightly exhilarating, a reminder of how easily Mother Nature could shrug him off the planet like a dog shaking off the rain, complete with ear-flapping sound effects (at least in his childhood head).

"Mom, can I help?" he asked, looking around. The damage wasn't too bad: A couple of mugs had fallen from the sink coun-ter, a single picture lay shattered on the floor. He bent to pick it up, carefully pulling the larger shards free of the frame. It was a shot of him and his sister taken when they were very young, her face serious, her yellow turtleneck making her resemble the world's smallest executive on a casual Friday. His own face was a complete contrast, his eyes dancing, his face alive with laughter, his tiny chest thrust out to show off his new T-shirt, purple with a yellow star. He knew it was one of his mother's favorite photos; maybe that explained her body language.

"We can get this reframed," Asher said to her, holding it up. "The picture itself is totally fine."

His mom leaned on her broom and looked over. "Oh?" she said. "Great." She hadn't noticed the picture, clearly.

"Are you OK?" he asked her. "You seem . . ."

"Not OK?" she replied, exhaling with a puff. "I'm fine, a little shaken maybe. Fixing the wall is going to be a pain in the ass, but whatever."

The front door banged and Polly flew into the room breath-lessly. "Everyone OK?" she panted. "I came as fast as I could." Her hair was in braids but she'd lost one of the elastics, and the braid was half-undone.

Asher and Maggie stared at her, and nodded.

"No need to panic," said Maggie mildly. "We're all good." She pulled open a nearby kitchen drawer and hunted for a rubber band. She handed it to Polly, who secured the braid and smiled her thanks.

"The garden wall fell down," said Asher, "so I'm not sure if Bob would say we're good. His tomatoes got completely squashed." He noticed how flushed she was—was it possible she had literally run all the way home? Where had she been? Maybe she'd been with some guy who'd made her look so pink, and it had nothing to do with coming home. He looked away. She was too pretty to look at; it was overwhelming.

Polly's eyes widened. "Really? We should totally make spaghetti sauce!" She laughed. "What a pity he wasn't growing avocadoes, we could have had guacamole."

"Or lemons," said Asher. "We could have had lemonade."

Polly stopped laughing and frowned at him. "Lemons grow on trees. The wall wouldn't have squashed them."

He frowned back. "The lemons might have been shaken out of the tree. Plus," he added, "avocadoes also grow on trees."

"They do?"

"How can you be a native Californian and not know that?"

Maggie had been looking back and forth, and now she interrupted. "Guys, the tomatoes were crushed into the ground, so I doubt they're edible." She leaned the broom against the sink, and walked toward the garden doors. "However, it's a valid point, so I'm going to go see if anything was salvageable." She left, muttering, "You guys continue bickering if you must."

"I wasn't bickering," said Polly to her back.

"Nor was I," added Asher, affronted. He turned to look at Polly. "Although, really, what did you think avocadoes grew on, bushes?"

She tossed her head airily. "No, I assumed they grew on vines, like bunches of grapes. I'm an actress, not a farmer."

"I thought you worked at the bookstore?" asked Asher.

"I do," replied Polly. "I can do more than one thing at a time."

"I didn't say you couldn't," said Asher, starting to feel the conversation sliding away from him. So pretty, but so cranky.

"I didn't say you said I couldn't, I simply said I could."

They both paused.

"Well," said Asher, "fine then."

"Fine," agreed Polly. Then she headed outside.

Polly had indeed been with friends when the earthquake struck, and all of them had paused their conversation and waited for it to end. Once it was over they were ready to keep talking, but Polly felt worried and made her apologies. She knew it wasn't a bad earthquake and she could simply have called, but she didn't. She leapt into her little orange car and zoomed home.

Entering the kitchen, she'd felt relieved to see Maggie was fine and nobody was hurt, and now as she approached the vegetable garden she waved at Laura and Bob, working side by side. Maggie was already there, leaning on the fence.

"Bad news," she said to Polly. "Those that gave their lives gave completely, and are not edible. Those that survived are to be left on the vine to recover, says their father."

"I'm not their father," said Bob mildly. "That would be God. Or something. I am merely their servant." He was pulling on what was left of a tomato plant, and it came out, showering him with dirt. "And their executioner, when necessary." He tossed the plant into a green trash can that stood nearby.

Maggie sighed. "Well, I don't know about the rest of you, but I do not feel like cooking now. We had pizza the other night . . . I vote burgers."

"Seconded," said Polly instantaneously. "I will even volunteer to go pick them up, such is my sudden desire for a chocolate milkshake."

"I'll go with you," said Asher, calling from the upper patio. "I'll put my shoes on, you gather everyone's orders." He turned to go back inside, presumably for his shoes.

"OK, bossy boots," muttered Polly, but she turned to the others as she pulled out her phone and looked for her notes app. "Orders, please?"

"Veggie burger with cheese for me," said Laura, "and a chocolate malted, if they have one." She paused. "And fries."

"Large or small?" asked Polly, her finger poised above the screen like a waitress holds her pencil.

"Large shake, small fries." Laura blushed a little. "I'm going to work it off tomorrow, I promise."

Polly looked at her curiously. "You don't have to caveat self-care, you know. You're allowed to nourish yourself." Having delivered this statement, Polly turned to Maggie. "And for madam? Something highly caloric and bad for your arteries?"

"Yes, definitely. Bacon cheeseburger with caramelized onions, large strawberry shake, no fries." Maggie cheered up. "I love a strawberry shake."

"And finally, Bob?" asked Polly. "Or has the death and devastation of your little minions put you off?"

"Nope," said Bob. "I'll also have a bacon cheeseburger, no shake, onion rings."

"Wait," said Laura. "They have onion rings?" She frowned. "Are they proper onion rings or are they the ones where you take a bite and the whole onion circle slides out and leaves you with a batter husk?"

They all stared at her.

"Sorry," she said. "I like onion rings."

"You can share mine," said Bob. "We can do a fry–onion ring exchange."

"Great," said Laura. "We can eat while we fill out your paperwork." She headed to the gate. "Come on, we can do most of it online."

Bob stared after her. Maggie raised her eyebrows. "What paperwork?"

Laura turned and kept walking backward, demonstrating her skills. "Bob's applying to grad school."

"Maybe," said Bob.

Maggie opened her mouth to comment, when Asher spoke from the kitchen door, his voice slightly raised.

"Mom?"

Maggie turned. "Yes?" Her brows contracted; she could see from his face that something was up. "What is it?"

"Sarah's here."

A woman stepped past him onto the patio. "Ash, I don't need an announcement, for crying out loud." She was smaller than he was, and her hair was long, a tangled mass of curls that fell around her shoulders. She was beautiful and immaculately put together, wearing the kind of casual clothes that were anything but: the perfect white T-shirt, the perfect pair of jeans, the perfectly distressed suede jacket. Laura saw wealth all the time in Manhattan, and recognized it.

The woman walked carefully down the steps from the patio and evaluated Polly, Bob, and Laura, switching on a pro forma two-second smile that barely wrinkled her nose, let alone her eyes. Reaching Maggie, she leaned in and kissed her formally on both cheeks, her hands lightly resting on the other woman's upper arms. Then she stepped back and looked around at the broken wall, the devastated vegetable patch.

"Bold landscaping choice," she drawled. "You've done wonders."

There was a pause, then Maggie cleared her throat and said, "Everyone, this is Sarah." She paused. "My daughter."

TWENTY-SEVEN

Sarah Morse was not what Laura expected. Having been introduced, Sarah made no effort to discover anyone's names, but merely waved a lazy hand and turned to start walking back to the house. Her walk reminded Laura of a winning racehorse circling the paddock, proud and aware of its own success. After a fractional pause Maggie followed her, and once they'd both disappeared inside, Laura turned to Polly and Bob.

"Um . . . are we supposed to follow them?"

Polly shrugged. "No clue." She clicked her tongue. "I'd forgotten how weird she was. She clearly doesn't remember me at all."

"She's very beautiful," said Laura doubtfully.

Bob sighed, and turned back to his vegetables. "Pretty is as pretty does," he said, which made Laura giggle.

"That's my grandmother's favorite line," she said.

Bob smiled a small smile and looked back at her. "Mine too."

Polly raised her eyebrow. "Your favorite line?"

He shook his head. "My grandmother's."

Polly made a noncommittal noise. "My grandmother's favorite line was *Who the hell drank the last of the scotch?*" She headed toward the house. "I'm going in. Something tells me Maggie might need backup."

Laura hesitated. "Maybe we should go, too?" She raised her voice. "Pol, should I come with you?"

Polly shrugged, and turned around. "No need, I can take her." Her eyes fell on the huge pile of roses. "Hey, can I have those roses?"

"Bob gave them to me," said Laura without thinking, then caught herself, "but of course, take them inside."

Polly raised her eyebrows. "Bob, she's giving away your flowers."

Bob was kneeling at the far end of the vegetable garden, completing his survey of the survivors. "I'll grow her some more," he said casually. "Take them in and put them in water before it's too late. I'll be in shortly, I need to finish staking these guys."

Polly came back for the roses, and Laura helped her. Then she stayed with Bob, saying, "I'll help you, then we can go in together."

Bob sat back on his heels and looked up at her, squinting into the sun. She moved, casting his face in shadow. "Scared of the new girl?" he said, smiling.

Laura nodded. "Is that dumb?"

He turned back to the plants, shaking his head. "Nope, she hasn't said a word to me and I'm already terrified." He staked the remaining unsupported tomatoes efficiently, searching the ground for the twist ties he'd put somewhere. They were green to blend in with the plants, but that also made them hard to find.

Laura spotted them and bent to pick them up, handing them to him one at a time. She giggled again. "Me too. Why is that?"

He shrugged, reaching out his hand for the next twist tie, which she slapped into his palm like a surgical nurse. "Beats me.

Her mom is the least scary person I've ever met." He looked up at the sky. "It's going to start getting dark soon. Shall we go in?" He stood and wiped his hands on his jeans. "Do you think we're still getting burgers?"

Laura nodded. "I think Polly was pretty determined." She paused. "I don't suppose there's another game on?"

Bob shook his head. "Not tonight, but we can always watch an old classic."

"How do you mean?"

"Well," he said, "there's this thing called the Internet . . . ?"

Laura put on a puzzled face. "It sounds familiar . . . I can't place it right now . . ."

"Well," said Bob innocently, "thanks to the magic of the Internet, we could watch the '81 World Series."

Laura narrowed her eyes at him; she was painfully aware the Dodgers had won that one. She said, "Or '77 or '78?" The Yankees had taken both.

They started walking toward the house. "How about this," said Bob. "We'll toss a coin, and the winner picks the game."

They climbed the steps to the patio and approached the kitchen door. "I like it," said Laura, pleased by this idea. "Then the other person can pick the next one."

"Deal," said Bob. "We can watch a new game every night."

"A new old game," corrected Laura. "And why stop at baseball? We can do Lakers-Knicks as well." She stepped back to let him go through the door. "The 1970 playoffs were fantastic."

Bob gestured for her to precede him. "Not for us," he said mildly.

As they walked into the kitchen, Laura was about to launch into a recitation of all the playoff games where the Knicks had kicked the Lakers, but when she realized they'd walked into a war zone, she forgot all about it.

Surprisingly, Asher seemed to be the most irritated person in the room. Sarah was leaning on the kitchen counter, as her mother often did, and though her expression was calm, clearly she was attempting to give as good as she got.

"I come over all the time," she was saying, "and I don't know where you get off bitching at me, seeing as you literally left the country four years ago and didn't visit once."

"He was working," said Maggie, her voice tight with the effort of sounding loose. "It's not like Tokyo is around the corner."

"Unlike, say, Beverly Hills," said Asher. It was clear from his face that this argument was hitting a big, fat nerve.

Bob looked at Laura, whose eyes had widened slightly. Both of them wanted to slowly back out the way they'd come. Failing that, Bob wondered if he could lower his head and glide through the kitchen unnoticed, while Laura wondered if anyone would see her if she dropped to her belly and crawled to the hallway. Instead they froze in place and pretended to be somewhere else.

"So was I, working," said Sarah, wounded. "You always take his side." She threw up her hands. "I don't know why I expected anything different." She snapped at her brother, "Clearly your Japanese colleagues failed to pass on any of their famous civility."

Asher scoffed. "This isn't about me, Sarah, it isn't even about you, although you probably think it is." He looked at Maggie. "Mom, when was the last time Sarah came over?"

Maggie looked at Polly. "So, Polly, would you like a cup of tea?"

Polly, who'd been watching the argument since it had kicked off a few minutes earlier, telling herself she was studying body language rather than stickybeaking another family's drama, answered immediately. "I would love a cup of tea, Maggie, thanks." She got to her feet and went to the cupboard. "Shall I get some cookies?"

Sarah turned to look at her mother. "Wow, Mom, it's like having your kids around, except these guys are actually helpful." She turned to look at Polly. "Even if they do dress like cartoon characters."

Bob looked at Polly, who was slowly turning back from the cupboard, and he started walking through the kitchen, keeping his head down. Laura was right behind him, but Maggie wasn't having it.

"Bob, Laura," she said, "I'm making tea, would you like some?"

"Which cartoon character?" asked Polly mildly.

"I don't know," said Sarah bitchily. "Someone minor. A sidekick."

"Uh . . ." said Bob.

"Great," said his landlady. "Polly, grab a couple more cups, would you?" She stepped into the hallway and raised her voice. "Libby! Do you and Anna want some tea?" Her voice was still calm, but Laura could hear a faint note of hysteria. Poor Maggie was not having a good day. Earthquakes. Walls. Arguments. A distant voice responded, and Maggie came back into the kitchen. "Two more for tea, that's fantastic."

Polly was having an internal argument, but decided to simply smile and restrain her tongue. She was learning to let shit go and gave herself a small pat on the back for progress. Then she wondered which element of her outfit provoked the comment—it could easily be the shirt; there was a definite Velma from *Scooby-Doo* vibe. To be fair, she'd been kind of fine with that.

Sarah had swiveled her sights back to her brother. "Mom, you can't let Asher talk to me like that." She folded her arms. "It's so easy to criticize, isn't it? God forbid you look at your own side of the street."

"What do you mean by that?" asked Asher, his voice much quieter now. He was aware they had an audience, including Polly, and wished this had never started. But his sister always did this, always caused trouble.

"You know," said his sister, going over to her purse, which sat on the table. She pulled out a pack of cigarettes and a Zippo lighter. "You let Madeleine walk all over you and then you fled the scene. Borrowing money from Mom to do it, am I right?"

Asher looked quickly at his mother, who shrugged. "I didn't say anything."

"I paid her back," he said to his sister. "I paid her back within a few months."

Sarah stuck a cigarette in her mouth, but didn't light it. "And now you're back, living with Mom."

"Sarah," said Maggie, "please don't smoke in here."

Sarah pulled the cigarette out of her mouth and crumpled it in her hand, holding it up high and letting the mangled pieces drop to the floor. "Sorry, Mom, forgot the rules."

"Only till I find a place." Asher pointed at his sister. "Maybe if I'm lucky, I can follow your example and marry someone wealthy and stupid."

Sarah laughed. "My husband is not stupid." She went to pull another cigarette from the pack, shot a look of frustration at her mom, and didn't.

"He married you, didn't he?" Asher couldn't help himself any more than he could have at twelve.

Laura was unable to hold in a gasp, and everyone turned to

look at her. "Sorry," she said, going bright red. "I . . . uh . . ." Her family argued all the time, but it was usually about some arcane point of knowledge, rather than ad hominem attacks on one another's character. Those they saved for one-on-one conversations, but for the first time Laura could see the silver lining in that.

The kettle was coming to a boil, and Maggie's eyes were glittering with emotion and embarrassment. "Guys, would it be possible to get together without it devolving into a screaming match?" She turned to Asher. "Stop insulting Jeff, he's not here to defend himself, and he and Sarah are very happy together." She turned to Sarah. "And stop poking at Asher because he borrowed a little money years ago. He paid it back, and I would have done the same for you." She paused. "I still would, not that you want my help with anything."

"What does that mean?" Sarah's quills were still sticking out all over, her readiness to defend herself pokily palpable.

Maggie sighed and raised her hands in surrender. "Nothing. It means I would help you. I would help Asher. I would help anyone who asked me, if I could."

There was a pause, and Laura could see Sarah's face working as she battled for the right comeback. In the end, she picked the wrong one. "Well, you're a fucking saint, aren't you? And I'm the miserable sinner who ruined your perfect reputation at the tennis club."

Maggie flushed and shook her head. "No, and you know that's not fair."

"Don't be a bitch, Sarah," said Asher. "You're too old to get away with it."

Sarah was gathering her things, putting the pack of cigarettes back in her bag, hurling the lighter after it, throwing the bag on her shoulder, and getting ready to leave.

"Don't make me any tea, Mom," she said sarcastically. "Not

that you asked me if I wanted any." She walked out of the kitchen. As she went down the hallway, she said loudly, "Bye, Asher, see you in another four years, maybe."

"Sarah . . ." he called back. "Don't leave."

"Why would I stay?" she asked as they all heard the front door open. "I've never been welcome here, and honestly, I'm cool with that." The door slammed, and the house shook for the second time that day.

TWENTY-EIGHT

Growing up in Manhattan meant Laura had plenty of experience flicking on the kitchen light at midnight and seeing cockroaches scattering in various directions. She knew, thanks to the kinds of conversations her family had at dinner, that the cockroach was one of the fastest insects on earth, capable of covering five feet in a single second. While no one in the kitchen could call on that much accelerative power, they all treated the slamming front door as a kind of starter pistol and took off, possibly to avoid the dense cloud of awkward settling over the room.

Bob kept going in the direction of his bedroom, with Laura on his tail. Asher headed upstairs, Polly ditto, and Maggie crossed the kitchen and hit the back stairs like a homing pigeon. Within seconds the room was empty apart from the dogs, who looked at each other with consternation, each silently accusing the other of farting.

When Bob reached his door, he turned to look at Laura. "Uh, do you still want to watch a game?"

She shook her head. "No. I was thinking I would go and pull the bedcovers over my head." She hesitated. "How long till we can pretend that didn't happen?"

"That what didn't happen?" Bob grinned at her, and Laura

was relieved. She hated scenes and avoided confrontation of any kind. She wasn't wired for it and definitely wasn't armed for it. Growing up she'd sit on the sidelines of spirited debates, occasionally being called on to give an opinion, an opinion she took too long to form, making her brothers throw up their hands and interrupt whatever stuttering attempt she was making. So she stayed out of the fray, which led friends to call her aloof and family members to call her a chicken.

She smiled at Bob and opened her bedroom door. "Another night, maybe?" she said.

"Definitely," he replied, giving a final friendly wave as he disappeared. Laura could hear Polly and Asher talking upstairs and quickly went into her room, in case they started fighting, too.

As it happened, Polly and Asher weren't fighting. Asher had reached the landing first, and turned to Polly, still angry.

"I'm sorry you had to see that. My sister is kind of . . . difficult." He was flushed, upset, and Polly shook her head.

"All families fight. But you were kind of a dick."

Asher was surprised. "She started it."

Polly shook her head again. "Nope. I was there for the whole thing and you definitely had a hand in it from the beginning. Sorry not sorry, that's the truth."

He stared at her. "You're very blunt, aren't you?"

"Only about other people," she said. "I'm completely in denial about my own shortcomings." She stopped abruptly. "Oh crap, the burgers."

Asher was calming down and realized hunger might have had something to do with the scene in the kitchen. "I can still go."

"Are you hungry?"

"Very," he replied. "And my mom definitely wants a strawberry shake."

Polly turned to go back downstairs. "Well then, let's go. I can point out more of your character defects on the way."

"Do you have to?" asked Asher, following her. "I'm already feeling bad for losing my temper. Maybe I should call Sarah and apologize."

"Eat first," said Polly wisely. "Blood sugar is your ally." She'd reached Laura's door and paused to knock on it.

Laura opened the door a sliver and peeped out. "Hi there," she said.

"Still hungry?" said Polly. "In all the excitement we forgot we were going to get food." Asher was standing close behind her, and Laura smiled at both of them.

"Yes," she said gratefully, "I'm starving. Do you need money?"

"You can send it to me after," said Polly, going to knock on Bob's door. Asher looked at Laura and smiled nervously.

"Sorry about that," he said. "Family stuff, you know . . ."

Laura nodded. "No worries," she said, catching Bob's eye across the hallway as he opened his door. "Forget it." Bob gave her a fleeting half wink as he confirmed his order for Polly, then disappeared back into the safety of his room. Laura abruptly remembered the cigarette on the kitchen floor, and her desire to be helpful overcame her need to hide. She went to clean it up.

What had been tobacco and paper was now dog vomit, and Herbert was sitting under the kitchen table regretting his life choices. Laura grabbed handfuls of paper towel and tackled the mess, pointing out to Herbert that smoking was very bad for you and she hoped he'd learned from this experience. But her voice was kind, and Herbert felt a little better. He was still a good boy.

After Laura had left the kitchen, Herbert walked over to the foot of the back stairs and tipped his head to one side, listening to the distant sound of Maggie crying. He looked around for a shoe, or something else she might enjoy. Finally settling on a circular from the AARP, which he pulled from a pile of papers on a kitchen chair, he grasped it firmly in his teeth and headed upstairs to see if there was anything he could do.

When Asher and Polly came back to the house and yelled, "Food's here!" it was like hitting reset. Maggie had washed her face and changed her shirt, and walking into the kitchen was like entering a totally different place and time. Polly, Asher, Bob, Laura, Anna, and Libby were all bustling around getting plates and napkins, speaking in that chirpy tone of voice that brooks no rehashing of recent arguments, old scores, or anything controversial at all. *Everything is fine*, the tone says. *I'm fine, you're fine, we're all fine.* Maggie sighed inwardly; from years of professional experience and personal failure, she knew the argument would lurk like old laundry until it was properly aired. Then she spotted her strawberry milkshake and decided to let it lie for now. The argument, not the milkshake; the milkshake she was going to suck down with no hesitation at all.

Polly was in charge, pulling burgers from the bag and announcing each like the guy in a white wig at the doorway to a ball. Caramelized onions and bacon! Veggie burger with cheese! Major Onion Rings and the Right Honorable Lavinia Fries! Laura took her veggie burger and turned to Bob, who was about to start dividing their sides. She lowered her voice.

"Game?" she whispered, and he looked up quickly. Barely nodding, he turned and carried his plate away, thanking Asher and Polly as he went. Laura lingered for a few minutes, chatting to Polly about the bill, and what to do if there was another earthquake. Maggie advised her to put a pair of shoes under her bed and a flashlight in the shoes, then headed off to her private aerie, clutching her dinner. Smiling around the group, Laura turned and left, congratulating herself on her subtlety. Once clear of the kitchen, she dashed to Bob's door and found it ajar. Pushing through, she saw he was already pulling up a game. She sat down ready to say very little and eat quite a lot.

He grinned at her. "Clean getaway?"

She nodded, reaching for an onion ring. "Is it bad we didn't invite everyone?"

Bob shrugged. "Believe me, no one else in the house cares about baseball. I've tried."

Laura nodded, comforted. She didn't want to leave anyone out, but it wouldn't be the same if she had to make conversation. With Bob all she had to do was watch and bicker pointlessly about the referee. It was peaceful, like being home with her grandmother, not that she was going to mention that. Bob might be mellow as all get-out, but no guy likes to be told he reminds you of your granny. Besides, Polly would never let her hear the end of it, however much she explained she and Bob weren't interested in each other that way. She looked over at him now, and waved her onion ring.

"These are good, you were right."

He nodded, picked up a handful of fries, and started making fun of the Yankees' starting pitcher.

It was heaven.

Back in the kitchen, Polly watched Laura leave and then turned to Anna and said, "A hundred bucks says Laura and Bob are hanging out."

Anna made a face. "Why wouldn't they hang out here?"

Polly shrugged. "Because they're both irritatingly private?

Who knows?" She sighed. "I'm starting to realize not everyone likes to live their life out loud like I do." She frowned. "I'm not even sure if I do."

Anna was confused and looked it. Polly smiled. "How's your food?"

"Insanely delicious," said Anna, reaching for a napkin to wipe her chin. She turned to Libby. "How much longer till we leave?"

Libby had his mouth full and held up both hands, fingers spread wide.

Asher said, "Leave for what?"

"Bridge tournament," said Anna, chewing the last bite of her burger while attempting to cover her mouth and talk at the same time. "It's the semifinals and I think we've got a pretty good chance." She went over to the sink to wash her hands.

Libby nodded and finished up his chocolate shake. "Of runner up, maybe. I think the Deadly Armenian Duo will be there."

Anna turned off the faucet and frowned at him. "Crap."

Asher laughed. "The Deadly Armenian Duo?"

Libby nodded earnestly. "Well, that's what we call them. They're a telepathic married couple from Glendale, the Markary-ans. They never speak, they never smile, and they never, ever lose." He looked at Anna. "Maybe one day we'll be that good."

Anna grinned. "What am I thinking now?"

Libby stared at her and closed his eyes. "Three of clubs."

Anna shook her head.

"Four of spades."

Anna shook her head again. "No, and we need to leave if we're going to get there in time."

Libby jumped to his feet and ran upstairs. Anna looked around for the shoes she'd kicked off earlier, and a jacket.

Polly looked at her. "I can guess what you were thinking," she said.

Anna finished shrugging on her coat. "I doubt it," she said.

"Why don't you tell him?" Polly asked.

Anna looked surprised and opened her mouth to speak, but Libby reappeared, coated and ready to go.

"All good?" he asked, rubbing his hands together.

Anna nodded, still looking at Polly. "You don't play bridge, do you?" she asked her.

"No," said Polly.

"Good thing," said Anna, walking out of the kitchen.

TWENTY-NINE

The next day was Monday, and Laura dropped by the bookstore on her way to the library. She found Nina and Liz reshelving earthquake-toppled books. Most of the shelved books were fine, held in place by their colleagues, but the displays on top of the bookshelves had been universally trashed. Liz was smoothing covers and reassuring the books they were still beautiful, and Nina was tutting over imperfect alphabetization.

"The question is," she said to Laura, who was trying not to look at Liz, who was making faces behind Nina's back, "whether you should subalphabetize books by their title, having already alphabetized them by author, *or*"—and she stressed this—"if you should suborganize by date of publication so people can read them in order."

Liz gave up making faces and said bluntly, "Neither. You should shelve them with the author's other books and not worry beyond that." She had decades more experience than Nina, and occasionally brought it to bear. "What about authors who write a series but occasionally write a stand-alone?"

Nina was ready. "You shelve the series in order, and the stand-alones separately."

"So you ignore the date of publication?"

"Yes, in that case."

Liz's expression made it clear she thought Nina was nuts. "So what about, for example, the Who Was? series?" This was a long-running series of nonfiction children's books, covering historical figures and events, places of interest, and natural phenomena. Liz pulled one at random from a nearby shelf: *Who Was Alexander Hamilton?* "Am I supposed to shelve these in historical order? What about the What Was—es? How do I shelve those? Do volcanoes go next to hurricanes, or next to mountains?" She plucked another volume in the same series and waved it. "What about Where Is—es? Do I provide a map? They publish two dozen books in the series every year, they've been going for nearly twenty years, and they'll never stop because history keeps on happening!" Liz looked triumphant as she held up the two books with their bobble-headed portraits of Hamilton and—incongruously—Elton John. "What do I do with these, Nina Hill?"

Nina looked at her and opened her mouth and closed it a few times. Then she shrugged. "This is why you're in charge of children's books."

Laura started to back out of the store: This was clearly an argument with a lot of legs, and both women seemed to be enjoying the debate rather than trying to win. She was familiar with this kind of argument; she'd had a very similar one with Bob the previous evening about the placement of outfielders. Her parents had one about talon evolution that no one else understood but that broke out any-time either of them had more than one glass of wine. And those were the arguments about relatively neutral topics; most families have several long-running, highly personal arguments . . . She wondered what the fight between Asher and Sarah had really been about.

"Wait!" said Nina, who had excellent peripheral vision and

could see her slinking away. "You remember the trivia thing is this Friday, right?"

"Yes," said Laura. "I'm going to read widely at the library, I promise."

"Good," said Nina. "No pressure. It will be fun. Unless we lose."

"No pressure then."

"None at all."

The semifinals of the East Los Angeles Pub League were being held—this year—at a bar called Donut Shoppe, which might in other contexts be ironic but which in Silver Lake meant a bar that sold donuts. Microbrew artisanal donuts.

The bar smelled of burnt sugar, and the floor was a multicolored oil slick of spilled beer and sprinkles. Nina handed Laura a cruller and took her over to meet QuizDick, Master of Trivia Ceremonies and stakeholder in one of the more successful YouTube trivia shows (you'd be surprised). His real name was Howard, but nobody called him that.

QuizDick looked at Nina suspiciously; she and he had history. However, Nina was determined not to be combative this year. She wanted to be more grown up, despite the streak of purple frosting on her chin.

QuizDick held up his hands, "I'm not cutting you any slack this year, Hill. Last year's finale was a fiasco, and your team wasn't even competing."

"What happened?" said Laura to Nina, who shook her head.

"It's a whole other story," she said. "Don't worry about it." She smiled peacefully at QuizDick. "I'm not here to fight, I'm letting you know we have a new team member."

QuizDick looked at Laura and transferred his suspicion to her. "Did you change your team details on the website?"

"Yes," said Nina.

"Did you order her a T-shirt in the correct size?"

"Yes," said Nina, "but it's ugly, and she refuses to wear it."

"And did you receive a new, printable team list to sign and submit today?"

Nina brandished a piece of paper and smiled an almost believably angelic smile. "Here you are, Quizmaster, all ready to go."

"I'll be the judge of that," he said crossly, taking the paper and checking it over. "Hmm, seems in order." He folded it and put it in his pocket. "You're up against Victorious Secret, another all-girl team." He leered at Laura. "Winner takes all . . . their clothes off?"

"Super doubtful," said Nina emphatically, "and unless you stop staring at our new player, I'll tell Leah you made that comment and she'll respect you even less than she does now."

QuizDick had a deep and abiding passion for Nina's friend Leah, whose knowledge of European history was the stuff of his wildest fantasies.

"No," he said quickly, "please don't." He turned to Laura. "I apologize if I offended you."

Laura shrugged. It was very loud in the bar and she'd had two donuts; the combination of noise and unusually high blood sugar meant she hadn't really heard him.

QuizDick turned back to Nina. "I love the way she says . . . Plantagenet."

Nina patted him on the shoulder. "I know."

Then she whirled around, gathered Laura, and headed back to their table.

Behind them QuizDick gathered his sheets of paper and tried not to think about Leah dressed as the many wives of Henry VIII.

Back at the table, Nina's boyfriend, Tom, had arrived and was debating the relative merits of donut holes and mini-donuts. Leah and Lauren both had strong feelings.

"It's a question of proportion," said Lauren. "A donut hole is mostly glaze, whereas a mini-donut preserves the ratio of glaze to donut. It's not so much a miniature donut as it is a donut in miniature." She said this last part sagely, as if she weren't actually paraphrasing a popular children's cartoon. (She was hoping no one else got the reference.)

Nina looked at her narrowly. "Did you just . . . ?"

"No," said Lauren quickly.

"Well, that's my point," said Tom. "I'm a glaze guy, which is why the hole is better than the mini."

Nina opened her mouth to weigh in on this vital topic, when her attention was drawn to the door. "Wait, isn't that Polly and Bob?"

Laura nearly twisted her neck to see that Nina was, indeed, correct. Not only Polly and Bob, but also Asher, Libby, and Anna. All five were headed in their direction.

Laura turned to look at Nina. "What if I mess up?"

Nina shrugged. "They're cheerleaders, not a hit squad." She waved at the newcomers, then turned back to her boyfriend. "Hey, Tom, have you met Bob before?"

Tom stood up and held out his hand to Bob. "I think so . . . didn't we meet at Clare's birthday party?"

Bob frowned, then his expression cleared. "Were you the one who made her the tiny bookcases for her fairy house?"

Tom blushed. "Yes." He looked at Nina. "Somebody made a good suggestion." He nodded at Bob. "And I believe you were the one who took her on a tractor, because that's how she introduced you."

"This-is-Bob-who-lets-me-drive-a-tractor? Yes, that's me."

The two men grinned at each other, then Tom said, "Shall we get some more beers while the nerds prepare themselves?" He looked past Bob to where Asher and Libby were standing, and leaned forward to extend his hand. "Hi, I'm Tom."

Asher grinned and shook his hand. "I'm Asher, I'm Bob's landlady's son."

Libby followed suit. "I'm Libby, I'm not related to anyone here."

Tom considered that, then said, "Want to help bring in the beer?"

The four guys headed off, and Laura turned to Nina. "Do you think we'll ever see them again?"

"Probably," said Nina, looking through her notes, "or they'll form an eclectic and tightly knit boy band, but hey, if you love something, set it free." She looked up at Laura fiercely. "Costello. *Focus.*"

Polly was gazing around as if she'd never seen a bar before. "I haven't been here in ages, was it always this . . ."

"Polly! I thought I'd lost you forever!" cried a large and inebriated guy, throwing his arms around her and lifting her off the ground. "It's been soooo long."

"Wow," said Polly, wriggling free and taking a big step back. "And yet not long enough—do I know you?"

The guy looked injured. "Yeah! We dated . . . kind of . . . before Christmas . . . you don't remember?"

Polly shook her head and looked around quickly to see if

Asher was nearby. He wasn't, but Anna and Laura were staring unabashedly, and even Nina paused in her last-minute preparation. Polly turned back to the guy, who was attractive, despite a beard *and* a man-bun. One or the other, people, make a choice.

"I'm sorry, I'm super bad with names . . . Mike?"

"No."

"Steve?"

"No"—the guy was frowning now—"Bartholomew."

"Really?" Polly covered her mouth with her hand. "I mean, sure, of course. Bartholomew . . . ?"

"Fenstremmer." The guy looked pretty pissed. "Barty Fenstremmer. Not a very common name."

"No," said Polly contritely. "I'm really sorry, I meet a lot of people and do a lot of things, especially around the holidays. Maybe I'm confusing you with—"

The guy interrupted her. "We met when you crashed your bike into the back of my car. You were dressed as Sassy Santa Claus and the hat had fallen over your eyes. We went to Echo Park Lake and made out in a swan boat. Then we got into a fight with another couple in a different swan boat because their boat was lit up and ours wasn't. Then you insisted we go climb the Hollywood sign, which you can't legally do, but somehow we did and then you stripped down to your underwear and took off down the fire road, which was when the park police showed up."

Polly tightened her lips and shook her head again. "Nope, sorry, it's not ringing a bell." She looked over at the four guys, who were fast approaching the table. "Oh shit, here come all my boyfriends. Run, Barty, run!"

As the guy lumbered away as quickly as he could, he looked back and mimed holding a phone up to his ear. Polly smiled broadly at him and nodded enthusiastically.

"Who was that guy?" asked Asher, handing Polly a tall icy bottle of Coke.

"No clue," she replied. "When does the competition start?"

One of the innovations QuizDick brought to his trivia contests was the decorative contestant podium. A member of each team would face each other across the podium—which today was a re-purposed condiment stand from a defunct coffee shop—and buzz in with their answers. It made for better YouTube footage and re-duced the chance of people simply googling the answers under the table. It also let QuizDick release his inner crafter, and he'd spent many happy hours hot gluing glass pebbles to create the stunning reflective effect he was going for.

Victorious Secret had come over from Pasadena, which was Tom's hometown. There was a short and spirited debate about whether he was allowed to support both teams, but in the end he decided to protect his safety while sleeping and stuck with Nina's team. The four ladies of VS had to be content with the entire Caltech astrobiology department, who had come out to support the team captain, who was one of their own.

Bob leaned over to Tom. "Regular people play this game, too, right? You don't actually have to be a rocket scientist?"

Leah heard the question and answered first. "No, and some-times education gets in the way of knowledge." She blinked. "Which sounds profound but isn't." Then she added, unable to stop herself, "Besides, astrobiology is not rocket science per se, it's rocket science adjacent."

After a pause to let that settle in, Tom shook his head. "Trust me, I am an incredibly average guy and I had my own team." He paused. "Which, now that I say it out loud, does sound a little bit weird."

"You quit your team?" asked Laura.

Tom nodded. "I don't have as much time as I used to."

Nina rolled her eyes. "You can make time. I am literally in the exact same relationship as you, I simply moved stuff around."

"What did you cancel?" he teased, his eyes dancing as he looked at her. "Tell the normal people what you moved out of your schedule to make room for both me *and* trivia."

"Additional reading," said Nina defiantly.

"Which was additional to?"

"Work reading," she said in a slightly quieter voice.

"Which was on top of?"

"Regular reading," she muttered.

Tom turned up his palms and grinned at Bob. "That probably answers your question."

"Everyone's an expert on something," said Bob, "I suppose." He looked at Laura and grinned. She grinned back, glad he was there.

She lowered her voice and leaned closer to him. "I'm nervous." She wasn't sure why, but she felt like Bob was on her side, in some indefinable way. A good friend.

Bob kept his voice low and said, "Don't be. It's not like you're competing for the honor of your state or anything."

Nina interrupted, having apparently turned her hearing up to bat-like. "Not her state, but her team. Don't minimize the challenge, Bob, this is serious stuff."

He raised his eyebrows. "It has 'trivial' *in the name*."

"Shush," Nina replied.

Bob looked at Laura and made a goofy face. She still felt nervous, but she was reassured at least one other person wasn't taking it too seriously. Nonetheless, when QuizDick rang a tiny golden gong—yes, really—she got ready to make a fool of herself.

The format was simple. Each team sent up a person to compete, and that pair of contestants were asked three questions on random subjects. The fastest buzzer got first chance. If they guessed wrong, the other contestant got to answer. If *she* didn't know, the first contestant could throw it to their team. If their team didn't know, the other team got a chance. No one understood the points system except QuizDick, which was completely intentional. It was calibrated to be *precisely* complicated enough that people would attempt to understand it for about thirty seconds, then give up and rationalize that it added an element of chance to an otherwise pretty cerebral game. Then they'd order another drink.

Captains went first, Nina up against Victoria One, whose doctoral thesis was about a subject so arcane and abstruse that there were only seven other people in the world who understood it. However, when faced with the question "Who wants to steal the Krabby Patty formula?" she completely blanked.

Fortunately, Nina had wasted her youth with the best of them, and was able to answer.

The next question, "How long can golfers search for their balls?" created such an uproar of hilarity that the contest was temporarily halted while everybody took a minute to grow up. It was particularly enjoyable to Nina, because it was clear QuizDick hadn't read the question out loud in advance and hadn't seen the problem until it was too late.

She waited for the commotion to die down, then said, "New question, please."

QuizDick shuffled his cards. "How many hearts does an octopus have?"

"Three." Nina was rock solid on sea creatures; she'd spent almost the entire summer vacation of her eighth year memorizing them. All of them.

"Last question," said QuizDick. "Which racehorse holds the record for the largest margin of victory in a race?"

Nina closed her eyes. Horse racing was the Achilles' heel of her Achilles' heel, i.e., the sport about which she knew even less than she knew about all the others. But there was silence; Victoria One didn't know, either. Nina hit her buzzer.

"Can I offer it to my team?"

QuizDick nodded. Nina turned and looked hopefully at Laura, her sports expert, who was looking at Leah, who was looking at Lauren, who had leapt to her feet and cried, "Secretariat." Then she looked at Nina in amazement. "How can you not know that? There's a book! There's a *movie*."

Laura turned to Bob. "Even I saw that."

Bob nodded. "He was a bighearted horse." He looked at Tom. "He still holds the world record for that distance on dirt."

"Shh," said Tom quickly. "Don't let Nina hear you."

THIRTY

It turned out the prize for winning the trivia contest was a dozen donuts for each team member, and by the time Bob and Laura climbed into his truck to drive home, both of them were as giddy as squirrels in a Snickers factory. The contest had come down to a final question about who was the very first player drafted in the very first NFL draft, and miraculously Laura had known the answer.

Bob was still laughing about it. "How on earth you remembered Jay Berwanger, I have no idea. I've never even heard of him."

"No one has, really," said Laura, shaking her head. "He didn't end up signing a contract and became a foam rubber salesman instead."

"You are making that up." Bob stared at her as he turned the key to start the engine.

"Nope," said Laura. "My grandma mentioned it all the time, because she's fond of missed-opportunity stories."

Bob pulled out into traffic. "Are there lots of those?"

Laura nodded. "Sadly, yes." She fell silent. "I think I'm having a sugar crash. Maybe the fifth donut was a mistake." For once she wasn't nervous to be in a car, but getting mildly drunk and stuffing herself with processed sugar probably wasn't an excellent long-term coping strategy. On the one hand she was relieved to be calm, and on the other she knew from experience that the occasional easy day doesn't mean the bad days are over. Recovery isn't that linear, any more than life is.

Bob laughed. "They were really good donuts, and you did win."

Laura smiled. "Nina was really pleased, wasn't she?"

"I think so," he replied. "She was very subtle about it, though."

Nina had literally leapt on the table and waved her fists at poor Victorious Secret, who hadn't taken their loss very well. They'd answered a layup question ("What has the Kepler telescope found more of than any other telescope?" Answer: exoplanets.) that had Nina crying foul because, as she furiously demanded, on what exoplanet was that a trivia question, and they thought they had it in the bag. But no, Laura had come through in the clutch and Nina was triumphant. She'd invited everyone back to her place for ice cream, but Laura had had enough sugar for one night, and Bob offered to drive her home. They both had to get up early, and to be honest, Nina wasn't sure her apartment would hold everyone anyway, so she'd hugged them both several times, very enthusiastically, and waved them off.

Laura giggled. "Nina's pretty wild. I like her, though. I wish I was more like that."

Bob shot her a look, his eyebrows drawn. "Like what?"

"Cooler, smarter. More . . . unusual." Laura shrugged, and looked out of the window, feeling her energy dissipating. "I'm very normal. There's nothing special about me."

Bob made a noise. "That's a dumb thing to say." He corrected himself. "Sorry, I didn't mean exactly dumb, but everyone is special."

Laura laughed. "If everyone is special, then no one is special, right?" This was literally something her mother said all the time, and Laura could hardly believe it had come out of her mouth.

Bob shook his head gently. "No, everyone *is* special, there's not a limited amount of special to go around. Everyone has something about them that's unique." He looked at her, his eyes very dark in the reflected streetlights. "Maybe it's hard to see it for yourself."

"Maybe," said Laura. "Polly has incredible style and charm, Nina's a whiz at trivia . . . I'm a regular woman who likes sports and dogs and human anatomy." *And is too scared to drive and panics when she hears a loud noise and may have to give up on her dreams and slink home to her parents . . .*

Bob reached over and prodded her gently. "You're a mean poker player. You swim very fast. You're extremely encouraging." He kept his eyes on the road. "I think you're special." *And beautiful, and kind, and incredibly sexy . . .*

She looked at him and smiled. "I think you're special, too."

They pulled up in front of Maggie's house, and Bob cut the engine and turned to Laura. "Honestly, Laura, there's a lot about you that's unique. You made me feel like going to grad school, for example."

Laura grinned. "See? So special you can't wait to leave town."

"Actually," Bob replied, "you being in the house makes it harder to leave."

Laura felt herself blushing. "Because you like having someone to shoot hoops with?"

Bob colored, too, and nodded. "And talk to, and watch games with, and sit next to in silence . . ."

Laura took a deep breath. "And hide from embarrassing arguments with, and fix trellises with . . ."

"Yes," said Bob, moving closer, "all that important stuff . . ."

They stared at each other, and then, at the exact same moment, both leaned forward to kiss. It wasn't even a conscious thought, it was simply what was happening. Not a huge kiss, not an intense, swooning kiss, but a promising one. A kiss that said there was potential for an endless supply of those kisses, should an endless supply be called for. As they pulled apart, both knew something had happened that was going to make a difference, they just weren't sure what difference it was going to make.

Bob opened his mouth to speak, when he noticed someone standing on the stoop of Maggie's house.

"Who's that?" he said, leaning down to look past Laura. She could smell his hair, the green scent of cut grass that always seemed to linger around him. She wondered if they were going to sleep together, if things were about to change that much, that fast. She wanted to quite badly, she realized. She brought herself back to the present and turned to see what he meant, happy for a distraction so she could get herself recalibrated.

Sadly, that wasn't what happened. Instead, she looked up at the doorway and caught her breath in a hiss, her intense attraction to Bob instantly forgotten.

"No. Effing. Way," she muttered, rapidly opening the door and stepping out, nearly knocking Bob's arm out from under him in the process.

"There you are!" said the tall man standing at the top of the drive, starting to walk toward them. "I've been waiting for ages. There's a friendly gray cat here who's been keeping me company, but he seems to be the only one home."

Bob felt his stomach drop, knowing from every step Laura took toward this guy that the kissing was done for the night. He sighed and climbed out of the truck. As he rounded the front, the other man reached the sidewalk and smiled at him.

"Hi there," he said. "I'm Nick." He swept Laura into a hug and whirled her around. "I'm Laura's fiancé."

Bob wasn't happy about it, but he couldn't help liking Nick. It was hard not to; he was friendly and good humored, and if he kept hugging Laura and kissing the top of her head, well, why not? Bob would have been doing something broadly similar if Nick hadn't been there. Besides, it was clear from Laura's reaction that Nick's sudden appearance was (a) surprising and (b) very unwelcome. If Bob hadn't been feeling a little thwarted by the turn the evening had taken, he might even have felt sorry for Nick, who was clearly digging himself a hole with every *sweetheart*, *babycakes*, and affectionate hair ruffle.

Laura was furious. She felt she'd made herself abundantly clear on the phone and yet here he was, her ex-fiancé, standing in her new life as if he'd been part of it all along. He knew she wouldn't cause a scene in front of anyone, because it wasn't her way, and she knew he was milking that advantage for all it was worth. A few minutes after they'd all walked in, Maggie had come downstairs to see what the excitement was about, and now Nick was holding court in the way he always did. He was asking questions, cracking jokes, waging the charm offensive that came so naturally to him. It was a large part of what drew Laura to him in the first place, and his social currency had been a lifesaver in high school and college. Now, however, she wanted to make her own capital, and spend it as she saw fit. She watched him drawing out Bob and Maggie with equal ease and felt uncharitable. Perhaps he was being a good friend, making sure she was settling in.

Maggie yawned. "Kids, this is way past my bedtime, I'm going back to bed." She smiled at Nick. "It was a pleasure to meet you, Nick. You're welcome to join us for dinner tomorrow if you'll still be in town."

Nick smiled. "I'll be here. I'm planning on staying as long as Laura will let me."

Both Bob and Maggie looked at Laura, who blushed and said nothing. This was classic Nick behavior, making her commit to something she didn't want to do by asking her in public.

Maggie smiled again and said good night, heading up the stairs to her bedroom. That left only Bob, which was awkward for all of them, so he quickly said good night as well, muttering something about an early start.

Laura waited until she heard his bedroom door close, then turned to Nick.

"My room, now," she said.

Nick grinned. "I was hoping you'd say that." He grabbed his suitcase handle and turned to leave the kitchen.

"You can put that by the front door," said Laura, leading the way. "You'll be leaving in a minute."

Nick said, "Why don't I leave it here by the door to your room? Maybe I'll be able to extend my welcome."

"You don't have a welcome," Laura replied, holding the door open and then closing it behind him. She turned to face him as he looked around the room. She gave him a second to take it all in, then said, "Nick, why are you here?"

He sat on the edge of her bed and grinned up at her. She frowned back. She was finding his good-looking, familiar face incredibly irritating. Nick shrugged. "I came to persuade you to change your mind and come home," he said simply. "Your family voted me Most Likely to Succeed, so I came."

"My family?" she said, her eyebrows as high up as they could go. "What do they have to do with this?"

Nick put on one of his favorite expressions, concerned intelligence. "Your parents and I are worried about you, especially now that you're so far away. What if . . . things get hard again?"

Laura snorted. "Nick, I'm fine. I've been fine for over a year. Ever since I made the decision to do this, in fact."

Nick shook his head. "Did you get a car yet?"

Laura felt her face flush. "No, but I'm working on it. The buses are fine. Why is everyone obsessed with me getting a car? Is it really that important? Aren't we supposed to be saving the planet?" She sighed. "I'm sorry you guys don't like my choices, but I do, and as I'm the one who has to live with the consequences of those choices, there's really nothing else to talk about."

Nick assumed a wounded expression. "Pussycat, we care about you, that's all. You've been through a lot, you shouldn't be making big decisions like this."

"Nick," said Laura sharply, "I made my decision. The fact that you don't approve of it doesn't stop it from being made." She stepped back and reached for her bedroom door. "Another decision I made was not to waste any more time rehashing conversations more than once. Conversations like this one." She swung the door open, and smiled politely. "I assume you have a hotel room somewhere?"

Nick wasn't happy, and for a second Laura thought he was going to lose his temper. She'd never given him reason to lose it until recently, having basically gone along with everything he wanted, and she'd been surprised by how little he enjoyed being resisted. Now he was looking at her as if deciding whether to blow his top or keep his powder dry for another day. She got ready to stand her ground, but Nick shook his head and got to his feet.

"I don't, actually, because I thought I'd stay with you, one of my oldest friends, but it's a big city, as you pointed out." He gave

Laura a brief and neutral smile. "It's late, why don't we talk about this tomorrow?"

Laura stepped back to give him room and lowered her voice. "We've got nothing . . ."

There was the sound of a body hitting a solid object, and the front door opened in a hurry. Polly, Asher, Libby, and Anna piled through in a cavalcade of color, sound, and motion. They spotted Laura standing in her doorway and burst into spontaneous applause.

"There she is . . . Miss America . . ." Libby started singing, surprising everyone with a pleasant and tuneful baritone.

Polly hushed him. "Libby, it's after midnight. Maybe you've never woken Maggie from a sound sleep, but I have, and she didn't buy cookies for a month." She was sober as a judge, but the others were very much the worse for wear, and Anna and Libby started giggling uncontrollably.

Laura said, "It's OK, Maggie only went upstairs a minute ago." She took a breath to downshift from the argument with Nick, but her heart was still pounding unpleasantly.

Asher looked at Nick and waved. "Hi there, I'm Asher, I live here." He paused. "Temporarily, currently, but permanently, previously."

Nick struggled to make sense of that. "I'm sorry?"

Polly grinned at him. "Don't even think about it, they've had too much to drink and far too many donuts."

"And artisanal ice cream, don't forget that," added Libby, who was swaying slightly but holding on to Anna's shoulder for balance. He looked carefully at Nick. "I had lavender and rose hip ice cream."

"Did you?" asked Nick politely, edging toward the front door with his suitcase creeping along behind him. "How was it?"

Libby looked up at the ceiling and gave it some thought. "You know when you pass a laundromat on the street, and the warm air and scent of detergent reminds you of your mom wrapping you in clean towels after bath time?"

Nick had never thought of laundromats in those terms, but he was in no mood to fight a poet. "Sure," he said.

"Well, it tasted like that," concluded Libby, "and it turns out that though it's an enchanting smell, it's an incredibly horrible taste." He shuddered and made a noise like a dog with a leaf in its throat.

Anna reached up and patted his hand. "We washed it away with two nice donuts, remember?"

"I can still taste it," said Libby dolefully. "I'm going fragrance-free from now on."

Bob's door opened, and he appeared wearing boxer shorts and a T-shirt. His hair was sticking up and wet, and Laura ached suddenly at the sight of him. How was it possible to be so deeply happy to see someone after only a few weeks of knowing them? He didn't look all that happy, however; he was frowning and looked at his wrist. "It's nearly one in the morning, some of us have to get up in five hours."

"Sorry, Bob," said Laura quickly. "Nick was leaving and then everyone else arrived."

Bob looked at her and saw something in her expression that softened his "No worries, I'll probably survive." He pulled back into his room, but not before he saw Nick lean over and kiss Laura soundly on the lips.

"Get some sleep, baby," he said, moving quickly before she could snap at him. "Lovely to meet you all, see you tomorrow." He disappeared out of the door, micro-pausing to get a full look at Polly, who returned the favor.

As the front door closed, a frowning Asher turned to Laura. "Who was that?"

"Yeah," said Polly, "who was that very tall, very handsome man?" She pointed at Bob, who was still standing in his doorway. "You left the bar with this guy. Did you kidnap the other one on the way home, or did Bob have him pre-stashed in the trunk?"

Laura shook her head. "That was Nick, my ex, and he was here when we got back." She held up her hand. "No, I have no idea what he was doing here, and I'd love it if he went back to New York on the first flight tomorrow." She looked at Bob. "I'm going to sleep, it's been a long day. Sorry, Bob."

Bob smiled at her, not ready to admit he'd been standing in his room listening to the rise and fall of her conversation with Nick, replaying the kiss in the car and wondering if it was ever going to happen again.

"No worries," he said, and this time he closed his door and Laura did the same. Both of them paused and sighed deeply, but for very different reasons.

Polly headed into the kitchen with the rest of the gang in tow.

"Who wants herbal tea?" she said brightly. She enjoyed a three-second period of self-reflection, appreciating the growth it had taken to become an herbal tea drinker. It hadn't been that long ago that the kind of choices she faced at midnight weren't as benign as that.

Libby groaned. "I don't feel so good, I think I'm going to bed."

Anna patted his hand for the second time. "I'll tuck you in," she said. "We have a tournament on Sunday, I need you fully recovered by then."

"You're too good to me," he muttered as Anna led him away.

"Probably," she replied.

Left alone, Asher watched Polly reach into the cabinet for

chamomile tea and then change her mind and take mint instead. He found her so attractive, and not only for her cute, idiosyncratic appearance. She was unfiltered, a pure distillate of Polly-ness, and she gave the overwhelming impression that if you didn't like her, she could 100 percent live with that. Asher felt himself sobering up by the second and decided to coast to success on the remains of his inebriation.

"Polly, will you go out with me?" he said. "I think we'd have fun."

Polly was silent, and as the kettle clicked loudly, she went very pink. "Thanks," she said, "but no."

"No? Just . . . no?" said Asher. "No, you don't think we'd have fun, or no, you won't go out with me?"

Polly felt a cramp in her serenity. She liked Asher, she definitely found him attractive, but as she turned to face him, her voice was firm. "No, I can't go out with you." She was really pink now. "I won't."

As Asher stood there, totally confused and with the last of his buzz ebbing away completely, Polly walked out of the room and headed upstairs to bed.

She didn't even wait for tea.

THIRTY-ONE

When Bob opened his bedroom door the next morning, the first thing he saw was Laura, who had just opened hers.

They looked at each other for a second, then started grinning.

"Good morning," said Bob.

"Good morning," Laura replied. "Fancy meeting you here." She'd been listening for the sound of his door, but there was no need to mention it. She'd woken a little earlier, and when her first thought had been Bob and the kiss from the night before, she decided to take a risk and catch him on his way to work. She wanted to see . . . well, she wasn't sure what she wanted to see, but she wanted to see him, and that was as far as her plan went.

"It is a strange coincidence," he said. "I was heading out to work."

"I myself," said Laura, "was going on a run."

Bob came all the way into the hallway, and closed his door. "Well then," he said, "perhaps we can commute together?"

"Of course," she replied. "We're going in the same direction, after all."

Smiling, Bob turned and headed out of the front door, with Laura right behind him. Silently, they reached the sidewalk and the truck. Bob turned. "Well," he said, "thanks for, um . . . foot-pooling?"

She laughed. "So much better for the environment." She took a breath. "I'm sorry about Nick showing up like that."

Bob looked at her, marveling at how familiar her face had become, how touching he found the pale trace of pillow marks on her upper cheek, the hint of toothpaste on her breath. First-thing-in-the-morning Laura was very beautiful. He felt overwhelmed and shy.

"It doesn't matter," he said, then realized that sounded . . . wrong. "I mean, it was probably for the best." *No, no, that's worse.* He hurried to make himself clear. "Not that I regret kissing you, or anything . . ."

Her face fell, then grew still and cool. "We've only just met," she said, nodding, "and we live in the same house, I get it."

"No," said Bob, horrified at himself. "I meant . . ."

"It's OK," said Laura, bending to tighten her shoe and cover her embarrassment. "I totally understand." She straightened. "Let's face it, donuts and alcohol are a dangerous combination. Have a good day at work."

Then she turned and ran away, and it was all Bob could do to not run after her.

For the first quarter of a mile, Laura didn't even feel her feet hit the sidewalk, she was so mortified. She heard the truck pull away behind her and looked resolutely at the horizon. She had made such a fool of herself, as if he would believe she coincidentally happened to be coming out of her room at that exact minute. He must have realized she wanted to talk to him, and did his best to free himself from her nascent stalking. She felt her eyes fill with tears, but she blinked them away and kept running, not slowing down until she was sure she had herself under control.

Even though she was calmer, she was still upset when she walked into her room, and almost without thinking she picked up her phone and called home.

Her grandmother answered, which was a surprise.

"Where's Mom?" asked Laura.

"Good morning to you, too," replied her grandmother. "How lovely to hear from you, how kind of you to remember our existence."

Laura frowned. "I'm sorry, Grandma. Nick showed up here last night and apparently it was Mom's idea."

There was a pause.

"Hold on." Her grandmother clearly held the phone against her chest, because the following conversation was muffled:

Her grandmother's voice, short, sharp syllables, ending in a rising tone of incredulity.

Her mother's voice, defensive syllables, tone moving very quickly from *I don't see a problem here* to *I refuse to see a problem here*.

Her grandmother's voice, one long string of sound that apparently rehashed every recent slight perceived between them, because at the end of it suddenly the sound got clearer and her mother's voice appeared on the phone.

"Laura?"

"Mom."

"It was Nick's idea to visit, I just thought it was a good one."

"Why?" Somehow the fact that her grandmother had been angry on her behalf had cheered Laura up a bit, and although she was still ticked, she felt better. It's always reassuring to have backup.

"Because I think you should come home."

"Well, I don't think so, and as I am a fully adult human being, my thoughts trump your thoughts when it comes to directing my actions." Laura was privately proud of getting this sentence out without tripping over her words, but unfortunately her mother was in unyielding mode, which was her default setting.

"You're not doing very well, Nick says."

Laura paused. "You already spoke to Nick?"

"He texted me last night."

Laura closed her eyes, suddenly exhausted. The feeling in her chest when Bob had basically backtracked the kiss welled up again, and she fought down tears. She had started this call willing to fight, but now all she wanted to do was stop talking.

"Mom, I have to go. Please stop interfering in my life, or I won't invite you to be part of it anymore."

Her mother was still speaking as she disconnected the call. Laura walked over to the window and gazed out at the garden. Daisy was sniffing around the lawn, with Oliver hiding nearby, clearly debating whether a pounce was worth the effort.

Laura reopened her phone, scrolled to her mother's number, and blocked it. Then she scrolled to her clock settings and set an alarm to unblock the number a few days later.

Her mother was never going to give her a break. She was just going to take one for herself.

A few minutes later, Laura went into the kitchen to grab some water and found Maggie and Asher sitting and talking quietly at the table.

Laura stopped short inside the door, but Maggie looked over and smiled.

"Asher was telling me about your triumph last night." She was still in her dressing gown, and looked relaxed and happy.

For a minute Laura wasn't sure what she was talking about, then remembered the trivia contest. Her mind had been so full of kissing Bob, then Nick showing up, and now the embarrassment of the morning, that everything else had faded away.

She shook her head. "It wasn't that triumphant, we got lucky." She pulled a glass down from the cupboard.

"Yeah, lucky you were on the team," said Asher, leaning back in his chair and reaching out to tip his coffee cup a little to see if it was empty. It was, and he looked at his mom. "Do you want more coffee?"

Maggie made a noise he obviously recognized, because he stood and took both their cups. As he came closer, he raised his eyebrows at Laura. "Would you like some?"

She was guzzling a glass of water and held up her finger for a second. Then she put down the glass and wiped her chin with her forearm. "No, thanks. I'm going to shower and catch up on some paperwork." She looked over at Maggie. "You didn't need to invite Nick to dinner, you know, he really isn't supposed to be here." She refilled her glass. "I wish he wasn't."

Maggie looked at her curiously. "But he is, and I like meeting new people." Plus, she thought to herself, I'm interested to see what happens because I'm a nosy old woman. Well, middle-aged woman, anyway.

Laura shrugged. "Fair enough. He's easy to hang out with, ask him a question and he'll never stop talking. You don't even have to listen." She was looking at Maggie as she said this, and saw an expression cross the older woman's face she couldn't place. Then she blushed as she realized Maggie thought she was being a bitch. She tried to backtrack. "No, but really, he's very interesting."

Maggie raised her eyebrows and looked at Asher, who had filled the coffee cups and was standing there holding them. He shrugged and said to Laura, "Don't overthink it, she collects people like pebbles. When she decided to turn this place into a guesthouse, the only person who was surprised was her." He went to the fridge to get half-and-half.

Laura headed to the shower, feeling awkward. Damn Nick, why did he always have to put his paws all over everything she did? He'd always loved to keep tabs on her, reporting his findings back to her mother because they'd always gotten on better than she and Laura had. Her mother exclusively exerted herself mentally, like the rest of the family, whereas Laura had endless physical energy, and needed to use it. She didn't want to sit and read for hours, or draw highly detailed plans of imaginary cities, like her older brothers; she wanted to play soccer, or tag, or soccer-with-tag-included. Laura sighed; she'd always felt like the daughter her mother never wanted, and Nick showing up had reminded her what a disappointment she was to them all. She turned on the shower and stepped into it, closing her eyes and waiting for her anger to fade away. Her anger at Nick at least; her anger at herself was going to take a lot longer than that.

Back in the kitchen, Asher put the coffee down in front of his mom and cleared his throat. As Maggie had known him all his life, she was familiar with his nonverbal communication: He was about to tell her something. She looked up at him and put on a pleasantly expectant expression.

"Thanks for the coffee," she said, to get the ball rolling.

"Mom," he said, and rubbed his nose.

Crap, it was going to be something she wouldn't like.

"I wanted to let you know . . ." He paused.

Ah . . . not only something she wouldn't like, something she would be mad about. She decided to cut the agony and hazard a guess.

"You spoke to Madeleine?"

Asher's mouth dropped open. "How did you know that?"

Maggie shrugged. "Please tell me you didn't invite her for dinner."

Silence.

Maggie threw up her hands. "Why? You were all set to move to Japan together when she was like, basically, sorry, don't love you, have fun in Tokyo."

Asher sat back down in his chair. "I do remember, Mom."

"You'd only learned Japanese in the first place because she wanted to."

"I *know*, Mom." He ran his hand through his hair, as he'd done ever since he'd been her boy, and Maggie reminded herself he wasn't that child anymore. He was an adult, and if she pushed him away, he might choose not to come back. Like Sarah.

She sighed. "Well, it was a long time ago. People change."

Asher looked relieved. "You're not mad at me?"

Maggie shook her head, amazed at her self-restraint. "No, but can I ask why you called her in the first place? Or did she call you?"

Asher blushed. "I called her. I don't know." He did know. He'd gone upstairs the night before, after Polly had turned him down, and almost without thinking picked up his phone and texted Maddie's old number. He'd half expected it wouldn't work anymore, but when he'd woken up this morning, she'd sent a response. She was *tickled* to hear from him, she said. That was the word she'd used, as if their relationship were an adorable friendship, rather than the hideous breakup and four years of silence it actually was. They'd texted back and forth for a while, obliquely ascertaining each other's romantic status, ferreting for signs of revivable interest. Finally he'd asked her if she wanted to come over for dinner.

"Your mother will shoot me on sight," she'd replied, with a laughing face emoji, followed by the gun emoji.

"Nah," he'd lied. "She's over it." (And she didn't own a gun.)

Now he looked at his mother with relief. "You promise you're going to be nice?"

Maggie levered herself up from the table and picked up her coffee. "I'll try, but if she puts one foot wrong . . ."

"You'll bite it off?"

Maggie grinned at her son. "And spit the toenails back in her face, machine gun–style."

Asher laughed. "That would almost be worth seeing."

Maggie shook her head and headed upstairs.

THIRTY-TWO

Nick showed up a little before six, bringing an excellent bottle of wine, a bouquet of flowers, and a box of mini-cupcakes from the hippest, happening-est bakery in town.

Polly was particularly charmed by the tiny cupcakes and made it clear.

"How did you even *know* about Cat's Tongue?" she asked, licking her fingertips after sampling a peanut butter and honey cupcake. "They only opened last month, the buzz has barely left the neighborhood, let alone spread to the other coast."

Nick was blasé, offering the box a second time and smiling encouragement. "The Internet, of course. When I go somewhere new, I like to do my research." He looked reproachfully at Laura. "I was hoping to take my best girl out to dinner, I made reservations at Cream of the Crop."

Polly literally clapped her hands together, which was unfortunate as she'd just taken a raspberry-studded cupcake. "You're kidding!" She whirled around to Laura. "Dude, you should one hundred percent go! It's a vegetarian paradise."

Laura smiled politely but shook her head.

"You can take me if you like," said Polly, wiping crumbs and frosting from her hands and shamelessly turning to Nick again. "I'm not vegetarian, but I'm prepared to make an exception."

Nick smiled at her, letting his eyes crinkle up the perfect amount to make it personal without making it flirtatious. "Sadly, I canceled the reservation once I realized Laura wasn't interested."

Polly frowned at Laura. "You don't like vegetarian food?"

Laura shook her head. "I've got nothing against the food." He's making me bitchy, she thought. She realized she didn't like the person she became when he was around, but genuinely wasn't sure whose fault that was.

Maggie looked over, concerned. "Nick, are you a vegetarian? I'm making steak salad."

"No"—Nick shook his head—"that sounds delicious, I'm glad I brought red." He helped himself to the deliciously salty, oily almonds that Polly had brought out for the table. He was starting to see why Laura liked Los Angeles. He carried on, "Laura always talked about going vegetarian but never did." He looked at Polly. "She doesn't like hard work, I guess."

Laura opened her mouth to defend herself, but Polly said, "Really? That hasn't been my experience of her at all."

There was a knock on the door, saving Nick from having to respond to this calm but inarguable statement, and Maggie asked Laura to go get it. She was more than happy to leave the kitchen and nearly tripped over Ollie in her haste to reach the front door. He'd been lurking in the shadows, a catnip mouse nearby, fresh teeth marks dimpling its damp surface. Even cats cut loose on Saturday night.

Outside, a rather short, nondescript girl with mousy hair was standing on the doorstep. She was wearing a simple long linen dress that Laura coveted but that would have made her look like the window display at a camping warehouse.

"I'm Madeleine," said the girl, not looking at Laura but scanning the hallway behind her. "I'm here for dinner." She shivered, despite the warmth of the early evening. "Is Asher home?"

"Of course, come on in," said Laura, remembering her manners and stepping back. "He's in the kitchen, I think, with everyone else."

The girl paused. "Is Maggie there? His mom?"

"Yes," said Laura curiously. The girl hadn't asked for her name, and now it felt weird to offer it.

The girl shivered again, although this time surely it was put on. "She hates me," she whispered.

Laura frowned. "Really?" She wasn't sure what to say to that, though what she wanted to say was *Good lord, what on earth did you do?* because Maggie was the friendliest person on the planet. "I'm sure she doesn't."

The girl looked up at her, and Laura realized her first impression had been wrong. Madeleine wasn't nondescript at all, she was simply well camouflaged. At first glance all her colors ran together, but now that Laura was looking closely she could see Madeleine's eyes were agate green, her skin was cream, and her hair was the color of an unskinned almond. To complete this all natural, earth-toned palette, God had seen fit to give her dark brown freckles and eyelashes that were so thick and black she appeared to be wearing makeup, when in fact she wasn't and probably never would. She was mousy only in the way a field mouse is mousy—delicately beautiful, finely drawn, and exquisitely trembly. She gave the impression she was easily alarmed and could possibly burst into tears if someone raised their voice. There had been a girl at Laura's high school like this, who'd thought it funny to appear terrified by Laura's size, all the better to highlight her tiny femininity to any boys nearby. Over the years Laura had gotten closer and closer to pushing her over with one hand and single-footedly stompling her into a nub, but had restrained herself. She was 100 percent ready to pick up where she'd left off, should this tiny creature also turn out to be a total pain in the butt.

Laura headed back to the kitchen with the mouse-girl in tow, and as she entered the room, she saw Asher's eyes seek out Madeleine's face immediately. Maggie wasn't looking, but when Asher said the girl's name, her back stiffened. She gave a very convincing impersonation of someone who hadn't heard a word, and if she stirred the salad dressing a little more vigorously, the difference was subtle.

Asher came over, his face bright with color, and after a brief hesitation he and Madeleine hugged. He had to stoop to embrace her, and once again Laura was reminded of tiny animals in nests held together with spiderwebs. Asher pulled away and smiled. "You look wonderful, it's so lovely to see you." He sounded . . . relieved, somehow.

Polly looked over, and Laura caught her eye. Almost instantly Polly looked away again, feigning disinterest and fooling no one.

"You too," said Madeleine shyly, and stood on tiptoe to kiss him on the cheek. "I'm glad you're home."

Then Maggie was there, holding out her hand. "Hello, Madeleine, you're looking very fit." This was ludicrous, as Madeleine resembled a consumptive on her last legs, but judging by the undertone, this was an old dig.

They shook hands, then Madeleine peeped at Maggie from under her lashes and said, "It's nice to see you. It's funny, you've gotten older but everything else looks exactly the same. Same furniture, same pictures, same spoons on the wall." She looked around and said softly, "Probably the same dust, but still . . ."

Maggie looked around and went a little red. "Yeah, maybe it's time for an update, but you know I've always enjoyed commitment."

"I remember you always said so," said Madeleine, raising her eyebrows at Asher, who was also a little pink. Maggie closed her eyes briefly and returned to her cooking, keeping her thoughts to herself.

"Laura!" It was Nick. "You're drifting away." He turned to the others. "She's an adorable girl, but a space cadet, am I right?"

"Sorry." Laura came back to the table and tried to gather what she'd missed. Unsurprisingly, Nick was leaning back in his chair, as congruous as a lizard on a hot wall. It wasn't the situation, it was simply him. He was born comfortable, and Laura had found it enormously attractive at first. They'd been kids together, but as they both crested the hill of puberty, he'd taken off in fine style and she was grateful to be dragged along. Everyone stared at him and saw her out of the corner of their eye, which was about all the attention she'd been ready for.

Polly brought her up to speed, pointedly ignoring the soft exchange of news happening between Asher and Madeleine on the other side of the kitchen. She raised her voice slightly. "We covered a lot of ground while you were playing doorman."

"Oh yeah?" said Laura, looking suspiciously at Nick.

Polly was clearly very amused. "Nick showed us photos of you guys at prom, and at high school graduation, and a very memorable shot of you dressed as a pirate."

Laura narrowed her eyes and shook her head. "You had all of those on your phone?"

Nick nodded. "I came prepared."

"Prepared to embarrass me?"

Polly interrupted. "They weren't embarrassing, they were hilarious. We're not laughing at you, we're laughing with you."

"I was laughing at you," said Nick, "but that's fair, because I was in all the pictures, too, and was therefore laughing at myself."

"You weren't in the pirate picture," Polly pointed out.

"He didn't even take that one," said Laura, and Polly was surprised to hear an accusatory tone. "He wasn't there." She paused. "Did my mom give it to you?"

Nick held up his hands in mock defeat. "Guilty as charged, madam. It's one of my favorites and she was nice enough to send it to me." He grinned at Laura. "Don't get mad, sweet cheeks, you look amazing in it." He held up his glass for a refill.

"You're a very tall pirate," said Polly, nodding. "It's pretty impressive."

"She was the tallest girl in school," said Nick, "from seventh grade onward."

"Can we change the subject?" said Laura, mortified. She could feel a painful tightness in her chest she thought she'd left behind in New York, but here it was, making its Los Angeles debut. Step right up, folks, and see the giant embarrassed lady.

The front door opened and closed, and Libby and Anna walked in.

"Ooh," said Anna, seeing the small crowd. "A party! How exciting. What are we celebrating?"

"Me," said Nick shamelessly. He stood up and extended his hand, applying his one-hundred-watt smile. "We didn't get properly introduced last night. I'm Nick, I'm Laura's fiancé, newly arrived in the beautiful City of Angels." He smiled at Anna, who dimpled. "I see the tourism board wasn't kidding."

Libby frowned and looked at Anna, who wasn't looking at him at all.

"Hi," she said, blushing slightly at the compliment. Inwardly, Laura rolled her eyes. Yes, Nick was tall and handsome and charming and smart and funny, but he was also a massive pain in the ass, and it drove her up the wall that everybody fell for his bullshit and encouraged her to put up with it, too.

"Ex-fiancé," she said loudly, aware she sounded petty, but it wasn't a minor distinction. Being engaged was binary; you were or you weren't. Furthermore, Nick wasn't a vague person, he was a scientist: He was using the power of presumption to influence her behavior, and it wasn't going to work and was seriously pissing her off.

"Laura," said Maggie, "can you come and give me a hand?"

"Gladly," said Laura.

"I'm actually fine," said Maggie, lowering her voice as Laura approached. "Is Asher still talking to Madeleine?" She handed Laura a tomato and a paring knife, as cover.

Laura waited a second, then risked a glance. Asher and Madeleine were standing against a run of low cupboards, close to each other, their voices quiet.

"Yes," she said.

Maggie sliced the steak against the grain, with firm, even strokes. "And does he look like a sick calf?"

Laura frowned. "I'll be honest, I'm not sure what that looks like."

Maggie made an impatient noise. "Does he look like he normally does? Alert? Amused? Intelligent?"

Laura looked and was surprised. "No, actually. That's weird. He looks . . . mildly unwell."

"Pink cheeked?"

Laura nodded.

Maggie made a clucking noise. "Eyebrows slightly drawn? Mouth open wide enough to insert a slice of toast?"

Laura looked at Maggie and raised her own eyebrows. "That's strangely specific, but yes, as it happens. Not a big slice."

"A regular slice."

Laura looked again. "Sure."

"What's he doing with his hands?"

Laura smothered a giggle. "They're clasped in front of him, it's actually very cute."

Maggie put down the knife and held her hands in front of her chest, as if she were a six-year-old flower girl unsteadily proceeding down the aisle. "Like that?"

Laura nodded.

"Fuck," said Maggie, picking up her knife and finishing the rest of the steak. "If I kill her accidentally, will you help me dispose of the body?"

The front door opened again and Bob walked in. He immediately looked for Laura and smiled hopefully. She hesitated, but smiled back, trying to push through her embarrassment. She turned back to Maggie. "Yes, of course. And Bob's here, he probably has a shovel."

"Excellent," said Maggie, sliding the pile of steak onto a platter. "We can hide her in his water feature."

She turned to the room. "OK, people, time to eat."

THIRTY-THREE

As Laura had anticipated, Nick dominated the conversation. A portion of the audience was engrossed, and the rest were using his monopoly as cover for social intrigue and sexual tension. Madeleine had turned out to be one of those women who get better looking the more you look at them, which is powerful magic in the wrong hands, especially when combined with the kind of reticence often mistaken for depth. As time passed, the men in the room started orienting toward her like iron filings in a physics class on polarity, with about as much control. Polly was studiously ignoring Asher, because having turned him down, she didn't think it was reasonable to feel as jealous as she did, but every so often, Laura would catch her looking at him or glaring at Madeleine. Anna was increasingly cross with Libby, whose attention was drifting, and he was vexed with her for giggling at everything Nick said. Madeleine didn't have everyone's full attention, though, and it was making her increasingly cranky.

It turned out Asher and Nick both enjoyed the physics of musical instruments and had connected over a shared love of wave formation (sound, not salt water). Maggie shouldn't have been surprised, but she was. Asher had been a gifted musician as a child, but when he'd left it behind after college, she thought he'd completely dropped it. But as he and Nick discussed the principles of harmonics and resonance, talking over each other with enthusiasm, she found herself relieved. He was a grown man, but the child he'd been was still in there. She was also pleased to see he was looking slightly less whacked around the head with a fish. His color was back to normal, and he was using his hands to wield a knife and fork, packing away his dinner like he hadn't eaten in a month. Maggie wondered if he'd been too nervous about seeing Madeleine to eat. She chided herself for failing Parenting 101: Blood Sugar, Enemy and Friend, and then remembered it wasn't her job any longer. All this knowledge she'd amassed over the two decades of child-rearing, all useless now. Like throwing out high school textbooks after graduation—*won't need these anymore.*

Having disappeared into her own reverie, she wasn't paying attention when the conversation moved from musical instruments to the subject of Laura Costello.

Strangely enough, Madeleine started it.

She looked at Laura, decided she needed to evaluate this other person living in the house with Asher, and asked, "So, Laura, what is it you do for a living? Asher says you're new in town?"

Laura, who had been peacefully letting the sounds of conversation wash over her while she contemplated the hand and wrist involvement in spoon use, looked up and hastily swallowed.

"Um, I'm going to grad school to study physical therapy. And yes, I've been here around a month. It's very nice."

Madeleine deployed a very useful muscle called the mentalis to pout a little. "Is that like a massage therapist?"

"No," said Polly, leaping in while Laura was mentally counting to ten before answering. (The conflation of physical therapy and massage therapy was a bugbear for both sides of the confusion, and Laura was tired of clarifying.) "Physical therapists help people recover from accidents and injuries."

"But you do do massage?" Madeleine said to Laura, ignoring Polly.

Laura nodded and opened her mouth, but Polly had her back up and was taking this one for the team.

"Sure, but she does a lot more than that. She helps people learn to walk again, things like that. *Useful* things."

"What do you do, Madeleine?" asked Libby, wading into undercurrents he was totally oblivious to.

"I'm an interior designer," said Madeleine, at which Polly made a snorting noise she quickly turned into a cough.

Madeleine had already identified Polly as her only competition for Asher's affections, even though she wasn't sure she was interested in his affections. She'd grown bored of the conversation about musical instruments and was ready to take back control of the evening. Despite the fact that she looked like a character from Beatrix Potter, Madeleine was . . . well, there's no other way to say it: an asshole. She'd had parents who were proud of her prettiness and very little else, and the fact that she'd always gotten what she wanted as long as she stayed quiet and smiled long enough made her resentful and sour. She didn't like other women, because they were friendly at first and then less so, whereas men were oblivious at first and then very obliging.

"Asher tells me you work in a shop, Polly." She made "shop" sound like "brothel."

Polly nodded. "A bookstore, yes. Have you read any good books?" She didn't add the usual "lately," but left it there.

Madeleine narrowed her eyes, and responded, "Yes, of course. Asher also tells me you're an actress."

Polly nodded.

"Have you been in anything I might have seen?"

Polly shrugged. "I don't know, I don't do reality TV."

Bob looked across the table at Laura, who was looking back at him with a mounting sense of panic. There was going to be a scene, she could feel it. He gave her one of his fleeting winks, and she flickered a smile. They would keep their heads down and the storm would pass over them. At least they weren't talking about her any longer.

"You know," said Nick conversationally, "Laura could have been anything she wanted to be."

And we're back to me again, thought Laura. Fantastic.

Maggie looked at Laura and then at Nick. "Well, isn't she being what she wants to be?"

"So she says"—Nick shrugged—"but she has a truly first-rate mind, she had offers from Caltech, MIT, Cornell, Stanford . . ."

Bob frowned. "Where did you go to school?"

"Columbia," said Laura quietly. "My parents are professors, it was free, why would I go anywhere else?" She looked at Nick. "Nobody wants to discuss this."

"But you could have been a scientist," said Nick incredulously.

Laura sighed. "I didn't want to spend my life in a lab, Nick, you know that."

"She has so much energy," said Maggie. "She would be totally bored sitting inside all day."

"Seriously," chimed in Anna. "Have you seen how much she runs every day? Have you seen her swim?"

Nick shrugged. "She could still do all that physical stuff, but she could have contributed to the world."

"I do contribute . . ." said Laura, but they were still discussing her.

Nick was a tiny bit drunk. "Yes, but you could have done your little physiotherapy thingy at Columbia, you didn't need to move all the way to the other side of the country. Maybe you thought the standards would be lower on the West Coast?"

"I bet it's super challenging," said Anna staunchly. "Not everyone likes thinking all day."

"I think—" asserted Laura, but Madeleine interrupted her.

"Maybe she doesn't want to be like her parents." Madeleine was proud of this insight, even though she never could have applied it to herself. "She came across the country for a reason, right?" She raised her eyebrow artistically at Nick. "Maybe she came here to get away from you?" She lowered her lashes. "Although why anyone would do that, I don't know . . ."

Asher frowned. "People change their minds, maybe she felt like a change."

Laura tried again. "I wanted . . ."

"All I'm saying," said Nick, finishing his glass of wine with a flourish and pouring himself another, "is that she's wasting her brain." He held up his palms. "But that's the thing with Laura, she's impulsive first and stubborn second. She leaps into things, and then refuses to change her mind."

Bob looked across the table at Laura and could see how much she wasn't enjoying this.

"So," he said to Nick, "you were explaining the difference between . . ."

It didn't work. "Although," said Nick, "that isn't totally true. After she had her accident, she changed her mind completely."

Madeleine looked vaguely interested. "You had an accident? What happened?"

Laura opened her mouth, but Nick pointed his finger and talked over her. "One minute she was all set to go to grad school and deepen her study of whatever it was she was interested in—can't remember right this second, this is excellent wine—and then she was like, yikes, broke my leg, guess I'll be a nurse instead." He laughed around at everyone, not that anyone else was laughing. "You can only imagine what her parents thought about that!"

Laura frowned. Nick was drunk and this was deeply annoying.

"What's wrong with being a nurse?" asked Libby, puzzled. He noticed Anna was frowning at Nick now, and welcomed this development. He hadn't liked the other guy from the get-go and was more than happy to help him dig himself a deeper hole.

"Nothing," said Nick, "if that's as far as your brain will take you, but Laura's much too smart for that. She has a gift for science, she could have changed the world." He looked at Laura and had another thought. "Of course she needs to get her mental illness sorted out, no one's going to take her seriously if she keeps bursting into tears all the time, it's hard enough being a girl already." He looked owlishly at the women at the table. "Sorry, but that's the truth, whether it's fair or not, and a scared little girl isn't going to get tenure, is she?"

Several mouths opened to respond, but then a new voice chimed in.

"Hey," said Nina Hill, who was standing at the kitchen door. "I knocked but nobody heard me, and the door was unlocked . . ."

"Who's that now?" asked Madeleine, who was getting very tired of everyone talking about someone else.

"I'm Nina," said Nina, coming into the kitchen. She looked

at Maggie. "I'm sorry for walking in, I wanted to bring Laura this." She held up a T-shirt that read *Trivia Bowl Semifinals*, with a truly repulsive design of question marks in various colors. "Our team got through to the semis and I wanted to discuss our plan of attack."

There was a pause, then Nick said, "Wait, you're on a trivia team?" His tone of voice would have been the same had he been commenting on her new hobby of trafficking stolen body parts.

"Not just any team," said Nina staunchly, "the best team. My team."

"And who are you again?" Madeleine was getting overwhelmed by the number of attractive girls in the room.

"She's my boss at the bookstore," said Polly.

"Oh," said Madeleine, "another shop assistant."

Nina frowned. Luckily for Madeleine, Nick was still on a tear.

"Jesus, Laura. You could have gotten a PhD and come up with a cure for cancer or something, and instead you're playing games and becoming a personal trainer?"

"It's not—" Laura couldn't get a word in edgewise.

"I bet you come home and put on pajamas and watch sports on TV, right? I blame your grandmother, she always encouraged the basic side of you."

"Hey," said Laura, "leave my grandma out of this."

Nick was now red in the face, and everyone else had gone quiet. "I bet you sit on your ass and talk about boring things with your boring friends instead of applying yourself." He paused and took a deep breath. "I'm starting to think I dodged a bullet. I came here to offer you a second chance, hoping you would come to your senses, but apparently you left them in New York." He looked around. "This is what you've sunk to? Retail workers, gardeners, therapists . . . Psychotherapy is a pseudoscience, it might as well be astrology!" He stood up, furious. "Honestly, Laura, we could have achieved so much, but you've always settled for so little." He finished his new glass of wine and put it down on the table a little too firmly. "I thought I could bring you up a level or two, maybe let you help me with my research, but I guess not."

Laura took a deep breath. She couldn't pretend this wasn't happening anymore, she couldn't pretend it was acceptable to be talked about and over like an object, and she certainly couldn't pretend Nick hadn't insulted everyone *and* told them she was an emotional basket case. Her cheeks were flaming, her eyes were smarting, and she could hear her mental clock ticking down to an implosion. She was determined to get the words out while she could.

"Nick, stop talking and listen to me. I've found something I actually want to do, not something other people think I will be good at. I like playing sports, I like my new friends, and I like trivia. You and I may have been friends since we were kids, but you don't know me at all. You're being incredibly rude and it's time for you to leave. Please go back to New York and break the news to my parents that I really am, one hundred percent, in every way, lost to science." She pushed her chair back, worried she was about to burst into tears, ashamed of not being able to control herself. "You can also tell them I'm very happy, not that any of you really care about that." She stood up and smiled tightly at her landlady.

"Maggie, thanks for a lovely dinner. Madeleine, I'd like to say it was nice to meet you, but you're kind of a bitch. Nina, thanks for the T-shirt." She took it from Nina as she passed her. "I'll call you tomorrow."

Then she left the room, walked to her bedroom, and shut the door.

After a second of silence, both dogs got up and followed her.

THIRTY-FOUR

After taking a long, hard run the next morning, Laura spent most of Sunday curled up and hiding in her room. In the afternoon she watched the baseball game, and when she went to the bathroom she could hear it playing in Bob's room, too. She hesitated. Part of her wanted so badly to go knock on his door and watch the game as if nothing difficult had ever happened between them. No freaking out repeatedly. No kissing. No loss of tempers at ex-boyfriends. But most of her felt too ashamed to be seen by anyone, and she returned to the game alone. Back under her shell, back behind her wall, back to the privacy of her own head. Maybe it wasn't the friendliest place to be, but at least it was the most familiar.

Sometime around the seventh inning, there was a knock on her door. Laura opened it a little and saw Polly. Being Polly, she pushed past Laura into the room and came straight to the point.

"Hey there," she said, sitting on the floor with the fluidity of a child. "Last night was super entertaining for me, but I imagine it sucked for you."

Laura nodded.

Polly nodded back. "Yup, I bet you hated every second of it."
She hugged her knees and rocked back and forth a little.

Laura gave another nod. Polly was so forthright she blew right
past Laura's defenses and made them feel unnecessary. Laura didn't
really understand the mechanics of it; one minute she was completely alone and feeling like crap, the next minute Polly was there
and she was feeling better. But if you'd asked her if she'd wanted
company, she'd have said no. *Do other people find being alive easier
than this? Surely to God everyone isn't struggling this much?*

"Which was worse," asked Polly conversationally, "the part
where we were all talking about you as if you weren't there, or the
bit where your ex revealed what a shit heel he really was?"

Laura frowned at her. "Neither. The worst part was when I
lost my temper and stormed out."

Polly looked at her quizzically. "That was storming? Dude, if
you'll excuse me for sounding all Californian for a minute, you
need to work on releasing your anger, because that was the polit-
est temper tantrum I've ever seen." She put her hand to her heart.
"Honestly, after you left, we felt like crap because you'd been so
self-controlled and hadn't ripped everyone a new one for commenting on you like a character in a telenovela."

Laura looked down at her bedspread and let a tear fall onto
her computer keyboard. Quickly she blotted it with her sleeve,
but it slipped between the K and the L. L for loser.

"I'm sorry, Polly."

Her friend leaned forward and poked her very hard on the
thigh, three times. "Quit it. I don't completely understand what
Nick was so peevish about, but you'll be pleased to hear he left
shortly after you delivered your wonderful exit." She hugged herself. "Oh my god, when you called Madeleine a bitch, I thought
I might die and go to heaven. It was amazing."

Laura started to smile. "Really?"

Polly nodded. "She was deeply offended, and when Asher didn't immediately leap to her defense, she stormed off herself." She made a face. "She has no issue accessing her anger, I'll give her that."

"What else happened?" Laura felt better, but she was still worried.

Polly shrugged. "We cleaned the kitchen and had dessert."

"No one said anything about me?"

Polly hesitated for a second, and Laura realized Polly was trying to decide whether to be honest or not.

"Please tell me," Laura said.

"Before he left, Nick elaborated on your . . . problem."

Laura blushed. "The panicking thing?"

Polly nodded. "Yes, he actually risked life and limb by calling it scaredy-cat syndrome, and was listing the various freak-outs you'd had, when Bob stood up and told him he could either leave or be thrown out, and he had ten seconds to decide."

"Really?" squeaked Laura. She picked up her quilt and hugged it, feeling confused.

Polly nodded. "Really. Nick was telling us how fragile you were, how a year ago you'd ended up in the emergency room, how you couldn't be in a car, or drive anywhere, or even be on the street, really."

Laura remembered the emergency room. She'd crumpled in a doorway on Eighty-Sixth and Broadway, overcome by anxiety, and someone had called 911. The EMTs had taken her in, and a very pleasant psychiatrist had talked to her for a bit. But she'd insisted she was fine, and as the guy in the next cubicle insisted his elbows had been replaced with *exact replicas*, the busy psychiatrist let her go without much questioning.

Laura hung her head. "It's true."

"So?" said Polly, as if they were discussing pizza preferences. "You'd had a near-death experience, you'd been through a lot, and God knows we all break down from time to time." She shook herself. "Honestly, like any of us is impervious to life, or able to fight our way through it alone." She made a puffing noise, then continued, "Anyway, Bob rose up like a really good-looking but slightly terrifying knight of old England, issued his warning, and literally started rolling up his sleeves. It was beyond awesome."

Laura raised her eyebrows. "He did?"

"Yeah"—Polly looked amused—"then Maggie chimed in with *If you really cared about Laura, you'd respect her privacy and not share her private medical information with strangers.* It's funny, isn't it, how sometimes the people who've known you the longest are the ones who know you the least?"

Laura gazed at her, not sure whether to smile at the story or be horrified. "And then he left?"

"Well, yes, but not before Nina told us that one in five Americans lives with a mental illness, with the highest proportion being young women between the ages of eighteen and twenty-five. She probably would have gone into exhaustive detail because that's how she rolls, but Nick got the message that he'd lost his audience and started sputtering apologies."

Polly looked at Laura, and her eyes were clear. "And *then* he left. I will say he looked ashamed of himself. Alcohol can make people say things they regret, you may have noticed that."

"What about the whole in vino veritas idea?"

Polly sighed and lay flat on her back. "Sure, yeah, but also not. It might be veritas, but it usually isn't very reliable veritas. Alcohol can loosen your tongue so you say what you've been wanting to say, but that isn't necessarily what you *should* say, if you get me."

Laura nodded. "What did Bob say then?"

"Nothing. We all changed the subject. He, Asher, and Libby went out for a drink—I think Nina might have been right about that boy band idea—and she, Anna, Maggie, and I made fun of Madeleine for a straight hour. It was very unsupportive of us, tearing down another woman like that, but it was deeply satisfying."

Laura sighed. "I wish I was more like you. Or Nina. Or even Maggie. You're all strong and interesting and funny."

"I'm not strong," said Polly, rolling over, surprised. "I can barely lift a box of books, Nina's always complaining about my noodle arms." She propped herself on one arm and waved the other like a fusilli.

"I didn't mean it that way."

"Hmm," said Polly, unconvinced.

After a pause, Laura said gingerly, "Polly?"

"Still here," replied Polly.

"Will you take me shopping for clothes? And maybe . . . to get a haircut?"

Polly stared at her, then sat up and threw back her head to make what could only be described as a yodeling sound. "Will I? I will! It would be my pleasure, though there's nothing wrong with the way you dress, and your hair is amazing, I won't lie. How about instead of cutting it I teach you to do lots of different styles instead? Short hair requires more maintenance, and you don't seem like a high-maintenance person, if you don't mind the continued uninvited commentary on what you're like."

Laura grinned at her. "No, that's totally true, but are you sure I shouldn't cut it?" She thought of something. "We'll need to make it all thrift store, I'm not flush with cash right now."

Polly nodded. "Thrift stores are the best, and we should bring

Nina, because she knows all these thrift stores in weird places like Torrance and Whittier and Rancho Cucamonga."

"That's a real place?"

"Yup."

Laura felt enthusiastic. "And, Polly, I want to try lots of new things. I know the things I like, but there might be all kinds of other things, right?"

"Almost certainly," said Polly. "I didn't know I liked paint by numbers until Instagram showed me the way."

Laura paused. "Well, not sure about paint by numbers, but I want to try dancing, and karaoke, and stand-up comedy, and . . ." She struggled to think. "And pottery!"

Polly got to her feet. "I'm one hundred percent down for making sarcastic or supportive commentary, as needed. We can start tomorrow." She shook herself and impulsively hugged Laura. "Right now I need to go meet with some friends." She stepped back from the hug and held up her hand. "One more thing."

"Yes?" said Laura.

Polly assumed a serious expression. "I understand your position that there's nothing between you and Bob, but he was there to support you on trivia night, and last night he was ready to throw hands in your defense. That's a lot of being present for a relatively new neighbor."

Laura shrugged. "You were there on trivia night, and Maggie stood up for me last night as well. Los Angeles seems to be full of people ready to go to bat for strangers." She smiled, covering the sinking feeling she had inside for not telling Polly the truth. "You're a fine one to talk, you invited a potential serial killer to move in after knowing her for less than an hour."

Polly narrowed her eyes at Laura, then made a face. "If that's how you want to play it, we can play it that way."

"How do you mean?" asked Laura.

"Distraction, deflection, denial, you know, the three Ds of self-delusion."

Laura stared at her.

Suddenly Polly grinned. "Sorry, I spent last Thursday reshelving self-help and I guess it rubbed off." She spun around. "I'll be back later, you can dodge more questions then."

She closed Laura's door behind her and looked across the hall at Bob's. She could hear Asher and Maggie laughing in the kitchen, and shook her head as she went upstairs to grab her shoes. If Laura wasn't ready for the truth, there wasn't much Polly could do about it, and it's not like she was any model of self-awareness herself. Reaching her room, she realized the shoes she wanted were in the kitchen, and hesitated.

When she came downstairs, Laura had just come out of her room and smiled up at her.

"You changed your whole outfit," she said. "I like those shoes."

"Me too," said Polly, heading out the door.

THIRTY-FIVE

The next day, after the bookstore closed, Nina and Polly took Laura to Goodwill, the first step in the Laura Costello Fashion Upgrade. Laura was already sporting her first new hairstyle, a simple pair of fishtail braids. The demonstration side was perfect, the other was . . less perfect, but Polly said it would come with practice. Then she'd added big red ribbon bows to the bottom of the braids, which she said would provide "visual distraction." Then she'd prevented Laura from undoing the braids and even now was watching her carefully.

Threading their way through a small tent city that had sprung up around the Goodwill's perimeter, Nina and Laura had to wait for Polly to greet someone she knew, and Nina sighed.

"It doesn't matter where we go, Polly always knows someone."

"Even in a homeless encampment?"

Nina nodded and Polly rejoined them.

"Sorry," she said. "Catching up with a friend." She smiled at them and gestured to the wide doorway of the thrift store. "Shall we?"

Laura was overwhelmed by the clutter and endless rows of racks, organized by color or by purpose. Outerwear. Women's tops. Men's shoes. Children. But Nina and Polly had obviously been here more times than they could count, and waved at the women working behind the counter.

"Miss Hill," said one of them, an elderly woman wearing a feathered hat and a determined expression, "I have something for you."

"Miss Johnson," replied Nina, "how very kind." She went over to investigate, and Polly took Laura by the arm and led her away.

"It doesn't matter where we go," she said. "Nina always knows someone."

"Huh," said Laura, hiding a smile.

"So," said Polly, "I saw your Pinterest boards, I get it. You like bold colors and big statements, and certainly you have the height for it, but I think we should work up to the seventies leather coat and Pucci pattern look."

"But I love that look," protested Laura.

Polly shook her finger. "Yes, but it doesn't matter how inexpensive the clothes are, if you never wear them, they cost too much. Especially if they lurk in your closet and make you feel bad every time you look at them."

Nina rejoined them, carrying a pair of stack-heel wing tips in a shade of red commonly referred to as oxblood.

"Score!" she said happily. "Gladys is my secret source."

Polly narrowed her eyes. "Why are we not the same size? I would rock those."

Nina shook her head. "No, you're too bohemian for wing tips."

"You're wrong, I could totally pull off sexy librarian."

They started bickering back and forth, and Laura wandered off to peruse the racks. Polly was right; she loved bright colors and big patterns, but at her size they drew more attention than she was comfortable with. She daydreamed about everyone looking when she walked into a room, gasping at her wonderful outfit, amazed by this tall, gorgeous woman in six-inch heels, gazing imperiously over everyone's heads . . . but even in her dreams she wanted them to go back to ignoring her after a minute or two. She remembered very clearly a middle school dance—Nick had been there, and the youngest of her brothers—where a friend had talked her into wearing a then-fashionable black furry coat, enormously fluffy and over the top. She had felt very glamorous in it, and walking through the snow in matching boots and a woolly hat, she'd appeared invincible. Several grown women had smiled encouragement at her, and once or twice she'd felt the eyes of young men on her and wasn't sure what to do with her face. Middle school had been agony for a girl taller than many of the teachers, in a society that judges people on their package rather than their contents. She'd walked into the gym, looking around for her friends, and a gang of middle school boys had burst into laughter and pointed: *Look, it's a gorilla!* Then they'd pretended to run away from her, screaming, and everyone's laughter had followed her across the room and everywhere she went after that. Gorilla Girl became a nickname she hated, and the joke of people running away when she came around the corner got old pretty much instantaneously. It faded away in high school, only to be replaced by *you're tall enough to be a model* (not, she always noticed, *you're pretty enough to be a model*) or *you must play basketball*. Grown men assumed she was older than she was—or didn't care— and approached her all the time, commenting on her height and scanning her up and down in a way that made her feel sick with confusion.

Polly and Nina sidled up to her, clutching a selection of funky T-shirts in bright colors. Nina also had some dark vintage jeans and a pair of chunky boots.

"Right," said Polly commandingly. "We've decided on a gradual approach. We're going to start by keeping your basic shape—pants and tops—rather than putting you in ball gowns right away." She looked at Nina. "I was ready to go full princess from day one, but I was overruled."

Nina nodded, ignoring the slight. "We're going to switch out leggings for vintage jeans. Get some cooler tees. And replace running shoes with boots, at least for when you're not literally running. Then, when you're good with that, we can go further."

"Further, how?"

Nina laughed. "I don't know, let's take it one outfit at a time."

Polly added, "Besides, leggings don't make the most of your incredibly long legs and ridiculous butt."

"What's ridiculous about my butt?" Laura lowered her voice as several people swiveled to see for themselves.

"The angle of elevation," replied Polly airily. "Go, try these on, you'll see."

After they'd finished shopping, Polly disappeared to meet some friends, and Laura and Nina decided to grab a quick dinner on Larchmont. Laura completely understood why she enjoyed spending time with Polly; she was hilarious and adorable and generally a force of nature. But she was surprised by how much she was growing to like Nina, too, despite the fact they seemed to have so little in common. Nina lived in a world filled with fiction and stories and words, while Laura experienced the world by moving through it, usually at speed. It wasn't that she didn't like books or movies, it was simply that her happiest times were spent in motion. Nina liked to wear clothes with character. Laura liked to wear clothes with spandex. Yet they found each other delightful.

It didn't hurt that Nina was still reeling from Laura's sports trivia prowess, and relived their triumph several times while they waited for their pizza to be ready.

"I'm pretty sure the Caltech folks bribed someone. There's no way QuizDick could have come up with that exoplanet question himself." She took a breath and her eyes widened. "By the way, an exoplanet is a planet that orbits a star other than our sun, and the only way to see most of them is by the minuscule disruption of other stars. It's fascinating. It's as if you had to find a single fish in the ocean by studying how the other fish were making room for it." She frowned. "I *think*. I may not have understood it completely."

"Huh," said Laura. "I guess you looked it up."

Nina nodded and literally hugged herself. "The only thing better than knowing something is NOT knowing something and finding out about it." She frowned again. "By the way, your ex-boyfriend is an idiot." Nina never met a subject she couldn't change in an instant.

Laura went red. "Oh yeah, I'm really sorry about that."

Nina shook her head. "He was remarkably uninformed for a scientist."

The pizza came, and Nina busied herself separating the cut slices, blotting the excess oil with a handful of napkins, sprinkling red pepper flakes, getting fresh water, and all the other things you do once the pizza arrives. Laura was fascinated by the speed and accuracy of Nina's small, pale hands flashing like the white gloves of a magician setting up a trick. She was like a little bird, one moment still, the next a flurry of movement. Laura thought of something and leaned forward.

"Did you know your hair exactly matches the plumage of the orange fruit dove?"

Nina raised her eyebrows. "Nope, I had no idea there even *was* an orange fruit dove, not going to lie."

Laura sighed. "You'll look it up later, I expect. Anyway, scientists can be dumb as bricks about things they don't know anything about." She added, "Which is, to be fair, true of everyone." She folded a long slice of pizza and took a big bite. "Oh my god, it's almost as good as New York pizza."

Nina looked around wildly. "Shhh! The owner will one hundred percent throw you out if he thinks you're dissing his pizza." She wiped her chin. "I guess I get what you mean. Your fiancé—"

"Ex-fiancé."

"Sorry, ex-fiancé, probably knows a lot about his area of whatever . . ."

"Membrane transport systems."

Nina paused, considered whether to dig deeper, decided she wouldn't be able to understand the answer even if she could formulate a question, and moved on. "I'll take your word for it, but he definitely knows next to nothing about mental health."

Laura got redder. Nina chewed her pizza and watched her new friend.

"There's no need to be embarrassed about struggling to deal with an emotional and physical trauma." She put her elbows on the table. "In some ways it's easier to understand than, say, social anxiety, which I have."

"You do?" Laura was puzzled. "You seem so confident."

Nina shook her head. "For some reason you don't make me anxious, and anyway, I do better one-on-one than I do in a group. Plus I've been going to therapy, and I take medication, which I don't always want to do but which I decided was part of accepting, once and for all, that I'm a grown-up." She looked around for the waitress. "I want a soda, do you want one?"

Laura shook her head and said, "I always thought being an adult meant being able to handle everything yourself."

Nina nodded. "Sure."

Laura frowned. "But then . . ." She tailed off.

"You don't literally handle everything alone, though, right? You wouldn't operate on your own burst appendix or install your own linoleum."

Laura shook her head.

"Right, so why is it more grown up to handle your own emotional and mental health? There are experts for that."

Laura finished her slice of pizza, and wished there were a dog to give the crust to. "I thought being a grown-up meant not needing help with anything."

"No," said Nina, "being a grown-up is *accepting* help when you need it." She grinned. "So get a therapist, work on your shit, and when you're up to it, I'll take you to my cranky tame mechanic and we'll find you a car." She pointed a piece of pizza at Laura. "Living here is fun, but getting out of town is even better. Joshua Tree, Palm Springs, Disneyland, Carmel . . ."

Laura nodded, and thought of a good way to change the subject.

"Hey, I'm going to sign up for the LA Marathon. I don't suppose you want to start running with me?"

Nina froze. "You promised you weren't going to try and make me healthy."

"I don't think I actually promised," replied Laura.

Nina shook her head. "There is no way I'm willingly going to run anywhere, unless it's to the bookstore, because it's on fire, and I'm carrying the last two buckets of water."

Laura frowned at her. "In the world? You'd throw the last two buckets of water in the world on a burning bookstore?"

Nina ignored her. "It would have to be pretty serious for me to run, let's put it that way."

"Nina," said Laura, "if you don't start exercising now, you'll regret it when you're older."

"Exactly," said Nina. "If I run around and get sweaty *now*, I'll regret it immediately, whereas if I wait, I'll have decades of not-regretting ahead of me." She changed the subject. "What's going on with Bob? Polly says you two have crushes on each other but aren't doing anything about it."

Laura frowned. "Polly lives in a dreamworld."

"You're not answering the question, you're telling me something I already know. Polly does live in a dreamworld, but that doesn't mean she isn't right. I saw the way he looked at you on trivia night. I saw how he looked at your idiot ex on Saturday night."

Laura sighed. "We kissed, after trivia, and I thought maybe it was going to be the start of, you know . . ."

"More kissing?"

"Yes, exactly, more kissing, but then he backtracked the next day, and I don't really know what to make of any of it." She looked at Nina. "I'm feeling very confused about everything, and Bob's one of the things I'm confused about."

Nina nodded. "Sure, who doesn't prefer a sense of cast-iron certainty and control? Trouble is it's an illusion, things could go kablooey any minute."

"Kablooey?"

"Yes, you know. Tits up. Pear shaped. Awry. I expected adult life to be long stretches of mastery, occasionally interrupted by a steep learning curve of chaos and excitement, but I learned recently it's the other way around." She looked at Laura and shrugged. "But what can you do?"

Laura narrowed her eyes. "You're very philosophical."

Nina looked around for the waitress. "Nah, I'm clutching at straws, like you. I'm simply older and more resigned to it."

"To what?"

"To life."

"You're resigned to life?"

"Better than resigning *from* it. Things always basically work out, so I'm plodding along, trying not to spin my wheels pointlessly. Someone once told me that anxiety lives in the unknown future, depression lives in the unforgettable past, and peace lives in acceptance of the present moment."

There was a long silence.

"I have no response to that," said Laura, feeling more perplexed than ever.

"I didn't, either," said Nina. "Shall we get ice cream?"

THIRTY-SIX

When Nina dropped Laura back at home, it was still pretty light outside. She left her thrift store haul in her room and checked her email. Nothing from the work agency yet, which was a relief because she wasn't entirely sure how she would handle a job, and a pain because eventually she was going to need more than the money she had saved. Sighing, she wandered into the garden. Polly wasn't home yet, and there was no one on the patio. Then she heard the *thwack thwack* of a basketball, and went to see who was shooting hoops.

It was Bob, and as she came around the corner, he turned and smiled at her. Since their uncomfortable conversation, Laura had been telling herself it didn't matter, that she barely knew him anyway, and she had way too much on her plate to even think of a relationship. But when he smiled at her, all of those sensible thoughts faded away to be replaced by the very real desire to kiss him again, and take it from there as far as it would go. And then shallowly wondering if he liked her braids.

"Hey there," he said, wiping his forearm across his forehead. "I'm practicing." He laughed and bounced the ball. "Trying to make it at least mildly challenging for you."

Laura smiled, relieved that the air between them appeared to have cleared. What she didn't know was that Bob had spent much of the previous day cursing himself for being so verbally clumsy. He'd replayed their conversation to his sister Roxy, and once she'd stopped making horrified noises and straight-up laughing, she'd advised him to stick to sports, gardening, and other safe subjects.

"You're a lovely guy, Bob," she'd said, "but that poor girl walked away convinced you're not interested in her, and seeing as you *are* interested in her, your best bet is to keep it to yourself for the time being." Her voice softened. "Let your actions speak louder than words. Take your time."

Now, as Bob threw Laura the ball and she immediately lofted it into the net, he decided to take his sister's advice. He lacked the confidence to just tackle it head-on: *Hey, you know how I clumsily made it sound like I didn't even mean to kiss you in the first place, and would definitely not want to do it again, well, that was a mistake, and although this explanation is already going on a really long time, I want you to know that I would definitely want to kiss you again, you know, if you ever wanted to do that, too, not that I'm assuming that you would, obviously, because that would be, probably, not great, although if you did want that, then that would be great, of course.* He shuddered just thinking of how many different ways he could screw up a speech like that. He could barely even *think* it straight.

Fortunately, Laura needed to get something off her chest.

"Uh, Bob?"

He caught the ball, threw it, missed, and said, "Yup?"

"Polly told me what happened after I left the other night. I mean, at dinner."

He looked at her briefly, and threw and missed again. "Dammit." He stopped, and bounced the ball, looking at his feet. "You know," he began, "it isn't anyone's business . . ."

"I wanted to thank you for standing up for me," she said. "You didn't have to."

Another quick look, then back to his feet. "Your boyfriend . . ."

"Ex-boyfriend."

He smiled. "Yes, ex-boyfriend. Anyway, he didn't deserve to be thrown out, probably, but he was pissing me off."

Laura smiled, stepped closer, and stole the ball. "He didn't use to be such a pill, but being on the tenure track is going to his head."

Bob frowned. "Not entirely sure what that means, but whatever, he was being a dick and I lost my temper a bit."

"Well"—Laura turned on one heel and arced a beautiful shot off the wall and into the net, the ball dropping through without touching a string—"I used to think I never needed anyone's help, but I'm starting to realize I was wrong." She caught the ball and stepped closer to Bob, reaching up a little and kissing him on the cheek. "Thanks."

"You're welcome," he said, snatching the ball and leaping surprisingly high, dropping a fairly creditable dunk.

"Wow," said Laura. "You have been practicing."

Bob nodded, although he suspected the surprising kiss was what really put wings on his heels.

"So," he said, "did you already eat? I was thinking of ordering a pizza."

Laura laughed. "That's what I had, with Nina."

"At Village Pizza?"

Laura nodded. "Yeah, if that's the one on Larchmont. It was excellent."

Bob threw her the ball. "I'm going to go get some actually, it's better fresh. I assume you don't want any more?"

She laughed. "No."

"Ice cream?" He was grinning at her. "I know you're not the

biggest fan of driving, but maybe a pineapple upside-down cake sundae might tempt you out . . ."

For a second he thought he'd messed up again, because her face grew still. But then she shrugged.

"You know what? I've discovered pretending something isn't hard doesn't actually make it easier. I'm having a tough time being in a car right now, yes, but I'm not going to give up driving forever, am I?"

Bob shrugged. "Uh . . . doubtful? This being the twenty-first century."

"Right." Laura sounded determined. "So yes, I will come with you, and yes, I will have some ice cream." She hesitated. "Although I did also have some of that with Nina, too." She took a deep breath. "But I need to keep up my strength."

Bob burst out laughing. "Wow, you sound like you're going to war."

Laura was reminded of Polly's description of Bob rolling up his sleeves, like a knight of old England.

"It feels a bit like that, but you've already seen me freak out twice, so it's not like you could think less of me."

Bob had started walking back into the house, but at this he turned. "Why would I think less of you for freaking out? Everyone's scared of something." He looked around for somewhere to put the basketball, and his hair fell over his face.

Laura shook her head, wishing she were close enough to push it away. "Not in my house. In my house no one admitted to being scared of anything."

"Well, if I can sort of quote one of my friends, pretending something isn't scary doesn't make it any less so." He turned back to the house, and Laura followed him. "I don't like rats very much, and I come across a lot of them at work. They nest in ivy, you know, and other plants like that, and every time one of them bolts out, I squeal like a four-year-old girl." He laughed ruefully. "Literally, I sound like one of my little nieces, except that they probably wouldn't run away like a flamingo, trying to keep their feet off the ground." He did a quick impersonation of himself, high-stepping, squealing, and running, making Laura laugh. He grinned at her. "By the way, I like your braids. Very cute."

"Thanks," she said, blushing. As they approached his truck, though, she felt herself slowing.

He turned and looked at her. "I can bring you some . . ." he said, but she shook her head.

"Listen," she said. "The panic comes and goes. I drove with Lili the other day and it was kind of OK. I can do this."

"I know," he said, opening the truck door.

"Or at least," she said, opening hers, "I can try."

They got in and Bob started the truck. He turned to her and smiled. "Patrick Ewing or Carmelo Anthony?"

Laura stared at him. "Why are you even asking that question? Sure, Carmelo Anthony was great, no question, but Patrick Ewing was a god."

"OK, but neither of them approach LeBron, let's be clear."

It turned out that arguing about basketball was almost as effective an antianxiety treatment as alcohol and donuts, and the debate carried them all the way through the drive, the pizza, and the ice cream.

As they sat on a bench outside the ice cream place a little while later, Bob turned to Laura and said, "Have you actually driven since the accident?"

"You mean behind the wheel?" She shook her head. "I used

to like driving, even though as a Manhattanite I didn't do it very often. It's a bummer. I mean, the whole thing is far more than a bummer, but I dream of driving sometimes, not nightmares."

They ate their ice cream in silence for a while, then she took a deep breath and said, "I'd like to try it sometime, but the traffic . . . there are so many other people I could hurt, or who could hurt me." She looked at Bob and her eyes were bright and clear. "People sometimes comment on my limp, you know, but they have no idea what a triumph it actually is. The doctors thought I was never going to walk again, and I was really scared."

He popped the last of his waffle cone in his mouth and nodded. "I would have been, too, honestly, who wouldn't be?" He wiped his hands on his jeans and stood up. "Do you trust me?"

She looked up at him and frowned. "Uh . . . yes, strangely."

"Come on then," he said, holding out his hand. "I have an idea."

THIRTY-SEVEN

I've never driven a truck before," Laura said as she stood irresolutely in the dark. Then she added, "And I've never been to Dodger Stadium, either."

The parking lot at Dodger Stadium can hold sixteen thousand cars, but that evening it was largely empty. It turned out Bob knew several members of the grounds team there, and a friend of his had met them at a side gate and let them drive in.

"You guys still here?" Bob had asked, and the guy had nodded.

"When they're not at home, we have to make the most of it, repairing the turf," he replied, and looked at his watch. "We'll be closing up at eleven. You're good for now." He'd shot Laura a friendly look and Bob a quick glance. "Have fun."

Bob nodded, then turned to Laura. "He thinks we're up to no good."

Laura giggled nervously, half wishing it were true.

They'd driven across the enormous parking lot and found a well-lit section away from the gates. Bob had spent the time explaining the difference between Bermuda grass, which is what they grew on the field here, and bluegrass, which they use in East

Coast ball fields. As always Laura found the sound of him talking calming, the familiar sense of being on firm ground. If Bob didn't want to complicate things by having a romantic relationship, then she would content herself with friendship, because there was something about his presence that made her feel safe. She was used to providing her own security while at the same time pretending she didn't need it.

Then Bob had parked and gotten out of the truck, leaving the driver's door open for Laura.

Now she stood next to the open door and worried.

"You'll be fine," said Bob, sliding into the passenger seat. "This is as easy to drive as any car, it's just higher off the ground." He leaned down and peered at Laura through the open door. "How about we start with you simply sitting behind the wheel? We won't even turn on the engine."

Laura nodded, and breathed slowly as she settled behind the wheel. She put her hands on it. Breathed some more.

"I'm fine," she said, looking at him. "I'm fine."

"Great," he said. "Do you want to swap back now?"

She raised her eyebrows. "Really?"

He nodded. "Yes. There's no rush, right?" He blushed. "We can come back every night if you like." He paused. "Unless they're playing at home, in which case the lot will be full." He perked up. "But we can go to SoFi instead, the Rams stadium." He laughed. "We can move from venue to venue as the seasons come and go."

Laura reached out and turned on the engine, feeling vibration through a steering wheel for the first time in over two years. Sense memory is powerful stuff, and as she put the truck in drive and moved forward, she was pleased to feel . . . normal.

"Or," said Bob, surprised, "you could drive right away."

Slowly, in a long curve, Laura crossed the parking lot and circled back to where she'd started. She parked, put her head down on the wheel, and wept. She was shaking, she felt light-headed, she wasn't sure *how* she'd done it, but she'd done it.

Bob sat there quietly, waiting.

Finally, Laura raised her head and looked at him.

"When the accident happened it was dark, like now, but there was snow on the sides of the highway. Not a lot. But some. I'd been snowboarding with friends . . . they stayed up at the mountain. I wanted to get back, I don't remember why. I was following a truck and rocking out to something on the radio, not going fast, not being distracted, but the truck hit its brakes and something went wrong." She looked at Bob, her eyes still glittering with tears. "I tried to avoid hitting it, but the back end was swinging around weirdly, and as I tried to pass, it swung back and basically I drove into it at the same time as it was accelerating toward me." She breathed some more. "You know how they say time sometimes stands still?"

He nodded, his eyes holding hers, his hand somehow holding hers, his heart keeping time with hers.

Laura's eyes were filled with tears, but they didn't fall. "Well, I remember the next few minutes as though they were hours. I'm super focused, right, on trying to steer around it, but it's coming toward me and I realize I'm going to hit it. There's no other option, I have no choice. I hit the brakes, but it doesn't really matter and we hit." Her voice died away as she remembered coming to, mercifully briefly, seeing the Christmas decoration spangle of the broken glass all over her, not seeing blood and thinking maybe she was OK. She'd drifted in and out of what felt like a dream but was so, so much worse than any nightmare. She couldn't understand why she couldn't see but learned later her eyes were so badly damaged by the airbags they'd swollen shut. Her body had been facing almost backward, wedged against the seat belt next to the door, her legs still the other way, trapped and twisted under the dashboard. Everything was wrong, the wrong textures, the wrong smells, the wrong sounds: faintly, the sound of sirens, the sound of brakes, the sound of voices. She smelled something like fireworks and tasted something like salt, and then suddenly her mind cleared and she was back in the truck, the lights of Dodger Stadium illuminating Bob's cheekbones and the wide eyes of his sympathy.

Laura took a deep breath.

"You can drive now. I think that's enough for one night."

Silently he nodded, and opened his door to come around and take the wheel again.

When they got home it was late, and Bob could see Laura was wiped out. He held her door open and walked slowly alongside her as they went into the house. She stepped into her bedroom and turned to him and smiled. She opened her mouth to invite him in, a decision she had reached on the drive home, but before she could say anything, he spoke.

"I'm sorry I pushed you," he said. "It's really none of my business. We're friends, I should have let you be."

"No," said Laura, biting back what she'd been about to say. "It was good, I'm glad you did. It kind of broke the ice." She sighed. "You know, Nina told me I should get a therapist and get my shit together, and she's right. I want to stay here, I like it, and if I don't move forward, I'll have to move home." She smiled slightly. "If you know what I mean."

He nodded. "I do."

Was it too late to kiss him again and see where it went?

It was. "Well, I'm across the hall if you need me." He turned away and went into his room, the faintest "good night" floating across the space between them.

"Good night," replied Laura faintly. She wasn't even sure if he'd heard her.

Fall

THIRTY-EIGHT

Sometimes you recognize an important moment, other times it passes unnoticed. The night at Dodger Stadium fell somewhere in the middle; Laura was aware of how important a step driving had been, but completely failed to notice how her feelings for Bob had changed. In her defense, she had a lot going on, but as the proverb says, there are none so blind as those who will not see. Certainly, Laura was one of only two members of the Maggie Morse household who didn't notice how close she and Bob were getting, and the other one was Oliver. Cats are notorious narcissists, bless their self-centered little socks.

Laura still found Bob deeply attractive, and would happily have admitted it, had anyone needed clarification, but he had also become someone she liked spending time with and looked forward to seeing. A friend, in fact. Several times she was tempted to ask him about that kiss . . . but she valued his friendship more and more and couldn't bring herself to risk it.

As summer wound to a close and September got underway, the Nina-Polly Plan for Laura's Enrichment (Polly suggested the name and only later revealed it was so she could refer to the whole endeavor by the acronym NiPPLE) moved into its second phase, which was new activities (indeed, Polly had suggested writing an Adventurous New Activities List, but Nina was onto her by that point).

Laura had started grad school, but only had classes during the day, which was extremely fortunate. It meant her evenings were free for Enrichment, and once a week she, Nina, and Polly would get together and try something Nina had come up with. This led to several major discoveries. The first of these shouldn't have been a surprise, which was that Polly was an excellent surfer. As Polly was a Long Beach native, it made a certain amount of sense, but the biggest surprise was how shocked Polly herself had been.

"Sure, I've surfed before," she said, having coasted onto the beach still on her feet and with both earbuds in place. "But I don't remember anything about it." She'd shrugged. "Mind you, I don't remember anything between the ages of fifteen and eighteen, so maybe I picked it up then."

Laura, on the other hand, had waded into the waves feeling smug and overconfident and had to be rescued twice by the lifeguard, who may have been a little too quick off the mark, honestly. Both times Laura had been rolling around under the waves for fewer than ten seconds, wondering if this was drowning and if she was ever going to see dry land again, when the lifeguard appeared, towing her to shore in a passable impersonation of a helpful dolphin. Not that she wasn't grateful, but his lack of faith in her ability to bob to the surface was a little embarrassing.

A second discovery was that Laura enjoyed pottery, a craft she'd never tried before. The introductory class had an inauspicious start, as the first thing that happened when the three women walked into the studio was that Polly leaned nonchalantly on a rack of drying pots and started a chain reaction of falling and crashing that resulted in a very tall, very fragile vase getting knocked off a table halfway around the room. As everyone in the studio had stopped to watch the disaster parade of momentum and gravity move its way through space and time, the vase had a moment of complete silence in which to gracefully topple to the floor and shatter into a billion jagged pieces.

Polly, being Polly, waited until the last tinkle had died away and then said, "Oops, we're here for the pot throwing class—I guess I started early," which no one found funny except for the three of them, and the teacher didn't really warm up to them until the second class. However, at that point she realized Laura was a bit of a ceramics savant and forgave them everything.

Polly never really took to it, and Nina found the whole process too "sticky," but Laura went back on her own regularly and produced a surprising number of mugs and dishes. All the animals had new matching food bowls, and she was working on a birdbath for Bob's water feature. She had also mastered the Heidi-style braid buns, which turned out to be a kick-ass look on her and kept her hair out of the clay. She also acquired a number of thin cotton men's dress shirts, which she wore for pottery class, and which for some reason drove Bob quietly insane with lust. He was much better at hiding his feelings than Laura was, but he did make an effort to be home on the evenings she went to the studio. He would look forward to the moment she walked in the door, her sleeves rolled up, thin shirt streaked with clay, hair coming loose and wild, and feel a kind of joy in her beauty that he never got tired of. He loved how willing she was to acquire new skills, how brave she was in tackling her challenges. He wished for half her courage, because maybe then he'd be able to tell her how he felt.

One day toward the end of October, Laura was in the garden lazily throwing a ball for Herbert. She was pleased to discover she could still run after the dog while wearing the boots she'd found at the thrift store recently, and the vintage jeans turned out to be as comfortable as sweatpants once you got used to them. She was just daydreaming about maybe putting the same boots under a summer dress when her phone rang and she answered it without looking, a decision she regretted as soon as she heard her mother's voice.

For once, though, her mother sounded uncertain.

"Uh, hi, Laura?"

Laura confirmed her existence, glad her mother couldn't raise her eyebrows at the *Visit LA: It's a riot!* shirt she was wearing.

"Um," said her mom, a syllable Laura wasn't sure she'd ever heard her use before, "we got your package."

Laura blushed. "Oh yeah? That came quickly."

"They're . . . lovely. Did you . . ." Again, massive hesitation. "Make them?"

Laura giggled nervously. "I did, yes."

"Oh." Her mom was silent.

Laura frowned. "It's fine if you don't like them," she said. "I just started, I'm sure I'll get better at it."

"No," said her mom. "No, I love mine. You never made me anything before."

And then, unmistakably, she sniffed.

"Mom, are you OK?" said Laura, her eyebrows disappearing into her hairline. "Is everything alright?"

"Yes," said her mom. "I was just touched that you made me a mug with 'Mom' on it, isn't that a normal response?" Her tone got noticeably sharper. "I believe it's appropriate to have maternal feelings of pride when one's offspring does something nice."

"Well, sure," said Laura. "I'm, uh, glad you like it." She added, "Did Dad like his?"

"I think so," her mom replied. "He filled it with coffee and took it with him to class."

"Wait, instead of his 'Hummingbirds Do It While Hovering' mug?"

"Yes."

"Wow," said Laura.

There was a pause. Then her mother said, "So, how's it going out there?" She coughed. "We miss you, you know."

"You do?" Laura bit her tongue, wishing she hadn't sounded so surprised.

But her mom didn't get annoyed. Honestly, if Laura had realized how effective handmade items were going to be in creating family rapprochement, she would have been knitting socks for years. "Yes," said her mom, "we do." She took an audible breath. "I'm thinking of maybe coming out to visit in early December, what do you think?"

"I think that would be great," said Laura, surprised to discover it was true.

Hanging up, Laura found herself smiling, looking forward to telling Bob about the conversation. She also wondered what her therapist would make of it. After the first night at Dodger Stadium, Laura had taken a deep breath and reached out to one of the therapists on Maggie's list. Although they'd begun by focusing on her trouble with driving, they'd quite quickly widened their scope to include other aspects of Laura's life, including her childhood. Now talking to Shannon was another highlight of her week. Shannon was the softest, gentlest person in the world, carefully listening to everything Laura said, then smilingly asking accurate, incisive questions that crowbarred years of accreted defenses. It was occasionally painful and often exhausting, but Laura felt herself lightening with every session. She and Bob had gone back to Dodger Stadium several times, and now she drove all over the parking lot without a problem.

Laura wasn't quite sure where she was going . . . but at least she felt she was getting there.

That evening Bob came to dinner looking like the cat who got the cream. He was the last one to arrive, and everyone else was already fighting over the corn bread.

"I'm going to Ithaca," he said excitedly, pointing at Laura. "You were right!" He sat down and snagged the last piece, despite a final lunge from Polly, who had a thing for corn bread.

"I was?" asked Laura, tipping her head to one side. "About what?" Ithaca rang a bell; what had that conversation been about?

"You joined the army?" guessed Polly.

"You're going to beauty school?" suggested Anna, grinning.

"You won an Oscar for Best Original Screenplay?" asked Libby.

"I'm trying to get into grad school"—he was grinning from ear to ear—"and they invited me to come out for an in-person interview and tour of the gardens." He turned to Maggie. "I really didn't think my application would go anywhere, or I would have mentioned it earlier, sorry." He looked at the piece of paper. "Not sure why I printed out the details, but I guess I was so surprised I needed to see it on paper." His face was flushed, his eyes were sparkling, and Laura felt her tummy sink. *Ah yes, that's right. Grad school.*

Maggie was smiling. "This is very exciting news. Tell us everything."

"It's thrilling," said Polly. "You should probably give me that corn bread in celebration."

Bob ignored her and handed Laura the printout. "See? I never would have done it if you hadn't encouraged me." He noticed she had her hair in the single long braid he longed to undo every time he saw it, and that she was wearing the tiny hummingbird necklace she so often did. He couldn't help noticing; she was his favorite thing to look at, and he did it as much as he could. It was painful, but he couldn't help it.

Laura smiled and read the letter. She looked up at him. "You did it yourself, I didn't help you at all." This was true. After their first conversation about it, on the day of the earthquake, it had never come up again, and Laura realized she hadn't pursued it. She'd been so wrapped up in her own concerns, she hadn't thought about his at all. Epic friendship fail. She handed the piece of paper back to him, and smiled. "You deserve it, I'm sure they'll welcome you with open arms." *I certainly would.*

Bob looked at the letter again, and a frown crossed his face. "I hope I can do it."

"Of course you can," said Laura emphatically, putting down her knife and fork. "Don't doubt yourself! You're smart, you work really hard, you have loads of experience already, probably a lot more than the other students, and you have fantastic ideas that will really make a difference! You're going to have a great time and they'd be really lucky to have you."

She looked around and realized everyone else was staring at her.

"Wow," said Polly, picking up her juice and taking a sip. "Don't hold back, say what you really think."

"Yeah," said Anna, "I wish I had a cheerleader like that. Jeez."

Maggie said nothing, just leaned down to pet Daisy and hide her smile.

Laura looked at Bob, who was blushing. "Uh, thanks," he said. "I'm not as confident about my chances as you are."

Laura was a little bit embarrassed, but wasn't about to back down. "You'll see," she said quietly. "It'll be great."

Bob shrugged. "Well, this is just an interview. I'm going to be gone for a couple of months, though. Edward hooked me up with a friend of his who's developing some new kind of soil additive, and I'm going to help her with it for a while." What he didn't say was that he'd been finding it increasingly hard to be around Laura and had leapt at the chance to get some space. He needed to work out what he wanted, who he wanted, and in fact, who he wanted to be himself. He'd thought everything was settled in his life, but then Laura showed up and made it both better and worse. "Her experimental farm is in Massachusetts, so I'll go there after the interview."

"Crap," said Polly. "Who's going to take care of the garden? Who's going to feed Pearl?"

"Not to mention Bob and Patrick," added Libby.

Bob had built his water feature, a koi pond, and Maggie had run out and bought three fish to live in it. They'd grown suspiciously fat, and Bob had accused multiple people of feeding them on the sly.

"Someone who can be trusted," said Bob firmly. "Someone with self-control."

"Not me," said Polly. "I'm not good at self-control, and they hate me."

Asher laughed. "Because you lean over the pond and scare them."

"Not intentionally," replied Polly. "I'm giving them advice."

"From your experience as a fish?"

Polly nodded. "I grew up on the beach, remember?"

"Which is exactly where fish do NOT want to be," said Asher, who'd gotten more relaxed about his feelings for Polly, despite the fact that they'd only grown deeper and stronger the longer he knew her. He wasn't sure why she wouldn't go out with him, but he was hoping she'd eventually change her mind. She woke something in him, something lighthearted he thought he'd lost forever. Something silly.

Polly shrugged and finished her dinner, pushing back her chair. "Thanks for dinner, Maggie. Congratulations, Bob, I guess this means I get my dog back?" She stood up. "I'm going out, see you guys later." She was dressed, unusually for her, in sweatpants and a T-shirt with a pigeon on it. Her hair was caught at the nape of her neck in a loose bun, and the whole effect was relaxed but incredibly pretty.

"Date?" asked Asher, completely failing to sound casual.

"Friends," said Polly.

"You have a lot of friends," he said.

"True story," she replied, leaving the room.

There was a pause as Asher gazed after her.

Laura cleared her throat. "Ash, why don't you tell Polly you like her?"

He looked around at the table. "I did, kind of," he said. "I asked her out over the summer and she said no."

"Ask her again," said Bob. "If she says no again, you'll know, and you can start getting over it." I'm familiar with the process, he thought to himself, and you might as well begin immediately.

"Plus, she might say yes this time," said Laura.

Maggie cleared her throat. "Yes, it's a good idea to tell someone when you're interested in them, rather than pretending you're only friends."

"Or roommates," added Anna.

"Especially," added Libby, "when everyone else can see how you feel and it's driving them all a little crazy that you're not acting on it."

Then all of them looked at Bob and Laura, who were completely oblivious and still nodding at Asher.

Even he raised his eyebrows at them, but then he smacked the table and got to his feet.

"I'll do it," he said, and left the room.

Laura was excited and looked around the table. Everyone was staring at her.

"What?" she said.

Polly was halfway down the driveway when Asher caught up with her.

"Wait," he said. "I need to talk to you."

Polly turned and smiled at him. She loved his face, the way it moved all the time, changing constantly in reaction to the things she said and did. It made saying and doing things so much more amusing.

"Polly," he said, in a rush, worried he wouldn't get it out otherwise, "are you seeing someone?"

She frowned, and shook her head. "No, I'm hanging out with friends." She looked at her phone. "I have to go . . ."

But Asher had a head of steam up.

"Because here's the thing, Polly. I had that whole thing with whatsername . . ."

"Madeleine?" said Polly, raising her eyebrow. "The one who broke your heart and destroyed your confidence? The one you hid from for several years in another country? The one your mother would like to run out of town?"

"Yes, that one," said Asher impatiently, "but this isn't about her, it's about you."

"You were the one who brought her up."

Asher felt himself losing the thread. "I know, but you don't make me feel like she did."

Polly frowned. "I don't make you feel like hiding in a foreign country? Uh . . . thanks?"

"No," he said. "Why do you always do this?"

"Do what?"

"Confuse me."

She shrugged. "I don't know, I seem to do it a lot, though."

Asher reached out and took her hands in his. "Polly, you're incredibly attractive."

"True," said Polly.

"But that's not what I love about you. I love that when I'm with you—assuming you're not driving me insane with confusion—I feel happy."

Polly stared at him.

He frowned; he wasn't getting his point across. "Like 'last day of middle school, favorite song on the radio with the sun shining and the windows open' kind of happy, like anything could happen and I would be fine with it." He dropped her hands and ran his hands through his hair in a familiar way. "Which is another thing about you. I never have any idea what you're going to say, you're like a different person every day but at the same time you're always yourself."

There was a silence as Polly digested this. It was a lot to digest.

He wasn't done. "And that's why I want to go out with you. I want to go everywhere with you and see what happens." He looked at her for a long time. "I know you said no before, but I really needed to ask you again."

Polly looked away, clearly trying to make a decision. "Look, your mother is one of my favorite people, so I'm going to take a chance that the apple is at least in the same orchard as the tree."

Asher nodded.

She took a deep breath. "The answer is still no."

Asher stared at her. "It is?"

"Yes, but I'm going to tell you why. I can't go out with you because I'm an alcoholic in my first year of sobriety, and you're not supposed to date anyone until you've got at least a year." She shrugged. "It's not a rule or anything, it's a strong recommendation."

There was a long silence. Asher's mouth dropped open a little. "But . . . you don't drink."

Polly stared at him for a full thirty seconds.

"Oh," he said eventually. "You *used* to."

She nodded slowly. "Yes. I drank all the time, I drank too much, and I couldn't stop on my own. Now I've got nearly ten months of sobriety and things are so much better I cannot even tell you, but that's because I've been taking all the suggestions I've been given by my friends in the program, and my sponsor, and I'm not going to buck the trend by going out with you even though I really want to."

It was Asher's turn to stare. "You do want to?"

She nodded. "I do, yes, but here's the thing." She sighed. "I'm happy that you like me, right now, but I have to tell you the truth. I don't even know who I am. I started drinking when I was pretty young, and doing everything I used to do drunk, while sober, is a surprising challenge. I haven't gone dancing—what if I can't dance? I haven't gone bowling—what if I can't bowl?" She looked at him, and Asher was surprised to see the beginnings of tears in her eyes. "I was lots of fun, everyone used to say so, and what if I'm no fun anymore? What if I'm not the same Polly everybody used to love?"

"Well," said Asher, "I don't know the other Polly, so I don't have anything to compare it to, but the Polly I know is hilarious and wonderful and about fifteen percent terrifying, so I'm not sure I could have handled the old Polly."

"Oh," said Polly. There was a long pause. "Well, if you're willing to wait, my sobriety date is January the fourteenth."

"So, dinner on the fifteenth then?" Asher pulled out his phone and put it in his calendar. "I can wait, as long as we can hang out in the meantime."

She nodded, looking worried.

"What's the matter?" he asked gently.

Suddenly she stretched up on tiptoe and kissed him thoroughly. Then she stepped back, looking much relieved.

"I needed to check the kissing part still worked," she said. "I hadn't done that sober, either."

Asher's face was very flushed, and he cleared his throat a little before speaking.

"That part seems to work very well," he said. "Thanks for checking."

Polly grinned. "You're welcome," she said. "I'm going now."

Then she turned and walked away. As Asher watched, she leapt in the air and clicked her heels together. Then she kept walking, not even turning around to see his reaction.

He smiled. Things might be weird with Polly, but they were never going to be boring.

THIRTY-NINE

Meanwhile, back inside the house, Laura and Bob—still oblivious to the rolling eyes of everyone in the kitchen—headed into Bob's room to watch a game and eat candy. It had started over the summer, and now it was a habit, and not simply because of the playoffs.

It was strange; she never invited him to do any of the activities with Nina and Polly, and he never again invited her to come gardening, or go to Denny's. But they shared their lives with each other. He'd offered to drive her to school every day, back when the fall semester had started. Laura was making a lot of progress in therapy, but still wasn't quite ready to face Los Angeles traffic. They'd discuss the previous night's game on the commute each morning, and Laura would catch the bus home. Her workload was pretty heavy and she'd gotten a teaching assistant job in the biology faculty, so she didn't have much free time. But what free time she had she spent with him, or with Nina and Polly.

She'd never known anyone like him, someone so accepting and calm. He didn't demand much of her; she didn't ask much of him. They . . . hung out. They watched the game, whatever game was on, they shot the breeze about this and that, and they slowly discovered they viewed the world in much the same way. Now, as she contemplated his leaving, she realized she looked forward to spending time with him more than any other aspect of her life and was going to be brokenhearted to lose it.

As they settled down on his sofa and popped a couple of beers, Bob looked over at Laura and said, "Did you bring . . . ?"

She nodded, reaching into her hoodie pocket and pulling out a bag of peanut M&M's. She tore it open and tipped some into her hand. Bob leaned over and picked out a green and ate it, then handed her a few browns.

"How was today?"

Laura rolled her eyes. "I spoke to my mother, or at least I think it was my mother, it might have been an alien pod person." She smiled and reached for the blanket she often snuggled under while they watched. She threw a fold of it over his legs, too, and wished she was brave enough to snuggle closer. "She was remarkably pleasant and didn't criticize any of my choices."

"That is confusing," he said, reaching for more M&M's. "Did you eat all the greens?"

"No," she said, tipping out the bag onto his wide palm. She loved his hands, they were strong and practical, and she watched happily as he moved the candies with his finger, sorting and dividing and sharing. He pushed the remaining browns toward her, and she took them.

"Laura," said Bob, settling back and throwing M&M's into his mouth more or less accurately. "Do you think there are fewer greens than there used to be?" He twitched the blanket to a better position, wishing he was brave enough to snuggle closer.

"No," she replied, realizing she was never going to be able to eat M&M's again without wanting to keep the greens for him. Or watch baseball games, or shoot hoops, or talk about flowers, or drive to school, or be on the bus, or . . . any of it. His friendship had become the most important relationship in her life, and now she realized it was so much more than friendship to her and she was never going to get up the courage to tell him so. She struggled to find the right words, to not fear another rejection, to be certain of his interest in her.

"So," he said, smiling, "when do you think your mother was taken by the aliens, and how come they gave her back?"

He watched the corners of her mouth turn up, and wondered if he would ever get tired of seeing her smile. And if he'd ever have the nerve to tell her how he felt.

A few days later Laura decided to talk to Polly and Nina about her revelation. They both simply stared at her.

"Sorry," said Polly. "You're telling us you've realized you fancy Bob?"

They were sitting on the floor in Nina's apartment, and Nina was sorting books. She'd sorted her books twenty-nine times, each time slightly differently. This time she was sorting by both author *and* historical chronology, which meant she had to look things up on the Internet. She was as happy as a toddler with a stir stick. Now she pulled her laptop closer. "Sorry, Laura," she said. "This is not news to anyone."

"I will say," said Polly, who was risking unemployment by occasionally—and very successfully—moving a book from one pile to another without Nina noticing, "that you may have missed the boat." She shrugged and turned her mouth down. "Sorry, but I have to be honest, it's my code. At first he was definitely interested in you, but lately he seems more . . ."

"Platonic," said Laura sadly.

Polly nodded. "I'm sure we can find you someone else to play with," she said. "Bob's very good looking but he's not exactly exciting."

"How do you mean?" said Laura a little defensively.

"Well, you know," said Polly. "He's so straight he doesn't need a ruler."

"Worst insult ever, Pol," said Nina, frowning at a stack she thought she'd already finished. "Sorry, but I have to be honest, it's my code."

"Fair enough," said Polly, "but you have to admit, he doesn't do much. He works, he watches football or whatever, he talks about work or football or whatever, and presumably he thinks about work and football or whatever." She shook herself. "I like a guy with a bit more fire."

Laura shook her head. "There's more to him than that, he's just not flashy. He's straightforward. We talk about all kinds of things, about the news, about what we both want to do in the future, about things we've done already, places we've been. He makes me feel . . . more than enough."

Nina looked at her. "Continue," she said.

Laura sighed. "I can't explain it. He doesn't interrupt me, because he knows when I'm done talking. He doesn't expect me to know everything but he doesn't assume I don't. If we're watching a movie, he'll make the comment I was going to make, or he'll look at me and I'll know what he means. He hands me a blanket thirty seconds after I feel cold, he wants a cup of tea at the same time, we're happy to be . . . hanging out."

Polly made a horrified face but Nina laughed. "Oh shit," she said. "You don't fancy Bob, you're falling in love with Bob."

"No," said Laura, "definitely not."

"This is serious," said Polly. "Nina's right. Although"—she

held up her hand—"maybe you're simply becoming good friends? Do you imagine him naked?"

Laura blushed.

"Do you want to kiss him?" Polly asked these questions as if completing a government form: *Do you have anything to declare?*

Laura nodded her head, bright red.

Polly rolled her eyes. "Yup, you're screwed. Thank goodness he's leaving for a while, we can try to shift your attention to someone else."

Nina took issue with this. "What's wrong with her and Bob dating? Why shouldn't she fall in love?"

"She just arrived!" said Polly, as if stating the obvious. "She's having fun on her own, with us!" She was unhappy. "If she cuffs up like you and Tom, then who's going to play with me?"

Laura leaned over and put her hand on Polly's knee. "Pol, nothing's going to change, nothing's going to happen. He's leaving and you're right, I don't want to get cuffed up, which is a horrible, horrible phrase."

"It's what the kids are saying these days," said Polly, her color returning.

Nina was holding a book in each hand and looking confused. "I don't understand what happened here . . ." She looked from one pile to the other. "This is completely wrong, I'm going to have to start the whole eighteenth century over again." She looked up at her friends and grinned. "Yay!"

"Not to change the subject or anything," said Polly, clearly happy to change the subject, "but the children's Halloween festival at the pumpkin patch is tomorrow, and you should totally come with us."

"Why on earth would I want to do that?" asked Laura.

Polly replied, "It'll distract you from Bob. There's easy pickings, if you like divorced dads and/or hunky pumpkin farmers who come to town for the month of October and make enough money to live like kings the rest of the year."

"How does a pumpkin farmer live like a king? What would that look like?" Nina wanted to know.

"Gilded tractors?" Polly hazarded.

Laura shook her head. "I appreciate what you're trying to do, but I'm not a big Halloween person."

"Not even Reese's peanut butter pumpkins? They're the best of the shapes," said Nina. "It's the perfect ratio of chocolate to peanut butter."

Laura looked at Nina with interest. "You really do spend a lot of time thinking about things, don't you?"

"'Fraid so," said Nina cheerfully, nodding. "It's what keeps me from gnawing my own fingernails off."

"Ew," said Laura. "And have fun at the festival."

"We definitely will, and so will you," said Polly.

FORTY

Polly wasn't wrong. The Larchmont Halloween Festival took place in a small empty lot at the northern end of Larchmont Boulevard. Whatever unicorns are responsible for it do a thorough job, and there were literally dozens of small children rushing about as high as jaybirds on sugar, hallucinating in polyester Disney costumes. There were face painters, bouncy castles, disaffected tweens trying not to have fun—it was bedlam, but fantastic if you didn't have any kids and wanted an excuse to dress up.

Unsurprisingly, Polly was a huge fan of dressing up, Nina was not, and Laura was somewhere in between. This resulted in the following disparity: Polly was dressed *as* a banana, complete with a giant foam costume and shoes made of fake banana leaves; Laura was dressed as a monkey *holding* a banana, which simply meant she was wearing a giant onesie with ears and a tail she'd bought on Amazon; and Nina was *eating* a banana and making fun of the other two. However, Nina was 100 percent down for the candy and had very strong preferences that were too complicated for Laura to understand. She herself wasn't a sugar person, so generally speaking Halloween had always been a bit of a bust, plus her parents hated the amount of candy dropped on the street, making the pigeons fat and giving the squirrels ideas.

But one of the things about Larchmont, and in particular the part of it where Nina lived, was that decorating for Halloween was the subject of serious civic competition. The local legend was that decades before, a scenic engineer who worked for Paramount (which is basically in Larchmont) had completely re-created the house from *Psycho*, largely for the fun of it, and unintentionally started an arms race of cobwebs and plastic spiders. Every year things got a little nuttier, creative types in the neighborhood showed off a little more, and kids came from farther away. These days they came by the busload, and Nina's only stipulation about attending the earlier pumpkin patch festival was that they needed to be home by six so she could lock her cat inside and hide from the children.

"Hey!" said a small voice, and someone tugged at Laura's sleeve.

"Hey yourself," said Nina, leaning across to bop Clare on the nose. "How do you know Laura?"

"She came gardening," said little Clare, who was dressed as a seagull, which meant a gray baseball hat with googly eyes and a bill made from a yellow pool noodle. Her mom had clearly forgotten till the last minute. "She teaches people to fly and isn't interested in Bob."

Laura frowned, but Polly and Nina were used to Clare.

"Where's the rest of your gang?" Polly asked her.

"Behind me somewhere," said Clare, looking in her candy bag. "I can see a Reese's peanut butter pumpkin." She looked up. "They're the best of all the shapes, did you know that?" She was asking Laura, but she didn't really wait for an answer, and Laura knew better than to bother. Catching and holding the attention of an eight-year-old child on Halloween is like trying to catch a hummingbird with a piece of dental floss. It's *theoretically* possible, but not very likely.

Lili and Edward showed up with a very small baby in a carrier. The October afternoon had a breeze, and the baby wore a little cream hat with red stitching that made it look like Lili was balancing a baseball between her boobs. Which was *also* theoretically possible, but not very likely.

Edward was talking to a taller little girl, who was presumably Clare's older sister. Laura tried to remember her name, but couldn't.

"Hey, Annabel," said Nina, saving Laura from asking. "How's the reading?" Annabel was in Nina's book club at the store and was responsible for snacks, a job she took very seriously.

"Good," said Annabel. "I'm on a dragon kick."

"Strong move," said Nina. "Eragon? Seraphina?"

"Yes and yes," said Annabel. She turned to Edward. "I really don't want to do any of the stuff, can I stay with you and read?"

"Sure," he said. "Or your mom can stay with you."

"She has the baby," said Annabel, who was teetering between wanting to be a kid and wanting to be a teenager, sometimes cycling back and forth many times a day. "You could take the baby." She looked up at him hopefully. He looked at Lili, who looked at Clare.

Clare looked back at them. "Give *me* the baby, I'll keep her busy."

In the end Lili gave Edward the baby and took Clare off to get her face painted, which didn't seem to be what Annabel had had in mind, but she accepted it. The baby was asleep, anyway, despite the sonic wall of toddler meltdowns.

Laura was sitting near Annabel and unexpectedly glimpsed Bob between the crowds of kids and parents. He was talking to a tall, beautiful woman who was holding his hands and smiling at him with a great deal of affection. Who was this chick? Not that it mattered, or was any of her business.

Taking a breath and exercising restraint, Laura looked over at the baby. "How old is she?"

"Six weeks," said Edward, smiling down at the oblivious baby. "Her name is Tess. She smiled the other day." He looked at Annabel, who looked up at him. "She smiled at you, didn't she, Bel?"

Annabel looked at Laura and Nina, who was also sitting there.

"She had gas," she said, and returned to her book.

Eventually Clare and Lili reappeared, and Nina got bossy about leaving.

"You don't understand," she said to Laura. "One minute it's all adorable empty streets except for really little kids who will be going to bed shortly, and ten minutes later it's Mardi Gras without the drunken girls showing their tits."

"Is it unsafe?"

Nina looked surprised. "Oh, no! It's totally safe, it's just solid people from one side of the street to the other, which is literally the backdrop to my nightmares."

"Really?" said Laura. "My nightmares are always about my accident, or a giant multiheaded spider who wants to wrap me up and suck my juices."

Everyone stared at her.

"Dude," said Clare, melted chocolate on her chin, "that's some dark thoughts right there."

Edward and Lili were heading to a local family restaurant that had fed more plain pasta and cheese to the children of Larchmont and the surrounding areas than you could ever imagine, and invited the three friends to join them.

Lili, bouncing up and down like you do when you have a baby in a carrier, explained, "We like to pretend we're feeding the kids so they won't eat too much candy, but we're actually having a glass of wine to fortify ourselves before hitting the streets."

"I can't," said Polly regretfully. "I have three parties to go to, and I want to hit the middle one during a very particular window."

Nina also shook her head. "Can't. I need to get inside before the screaming teens arrive."

Lili looked at Laura and raised her eyebrows. But Laura was a sticker, and she was sticking with Nina tonight.

When they reached Nina's apartment, Nina was relieved to find Phil already inside, grooming his paws and sorting his candy. Her boyfriend, Tom, who was good with his hands and therefore a keeper, had put in a cat door. Phil had been delighted, and capturing and transporting things from outside to inside became an all-consuming hobby. He was currently working on a collection of leaves, and Nina rarely woke up in the morning without at least one on her pillowcase. During a dark but mercifully brief period, it was snails; one time she opened her eyes to see a small cellar glass snail not two inches from her nose and created motion from rest that would have impressed Newton. Leaves were a big improvement.

Nina looked closely at the floor. "Check carefully before you sit down. He brought in one of those giant cockroach things the other day."

Laura turned to leave.

"I'm joking," said Nina. "He's too single-minded for that. He's one hundred percent focused on killing all the bougainvillea." Three of the little red leaf-pod thingies were strewn about the floor, each punctuated by tiny pairs of teeth holes. The fight had been brutal, and years of cat experience told Laura it probably hadn't even been brief.

"Moment of silence for the fallen," said Nina lightly, picking them up. "It's a pity he's not bigger. The neighbor has a lemon tree he could raid." She looked at Phil, who paused in washing his leg, the tip of his tongue still barely visible. "He's turned out to be such a ninja." Phil had resumed his bath, and was struggling to balance on his butt. He gave up, and toppled to one side on Nina's bed. Within seconds he was asleep.

Nina sighed. "Like I said, a warrior."

She went over to her tiny kitchen and pulled a half bottle of wine from the fridge.

"I'm glad that annual experience is over," she said, fake shuddering. "I always love the *concept* of these traditional things. There are loads—a spring fair, a summer festival, this pumpkin thing, Christmas caroling—but they're better in theory than execution. I love the two weeks of pleasant anticipation, and I'm always glad I actually (a) left the house and (b) did something I said I would do, which feels virtuous." She pulled the cork, which scared the cat, and added, "Plus a sense of contributing to the common something or other, then the genuine joy of arriving at whatever it is and smelling the same smells, seeing the same things, and getting a full, fat five minutes of deep joy." She closed her eyes briefly, remembering, then snapped them open. "But then I can't wait to get home."

Laura looked at her. "You're a little bit of an overthinker, aren't you?"

Nina laughed. "What gave it away?"

"Why keep doing it then? You could always say no."

"Sure." Nina lifted up the cat briefly and sat on her bed, replacing him more or less where he had been. "But if I say yes, then I get the chance to cancel a couple of days in advance, which is one of my favorite things to do." Nina giggled. "The only thing better than canceling plans is getting a text from the other guy canceling plans, am I right?"

"No," said Laura. "I like doing things."

"I've noticed," said Nina. "It's exhausting."

"Not to me," said Laura calmly.

Nina looked at her new friend's profile and felt a rush of affection for her. As efficient as Mary Poppins, as honest as Scout Finch, as calm as Galadriel. Laura grinned back and Nina added impulsively, "Don't you think maybe you should tell Bob how you feel? You know, before he goes away?"

Laura shook her head. "What's the point? I think Polly's right, he doesn't seem interested anymore." She hesitated. "I think he might be seeing someone else, anyway."

Nina shrugged. "You don't have any actual evidence of that, but if you want to use it as an excuse not to say anything, fair enough. I've used stupider excuses for sillier things." She poured herself a glass of wine. "Besides, you should probably kiss him again, you're an actions-speak-louder-than-words kind of person."

Laura sighed. "Everyone says so, but I'm not sure what kind of person I am, to be honest."

Nina sipped her wine. "I know what kind of person you are, I've given it some thought."

Laura looked at her friend wryly. "No, really?"

"Yes, really. You're the kind of person who walks into a room and makes everyone feel better."

"Better than what?"

"Better than they were before. You're calming. Competent. Capable."

"Despite my crappy fashion sense and inability to drive a car like a normal person?"

"Well, first of all, your fashion sense is improving and wasn't crappy in the first place, and as for driving, what on earth's a normal person? What does that even look like?" said Nina. "You had a traumatic experience and you're processing it. Jeez, give yourself a break." She looked into her wineglass and fished out a tiny piece of cork she then flicked at Laura. "Anyway, I think you're very brave because you keep trying, and as a very wise person once said, 'It's hard to be brave when you're only a Very Small Animal.'"

"Who said that?" asked Laura.

"Piglet from *Winnie-the-Pooh*," said Nina, and added, "I worry, on the other hand, that I'm the kind of person who radiates my inner anxiety into the world like a wireless signal. It hasn't escaped me that whenever I join a group it isn't long before people start leaving it. I think I put people off because I talk too much about random things." She looked at Laura. "Everyone contributes something, and I guess I bring the awkward." She held up one hand and waved a small, imaginary flag.

Laura reached over and patted her friend on the leg. "Honestly, I think you're really interesting, and the fact that you talk a lot makes it easier for me not to." Nina made a face, so Laura moved on. "What does Polly bring?"

"Unpredictability."

"Maggie?"

"Acceptance."

"Tom?"

Nina looked at her. "Sparks." She grinned. "And what does Bob bring?"

Laura closed her eyes and thought about it. "Things that sound boring but aren't."

"Like?"

"Friendship. Kindness. Comfort. Easiness, if that's a word." She shrugged. "I'm not doing a good job at describing it."

Nina laughed. "You're doing a fine job, because I think the word you're looking for is 'love.'"

"No, don't be silly," said Laura.

"I'm not being silly," said Nina. "Correct me if I'm wrong, but you're saying he makes you happy to be yourself, and happier still to be yourself with him. That there's nothing wrong that can't be handled, that you're exactly where you're supposed to be."

"Well . . . yes, I guess." Laura felt tight chested. "When I leave the house every morning, I feel better knowing that at the end of the day I'll be coming back to where he is."

"Sounds like love to me."

"I think love is supposed to be more exciting than that."

"Nope," said Nina. "I think new relationships are definitely exciting, but I also think love sometimes feels like sailing into harbor." She finished her wine. "Like running into someone you've known a long, long time but never met before."

Laura gazed at Nina.

"That doesn't even make any sense."

"And yet," said Nina loftily, "you know exactly what I mean."

FORTY-ONE

Laura wasn't the kind of person who worried about crowds—being very tall has certain advantages—but when she eventually left Nina's and stepped out onto the street, she was startled to see police cars parked at the intersections, and about forty-seven thousand people between her and the distant horizon. It was fully dark now, and dozens and dozens of kids carrying glow sticks and flashlights bumbled around at knee height while their parents tried to keep their heavily disguised offspring from wandering off. It was a lot, especially as many of them were wearing *exactly the same disguise*. All four-foot Elsas look very much the same, particularly from above. Laura took a deep breath and started to move steadily through the crowd, wanting to walk home in the cool, sparkling evening. She had lots to think about.

"Laura!" said a now-familiar voice, and Laura looked down to see Clare, still in her seagull hat. She appeared to be alone.

Laura crouched down so she could hear her. "Where's your mom?"

"I don't know," said Clare, who looked green and worried. "She was right behind me and then she wasn't." Laura knew that look from years of babysitting; too much candy, sudden adrenaline spike, imminent collapse of small party.

Laura took Clare's hands and looked her in the eye. "Hey, Clare, your mom is looking for you right now and she's probably pretty close, so all we need to do is stand here and she'll find us, right?"

Clare nodded. Around them rivers and tributaries of kids and parents and bags and costumes parted and reunited, but Laura held her space for Clare and waited until the little girl had regained her composure.

"You good?" asked Laura.

"Yes." Clare nodded gratefully.

"I'm going to pick you up and put you on my shoulders, OK? Then you can see a really long way and everyone can see you. Was Edward with you?"

"No," said Clare as she stood up and raised her arms to Laura. "He took the baby home. Bob was."

Of course. Because she was wearing a monkey onesie with ears and Polly had insisted on coloring the end of her nose brown with eyeliner. Laura lifted Clare smoothly, turning the little girl and plopping her onto her shoulders. She barely weighed anything, and Laura held her knees and turned slowly around, a lighthouse in the center of a storm.

"Can you see Bob?" Laura asked, trying to sound nonchalant. "He was at your house earlier?"

"Yes," said Clare, looking around. "With my aunty Rachel."

"You said your aunty Rachel was married."

"She is," she said. And then: "There he is!" She giggled, clearly enormously relieved. "He has Annabel on *his* shoulders!" This was hilarious, obviously. Then Clare added, in the way children sometimes tell you things they simply overhear, "Aunty Rachel has an open marriage."

Laura nearly sprained her neck looking up at Clare. "I beg your pardon?"

Clare was waving at Annabel, who had spotted them and was advancing through the crowd, kicking Bob's shoulders like a medieval knight on her steed. "She said so. She was hugging Bob."

"Where was your uncle?" asked Laura quickly, seeing Bob herself through the crowd, getting closer.

"I don't know, I haven't seen him in ages. What *is* an open marriage?" Then Bob reached them and the two girls grabbed each other into a hug, which dragged him and Laura together as well. After a second of confusion they both laughed awkwardly, and Laura was glad he couldn't see her face while she processed what Clare had said.

Then, from beyond Bob's shoulder, she heard Lili's exasperated and panicky voice. "Clare! What happened? We had a plan, we had an *agreement*."

Clare nodded solemnly as Laura lowered her into her mother's arms. "I know, but the crowd tore me away."

Lili looked at her daughter. "Really?" Relief at seeing her daughter was giving way to irritation at the frequency with which this kind of thing happened.

Clare's lip wobbled. "It was dark and I kept thinking I had found you so I'd reach for your hand and you'd hold it but then you'd look down and it wasn't you it was some other mom and I said sorry and it was a bit scary." Clare hugged her mom a little tighter.

Lili hugged her back, knowing both she and Clare felt equally horrible about losing each other. Then she stood and smiled at Laura. "Thank you so much for finding her."

"Of course, it was pure luck," said Laura, happy to have helped and trying not to look at Bob, who was standing right there, still with Annabel on his shoulders. They'd spent hours and hours together but now she felt shy. *Fantastic.*

"Hi, Laura," he said, smiling. "Always in the right place at the right time."

"Hi," she said, which was a start at least. "I guess."

Lili turned to the woman standing next to her, holding a variety of Halloween costume accessories and plastic pumpkin buckets.

"This is my sister, Rachel," said Lili. "I don't think you two have met." She paused. "Rachel, this is Laura."

Laura smiled and shook the tall, beautiful woman's hand. "Hi there."

"Hi," said Rachel, with the same smile Laura had seen her smiling at Bob earlier, when she was holding his hands. *Bob used to be my aunty's boyfriend, you know.*

"Nice to meet you," said Laura.

Rachel grinned at her and then looked at Bob. "What a team you two make," she said. "Not to mention the handy lookout." She reached up to Annabel, who bent down to hug her aunty. The image of the three of them—Bob, this woman, this child—hurt Laura.

"Anyway," she said, starting to back away, "I've got to get home, so . . ." She turned to leave, narrowly avoiding squashing a ninja turtle who barely came up to her thigh.

"I'll drive you home," said Bob, lowering Annabel to the sidewalk.

"We're all heading that way," said Lili, looking tired. "We parked in Larchmont, too."

So the procession turned and made its way through the crowd, the kids chattering the whole time. Lili and Rachel kept close behind them, leaving Bob and Laura to bring up the rear. Laura was painfully aware of him next to her, as the crowd occasionally pushed them together, but she didn't say anything. He had spent the weekend with an old girlfriend, he was going away for a few months, and then he was going away to grad school; there was no way they were going to be a thing, and she should be grateful to have met and made friends with someone she liked so much.

That was going to have to be sufficient.

FORTY-TWO

The rest of the week passed uneventfully, and gradually the candy wrappers on the streets disappeared, replaced by leaves and occasional rain puddles. Laura found herself avoiding Bob, not wanting to bring up Rachel, or really anything at all. He was leaving, and that was that. The air between them thickened, and though both of them were perplexed and cranky about it, neither was convinced it wasn't all in their own head anyway.

One evening Laura came home from school quite late and found Maggie sitting in the kitchen, alone. Only the oven light was on, and at first Laura didn't see her at the table. When she flipped on the overheads, Maggie jumped.

"Oh, sorry!" said Laura. "Sorry . . ."

Maggie shook her head. "No worries. I should go to bed anyway."

Laura frowned at her. "Are you OK?"

"Sarah called Asher today," said Maggie. "She's pregnant."

"That's great," said Laura reflexively. She paused. "Right?"

Maggie nodded, pushing her wineglass back and forth on the table. "Sure. Who doesn't want to be a grandma?" Her eyes welled up suddenly, and Laura walked over and sat at the table. "If she even lets me," Maggie said.

"Why wouldn't she?" asked Laura. "I mean, I get that you guys argued last time, but it's been months, surely you can patch it up?" She was ready to listen.

Maggie looked at her, her eyes dry again. "It might not be patchable." She sighed. "Quite a few years ago now, after Sarah finished college, she came to live here for a while, a month or two while she looked for work. She started an affair with one of our neighbors. He was much older, he was married, he had kids, and I was . . . critical."

Laura stayed quiet and let Maggie talk.

"His wife was furious and devastated and so was I, as if it was happening to me. I couldn't believe a child of mine could do something so selfish, so careless. I thought I'd raised her better." Maggie's voice was bitter. "I thought, in fact, it was all about me. My husband had left me, too, though not for another woman, and Sarah had been angry about it. Angry with him for leaving, angry with me for not caring more. We bickered pretty much the whole last half of her teens. When the scandal broke, and it really did, with neighbors taking sides and not talking to me . . ." She shrugged helplessly. "I didn't handle it well."

Ruining your reputation at the tennis club . . . Laura knew what that argument had really been about.

"I tried to get her to end it with the guy, so he could maybe go back to his wife, but she pointed out not all marriages are worth saving, like mine and her father's." Maggie's face was drawn. "We said terrible things to each other and then we said nothing, for over a year." She turned up her hands. "Now it's several years later, she and Jeff are married, they're having a child, and you saw how we were . . . it's still not good."

"But she talks to Asher?"

Maggie nodded. "Sometimes. They fight, too, like you saw, but it blows over. I let her down and she won't forgive me. I'm not sure I'll forgive myself." Her wineglass was empty, and Laura got up to get the bottle from where it stood on the counter.

"You know Carl Jung?" asked Maggie unexpectedly.

Laura smiled. "Not personally."

Maggie smiled back and shook her head. "Well, Jung talked about how the heaviest burden a child can carry is the unlived lives of its parents." She shrugged. "I'm paraphrasing."

Laura raised her eyebrows and thought about that. "Deep stuff," she said.

Maggie nodded. "Yes. He wrote it in the 1920s and I didn't hear it until a few years ago, not quite sure how I missed it. I have a psychology degree, for crying out loud. But maybe it's like when you're pregnant and you see pregnant women everywhere? Maybe I read it a hundred times and it never clicked with me. Then, when I wasn't talking to my daughter, it rang inside my head seemingly all the time."

"Why?" asked Laura.

Maggie looked out into the dark garden, though she couldn't possibly see anything except the reflection of herself and Laura in the black window glass. "At first because I wondered what I had pushed on my daughter that contributed to the decisions she had made." She looked at Laura and smiled sadly. "Honestly, I wasn't a very good mother. I worried far too much about the next thing we needed to achieve, the next hoop to be jumped through. I looked at all her opportunities and thought about what I could have done with them, if I'd had the chance. Worse still, I told her. Asher was an easier child, or maybe I was a more relaxed parent, I don't know. But I had a litany of mistakes to go over in my head while the silence between us got louder and louder."

"I'm sure it wasn't as bad as you think," said Laura, trying to be encouraging.

Maggie looked away from the window. "I bugged her about her grades, I talked to her about my divorce, I bad-mouthed her father, I compared her to her brother, I said people would think less of her if she went out dressed like that, I asked her if she was worried about her acne, I said she should get a personal trainer to help with her weight, I pushed solutions for every single problem she tried to share with me, I pressured her to take more AP classes than she needed, got her tutors for everything, and made her take fencing because someone told me it would help with college applications." She shrugged. "She hated it. And that's what I remember off the top of my head, I could go on and on." Her face was calm, her eyes dry, but Laura found it hard to look at her. "Never once did I pause to ask myself if this was something that would matter in ten years. Am I making decisions that will strengthen our relationship for the next forty years, which is when most of it will happen?" She shook her head. "Not even once." She paused. "Not until it was too late." She let tears overflow and run down her cheeks unstopped. "You convince yourself you're building a safety net for your kids when in fact it's a trap they'll spend the rest of their lives trying to get free of." There was a pause, then she said, "I think I'm drunk. I'm talking bullshit."

Laura stood and took Maggie's glass over to the sink, looking at the clock and wondering if it was too late for a cup of tea. "Maggie, why don't you go to sleep now, and tomorrow go see her? Go to her, to her house. Take her a present for the baby and tell her what you told me. Don't spend any more time thinking about it, fix it."

Maggie stood up and swayed a little, putting her hand down on the table to steady herself. "Sarah once said I became a therapist to prove I was a nice person, to cover up the fact that I'm not a nice person at all. She said I talked a good game, but when it came down to it, I did nothing to support her at all." Maggie wiped her eyes with the back of her hand. "And she's right, and even though I feel differently now and I'm not the same person, she won't let me close enough to show her."

"So don't wait for her to come to you," urged Laura. "Go see her. Go take the biggest, dumbest toy you can find, and throw yourself down in apology." She hurried to add. "Not literally, don't break a bone." She hugged Maggie, and thought of something else. "You know what else? Once she has the baby, she's going to need your help, and you'll be able to take action every day to help her, and show her how much you care. Plus," she added, "she'll see how hard it is to be a mom, which might help her cut you a little slack."

Maggie smiled at her. "You're very encouraging, you know that? You make difficult things seem eminently possible."

Laura was surprised. "Really?"

Maggie nodded. "And not because you say it, but because you do it, too. I said it when we first met and I'll say it again, you're kind of a legend." She headed for the stairs but paused. "Laura?"

Laura was clearing the table, and looked up. "Yes, Maggie?"

"Thanks."

Laura shrugged and tipped her head to one side, not sure what Maggie was thanking her for. Then she finished cleaning the kitchen and went to her room.

FORTY-THREE

Because life rolls on regardless of whether you want it to or not, Laura didn't have much time to think about Bob over the next few days. Polly and Nina were very focused on an upcoming store event, and when Liz announced she was going away for the weekend with her boyfriend, Nina called Laura in a panic.

She'd obviously had a lot of coffee and should have been cut off cups and cups earlier. "The creator of SnaggleBuggle is coming to the store for a special daytime event, and it's going to be a total shit show. We need all hands on deck, but Liz is taking her hands and running for the hills. She says it's for love, but I think it's because she doesn't like the publisher of SnaggleBuggle and is objecting the only way she knows how." Nina's voice got higher. "But who's really paying for her industrial action, eh? Me! Me!"

This entire speech had meant nothing to Laura, but she was happy to pitch in, and showed up early on the day in question, as calm and mellow as Nina was frantic and stressed-out.

"We're not serving juice," said Nina. "We had the carpet cleaned last month, and they're going to be overexcited enough as it is." She was slowly looking around the bookstore, evaluating the beanbags and chairs Laura and Polly had put out. They'd pushed back all the freestanding bookcases as far as they could, but Nina was still worried there wouldn't be enough room.

She sighed and checked the time on her phone. "Well, there's nothing more we can do unless we start demolishing walls, so let's go take a quick break and drink some coffee. We'll need our wits about us."

Laura frowned. "Isn't it only a kids' book?"

Polly and Nina laughed, and Polly shook her head. "You'll see," she said. Then she turned to Nina, and added, "No more coffee for you, madam."

SnaggleBuggle had started life as a semi-joking online spoof of a very successful children's book about a beleaguered bunny. Snaggle-Buggle was every bit as uncute as the bunny had been cute, and for some reason his antihero nature amused parents looking to subvert parenting norms. He'd spawned an actual soft toy, a TV show, a stage show (*SnaggleBuggleBoogie*, try not to imagine it), and, of course, a series of picture books, chapter books, and now graphic novels. The small children of America united as one, not to ask for world peace or food for the hungry, but for access to SnaggleBuggle merch.

The news that SnaggleBuggle and his human helper, Darren, were going to be appearing at Knight's had spread like wildfire. Darren had literally created SB in half an hour while extremely high and was seizing the opportunity and riding the horse till it threw him off. He'd hired a crack social media team comprising two fifteen-year-old girls whose energy and technical dexterity could probably have brought peace to the Middle East, had their interests lain in that direction. When Nina, Polly, and Laura finally came out to open the doors, they were horrified to see approximately three hundred children pressed up against them, leaving smeary handprints and breath clouds.

"There's a *Star Trek* episode, original series," whispered Nina, "where a planet is so overpopulated that when they pull back the curtains, everyone is all pressed up against the window. That image haunts my dreams to this day and now it's come true." She added, "It's called 'The Mark of Gideon,' and it wasn't a great episode apart from that one shot, just saying."

Laura looked at the doors. True, there was a pretty solid crowd of kids out there, but it was not apocalyptic.

She said, "You have a tendency to be overdramatic, did anyone ever tell you that?"

"No," said Nina.

"Constantly," said Polly.

"Besides," said Laura, "if I were you, I'd be more worried about the fact that it's twenty to one and SnaggleBuggle himself is a no-show."

"He'll be here, he's a professional," said Nina, unlocking the bottom of the door and preparing to open it. "Stand back."

The kids flowed in like a mighty river and arranged themselves clumpily, in the fashion of children. Those who couldn't fit sat on the sidewalk. Parents gave up and stood nearby looking at their phones. SnaggleBuggle showed up at 1:04 p.m., which was about thirty seconds after Nina's blood pressure started elevating.

Lili and Clare showed up, too, which was a pleasant surprise.

"Isn't Clare a little old for this?" asked Nina, with interest.

Lili shrugged. "She was an early adopter. You know, before SnaggleBuggle sold out and licensed his image."

Indeed Clare had taken a position at the side of the store and was regarding SnaggleBuggle with some skepticism.

"I hope she's not going to rabble rouse," said Lili worriedly.

"I hope she is," said Polly, though she had to hand it to Darren, he had them all sitting silent as church mice. The social media team, both of whom were called Sophie, were livestreaming and livestreaming the livestreaming, respectively.

"Hey, Laura," said Lili quietly. "Could I possibly talk to you?"

"Sure." Laura followed Lili outside.

"What's going on with you and Bob?" asked Lili, getting right to the point.

Laura immediately felt herself going red. "Nothing. What do you mean?"

"Bob came over the other night for dinner and basically spent the whole time talking about you."

"What? He's sleeping with your sister, isn't he?" Laura gasped and put her hand up to her mouth. "I'm sorry, that popped out."

Lili was staring at her. "What?"

Laura was embarrassed, and started making babbling noises of an indeterminate nature. "Well, I mean .. not that ... it's ... I'm sure ..."

Lili was firm. "No, really, what did you say?"

Laura was bright red. "That Bob was sleeping with your sister." She saw Lili's face change and took a big step back.

Lili said, "That's totally untrue, Rachel's happily married."

"Clare told me." As she said it, Laura realized how daft it sounded.

"Clare? What did she say, exactly?" asked Lili, still a little ticked at the slight to her sister.

"She said Rachel said she had an open marriage. That she hugged Bob." She was flamingly hot and embarrassed. "At the time ..."

Lili burst out laughing, loud enough that SnaggleBuggle paused in his rendition of "Sna-gaggle Bu-google," and one of the Sophies caught it on her phone and for two hours #crazymomlaugh trended on Twitter.

"Sorry," said Lili to the store at large, then dragged Laura a little way down the street.

"Listen, Rachel and Edward and I were having dinner with Bob before Halloween. Clare and Annabel were there, of course. Richard, Rachel's husband, was in New York for work." She hesitated. "All Bob talked about then was you, too. He's been trying to give you plenty of room and space to sort yourself out and he was panicking that he'd missed his chance with you."

Laura felt warm, and Lili watched and grinned as the color mounted the other woman's face. "You feel the same way about him, don't you?"

Laura nodded. "So why did Clare . . ."

Lili shook her head impatiently. "Listen, Bob was talking about how being with you made him realize why people wanted to get married, and Rachel was talking about how she'd never wanted to get married again after her first marriage fell apart, but that meeting Richard made her *open to it again*. That was literally all she said."

Laura looked blankly at her.

"Clearly, Clare got the wrong idea, because honestly, that child only needs the slightest encouragement to go rogue," said Lili, bouncing up and down to keep the baby in the carrier quiet. She made a stern face at Laura. "The day I met you, I *warned* you not to listen to Clare, she lives in a world of her own making."

"So now what do I do?" Laura looked into the store, where SnaggleBuggle had finished singing and was getting ready for audience Q&A.

Lili smiled. "I think you better find him and tell him."

"Tell him what? He's leaving to go away for a few months and then probably he'll go away again to grad school, and I have grad school, too, and why complicate things any more than they already are?"

Lili shrugged. "Dude, you're welcome to come between yourself and your own happiness if you want to, but nothing you just mentioned is a good enough reason not to tell someone the way you feel about them. That's a dilemma you're going to have to work out for yourself." She flicked a glance over her shoulder to where Clare had her hand up and was definitely about to ask a question SnaggleBuggle wasn't going to want to hear. "All I can suggest is you not ask Clare for input."

FORTY-FOUR

When Laura got back to the house, she saw Maggie making her way up the driveway carrying a stuffed giraffe almost as large as herself. Polly had given Laura a ride to the store, but rather than wait for SnaggleBuggle to extricate himself from an argument with Clare about brand authenticity, Laura had decided to walk home.

She'd ended up essentially running, because she really, really wanted to tell Bob . . . whatever it was she was going to tell him. She could have called him, of course, or texted, but she was hoping that the time it took to find him would give her the time she needed to work out what to say. She was overwhelmed with the desire to tell him *right now*, before he went away and buried himself in soil additives, so to speak. What if he met someone else? What if his feelings simply faded as hers grew stronger and their diverging paths took them farther and farther apart forever?

"Hey," she said to Maggie as she caught up to her, panting a little.

"Hi there," said Maggie, smiling. "Do you like my giraffe? I decided to take your suggestion, and this was the biggest thing they had at the store." She paused. "I could have ordered something bigger online, but then I wouldn't have been able to feel it, and I think you should feel . . ." She stopped. "Sorry, you're politely waiting for me to finish, what's up?"

"Is Bob still here?"

"No." Maggie shook her head. "He left a while ago. He told me to say goodbye." She opened the front door and let the giraffe go first, sliding its hooves across the wooden floor. "Did you need him for something? I assume they'll have phone service on the East Coast."

"No," said Laura. "I mean, yes, but no. I wanted to say goodbye in person."

Maggie preceded her down the hallway, having parked the giraffe. "Did you ever get around to telling him you're falling in love with him?"

Laura paused. "I . . . No." She sighed. "Does everyone know about this but me?"

Maggie turned on the kettle, which Laura had come to realize was her signature move. "Well, everyone who's ever spent longer than ten minutes with the two of you. And why not? You get along super well, you like the same things, you're both doers, not sayers, if you know what I mean." She leaned against the counter and folded her arms. "You like to go out and do stuff instead of simply talking about it. That's as good a foundation for a relationship as any."

Laura stared at her. She had never thought of it like that.

The kettle clicked and Maggie smiled. "Tea? I think I have a to-go cup somewhere." She looked at her watch. "His flight doesn't leave for another couple of hours, you can probably catch him if you hurry."

"I don't have a car," said Laura. She blushed bright red. "And if I did, I probably couldn't get up the nerve to drive it anyway."

Maggie frowned. "I thought you've been driving Bob's truck with him?"

Laura got even redder. "How did you know about that?"

Maggie shrugged. "Bob told me. He was very proud of you." She smiled. "You've come a long way since you got here, Laura." She snapped her fingers. "Why don't you take the truck? He left me the keys."

"Wait, what?" Laura was confused. "Didn't he drive the truck to the airport?"

Maggie shook her head. "No, he took a Lyft and parked the truck in the driveway. By the basketball hoop." She laughed. "He was actually worried in case you got pissed that he'd blocked the hoop, which is why he left me the keys. He wanted you to be able to move it." She walked over to a ceramic chicken that lived on the counter and contained all the keys, and fished around. She held up Bob's keys, the Dodgers key fob turning in the light.

"See?" she said, and smiled.

"I can't . . ." said Laura, feeling panicked. "I don't even know how to get to the airport."

"Doesn't the truck have GPS?"

Laura shook her head. "It's too old, it has a CD player, for crying out loud."

Maggie shrugged. "Use your phone."

Laura shook her head. "I can't."

Maggie sighed. "So call him. Call him and tell him how you feel."

Laura gazed at her. Maggie was right, she could call him. Or even text him, maybe. She'd waited weeks already, holding her feelings close to her chest, but now waiting another day felt impossible, and telling him in person felt imperative. She wanted to see him, *now*, tell him, *now*, and kiss him, *immediately*.

She took a deep breath, and shook her head.

"No," she said. "I'm not so good at talking, I think I better do it in person."

"Bold choice," said Maggie, and threw her the keys.

Laura climbed into the driver's seat of the truck. It smelled of Bob, and reminded her of all the times she'd driven, and how good it felt sitting next to him when he was driving, and how good it felt sitting next to him wherever they were.

"You can one hundred percent do this," she told herself, and pulled out her phone, plugging in the address for LAX.

She started to feel dizzy and nauseated. She called Polly.

"Hey," said Polly, who was apparently answering the phone while standing in a nightclub. "What's good?"

"Not much," said Laura, trying not to hyperventilate. "I'm about to start driving to the airport to try and reach Bob before he leaves so I can tell him that I think I'm falling in love with him."

"Fair enough," said Polly, as if people said that kind of thing to her each and every day. "How can I assist?" There was a particularly raucous burst of yelling, and Polly covered the phone. Then she returned. "I would come and drive you myself, but unfortunately Darren—the SnaggleBuggle guy, do you remember?"

"Yes," said Laura, wishing Polly could stay on one topic at a time.

"Well, he decided in his infinite wisdom—and I'm not saying he was stoned, I'm just saying his wisdom may not have been *naturally* that infinite—to buy every child here an ice cream cone."

"Oh," said Laura, frowning, "I bet Nina wasn't pleased about that."

"No," said Polly. "So I can't really leave until we get all the kids down from the bookcases and Nina is able to damp cloth the surfaces."

Laura opened her mouth to ask . . . and then closed it again.

"Polly," she said, "will you stay on the phone with me while I drive, in case I get lost?"

She put the key in the ignition, and turned it. The engine came on, and she had a flash of clear, blind panic. Then she heard Polly's voice.

"Of course, I'll be all mission control or air traffic control or some other kind of control." She held the phone away from her mouth and yelled, "Hey, Nina!"

Laura put the truck in gear, closed her eyes, said a prayer, and stepped on the accelerator. She heard Nina's muffled response, then Polly said, "Laura's driving to the airport and needs support, I'm going to conference you in."

Then she disappeared for a second and came back, and two seconds later Laura heard Nina saying, *"No, you can't jump from one bookcase to . . ."* and then her voice went away again and Polly said, "I'll get her back in a minute. Where are you now?"

Laura looked left and right and pulled out. "I just left the driveway."

"Alright!" Polly laughed. "Dude, you are crushing this already."

Laura tried to smile. "I have literally driven half a block."

"Half a block more than you could six months ago," replied Polly. "It's progress, not perfection, you know."

"Good point," said Laura, waiting at the intersection of Third and August. "There's a lot of traffic."

"Yup," said Polly, and then Nina's voice was there again.

"The good thing about traffic," she said, calm despite the absolute chaos that was clearly going on in the background, "is that it means no one's going very fast."

A car shot by on Third doing at least sixty.

"Uh, I don't think that's true," said Laura, trying to slow her breathing. She thought about what her therapist had told her about focusing on her breath, about being in the now, and decided maybe she should pull over and give up on this.

"You know," she said to the phone, "maybe this was a bad idea. What if I get into an accident?"

"You won't," said Polly. "Don't quit before the miracle. You can do this, we are right there with you, aren't we, Nina?"

"Yes," said Nina, "although I am also here, and if that curly-haired little monster doesn't stop throwing bookmarks up into the ceiling fan, I am going to leave the phone call and go directly to jail, passing him on the way and dragging him with me."

Laura laughed, and the laugh took some of her anxiety away. They were right; she could do this.

A fourth voice joined the call. "Turn right on Wilton Place."

"Who's that?" said Nina.

"GPS," said Laura.

"Really?" said Nina. "I'm not sure Wilton is the right call, honestly."

"Nina," said Polly firmly, "let the GPS lady do her job." She sighed. "Don't listen to her," she said to Laura. "Nina has never met a GPS system she doesn't second guess."

"I grew up here, they didn't," said Nina.

Laura turned right on Wilton Place. The other cars seemed awfully close, but she was doing it.

"Stay on Wilton Place for two miles," said the GPS lady.

Laura kept driving, feeling the familiar wheel beneath her hands, starting to get comfortable.

"What happens after Wilton Place?" she asked Polly and Nina.

"The freeway," said Nina, adding, "Put that down please. If you get ice cream on the flaps, they won't open anymore, and then your mommy is going to have to buy the book, which, judging by your nascent facial hair, is probably a bit young for you."

Polly giggled.

Nina lowered her voice. "Why is a teenager attending a Snaggle-Buggle event, anyway? Is he being ironic?"

Polly said, "I think you're being unfair. Maybe he brought a younger sibling."

Laura was having trouble breathing. "I'm sorry . . . did you say 'freeway'?"

Nina made an affirmative noise. "I mean, I guess you could take surface streets all the way if you want to avoid the freeway."

"Would that take longer?"

"Well," said Nina with the air of someone about to embark on a very long explanation, "that entirely depends on the time of day and *which* freeway and *which* surface streets we're talking about." She took a huge breath, but Polly interrupted.

"Yes," she said, "it would take longer. Do you know what time Bob's flight even is?"

Laura slowed down to pass a truck and nearly threw up in her own lap. "Hey, guys, I don't know if I can do this, I feel really sick."

"You're already doing it," said Nina, "but if you think you're going to puke, you should definitely pull over." She paused. "We'll wait."

Laura pulled over to the side of the street and stopped the truck. She leaned her head back against the driver's seat and tried to breathe calm back into her body.

After a second or two, Polly said, "Are you still there?"

Laura said she was.

"And did you throw up on yourself?"

Laura said she hadn't.

"Score," said Polly.

Laura opened her eyes and looked at the roof of the truck. The sun was low and she felt her eyes tearing. She folded down the sun visor, and noticed a piece of paper taped to it.

She sat up a bit and looked more closely.

"Hey, guys," she said softly.

"Yes?" said Nina and Polly in unison. It had gone quiet in the store; clearly they had chased out the last of the ice cream–dripping customers.

"Do you remember I told you Bob and I went out to Denny's one time, after we went gardening?"

"Yes," snorted Polly. "The worst date ever? That one?"

"I don't know what you have against Denny's," said Nina. "I love Denny's."

Polly snorted again.

"Anyway," continued Laura, "Bob has the receipt for that dinner taped to his sun visor. And he's written my name on it."

There was a pause. Then Polly said, "Maybe he wants to remember to get your half of the check back?" There was a thump, and she said, in a hurt tone of voice, "I can't believe you threw a book at me."

Nina said, "Laura, I realize you're freaked out by driving, and that it's a lot to ask, to drive in a strange city and on the freeway, but the guy taped a Denny's receipt where he could see it several times a day, for crying out loud, so I really think you need to pull it together and get back on the road."

Laura took a deep breath. "You're right," she said, and turned the engine back on. She looked at the receipt again, and felt desperately keen to both see Bob and kiss him quite a lot.

The 10 freeway, which was the freeway Laura was about to cautiously merge onto, is the southernmost interstate highway, running from Santa Monica in the west all the way to Florida in the east. It is regarded as a fairly sporting freeway by Los Angeles natives, who enjoy its generous speed limit and tend to think of it as "indicator optional." Laura was pretty scared as she joined the heavy traffic traveling en masse at speeds of around seventy miles an hour, and once she was on it, there was no way in hell she was going to try to get off.

"Are you on the 10?" asked Nina.

"Uh-huh," said Laura, swallowing hard. Cars whizzed by and then slammed on their brakes for no reason, vehicles changed lanes like teens at the roller rink, and every so often an extremely fast car with zero muffler whatsoever would speed past, cutting in front of her so closely she could count the piercings in the driver's ears, and then nip into yet another lane, as if the point of the exercise were to cross the white dividing lines as many times as possible. Maybe it was.

Somehow, however, Laura managed to claim a spot in the slower lane and stick to it, keeping her panic under tight control while also keeping up with traffic.

"After another mile, take exit 3B onto the 405 freeway," said the GPS lady.

"Oh yeah," said Polly. "I'd forgotten you needed to get on the 405." She gave a nervous giggle and then tried to cover it with an even more nervous cough. "Sorry . . . I, uh, had a crumb."

"You won't be on it for long," said Nina reassuringly. "It's on and off, no worries."

"Follow the 405 for ten miles," said the GPS lady.

"Right," said Nina. "Ten miles, like I said, nothing at all."

Laura looked in her rearview. The traffic behind her was solid, wall to wall, lane to lane, bumper to bumper, yet somehow all traveling at speed. The traffic ahead of her was the same.

"I'm scared," she said, her voice trembling. "How am I supposed to get off this freeway and onto another?"

Nina's voice was very calm. "Laura, you're in the right-hand lane, right?"

"Yes."

"Then stay where you are and follow the signs. The lane you're in will turn into the exit and you can keep going. I don't know how freeways work in New York State, but they're pretty idiot-proof here, you can do it."

"I can't."

"You can," said Nina.

"You have to," said Polly, always the realist. "You can't vanish from the middle of the freeway, this isn't Hogsmeade."

Laura frowned. "What's Hogsmeade?"

Nina caught her breath. "We'll talk about that later, for now just stick to your lane and try not to worry."

"I'm worrying."

"Well, try not to," she replied.

Laura saw the signs for the 405 coming up and realized Nina was right. The lane she was in was going to merge automatically onto the second freeway, and all she had to do was stay the course. She could do that. She could do that for Bob.

By the time Laura was approaching the airport, she had herself essentially under control. Her body felt calm, and if her heart occasionally raced as she passed something much bigger than the truck, she could handle it.

"How do I know which terminal to go to?" she asked Polly and Nina. "I don't know which airline he was taking."

"JetBlue," said Polly. "We talked about it the other day."

There was a pause, and then Nina said, "Um, I really hate to ask this, but if it's JetBlue, are you sure he's flying out of LAX and not Burbank?"

"Burbank?" asked Laura, starting to scan the signage as she approached the airport, looking for JetBlue.

Polly's voice was small. "It's the other airport. It's closer to our house. And JetBlue flies from there to New York, too."

Laura's vision blurred for a second. "Wait, what?"

"I'm going to hang up and call Maggie," said Polly. "She might know."

Laura thought back. "She never said *which* airport, she only said 'airport.'" She spotted JetBlue's logo, and headed toward the terminal. "I have to park, please try and find out if I'm even in the right place."

"Got it," said Polly. "Hanging up."

"Wait," said Nina. "You conferenced me—"

And then both of them were gone, and Laura was alone.

FORTY-FIVE

Bob had spent nearly an hour in the security line and wasn't sure he'd moved more than six inches. He found himself thinking about Laura, and wishing he'd been able to say goodbye in person. He'd waited as long as he could, but she was helping at the bookstore, and he knew she wouldn't leave until it was finished.

That was the thing with her. She did what she said she would. You could count on her. He thought about the curve of her ear, how she tucked her hair behind it. He thought about all the little jewelry she wore, the tiny bugs and butterflies and birds she favored. He looked out of the big windows and saw birds flying low across the runway, and realized that if she were there, she would probably know what they were. Before he'd left, Maggie had encouraged him to tell Laura how he felt, but she'd also understood why he was being patient. They'd both seen how hard it was for Laura, how much effort it took to push through her anxiety and panic. Bob wanted to support her, not add to her stress. He could wait. And he would.

He looked out of the window again. LAX was an enormous airport, and on the water. Storks, herons, shorebirds of all kinds.

Burbank was a lot easier to fly out of, though, which was why he'd picked it.

But Laura would prefer the birds at LAX.

When Polly called Laura back and told her the news, she'd put her head on the steering wheel and cried. She knew intellectually it was silly to be so upset. She could call him, she could FaceTime him, there were any number of ways she could tell him how she felt, and he was going to be home in a couple of months anyway. But she wasn't sure she'd ever wanted anything as much as she'd wanted to see Bob *right then*. It was all very well to know something in your head, but if your heart felt differently, it was going to pull rank and bring all the viscera along with it. And once your heart *and* your tummy set their sights on something . . . forget it.

So she cried for a while until her bitterly disappointed inner child got it out of her system and then she gathered herself together and turned the truck around. If anything, driving back was worse. On the way she'd been propelled by hope, with the wings of optimism pushing from behind. This time she was scared, and panicked, and worried that not only had she not gotten to tell Bob how she felt, but she was going to crash his truck and die before she even reached home. Nina and Polly got back on the phone and coached her the whole way, distracting her not only with traffic updates but with a fully researched and highly informative lecture from Nina about the politics of freeway construction. Any other day it would have been fascinating, but Laura was still fighting her panic when she turned onto August Boulevard.

As she pulled up in front of the house, Polly, Nina, and Maggie were waiting for her on the sidewalk, and Laura felt her throat tighten up again. Not with sorrow this time, but with gratitude. She'd come to Los Angeles to start a new life, alone, and had found friends who would be part of it forever. They had changed her, but only by showing her sides of herself she hadn't seen before. She wished she didn't feel quite so sick; it was going to be hard to tell them how much she appreciated them while desperately needing to lie down.

She climbed out of the truck and waited politely until Nina completed her thought about the politics of freeway construction, and ended their call. Suddenly a green-and-white taxi pulled up with a screech. The door flew open and Bob was there, moving fast in her direction, saying, "Ladies," to the others as he passed them. They froze on the sidewalk, and Polly reached for her phone, ever ready to capture a precious memory. Nina slapped her hand.

Bob started talking before he'd even reached Laura. Apparently Polly was rubbing off on him.

"Laura," he said, which was an excellent start, "I'm not very good at talking, as you know, but I've been thinking this over for ages so I'm going to get it out and you don't have to say anything back, or respond in any way." He took a deep breath. "You know when you're wandering around a new city and nothing looks familiar, and suddenly you turn a corner and know where you are?"

She nodded, her head swimming. The last few months had been filled with moments like that.

He reached out and took her hands. "That's how you make me feel. Like I'm not lost anymore. Like I know where I'm going. Like everything's settled into place." He smiled worriedly, but kept going. "Ever since we kissed that night after trivia, I've been carrying your face in my mind all day, hoping that you're happy. When I'm working and see hummingbirds I think of you, and when I'm driving and see pigeons I think of you, and I know you need time and space to take care of yourself, and I'm not asking you for anything, but I was standing in the airport and suddenly realized I couldn't leave without telling you how I feel." He squeezed her hands. "In person."

She stared at him, then stepped in close and kissed him, holding as tightly as she could, feeling overwhelmingly joyful and at the same time incredibly stressed by the entire day. The conversation with Lili, the running home, the driving, the wrong airport, the driving, and now this. It had been such a lot.

After a minute or so they stepped apart and looked at each other.

"I'm falling in love with you," said Bob.

"I'm falling in love with you, too," Laura replied. And then she said, "I'm so sorry," and threw up all over his shoes.

That evening at dinner Maggie stood and tapped on a wineglass for silence. She got it.

"I'd like to propose a toast," she said, looking around at everyone. It was a full house, and she felt a lump in her throat. All these people were very dear to her, and several of them were in love with each other, which made for a very pleasant atmosphere.

"To Laura, who arrived to start a fresh chapter of her own life, and managed to bring a lot of new life with her." She smiled at Laura. "And here's you thinking you moved here for you, when in fact you clearly came here for us."

"I'm not sure what you mean," said Laura.

"Well," said Maggie, "you pushed Bob to go to grad school, which might not have worked out so well for you in the short term, but is great for him." Everyone laughed, especially Bob, who hadn't let go of Laura's hand for several hours. When Laura had finished throwing up on him, he'd given her a sweet look and asked her if she felt better. She'd nodded, and he'd wiped her clammy face with his sleeve and kicked off his shoes then and there. Then they'd gone inside and she'd had a shower and brushed her teeth and he'd made her tea and tucked her up in a blanket nest on the sofa next to him, and they'd watched an old baseball game until she felt totally recovered. They both knew they were going to spend the night together, that it was only the first of many, and it wasn't clear which of them was happier about it. Bob was still going to the East Coast the next day, but Laura was going with him, and then—maybe—they would pop into the city and surprise her family. *Maybe.*

Maggie continued, "You helped me fix things up with Sarah, and reminded me I was too young to sit around and wait to get old."

"You encouraged me to tell Polly how I felt about her," said Asher. He and Polly were spending a lot of time together these days, and though it was still entirely platonic, it was making them both very happy. Even if she still drove him around the bend on a regular basis.

"You restored the honor of Book 'Em, Danno," said Nina, "which might not matter to anyone but me, but it matters to me quite a lot." She remembered something. "Speaking of which, the finals are coming up next month, we need to get back to work." She turned to Bob. "I realized you know a lot about horticulture, and I was wondering . . ."

"No," he said, "not a chance."

Nina made a face, then shrugged. "Maybe after grad school?"

"No," he said, "but I'll join Polly in the cheering section."

Laura rested her head on Bob's shoulder and sighed happily. She wasn't perfect, she wasn't cured, she still had issues and problems and worries . . . but she was doing her best, and her best was getting better every day.

It was more than enough for anyone.

EPILOGUE

Los Angeles Marathon
Entrant Laura Costello, 3.5 hours

Larchmont Easter Bunny 5K run
Entrant Nina Hill, 42 minutes

Larchmont Easter Bunny 1K costumed three-legged hop
Team Polly Culligan and Clare Girvan, 9 minutes

West Hollywood Bridge Invitational
First place: Markaryan and Markaryan
Second place: Libby and Shardanand
Third place: Costello and Morse

ACKNOWLEDGMENTS

This book took longer than usual to write, which I'd like to blame on the pandemic, but which was really just me not having my shit together. Without the patience and support of the whole Berkley team and especially my editor, Kate Seaver, I would have melted into a puddle and given up many times along the way. They gave me room but never gave up on me, and I'm enormously grateful. We got there in the end, but a lot of the credit is theirs.

I was fortunate enough to have Nancy Dudley Potter, DPT, to help me with the many physical therapy questions I had. She gave extensive and thoughtful answers, and any errors that crept in are entirely mine. If anyone out there breaks a limb or two, they should go look for her. She knows her stuff.

ADULT ASSEMBLY REQUIRED

Abbi Waxman

Questions for Discussion

1. Laura moves to Los Angeles for grad school but has several other reasons for wanting to leave her hometown. How often do we do things for reasons other than the one we're willing to admit to?

2. Having experienced trauma, Laura struggles with activities that used to be easy. While trauma is often depicted as having big, dramatic impacts, it can also create chronic smaller problems. How could you see this affecting everyday life?

3. These days there's a great deal of understanding about the importance of mental health, at least in the media. However, Laura comes from a family that still views mental health problems as a sign of weakness. Have you personally noticed a change in the way your own family discusses these things, or do you think there is still stigma attached to mental health?

4. Laura falls in with a group of people who are quite different from her. Have you personally found the best support

comes from like-minded people or those who bring a totally different life experience to bear?

5. At the beginning of the book, Laura is determined not to get into a relationship, because she wants to remain single for a while. What do you think are the advantages of being single, particularly when going through a life change of some magnitude?

6. Polly is somewhat scornful of Bob for being boring. How would you describe him, and do you prefer a partner who brings excitement or stability?

7. Maggie has come to regret the way she raised her daughter, and wants to restore the relationship. What role do forgiveness and acceptance play in your own family dynamic?

8. Nina Hill is a character who worries a lot about how other people perceive her. How do you think each of the characters in the book sees her? Does Laura see her in the same way Polly does, for example?

9. At the end of the book, Laura is able to handle something she couldn't earlier, but it is still very challenging. Is it better to force yourself to tackle a challenge, or give yourself time and space to overcome it? Is there a right way?

If you enjoyed *Adult Assembly Required*,

discover the previous novel featuring these characters . . .

Meet Nina Hill: A young woman supremely
confident in her own . . . shell.

Nina has her life just as she wants it: a job in a
bookstore, an excellent trivia team and a cat named Phil.
If she sometimes suspects there might be more to life than
reading, she just shrugs and picks up a new book.

So when the father she never knew existed dies, leaving
behind innumerable sisters, brothers, nieces, and
nephews, Nina is horrified. They all live close by!
She'll have to Speak. To. Strangers.

And if that wasn't enough, Tom, her trivia nemesis, has turned
out to be cute, funny and interested in getting to know her . . .

It's time for Nina to find out if real life can ever live up to fiction . . .

'Book lovers will absolutely relate'
O, The Oprah Magazine

Available now from Headline Review

REVIEW

Bookends

When one book ends, another begins . . .

Bookends is a vibrant reading community to help you ensure you're never without a good book. It brings together the best reads from three publishers: Hodder & Stoughton, Headline Publishing Group and Quercus Books.

✉ Sign up to the Bookends newsletter.
www.welcometobookends.co.uk

You can also follow us on:
🐦 @TeamBookends

📘 /WelcomeToBookends